# The Irish Duchess

*Patricia Rice*

# The Irish Duchess

Patricia Rice

Copyright © 2012 Patricia Rice
First Publication:
Book View Cafe, November 2012

ISBN 978-161138-232-7

Cover design by Hot Damn Designs

ALSO IN THE REGENCY NOBLES SERIES:
*The Genuine Article*
*The Marquess*
*The English Heiress*

# One

*August, 1822*

"Confound it, Your Grace, a bloody damn duke should act like a bloody damn duke, not hold hands with these puling malcontents who would save the world at our expense!" Lord Townsend paced the ducal study, shaking the papers in his fists.

Golden brown head bent over the bill under discussion, His Grace, Neville Perceval, the Duke of Anglesey, ignored the hostilities raging around him as he impassively scribbled notes in the margins of the bill.

The forbidding third man in the room, the Marquess of Effingham, threw the silent duke a look of exasperation and retaliated to Townsend's diatribe. "You've been living at the expense of the commons for centuries, my lord. It's damned well time you pay them back!"

As the argument died to an expectant silence, the duke raised his head. Their quietness had gained his audience the attention their earlier shouts had not. Arching a shaggy eyebrow in an expression that delineated anything from derision to surprise, he halted the scratching of his pen and raised his quizzing glass. Realizing both combatants glared at him, he waited for an explanation. Some days, he never had to use his voice at all.

"Devil take it, Your Grace, you're a duke of the realm! You cannot support Effingham's bill for Catholic emancipation. The king will have an apoplexy! Your grandfather would spin in his grave if he heard this sedition. If Castlereagh had some inkling of this, it's no wonder he killed himself. The mobs will tear London apart if we acknowledge papists. Imagine what will happen in Ireland should Catholics take office! Act like the duke you are and tell this bloody American to get the hell back where he belongs!"

The dark eyebrow remained quizzically lifted as the duke raised his ornate walking stick and slammed the gold knob on the table. The room's dignified occupants jumped several inches in startlement.

"I've already agreed to support the bill, Townsend, so sit down and listen or depart," he said impassively. "Was that ducal enough for you?"

The tall marquess grinned as much as his scarred features allowed.

Townsend, on the other hand, grumbled. "Liverpool won't appreciate your defection. You won't have the support of any but a few closet Whigs and Irish scoundrels. You'll regret this, Your Grace."

"What will you do? Take away my title?" In blatant dismissal, the duke picked up the pages before him, leaving the older politician to continue blustering or depart, as he so chose.

Glaring at the marquess, Lord Townsend grabbed his leather-bound files from the table and stalked out.

"You've made a dangerous enemy there, Neville," Effingham stated bluntly as the door closed.

The duke didn't even lift his head. "I repeat, what can he do? Have me thrown from the Lords? Strip me of my estates? Have the archbishop excommunicate me? You do realize, if it were not for all those disreputable blights upon the face of the earth that we call princes, I could conceivably be in line for the throne? If Edward hadn't married and finally legitimized one of his progeny, King Georgie truly would have had an apoplexy."

The Marquess of Effingham offered a decidedly unaristocratic snort. "So that's what's frustrating Townsend. No matter what your politics, men will still court your influence. You'd best watch your back then. Heirs to royalty often have short lives."

Unperturbed, the duke flipped another page. "If that were true in this day and age, the government would have been relieved of the considerable burden of Farmer George's repulsive offspring by now. Instead, they romp around the country, polluting blood lines with their bastards, driving us to financial ruin, and giving the scandal sheets more material than they can reasonably print. It continues to amaze me that they haven't killed each other yet — a certain sign that they aren't true royalty."

"Gad, you're a cynical bastard." The marquess pulled out a chair as the duke raised his speaking eyebrow again. "I know, you wouldn't be duke if you were a bastard." He took a seat but didn't pick up the papers before him. "You know, you're becoming a little too like Castlereagh — stiff, uncompromising, concerned only with having your own way, completely out of touch with the feelings of the people around you. It's not healthy, Neville. You see what happened to Castlereagh."

The duke replaced his quizzing glass and returned to his papers. "I'm in no danger of cutting my own throat, I assure you."

"I think I liked you better as a young pup who still believed the world was made of black and white," the marquess said.

"Pardon my straying from the straight and narrow," the duke replied dryly. "But I believe you and that dratted brother of yours might have had some influence in the matter of recognizing shades of gray."

"Don't lay the blame on me and Michael," Effingham protested. "It's your cousin Blanche who sits serenely in her country nest, pulling all our strings."

Neville frowned at that. "Money talks," he agreed bluntly. "But Michael has a way of twisting arms. He's even made me believe the only way out of an Irish revolution is to pass this bill. I don't give a damn whether Catholics hold office or jump in the ocean and swim the sea. The country simply cannot afford a revolution."

Before Effingham could comment on the cynicism of this declaration, the door burst open, letting in a whirlwind of silk and blazing fury.

"You monster! This is the last time I allow you to make a fool of me! I care not if you are the king of all countries, you will never pass through my door again!"

A parasol smashed onto the table, fracturing several delicate ribs. As the beautiful virago beat it against the backs of two empty chairs in a fit of frustration, it fragmented entirely. The duke raised his head with what would pass as a flicker of astonishment. When a reticule whizzed by his left ear, his expression went blank again.

"Take back your petty gifts! I will have naught to remind me of your faithlessness." A glove box dented the table, sliding off one side and falling to the floor in a splinter of carved rosewood. "No more will you make this place your mistress and me your rug to walk upon!" Apparently dispossessed of any further gifts to heave, she reached for an inkstand and flung it instead. "Never will you leave me waiting again! I am gone."

With a dramatic twirl, she stalked out, leaving a heavy trail of perfume.

The ensuing silence was broken by the duke's wry words. "I notice she did not throw back the enormously expensive bracelet for which I still owe an ungodly sum."

The marquess laughed. "I take it back, Your Grace. Perhaps you're not the dusty stick you seem."

Recovering, Effingham returned the front legs of his chair to the floor. Ignoring the trail of ink across the table, he shoved his chair back. "But it wasn't necessary to stay so late when you had a beautiful woman waiting. You cannot love duty more than a female like that."

The duke flicked a spot of ink from the pages he'd managed to save from the whirlwind. "To tell the truth, I would prefer listening to Townsend than argue with a woman. I cannot fathom why I fell in with her in the first place."

"Because she's free and easy and you're a man, despite all evidence to the contrary," Effingham replied bitingly. "Come along. We've done enough for the evening. My wife's holding a small soiree and the company will be delighted with your presence. Besides, there's food. You can cut a swathe through the swooning ladies and make it easier for us to reach the buffet table."

Neville balked at the idea of confronting a Whig party, but Effingham's greater stature and his own hunger steered him into the chilly autumn evening.

Realizing the night was yet young, the duke resigned himself to socializing. Effingham had sufficient brains to prevent boredom, but his young wife's sense of humor frequently tipped her entertainments to the wrong side of propriety. And if Effingham's stepbrother, the Irish Earl of Aberdare, attended, the evening could disintegrate into a nightmare of practical jokes. Neville wasn't certain he would ever forgive his cousin Blanche for marrying a madman.

Fortunately, the crowd assembled at Effingham's townhouse was a respectable one. Despite the marquess's predictions, no ladies swooned, giving easy access to the food. Rather, they congregated in the duke's path, making forward movement practically impossible.

Scowling as a grinning Effingham blithely left him to the vultures, Neville escaped behind a mask of boredom. At a particularly foolish comment upon his appearance in a Whig stronghold, he raised his quizzing glass, and lifted an eyebrow, cowing his opponent into backing away. With practiced ease, he took the opening provided and located a quiet alcove away from the babbling horde.

That he found the alcove already occupied came as no surprise. Signaling a servant to bring a plate, Neville took a seat beside a quiet young woman doing her best to disappear into the woodwork. Since she towered an inch or two above him, she attempted the impossible.

"Good evening, Lady Gwyneth. We meet again, it seems. I assume you have a chaperone hovering nearby to keep away the worst of the sharks?"

A shy smile tilted her pale lips. Although her statuesque size kept many suitors away, she possessed a fair face and considerable intelligence, in Neville's opinion. Her much-heralded wealth added all the impetus he needed to forward their acquaintance. He despised the necessity of such a mercenary relationship, but as Effingham's brother despicably said, *needs must when the devil drives.*

"My mother is in that chair by the palm," she said in tones barely above a whisper.

Reassured that the proprieties were upheld, and he was in no danger of binding himself irrevocably before he'd made the decision to do so, Neville nodded. He'd encountered the lady before whenever he forced himself from the halls of government in his reluctant pursuit of wife, wealth, and heir. He knew his duty. He must marry. But ever since his wealthy cousin Blanche had thrown him over for an irrepressible Irishman, he hadn't had the interest to pursue anyone else.

After the scene with his raging mistress earlier, Neville heartily wished for the serenity of hearth and home and a quiet wife so he need not seek comfort elsewhere ever again. Certainly, Lady Gwyneth could provide serenity. He just wished she could stir something a little more. Her height made it difficult not to admire her statuesque bosom, but Neville sensed her tension and corrected his impropriety by watching the milling crowd.

He was the Duke of Anglesey. His rank alone placed him beyond common human conditions such as lust or love. His responsibilities allowed no room for indulgence.

Gwyneth would make an excellent duchess. She would overcome her shyness in time. A duchess couldn't lurk in corners, obviously. Neville supposed breeding heirs on a reluctant wife would be a formidable task, but challenges didn't disturb him.

What did disturb him was the vague notion that he could not honor his vows for long with a woman who might not enjoy the duties of the marital bed. He didn't like breaking vows, but he knew himself too well to believe he could settle for weekly conjugal visits. Perhaps these annoying urges dissipated with age.

His food arrived without Gwyneth intruding upon his reverie. He should be delighted with such a quiet woman. No more violent emotional scenes and flying inkpots. But a little conversation added spice to a meal, so he sought a suitable topic.

"Do you ride, my lady?" Neville inquired.

The first sign of life stirred in her face. "Oh, yes, Your Grace. Whenever I can."

Of course. He should have known. A bruising rider who would follow the fox if she could. Oh well, that was acceptable behavior for a duchess, he supposed. "I find myself neglecting my stable of late. I don't suppose you would be interested in an unfashionably early jaunt about the park, would you?"

She seemed torn between two desires, but knowing duty as well as himself, she forced a nod. "I'd like that very much, Your Grace. I am an early riser."

"Good. Is tomorrow too soon?"

"That would be perfect, Your Grace."

He knew she could speak with intelligence when she wanted. He'd heard her do so. He supposed his title awed her and the prospect of his courtship daunted her. "Have you tasted the apricot fritters? They're quite good." He held out the delicacy on his napkin for her perusal.

Instead of accepting it, she shook her head. "I cannot, but thank you very much. They look delightful."

Neville sighed. Another young lovely wasting away in pursuit of a trim figure. He could tell her she could eat all the fritters she liked and it made no difference to him, but she wouldn't believe him.

He had the rather cynical notion that once married—if he made it clear that heaviness repulsed him—she would dig into every plate set before her. He suspected that was what his mother had done. His loving, very large mother had never carried another child after him.

Gloomily considering his future, Neville cleaned his plate while listening to the terrified Lady Gwyneth converse nonsensically on the weather. He should also take into consideration that he neared thirty years of age while this poor girl barely possessed nineteen. She probably still had foolish notions of love and white knights. Grumpy, taciturn old men probably didn't qualify. Not that he considered himself old, but to a nineteen-year-old...

Deciding he'd paid her the requisite amount of attention, he handed his empty plate to a passing servant, bowed, and excused himself. She colored prettily and seemed relieved at the same time. So much for dazzling the damsels.

He still had time for a drink or two at his club. To keep expenses down, he didn't keep a carriage in town. Actually, he didn't have much of a stable either, but one must maintain appearances. So he frequently walked damp gray streets beneath flickering gaslights. He sometimes did his best thinking then.

Right now, Neville pondered the lack of mutual attraction between himself and Lady Gwyneth. He didn't think himself particularly ugly. True, he had a long face and a rather stern jaw that might pass for formidable in some circles. His blasted thick eyebrows emphasized the noticeable ridges of his brow. But his hair was an unremarkable brown, and he was of only an average size. In all, he bore no attributes even remotely dangerous or displeasing to a lady.

He was a damned duke, for heaven's sake. Women swarmed him like flies. Elizabeth had found him well enough for her bed. He'd had other women before her. None had complained of his appearance. So why couldn't a simple girl look at him with something of appreciation?

Thinking he heard a step behind him, Neville halted beneath a gaslight and adjusted his gloves. The streets were fairly well traveled this time of night. A pair of revelers staggered and sang their way down the boulevard in front of him. The night watch lifted his cap in respect and strolled on his way. Neville heard nothing further from behind. A man in his position couldn't be too careful, but he couldn't give himself fancies either.

Deciding he'd only heard a servant scampering for the backstairs of a nearby kitchen, Neville proceeded down the wide street with the revelers. Light gleamed through the front windows of his club, and he hurried up the stone steps, handing his beaver hat to the doorman.

The rich leathers and glowing lamps of the interior welcomed him. He knew every man in here, had gone to school with most of them, fought verbal battles in the Lords with half. They nodded at him with respect and didn't expect gay sallies in return. He didn't have to laugh and flatter, be witty and flirt. He could have a good glass of brandy, turn a card or two, and engage in an animated discussion on the future of railroads. No wonder men didn't marry unless forced.

One of the men he expected to see stood in a corner conversing with some younger fellows who appeared ready to leave. At a wave from a former school chum, David Morrow, Neville strode in their direction.

"Whoa, old boy, didn't expect you here tonight. The Fair Elizabeth made it quite clear you were meeting her at Liverpool's," Morrow said.

Neville shrugged. "Duty called. I'm looking for a quiet evening."

"We're off to explore a new gaming house over on St. James. Supposed to be quite the thing. Come along with us," one of the younger men suggested.

"I've just come for a brandy. Thank you." Neville continued on his way.

"Thinks demmed well of himself, don't he?" he heard the heir to an earldom mutter.

"Guess he's too high in the instep to go gaming with the likes of us," another agreed.

In the mirror on the far wall, Neville watched Morrow cuff the closest speaker. He did his best not to wince at his friend's defense.

"He hasn't got the wherewithal to gamble with, fool," Morrow said. "Everyone knows Anglesey is just this side of bankruptcy, and the duke won't let his lady cousin pay his gambling debts. Don't let me hear you speak ill of your betters again."

~

Finished with the news sheets, Neville drained his brandy glass, picked up his walking stick and high-crowned hat, and set out for home. He had a stack of estate papers on his desk that needed his attention. And Blanche had yet another mad scheme for improving the Manchester mills that he must discourage in some manner.

He couldn't believe he was placed in the position of acting as a bloody tradesman just to keep his wretched cousin from sinking all her coins into improbable schemes for benefiting the welfare of mankind. Mankind was scarce worth the effort.

Neville allowed instinct to guide him home while he lost himself in thought. The Anglesey townhouse occupied a rather large chunk of real estate in one of the older sections of town, one where gaslights had not yet been installed. Accustomed to the dark shadows of trees from the park, Neville gave his surroundings little notice. Even the clammy fog obscuring the pavement did not deter him. He could find his way home blindfolded if needed.

Only the sound of a footstep where there shouldn't be one finally dragged him from his reverie. One too many violent incidents in these past years of political chaos had taught him caution. Had someone followed him from the club? Why?

One of the things he had learned from Michael, Blanche's new husband, was how to act quickly and defend himself. Over the years, his lessons with Gentleman Jackson had given him a much needed outlet for frustration. Neville needed no more than the snap of a twig to jump from absentminded thought to full alert.

The scoundrel crashing through the shrubbery caught the full force of the gold-plated knob of Neville's walking stick. The second scoundrel suffered the brunt of Neville's fist plowing into his face at such an angle that his jaw fell slack. Neville cursed as still a third leapt from the bushes, and footsteps behind him indicated he'd attracted a crowd.

Giving up any pretense of politeness, he flicked open the sword in his stick, slashed at the man advancing from his side, kicked at the one rising from the street, and heard the sweet sound of a groan as he connected with his soft target. Any triumph he might have felt dissipated the moment a cudgel cracked across the back of his skull.

With a growl of fury, Neville swung and slashed at his opponent, but he'd already realized the futility. There were just too many of them.

As someone grabbed his sword and twisted it from his hand, Neville plowed his fist into still another jaw and had the satisfaction of hearing it crack before the club came down on his skull again.

This time, the Duke of Anglesey crumpled to the street, swearing as the blackness of unconsciousness threatened. He had no heir. He couldn't die.

# Two

McGonigle lifted his tankard at the bar in the dark Irish tavern and gestured at an audience as poorly dressed and world-weary as he. "The bleedin' English are after drainin' us dry as stones. We cain't be lettin' them take what little we possess. Those are our homes! I say we drive the bastards out, let them know we won't take their thievery any longer!"

His diatribe was interrupted by a shout from the doorway. "William McGonigle, you're a scabrous, lying layabout with naught for brains but the whisky in your hand!"

The men in the smoky tavern turned, although the feminine pitch of the words identified the speaker.

Beneath the low portal stood a slender figure in boy's jerkin and breeches, hands on hips and arms akimbo. Her green eyes caught the lantern light in the malodorous dusk of the tavern. Thick auburn curls tumbled in dishevelment around a delicately-boned face that might have captured a man's interest—had ruby lips not tightened into a thin, disapproving line and her milky brow not been marred with a too-familiar scowl.

Even before she strode into the room, the work-hardened men inched out of her path. That she carried a riding crop in one hand had little to do with their unease. That she had the sharp tongue of an adder had a good deal more, especially when she unleashed it.

"Lazy, conniving troublemakers, the lot of ye!" she shouted into the silence, falling into the vernacular with the ease of experience. "You blame your sorry troubles on everyone but the ones who caused them—your own bleedin' foolish selves! You knew that thievin' Owen had no right to lease those lands, but you went on believin' his lies because it suited ye. And now the rightful owner returns and wants to improve them, and the lot of ye sit here whinin' like a bunch of pulin' babes about bein' robbed. You ought to be ashamed of yerselves!"

"Fiona, ye're after interferin' where you don't belong," one of the older men intervened. "The earl won't fancy it none, and yer uncle will take a switch to ye."

A low murmur in the background sounded suspiciously like "we wish," but at the glare of green eyes, none spoke the words out loud.

"I'd not be in here like this if the lot of ye were out moving your belongings like ye were supposed to be. It's costing the earl enough to drain and fill those bogs ye call fields. Don't expect him to up and move your lazy selves as well. I'll tell him myself to plow your wretched hovels under! Did ye leave your poor wives to pack the babes and your belongings too?"

Several of the men winced at her scorn and looked longingly at the door. McGonigle stood up. Larger than most of the men there, he towered over Fiona's slight figure by a foot or more, but she didn't flinch at his approach.

"Those are our homes, Miss Fiona, and don't ye be forgettin' that! Our daddies built those houses. We grew up in them. You can't be just throwin' a man out of his home willy-nilly and expect him not to fight back."

Exhaustion lined her pale features, but her reply remained forceful. "You know the law, McGonigle. Your father knew the law when he built that place on rented land. Improvements stay with the owner, and the owner has the right to do what he will with them. You're blamed lucky the earl has provided other housing for you. There's not a bloody English lord out there who would have done the same. Michael is as Irish as you or me. He's looking after you, if you weren't too damned backward to see it. Once he drains those bogs, we'll have twice as much land to farm. The fair has raised the funds for looms. Once we build those, we'll see a difference."

"The bloody damned law needs changing!" someone in the background shouted.

Fiona sought the face of the troublemaker, but her gaze was distracted. A girl with a shawl wrapped about her head and shoulders searched the interior, and Fiona knew what that meant. Glowering at the angry crowd, she shoved her way toward the child.

"A whole lot of bloody damned things need changing around here," Fiona shouted, at no one in particular. "And men who don't keep their pants on and stay home where they belong are one of them."

A guilty silence fell behind her as she strode out and the child hurried in her path. Every man jack of them recognized the girl and knew what her arrival meant. Fiona had no idea how many of those men in there had lain with the child's mother. She certainly didn't want to know. She just wanted those responsible for the children that resulted to step forward and take their share of the burden. Not bloody damn likely in this lifetime, she muttered to herself, as she hurried down the village street.

The western sun cast an unflattering light over the stone huts and muddy lane, shadowing the flowers at the doorsteps and illuminating the garbage and the pigs, but Fiona had lived with this setting so long she scarcely noticed it. As she reached the tumbledown hovel set far down a back lane from the main road, her attention turned to the terrified children huddled in what passed for the front yard. The screams from the interior curdled her blood.

Fiona stopped and hugged the eldest, a too-skinny boy of nine. She whispered in his ear, and sent him off with the others on an errand she made up on the spot. They knew her as the lady who brought them milk and bread, so they eagerly obeyed her. Sighing, Fiona watched them scamper off. Why the devil didn't the neighbors look after them at a time like this?

She knew the answer to that, but she didn't like thinking so cruelly of others. Despite the low portal, she didn't need to duck upon entering the darkened cottage, one of the few advantages of her unlofty stature.

The old woman in the corner continued rocking with grief without acknowledging Fiona's presence. The younger one straining in the last stages of childbirth wasn't conscious enough to notice. She gripped the filthy sheets over the rough pallet and screamed in an anguish Fiona recognized as abnormal.

Feeling the fear come upon her, she looked for a basin of water in which to wash her hands. She wished she had more knowledge, but as a woman and a Catholic, she was denied an education. Her mother had taught her to read and write, but that couldn't teach her what to do now. She could rely only on what little she had learned from experience.

"Bless the Lord, and may the sainted Mother of God deliver us," the terrified old woman whispered as Fiona wrapped the squalling babe in clean linen. "Ye've done it, lass. Let me have him, then, though it would have been better had the wee bairn never been born."

Fiona mentally concurred, but exhausted, she wiped sweat from her forehead with her sleeve, and returned to the unconscious woman on the pallet. Those six children outside needed a mother, even a poor one such as Aileen.

Cursing everyone from her parents to the bigotry of society, Fiona vented her anger and fear while she worked over her patient. The babe she'd saved wailed lustily.

"Blessed Lord Jesus, why!" Fiona screamed some time later, as Aileen's life ebbed with the flow of blood, and the old woman hastily murmured the sacraments.

The new mother issued a sigh of peace and fell still despite Fiona's frantic efforts. Beating the dirt floor with her fists, Fiona cried out her frustration and grief. She'd never had anyone die on her before.

"Ye done the best ye could, *cailin*," the old woman whispered as it became evident her daughter would not breathe again. "Do not greet so. She's at peace now. Just look at her. We'll see to the babes. Ye get yerself home before it comes dark."

Numb, Fiona listened to the babe wail and wondered how they would feed it. And the other children. What could one old woman do to feed those six children and a babe? The priest would take them away. They had orphanages in Dublin. Perhaps the children would have some chance of survival there.

Even as she thought that, she heard the children sneaking into the hut, weeping and clinging to their grandmother. Stairstep, all of them, each one a head taller than the next. The eldest was but nine. Some had their mother's red hair, others had the dark curls of their various fathers. If not for the dirt, they'd be a handsome lot.

Guilt ate at Fiona's innards as the old woman rocked the wailing babe and the next youngest wept. Sean, the eldest, looked at her anxiously. It was well past their supper times. They'd come to expect their mother's frequent lying-ins. They hadn't quite realized this one was permanent. They waited for an adult to provide.

Driven by curiosity, one of the neighbors arrived, took one look at the corpse on the pallet, and throwing Fiona a sympathetic look, herded the children toward the door. "I'll send Maureen to lay her out. Ye get yerself home now, Miss Fiona. I don't know what's to become of these chicks, I really don't." Shaking her head, she ushered them out.

"I failed her, I did," the old woman wept from the corner. "I tried to bring her up right, but what's a mother to do? There's naught for us here. I used to weave the most beautiful cloth, but they've taken that away. And even the wool is worthless now. How's a mother to support her babes, I ask? They've destroyed us all, the royal bastards."

The bitterness fell from her lips with the resignation of much repetition. Fiona knew the tale only too well. "My cousin's trying," she whispered, as much an apology as she could offer. "But he can't move mountains. And he can't spend all of his wife's money on charity. Whoever heard of a landlord paying tenants to use his land? It's not done."

"We know, lass. Don't fret yerself. The earl's made all the difference, giving the men jobs and their self-respect back. He can't do everything. We'll manage. Ye go on home now."

Glancing around the dismal cottage, Fiona felt the rage building again. She had traveled to England, seen the great houses and the glittering chandeliers and the wealth. It wasn't fair. Why should so few have so much, and so many have so little? It wasn't because they hadn't tried. Every attempt at saving themselves had met with the booted feet of the bloody rich crushing them back into the soil. It was time the nobles paid for their sins, but not the way the men in the tavern hoped to do it. Violence wasn't the answer.

Clenching her teeth and straightening her weary shoulders, Fiona started for the door. "I'll find a way, Mary. There's wealth enough out there to be had, and I'll have it someday, if I have to marry a bloody English lord to get it."

Had the worn leather hinges of the door allowed for it, she would have slammed her way out. As it was, she stalked into the lowering rays of the sun in a guilty fury that would have murdered the first man crossing her path. Sensibly, no man in the village left the shadows of their doorways while Fiona MacDermot stalked the streets.


"Fiona, where the devil have you been? We've been looking for you for hours." Seamus clattered down the stairs, waving two sheets of expensive paper in his hand. "We've got letters from Blanche."

"Lady Aberdare," Fiona corrected wearily, pushing past her brother and up the massive front stairs toward the security of her room and a hot bath.

"She doesn't stand on formality," Seamus replied without heat, following her up. "She wants you to join her in London, says it's much too boring otherwise, and Michael has business in the Lords, so she can't leave. She says she'll give you a come-out. You can find yourself a wealthy husband who can finance my campaign when I graduate."

Fiona snorted inelegantly at this specious bit of selfishness as she continued trudging up the stairs. "Marry a wealthy widow and support your own campaign."

"You can't disappoint Blanche after all she's done for us. I'm to escort you to London when I return to Oxford. It's time you left the muck of this place and become the lady you're supposed to be."

Seamus was her elder by two years, but Fiona had decided long ago that his brains were ten years younger. "I am not supposed to be a lady!" she shouted down at him where he hesitated on the landing. "And I'm bloody well not returning to that den of iniquity they call London!"

"You have no choice," he shouted back. "Michael has sent the fares and Uncle William has already arranged our transportation. We're to leave the day after tomorrow."

That she damned well was not. She had Aileen's children to worry about. Someone must find them food and homes. And the other women without menfolk in the village would starve this winter if she did not find some means of providing for them.

Mr. O'Donegal was supposed to teach them the old ways of preparing the flax they grew this summer so they could earn coins by weaving cloth. She had hope that quality linen might save the village, once the money they'd raised at the festival bought the looms. Burke would see to that on trade day.

Fiona heard her Uncle William calling her from the study above. The emotion of the day finally hit her with the impact a cannonball. She couldn't face him now. She simply couldn't.

Without further thought, Fiona took the back stairs two at a time, rushing out through the kitchen and past the startled cook, heading for the stable. Once upon a long time ago the earls of Aberdare had kept the finest stables in all of Europe. Those horses were long since lost, and the new earl resided in England and had little use for more. But they still had two fine mares eating them out of house and home. Fiona had practically grown up on the back of them. They were her one comfort in times of distress.

The roan tossed her head and nickered in greeting as Fiona grabbed a bridle.


Neville's duties kept him from traveling often. He had never visited Ireland for pleasure, and had certainly never expected to be fascinated by greenery lush to the point of opulence. Dusk created dancing shadows over the rolling fields he could well imagine peopled by cavorting elven folk. The mist and the lowering sun spun even the animals in the field into creatures of imagination.

The blows to his head must have warped his brain. The persistent headache had faded recently, lulling him into a false sense of well-being. The pain returned full force now, after an exhausting day of riding rough roads and losing himself in the byways by failing to understand the directions given when asked. If he didn't find Aberdare shortly, he'd be forced to sleep in the hedgerows.

Glancing toward the setting sun in hopes of seeing civilization ahead, Neville nearly fell from his saddle as a silhouette of a fey creature on horseback flew from the woods, hair streaming in silken lengths behind her. He imagined a lady centaur, or a fairy thieving some poor farmer's best mare.

Not once did he consider that the animal had taken control and endangered its rider. Even through the lengthening shadows Neville could see slim limbs and confident hands guiding the racing animal over potholes and ruts and into a breathtaking leap over a crumbling rock wall. The amazing sight not only tore the breath from his lungs, but aroused a lust he'd neglected for so long, he scarcely recognized it for what it was.

Forgetting headache and weariness, he steered his mount on a connecting path with the wayward rider's. Despite her apparel, he knew the equestrian was female. She was a woman wearing breeches. Perhaps she had a liberal view of other things besides attire.

Her mount nearly collided with his in the shadows of the trees as she raced across the road he traveled. She reined in, rearing her horse to a halt. "Who the devil are you?" she demanded imperiously.

Instead of grinning at her brash introduction, Neville scowled at the familiarity of a voice he hadn't heard in years. "Fiona MacDermot! You damned well haven't gained a particle of sense since I saw you last." So much for any brief hopes of pleasure.

The feminine figure stilled, then as recognition dawned, she responded in outrage. "His bloody majesty, it is! And a fine damned ending to one of the worst days of my life this is. If it's paying for me sins I am to have the likes of you about, then I'll do penance and never sin again." She swung her horse around and started to ride away.

Realizing she could lead him to Aberdare, Neville grabbed her reins, earning a crack across his gloved hand with her riding crop for his imposition. He snatched the weapon from her grasp before she could strike again. "Bigad, I can't believe Blanche wants a hoydenish creature like you anywhere near her. What the devil are you wearing?"

"Why, and it's me finest skirts, I'm sure," she replied mockingly. "Do not the ladies of London know the fashion?"

Neville had the distinct recollection of his urge to beat her the last time he'd seen Michael's cousin. She had the tongue of a harpy and the soul of a demon. She'd been a skinny nineteen and wearing rags and baggy gowns. He couldn't remember her ever looking like a woodsprite with curves to match the lushness of his surroundings. The only thing that kept him from an unholy state of lust was her stench.

"What have you been rolling in? A sty?" he asked unrepentantly, ignoring her mockery.

"Sure, and would your nobleness know what a pig smells like? Let go my reins. I'm going home."

"So am I, and I'm not letting you out of my sight while I do it. There are brigands in these woods this time of night."

"Do you need me to protect your precious hide?" she asked with grating innocence. "Sure, and a fine nobleman like yourself might look out for the dirty Irish bastards who'd steal the hair off your head did you let them."

"Shut up, Fiona, and start moving. I always knew my cousin was dicked in the nob, but now I'm certain she's lost all wit to ask the likes of you into her home. Michael should put a snaffle on you."

"A snaffle! Damn you for an arrogant..."

Neville jerked her rein when she tried to twist her horse away. "Stop it, Fiona. Behave like an adult for a change. If you're old enough for a come-out, you're old enough to mind your tongue. I'll not have you embarrassing Blanche if she insists on your company."

"I'll have you know I'm twenty-one and long past the age for a come-out. I want no part of the lady's invitation. Lady Aberdare is all that is kind, but I have no such opinion of London society. So you and my brother may return to merry old England without me."

"I don't think it works that way," Neville replied grimly. "I gave my word I'd escort you to London safe and sound, and I have no intention of going back on it."

The ache in the back of his head pounded in earnest at this reminder of his obligation. He was here as a kind of holiday, a break from his duties after the painful and humiliating incident that had left him bleeding and unconscious in the street. He'd never quite understood why the scoundrels had left him alive. He might have been happier had they not.

As it was, the overwhelming concern of everyone from the lowliest maid to the prime minister himself had driven him out of London. He'd dallied at Anglesey rather than make the journey to Ireland as he'd been instructed, but he hadn't been able to put off the task any longer. He was here now, and he was leaving in two days' time. And the imp from hell and her brother were going with him.

For Blanche's sake, Neville would take Fiona to London in a sack if necessary.

# Three

Halting on the castle's stone staircase the next morning, Fiona gritted her teeth and studied her nemesis.

The duke loomed in her path, blocking her way to the medieval front doors. Tinted light from the recently restored leaded glass windows splintered his arrogant features into shards of color and shadow. Dukes didn't even look like normal people, she mused. His hair wasn't brown, but golden brown; his eyes not gray, but silver. Even his odious quizzing glass glittered like a large diamond. Compared to the men she knew in their bulky woolens, hands callused with hard work, the duke appeared a polished gemstone, all sparkle and fire. She had never quite thought of the studious duke as a man of physical power, but he mirrored the morning light like a knight in sturdy armor.

Fiona feared he would not take opposition lightly.

"You cannot leave here looking like that," were the first words out of his mouth.

"If I left looking like anything else, people would not recognize me," she replied, testing the duke's measure. She wished she'd never come across him last night. Perhaps he'd still be wandering the dirt roads or found his way back to Dublin.

She stepped deeper into the shadows of the massive stairway. Like many of her forebears, she knew how to get around insurmountable objects.

"We leave on the morrow. Shouldn't you be packing your trunks?" Neville advanced across the foyer, his gaze never once leaving the place where she stood.

Fiona had never recognized authority and didn't accept it now. With a look of disdain, she observed his polished boots and blindingly white linen. "You may have use of all the trunks you need. I'm not one for wearing frills and furbelows."

"Fiona!" her uncle bellowed from above. "Is that you I hear? Mary's after scouring the halls for you. Get yourself back here now!"

The fiendish smile on the duke's angular face did little toward appeasing her temper. "Coming, Uncle," she called sweetly. With a swirl of her long braid, Fiona turned and dashed back up the stairs.

Her Uncle William seldom left the library long enough to actually track her down, giving her years of experience at avoiding his careless supervision. Slipping through the shadows of the formal dining hall, Fiona ran out the servants' door in the rear. Practically skipping with pleasure at deceiving those who would deny her her freedom, she dashed down the narrow back stairs.

She had things of importance to do this day. She didn't need the interference of her well-meaning family. The earl and his wife had her best interests at heart, she knew, but sending the haughty duke after her was a fatal mistake. She wouldn't travel one footstep in his company.

It had been two years since she'd seen the duke, but the memory of their one personal encounter still burned through her in every shade of embarrassment known to mankind. She remembered his furious disapproval, his scorn, his harsh words as if they had happened just yesterday. And she remembered how his arms had caught and trapped her and held her so close she couldn't have escaped had she tried.

She skidded to a halt in the mud as the early morning mist parted, revealing the object of her disdain standing, arms crossed, in front of the stable doors. There was something decidedly wicked about him as he lifted those expressive eyebrows and rested the broad shoulders of his tailored coat against her only means of escape.

"Going somewhere?" the duke asked pleasantly.

"I have errands, your bloody awful lordship," she spat out. "I have work to do, something I'm sure you're not familiar with."


Neville felt the return of his headache as he regarded the recalcitrant female in breeches. He couldn't think of one good reason why his cousin insisted on inflicting this Irish banshee on London society, except that Blanche had always possessed a fiendish sense of humor.

Unfortunately, he'd been condemned for having no humor at all, and he certainly saw none in his current situation. "What could be of more importance to a female than packing her fancies for a trip to London?" Neville asked with as much pleasantness as he could muster.

"How about a house full of orphans, a starving village, and the opportunity for providing a way out of poverty?" She tossed her long braid over her shoulder.

Neville stared at the tendrils of auburn escaping about her face. Everything about the brat screamed rebellion. She represented everything Irish he'd ever despised: disrespect for authority, hot tempered passion, illogical behavior, and a careless disregard for everything civilized. They still worshipped statues, for pity's sake.

"You're going to do all that in one morning?" Neville inquired. "Perhaps you'll rearrange the moon and the stars this evening for our entertainment?"

"Devil take you! Get out of my way, your royal arse. I have people waiting for me."

Her creative variations on his title amused rather than irritated him, though Neville had no intention of letting her know that. He'd acquired years of experience since the dukedom had so unexpectedly descended on his shoulders. They had taught him that dour authority worked far better than kindness. He didn't have the time for mincing words and twisting arms, and with his upbringing, charm had never been his strong point.

"Fine, then I'll accompany you. I'm certain Blanche meant to clothe you in something a trifle more respectable in London, anyway. It's a fine morning for a ride, don't you think?" Neville swung open the stable door and with a mocking bow, gestured for her to enter first.

He briefly considered closing the door after her and throwing the bolt, but then he really would have to consider tying her up and carrying her in a sack to the ship on the morrow. He would try more civilized methods first.

She gave him a glare intended to reduce him to sawdust. With a face and figure like that, she'd probably reduced most of the men around here to blithering idiots. But surrounded by the fawning attentions of every beautiful woman in all of England since he'd come into his title, Neville let the glare bounce right off him. Women had one purpose only, and this female scarcely registered in that category.

His duchess could be ugly as sin for all he cared, but she would have manners and deportment and more money than Croesus. Anyone lacking those commodities couldn't hold his interest.

Well, he'd take that back, Neville amended a moment later as Fiona threw a bridle on her horse, stepped on the mounting block, and leaped on the animal's back with the lithe grace of a cat. He couldn't help noticing the sway of her hips or the bounce of her breasts. The little she-devil wore no undergarments.

Swearing at the surge of unfamiliar lust resulting from that discovery, Neville decided she'd hold his interest as a mistress — if not for her unfortunate kinship to the earl.

Hastily mounting his own unsaddled horse, he followed her across an open meadow still glistening with dew. The sun hadn't broken through the mist, and dampness clung with diamond brilliance to Fiona's hair. In linen shirtsleeves, she spurred her mount into a gallop.

Suddenly enjoying the exhilaration of the morning and the straining horse beneath him, Neville gave his gelding its head. In his student days, he'd enjoyed the pleasures of a morning ride. He'd missed the wind whipping through his hair and the invigorating rush of his blood as his horse cleared a fence. His larger mount could easily out-stride Fiona's, but he kept the horse reined in to stay abreast of her. She laughed as she glanced in his direction.

His pulse raced faster, but Neville didn't allow himself the luxury of believing he'd earned her respect or obedience. Like any heathen, she was simply enjoying the moment. He grinned back, and pointed to a stream ahead. Understanding, she spurred her mare to greater speed.

They sailed over the trickling water, landing side by side on the boggy soil of the other side. Fiona's laughter rang through the crystalline air as Neville's gelding disapproved of the oozing mud and reared, but she paced her mount to his as they slowed the gait of their horses to cool them off.

"That's a fine animal you have there, your noble lordship," she said without her usual mockery. "I wish Michael would bring in more of the same. Aberdare used to be known for its fine horseflesh."

"You don't have to use my title, or your warped version of it," he answered without insult. "I'm family of sorts, and you call Michael by his given name."

She shrugged and didn't deign to look at him. "Michael is my cousin and Irish to the bone. You're none such."

The coldness descended between them again. Fiona was out of bounds for the thoughts he was having anyway.

"Ireland and England are one country now," he reminded her. "We have the same government and have had for twenty-two years. Why do you continue fighting a war that's long over?"

"One country, is it now?" she asked with scorn. "And who's to represent me and mine in your precious government? And don't say Seamus," she warned. "He's a bloody turncoat. He gave up the religion of his mother to call himself Protestant so he might attend Oxford. I'll have naught to do with his notions. Ninety percent of this country is Catholic and cannot hold office. I'll show you what your wretched representation does for us."

She dug in her heels and sent her mount flying down the road.

Cursing at ever presenting such a topic of conversation to the hothead,

Neville raced his horse after her.

They arrived in a lane of suspiciously new stone cottages. Neville resented every penny Michael spent, money that should have gone to Anglesey had Blanche married Neville as she was supposed to have done. But watching these women in their woolen shawls and unfashionable skirts hauling their pitiful belongings down the dirt lane in wagons and carts to the new cottages, Neville reluctantly admitted had he been in the earl's shoes, he would have done the same. The care of an estate's tenants came first.

Fiona had a greeting for everyone, although she neglected to introduce him, Neville noted with amusement. Perhaps she believed he would disappear if she pretended he didn't exist. He watched as she lifted a heavy parcel from an elderly woman who apparently had no cart. He didn't understand the exchange of Irish that followed, but the old woman gave him a nearly toothless grin.

His cousin Blanche had grown up on the estate and had always attended the tenants of Anglesey. Neville had come into Anglesey only when his uncles and father had died, and his grandfather grudgingly accepted that his despised grandson remained the lone heir. Neville had barely been twenty. Inundated with responsibilities he hadn't been trained to undertake, he'd gladly left the welfare of the tenants to Blanche.

Only Blanche didn't live at Anglesey anymore. Now the burden of tenants and land and duty all fell to him. Without the wealth to hire enough help, he neglected more than he should.

Reaching for the parcels carried by a young mother with two children clinging to her skirts, Neville contemplated whether Lady Gwyneth would take over the duties Blanche had abandoned with her marriage. He had difficulty imagining the shy woman as Lady Bountiful. She would learn, he decided optimistically.

Ahead of him, Fiona deposited her burden at a cottage where she conversed in Irish with the women gathering around her. They accepted her completely as one of them, not as any Lady Bountiful.

Neville frowned. Fiona was the granddaughter of an earl. She must learn her proper station if she took her place in London with Blanche.

Yet somehow, despite the breeches and shirt and disheveled braid, Fiona had the look of a lady about her. Perhaps because of the way she rode her horse, or the delicacy of her build. She would do, once Blanche cleaned her up and put her in decent clothes. She'd do, Neville amended, until she opened her mouth.

Neville followed Fiona as she progressed through the wretched village, blessedly holding her tongue and pretending he didn't exist. The place was little better than a pig sty, a far cry from the neat lanes and cozy cottages of Anglesey. The poverty was appalling. Didn't any of these people work?

He recognized a tavern and several shops before Fiona turned off the road for a back lane where the horses waded through filth. Neville decided they'd gone quite far enough. He wouldn't have Fiona carrying the diseases of these hovels back to Blanche and her children.

"I can see why you smelled like a sty yesterday," he said acidly as he rode up beside Fiona, and caught her reins. "I think you've wallowed in the mud long enough. You've proved your point. Now let us depart before you pick up some unspeakable disease."

"Oh, I forgot," she simpered, batting her unnaturally long lashes. "Dukes shouldn't expose themselves to the peasants. Whatever was I thinking? Do go on, your noble lordship. I perfectly understand."

She slid off her horse. In seconds, she was surrounded by a swarm of ragged urchins, all chattering in their heathen language. She hugged the tallest, tousling his dark curls as she listened intently to his urgent speech. "In English, Sean. Show the gentleman your learning."

The boy sent Neville a decidedly defiant glance but proceeded in fluent, if heavily accented English. "I shall work for the earl, Miss Fiona. I run fast as the wind. I can fetch and carry, groom the horses. I can earn enough, I know. Don't let them take the babes away."

For a moment, Neville thought he saw tears glittering in Fiona's eyes, but then she tossed her head, and the illusion dissipated. "It's a child you should be, Sean, not a man who must support such a family. It's schooling you need. The priests will see that you get it."

"But they'll take us all away!" the boy wailed. "I'll see naught of any of them again! Don't let them, Miss Fiona! I'll do my book learning in the evenings. I can do it, I know I can."

Briskly, she walked toward the cottage. "I'm after looking to it, lad. Give me peace till then."

Knowing better than to let the little witch out of his sight, Neville swung down from his horse and followed her. The two urchins who had been peacefully building castles of stones in the dirt yard suddenly took a turn toward warfare and used their building blocks as missiles, pelting each other and any target in their path. Before Neville could run their gauntlet, he had to collar them both and empty their hands of stones.

Dragging the unrepentant little brats with him, he entered the cottage.

Fiona had vanished. A brisk breeze blowing through an open window in the rear wall showed her means of escape.

"Burke! Burke, where are ye, man?" Fiona called as she approached the farmhouse. She was late. She'd expected Burke to be on his horse, impatiently waiting for her. She regretted leaving her own mount behind as she climbed the stile and crossed the rocky field on foot.

She didn't like the silence emanating from the farmhouse. Burke's wife had died years back. His children had grown and moved to the city, leaving him alone. He wouldn't have gone wandering when he knew their task this day. Fiona shivered as a crow cawed overhead. She wasn't superstitious, but she didn't need bad omens on an important day like this.

A cool wind traversed the barren hill, prompting another shiver. Just the cold, she told herself as she reached the gravel path to the house. She should have worn something warmer.

The old leather and lathe door creaked in the wind. Burke must be out and about if he'd left the door unlatched. He should have heard her by now. Fiona lifted her hands to her mouth and shouted again. "Burke! Where are ye?"

Cursing when she received no reply, she shoved open the door, hoping for a fire in the hearth. She would fix some tea before they set out and look for an old coat she might wear. They had a long journey ahead.

She wondered where he'd hidden the money the villagers had made last week in the autumn festival. All things considered, she thought they'd been quite successful, yet even so, she feared it wouldn't be enough for the looms. Perhaps they could buy a used one. Some of the men were talented with their hands. They might copy it and make it new.

Thinking wishfully of the steam looms Michael had described in the manufactories Blanche owned, Fiona traversed the empty front room for the kitchen. A steam loom would be splendid. They could turn out linen faster than they could grow the flax, and the women could sew it into fine garments. They'd be as rich as the merchants in Belfast soon enough. But that day was a long time coming.

The dog's whimpers should have warned her, but her thoughts had traveled too far to react in a timely fashion.

She walked into the kitchen and almost stumbled over Burke's body. Fiona didn't scream until her gaze encountered the bloody knife in his back.

# Four

Some trick of the wind carried the cry over hill and down dale, straight to Neville's ears. He dislodged the toddler climbing his leg and tried to listen more closely. The racket of six children and a wailing babe obliterated any immediate recognition of the sound. For all he knew, he'd heard the cry of a banshee or the screams of his own mind. The chaos of the morning had not relieved the pounding in the back of his head.

He strode out of the cottage and into the relative peace of the rising mist. A crow screamed overhead. Perhaps that's what he'd heard.

Fiona's mare whickered and pawed at the ground. Neville had just about decided to let the wretched brat do as she pleased and to leave for London without her. He'd tell Blanche she had measles or some such, anything to keep Blanche from running here with her children and embroiling herself in this mess.

But the cry rang out again, and the hair rose on the back of his neck. Responding to instinct, Neville mounted the gelding and kicked his heels, guiding the nervous animal in the direction of the wind.

He saw Fiona's slight figure flying over the rocky terrain even before he heard the scream again. If he could believe his own ears, she cried his name. He'd never heard her call him anything but "your bloody lordship" or something similar.

Swinging down from his horse, Neville caught her as she stumbled down the hillside. Fiona fell into his arms, gasping for breath and clinging to his coat sleeves.

"Burke! They've done for him! Holy Mother of Jesus, he's dead!" The words spilled out in ragged breaths as she shook his arms. "Help him! What can we do?"

Neville glimpsed the emerald of her eyes beneath windblown curls, before she apparently realized who she was talking to and jerked away, limping back toward town. "Uncle William! We must fetch Uncle William."

For one brief moment, Neville had felt the living flame imbuing her spirit. A chill wind spiked through him with her departure. Without thinking further, he caught her waist and threw her up on his horse, then joined her in the saddle.

His mind should have loftier goals than noticing how Fiona's rounded rump pressed warmly into his crotch, but his body knew what it wanted. Neville inched backward, relieved that she didn't seem to notice. She clung to the horse's mane, staring blindly at the farmhouse rising ahead.

"He's dead," she whispered. "There's nothing you can do."

"We'll make sure he's dead, then, won't we?" Neville intended reassurance, but the words came out wrong. They'd exchanged too many antagonistic barbs for anything he said to reassure.

Fiona stiffened in his arms but didn't reply.

The reason for her unnatural silence walked out of the farmhouse ahead. A burly man in farmer's tunic, followed by several shorter fellows cut from the same cloth stopped in the yard at the sight of the horse and its riders. Several removed their rough caps when they recognized Fiona. The burly one made no such gesture of respect.

"McGonigle," Fiona murmured, sagging briefly against Neville. She straightened before he had the chance to wrap his arm around her. Then like a will-o-wisp, she was off the horse and striding toward the stricken men as if she were as big and tall as they were.

"Sure, and weren't you supposed to be with Burke in Dublin this day?" the tallest man asked coldly.

"I was late. I looked in on Aileen's orphans first. When I arrived, I found him like that. He's dead then?"

One of the men who'd doffed his hat nodded and opened his mouth to speak, but the man called McGonigle overrode him. "And the money then? Do ye have the money we earned with the hard sweat of our brows?"

Neville had no idea what this was about, but he refused to stand aside and let the crude ruffian intimidate a female. Dismounting, he grabbed Fiona's hand, and slapped the reins in it. "Go fetch William, Fiona. He's the earl's man. This is his place."

She would have resisted if he'd said, "This is a man's place." But he was right, Fiona realized as she grasped the reins. Argument would get them nowhere. She looked for a mounting block to help her onto his larger horse.

She gasped as Neville caught her waist and lifted her. She almost slipped off the other side in surprise. Her cheeks burned, and she refused to acknowledge him as she urged the horse down the road. She'd done it again, let him manhandle her as if she were naught but a sack of grain. She wished she had some way of retaliating every time he made her burn like that, but he'd be gone on the morrow, and she had more pressing business.

Fiona knew in her heart that the money was gone, that the savings of an entire summer and the profits from the festival were all lost, that Burke had given his life to stop a thief. Not just any ordinary thief—the kind that stole money and ran—but a thief who stole hope, who stole the future of children and the hearts and souls of every single person in the village. She couldn't believe anyone in the village could have stabbed them all in the back, just as surely as they had stabbed poor Burke. But only the village's inhabitants had known that Burke kept their savings.

"There's naught to be done, lass," William said mournfully later that evening, sipping his port beside the fire. "We can question the entire town, but who's to say when the man died? Last night? This morning? Do you think everyone had a witness with them every waking minute?"

"You could watch for someone spending more than they should have," Neville suggested, leaning an elbow on the mantel and regarding the flames.

Fiona could see little more than the white of his linen and the sparkle of gold in his hair. The crystal goblet in his hand caught a flicker of light as he lifted it. Uneasiness shook her as she realized she sought his hand and mouth in the gloom instead of listening.

"I can't keep the men from going where they will," her uncle was saying. "If one leaves and doesn't return, we might have some right for suspicion, but that doesn't make him a murderer."

"Whoever the thief is, he must not have been close enough to the deceased to know his hiding places," Neville pointed out. "He waited until Burke uncovered the money before he killed him."

"Burke kept to himself. He'd not brag to his drinking buddies about the money's whereabouts. That's why I gave the funds to him." She'd killed Burke, Fiona thought as she spoke. It was all her fault.

She'd killed Aileen with her ignorance yesterday while delivering the babe, and now she held herself responsible for the death of a man who wanted only to better himself. She owed the children, and she owed the village for those losses.

"And you're certain that the money is gone?" William asked with his usual optimism. "It might be the thief came too soon."

"The money's gone," Fiona replied wearily. "We've practically torn the place apart stone for stone. There's a vault behind the fireplace. It's empty but for a few trinkets."

She rose from her chair as the duke began to speak, slipping away before he could say more than her name. She couldn't bear it if he said another kind word. She much preferred him insufferably arrogant and rude.

She couldn't go to bed. The shadows haunted her, and her thoughts churned, searching for some solution to the village's poverty, the orphans' plight, Burke's death. McGonigle had all but accused her of stealing the money for herself. Feelings were running high. They'd never had a murder in their midst. Sure, and there'd been the fights and stabbings in the tavern, but nothing like this. Evil lurked in the village, and she didn't know how to fight it.

She sought her mother's parlor. The castle had fallen to wrack and ruin when the Crown had claimed it these many years past. Not that it had been in good repair anytime in living memory. The earls of Aberdare had never been rich. But her mother had once taken her through the castle while the old earl still lived, pointing out places she'd loved as a child. The sitting parlor with its lady-sized chairs and embroidered footrests had always called to Fiona as a place meant for real ladies. Her mother had been the gracious noblewoman that Fiona had never been.

The new earl and his countess spent little time here, though their renovations of the old castle and its contents had given jobs to many and brought satisfaction to the countryside. Temporarily, at least, Fiona thought with contempt as she settled into a high-backed wing chair. There were always hotheads to complain of something.

The servants kept the rooms spotless from respect, not because of Fiona. She knew little of the chores of maintaining this monstrous place. Her mother had died years ago, and they'd been living in William's small farmhouse then. They'd only lived here in the last two years since the heir's return.

Fiona sighed and leaned her head against the chair back. All the best wishes in the world couldn't restore this cavernous edifice to a bustling, well-tended home. The wind blew down the chimney and rattled the window frames. She could well understand why Michael wouldn't allow his delicate wife to live in this mausoleum for any length of time.

Her mind jumped and skittered from one topic to another with the flightiness of a grasshopper. The duke had called her a grasshopper once, and recommended Michael put a jar over her head. She'd thought it rather funny at the time. She had been younger then.

As if her thoughts had conjured the devil himself, a shadow entered her hideaway. "A light would have made it easier to find you," an unwelcome voice admonished.

"Go away, your holiness," she muttered. "A man of intelligence might recognize the lack of invitation in the darkness."

"A man of cowardice might turn down the challenge, but I'm not that man."

She heard him pull up one of the other fireplace chairs. They were made for a lady's smaller size, and Fiona could imagine him squeezing his wide shoulders between the narrow wings and settling his masculine frame onto the flowered chintz. Perhaps he wore his quizzing glass to survey his surroundings in his usual stiff-rumped manner. Maybe she should have lit a candle, after all, to see the sight.

"Oh, excellent, I do enjoy a man who's so full of himself that he does not know when he's not wanted." She kept the edge out of her voice. Maybe if she just sounded weary, he would go away.

"I have a proposition for you," he said, apropos of nothing.

A proposition. Oh, fine and dandy. He would make her his mistress and give her fine jewels, perhaps. For a moment, Fiona considered the possibility. Jewels would buy food for orphans and widows. He spoke again before she could decide whether to kill him or accept him.

"I don't want Blanche burdened with an obnoxious brat. Her generosity stretches her strength too far. I considered leaving you here, but it's obvious that isn't a safe solution either."

"There's an understatement for you," Fiona murmured, staring at the empty grate. "If I kill McGonigle, someone would feel called upon to see me hanged. And if I don't kill him, I'll provoke him until he kills me. One of us has to go. And since it's not likely McGonigle is looking for a solution to our problems, then I suppose it's up to me. You wouldn't happen to know any rich men, would you?"

She hadn't meant to speak her thoughts out loud, leastwise, not to the wretched duke. But once said, they took on a life of their own. She'd threatened it before. She hadn't really meant it. There wasn't a man alive she could consider as husband. But a wealthy man, now... That had possibilities. An old man, one who would leniently smile on her wishes as her Uncle William did. One who would give her funds to buy looms and provide for Aileen's orphans.

"I know a great many rich men."

She'd like to slap the smug expression off his face, even if she couldn't see it. But she was learning not to underestimate the duke. She might despise what he stood for, but she couldn't despise his intelligence.

A man of rank and power had loftier responsibilities than concerning himself with a lone female in a distant land. Yet now that he was here and doing just that, she would exploit his knowledge.

Rather than leap at his declaration, she waited, almost feeling his sharp look when she didn't reply. She suspected his gray eyes grew cold as stone when he was thwarted.

"I could sponsor you in London, see that your come-out is a huge success, arrange for every wealthy bachelor in the country to beg at your door."

"In return for what?" Fiona asked with instant suspicion.

"In return for your complete obedience," he replied with the satisfaction of a cat purring over cream.

She didn't even know the meaning of the word "obedience." He didn't know what he asked.

"I'll not have you giving Blanche a moment's concern," he warned. "You'll deck yourself out in the clothes of her choice, speak politely or not at all, and behave as every other young female in society. In return, you'll have your choice of wealthy husbands. Defy me, and I'll cut you cold, and all society will do the same. Believe me, a duke has that power."

He didn't say, "*I* have that power." He'd said, "A *duke* has that power." Fiona didn't know why that made a difference to her, but it did. It was honest. Had he not held the title of duke, he couldn't have made any man in England look at her twice. But a duke...

There was something perversely gratifying in knowing she could use the aristocracy she despised for her own purposes. How long would it take to wrap a man around her finger and get her hands in his pockets? Other women did it all the time. She could do it too—for Aileen's children, and the looms, and for poor murdered Burke, may he rest in peace.

"All right," she agreed, "You see before you the very model of obedience." She ignored the duke's exceedingly impolite snort.

# Five

Entering the shadowed foyer from the sunshine outside on the morning of their departure, Neville blinked and paused to orient himself.

He'd given Fiona additional time for packing, not out of the kindness of his heart but because he had wanted to make a few discreet inquiries in the village. Aberdare needed to know all the pertinent facts about the murder. The village folk hadn't liked talking to an Englishman, but they'd all wanted Burke's murderer caught. Neville hadn't found a soul who disliked the man. And the disappearance of the village's hard earned savings had stirred a tempest that could grow to hurricane proportions if some action wasn't taken soon.

Neville wished he could pin the evidence on the obstreperous McGonigle, but it seemed the man's tirades had an audience almost every waking minute, and he possessed a wife who witnessed his sleeping ones.

Hearing sounds from the little-used parlor to his left, Neville strolled in that direction. The chill of the downstairs chambers reflected the great hall they had once been. Without a tree burning in the huge fireplace, the rooms were never warm.

"Eamon! What the devil brings you here?"

Neville heard Fiona's surprise as he lingered in the gloom of the massive doorway. The only light in the towering chamber came from arrow slits.

A shaft of sunlight struck Fiona. Resting his shoulder against the stone, Neville admired her wide, intelligent brow and curved dark eyebrows that expressed her emotions more freely than she knew. If it were not for the hint of rose in her cheeks, her skin would be pure white, untouched by the freckles sported by most red-haired women. Stubborn determination jutted her little chin as she confronted her visitor.

"I heard about Burke, and I heard a rumor you were leaving. I'm after thinking that's not wise, Fiona," the man said, seemingly unperturbed by her acerbic greeting.

The man pronounced her name with the long "a" — "Fey-onah." The accent jarred Neville's memory. If he remembered correctly, two years ago the man standing here now had been a wanted criminal. Aberdare had allowed him to escape in return for his services to Blanche. Neville didn't think the earl would appreciate knowing a known traitor haunted the halls of his home.

"As if you could teach me wisdom," Fiona replied with bristly sarcasm.

"I thought you well on your way in America by now. You're mad to return here."

Eamon O'Connor brushed a thick lock of dark hair from his face. Neville could see little of his features, but he remembered the Irishman as young and handsome, and a rebel to the bone, the perfect companion for someone like Fiona. Neville was amazed they hadn't run off together. He was further amazed at the stab of irritation he felt at the thought.

"A thing or two has turned up since we spoke last," O'Connor said laconically. "Your cousin has a magic way with the courts, it seems, and I'm no longer a criminal. But I'm not here to talk of myself, lass. The word is you've taken the villagers' money for your own, to spend it on fancy clothes in London and find yourself a fine husband. If you leave now, they'll think it's true for sartin."

Neville stifled a groan. He'd hoped to hustle Fiona out of here before she heard the rumor. Before she could do more than emit the first screech of outrage, Neville stepped into the dust-moted light where O'Connor could detect his movement.

"It's McGonigle's doing, you know that, Fiona," Neville said dismissively. "The man's a troublemaker. If your friends do not believe better of you than that, then they don't deserve your time or care."

Neville turned his attention from Fiona to the lanky visitor. "You had no need to disturb her with such idiocy. Michael should have turned you over to the courts and let you hang."

O'Connor shoved his hands into the pockets of a shapeless tweed coat and regarded Neville with the same expression he'd give a particularly loathsome insect. "And the same to ye now," he replied with remarkable placidity. "If ye must know, I've come to save Fiona from yer filthy clutches. I'd have her for wife, which is more than you can say."

The hard slap of Fiona's hand across O'Connor's long jaw echoed in the empty chamber. Neville stared in astonishment. O'Connor merely rubbed the sore place and regarded her without expression.

"You'd not have done that had you not already thought the same yourself," Eamon responded with the first hint of anger. "You'll do whatever you must to feed your orphans. I know you that well, Fiona MacDermot, so you needn't deny it. I'm here to stop you from making that mistake."

"You're a great, lumbering jackass, Eamon O'Connor, and I want you out of here this instant!" Furious, she spun around to confront the damned duke, and caught a moment's unguarded anger in his expression. She didn't know whether it was at the insult to her or to himself and she was past caring.

"To hell and damnation with the lot of ye!" Throwing up her hands, Fiona walked out.

"Don't say I didn't warn you!" Eamon shouted after her.

Warn her — of what? Of falling for the duke's cold charms? She'd as likely fall for a viper in her sewing basket. Since she didn't own a sewing basket and had no taste for snakes, the likelihood was nil. Fiona snarled at the stupidities of the male of the species. Wave a female in their faces, and they transformed into lust-crazed jackasses.

The bloody boring Duke of Anglesey would never do something so common as fight over a woman's honor. He'd probably pass a piece of legislation making it illegal for a man to insult a woman — or more likely, a duke — and assign the death penalty. That's all the damned English Parliament was good for anyway.

Despite her scorn, Fiona thought twice before taking the action Eamon's news demanded she take. She would disappoint Lady Blanche, and she truly would hate doing that. Blanche was the only woman Fiona had ever known who fit the description of ladies in the old folk tales. One simply didn't disappoint legends without good reason.

Ignoring the maid buckling trunks, Fiona changed into her boy's breeches and shirt. For a moment she felt a spurt of regret that she would not have the opportunity to snare a rich husband and make life easier for everyone, but nothing had ever come easily in her life.

She slipped down the back stairs, through the nearly empty kitchen, and into the straggling walled garden. She'd thought to make the garden a thing of beauty as well as practicality, but she'd never had time to do more than plant a few herbs and a rose sucker someone had given her. The cook had planted potatoes, but the vines had died back at the end of summer. They'd need digging soon.

She peered around the wall to the stables, prepared to avoid the duke if he blocked her way again. But she saw no sign of him. She didn't think either he or Eamon cared enough to fight over her now that she'd left their presence. She supposed Eamon would crawl back into whatever hole he'd crawled out of, and the duke would be in the drive overseeing the loading of the carriage. He learned quickly, she must admit. The castle had few servants and those were untrained. If a person wanted something done, they'd best do it themselves.

Slipping past the wall, Fiona hurried across the stable yard. She didn't need a saddle to ride Maeve. She could be gone before anyone missed her.

The horse nickered and took the carrot Fiona had snatched from the garden. After the drafty castle, the stable seemed almost cozy. Fiona felt more at home here than anywhere else. Giving the mare a hug, she used a crate as a mounting block and climbed on. Even if the duke should see her leave, he couldn't catch up with her.

She didn't count on finding him waiting for her as she rode out of the barn.

He grabbed the bridle before she could kick Maeve and fly past him. "You're becoming predictable, Fiona," he said coolly, holding the dancing animal without a hint of strain.

"So are you, your gracious lordship." Fiona could have sworn she almost saw a tug of a smile at the corner of his mouth. She hauled on the mare's reins, hoping to dislodge his hold. "You'll have to be off to London without me."

"I rather suspected that would be your response after that blackguard's visit. That's what he wanted from you, you know. He knows well how to manipulate you."

Fury shot through Fiona. "And dumb female that I am, I do as he says, don't I, my lord? Sure, and that's the way of things. A woman must always answer a man's call, and I'm no better than the rest."

Before Fiona even knew he'd moved, the duke hauled her off the horse, and she slid down his frock-coated torso. The shock of that closeness momentarily unnerved her, and she stood frozen, clinging to his lapels for support.

"And am I not a man, my lady sharp-tongue? It's my call you'll answer now. You gave me your word, and I'm holding you to it." The duke caught her loose shirt back and steered her in the direction of the castle.

Fiona planted her boots firmly in the soft ground and refused to budge unless he bodily hauled her. "I only promised to behave if we went to London. I'm not in London, nor am I going. So we have no bargain. Stop it, Your Grace! Leave off!" She reached behind her to twist his fist from her shirt.

He stopped, but he didn't loose her. In spite of the chilly morning, heat shimmered from the duke's body as he stood toe to toe with her. He hovered a head taller, and her nose nearly pressed into his cravat. She could smell the clean starch of the linen, and another scent, a tempting manly scent that she didn't want to acknowledge.

"Is running away the only answer you have to your problems?" he demanded.

Fiona jerked her head back to meet his gaze. "I am not running away," she informed him coldly. "Going to London is running away. Staying here and finding Burke's murderer is the responsible thing to do."

"You are not the magistrate; you are not responsible for finding a murderer. You're not the earl; you're not responsible for the village. You're not even related to those orphans back there and you have no responsibility for them. Pretending otherwise is foolish."

"There is no magistrate to punish poor Burke's murder! The earl isn't here, and there's none else to care." Fiona shook free of his hold. Tears wetting her lashes, she stared blindly at the horizon. The duke's harsh words were like nails, piercing her armor and crucifying her. She'd made the earl's castle her home, borrowed her mother's brother for family, adopted the village as hers when it was no such thing. But they were all she had.

"Someone must take responsibility sometime," she said distantly. "Who else will do it?"

Neville watched her quivering lips and a brittle bit of his soul cracked. He had thought of Fiona as a wild hellion, a kind of Queen Maeve rescuing the undeserving. Yet for just this moment, the glitter of tears reminded him of Blanche as a child. She'd bravely fought her tears after some childish accident but willingly buried her grubby face in his cravat and sobbed when he comforted her. Neville had the urge to comfort now, but he retained sufficient sense to realize that just because she was petite, Fiona was no child.

"I can't return to London without you," he told her flatly. "I meant to return early so I could consolidate my position behind the reform bill before the session begins..." He sighed and clamped his mouth shut as he realized what he was about to say, yet in the next breath, the words came out anyway. "I can postpone the matter for a week, no more."

Hope bloomed in Fiona's expression as she turned to him. He could almost see the sun breaking through the gray gloom.

"If you'll help me, I promise to go quietly to London without further argument."

He didn't like the way she looked at him when she said that. For nigh on ten years now he'd worn blinders to keep from seeing anything but the narrow path of duty. Fiona didn't fit on that path. Doing anything in her company would be a reckless deviation.

Neville frowned. "Don't make promises you can't possibly keep."

He caught Fiona's fist before it could strike his jaw. For a moment, he knew jubilation. He'd reacted faster than the Irish scoundrel, Eamon, more quickly than Fiona herself. He wasn't entirely washed up on the shore of stodginess then. With a widening grin, he braced himself. "Didn't anyone tell you ladies do not use fists like pugilists?"

She lunged at him then, pounding his chest with both fists. Catching the angry sprite and swinging her from her feet, Neville laughed loudly. The sound surprised even him.

# Six

"It's no mystery who needs the money most." None too pleased at being dragged into a murder mystery when he was supposed to be escorting Fiona to London, Seamus kicked at a peat block drying in the sun outside Burke's empty kitchen. "If you discount Aileen's orphans, the finger points at Colin. He's gambled himself into a pit in Sligo, then had to marry Patsy, and now with the new babe comin', he's lost his position at the granary. He's in desperate straits, he is, and there's naught to save him but a ship to America."

"Your fancy Oxford accent is fading fast, big brother," Fiona said scornfully, checking for clues in the weeds beside the porch. "You'd best get yourself back to university before they tar you for a Paddy again."

"I'd be on my way to university now if it weren't for your meddlin', interferin' ways, brat. It's because you had a crush on the charmer Colin yourself that you bite at me. He's a rogue, and you know it."

"Just because he has looks and charm doesn't make him a rogue." Feeling irritable, Fiona took up the argument more heatedly. "Colin never hurt a soul but himself."

"Fighting amongst ourselves isn't getting us anywhere," the duke intervened without looking up from his appointed task of looking for traces of a murderer. "Colin will go on our list of suspects. He has the motive. Desperate men may do desperate things."

There stood most of the reason for her irritation, Fiona fumed, glaring at the man poking his dandified walking stick through the weeds of Burke's potato patch. The sun caught glints of gold in the duke's hair, reinforcing the whole Golden Ball image he projected. She knew little of London fashion, but she recognized the constraining fit of his broad-shouldered frockcoat as the result of expensive tailoring. And the polish of his high top boots didn't come from walking muddy fields. She suspected real gold and not cheap brass made up the knob of his cane, and briefly, she wondered how much a stick like that would fetch in a pawn shop. Probably enough to feed Aileen's orphans for months.

She ignored the odd tug of interest she felt when the duke lifted his tawny head and watched her as if awaiting her reply. "Fine then," she answered with scorn to hide her wayward notions, "if money's a motive, you can add every man in the village to your list."

"And how many of the women?" the duke asked in that same placid tone that had escalated her irritation earlier. "A knife in the back is the work of a woman as much as a man. He knew his murderer, opened the door for them. Was he seeing anyone?"

"The Widow Blackthorne," Seamus answered. "But she's a wee bit of a thing and stood to gain more by marriage to Burke than from his death. I don't fancy her as a murderess."

"Mrs. Blackthorne is a harpy," Fiona replied with scorn, giving up on finding anything in the weeds and heading for the house. "Burke had more sense than to marry her. I wouldn't put it past her to suggest they take a share of the village's money. Burke would have told her where to go, and that would be that. Very likely, if you ask me."

"Women," Seamus muttered, following his sister inside.

"Don't ignore them," Neville recommended. "They see things we don't often enough."

Both Seamus and Fiona turned and stared at him in surprise. Neville shrugged and let his eyes adjust to the dimness of the kitchen. McGonigle and his friends had already torn the place apart looking for any sign of the money. If there were clues here, they'd be hard to find.

"Just precisely what are we looking for?" Fiona asked as she scanned the contents of the cupboard. "Burke had no family. People have been in here scavenging his larder already. If there was anything valuable lying around, it's gone now."

"It seemed reasonable to search for something that might have belonged to the murderer. We'd have to look for something that doesn't belong here, a loose button, perhaps. Did the knife match the ones in his kitchen?" Neville glanced around the humble room with distaste. The task seemed impossible. Or improbable.

Both Seamus and Fiona rewarded his suggestion with looks of scorn.

"Matching knives?" Fiona of the hasty tongue replied first. "Whoever heard of such? Burke might have a knife handed down from his grandda, or from his late wife's family, or if what he had was worn to a nubbin, and he felt particularly wealthy, he might have bought new from a tinker. But who's to say what his knives looked like?"

"The Widow Blackthorne," Seamus answered before the words were scarce out of her mouth.

Neville nodded thoughtfully. "Your Uncle William has the knife now, doesn't he? Why don't you have him take it to the widow and ask if it came from this kitchen? It's a pity we can't show it around town and ask to whom it might belong if it's not Burke's."

"It'll be Burke's," Fiona replied wearily, slamming the cupboard doors.

"There's none here, and a man wouldn't leave his own knife behind."

"That could mean whoever did it, didn't mean to commit murder when he came in." Despite his irritation at the delay, Neville found the puzzle intriguing. He supposed he could give the earl a full report when he returned, and the effort wouldn't be entirely wasted. Michael had a strong sense of justice.

Keeping his mind on the puzzle didn't keep Neville from noticing the smudge on Fiona's cheek and wishing he could brush it away. He'd never seen a woman in such dishevelment before, and he found it oddly disconcerting that she had no care for her appearance in his company.

If he had a shilling for every female who'd thrown herself in his path these last ten years, all gowned and coifed and reeking of expensive scents, he'd be a rich man today. But those same women hadn't given him a second look when he'd been a lonely student and the son of a younger son, far from the grandiose title of duke. He'd never learned how to talk with those women in his formative years. That's why he'd decided on shy Gwyneth. But even Gwyneth didn't go about in boy's breeches with dust on her face — not in his presence, anyway.

Without a care to how it looked, Fiona got down on her hands and knees to explore the space behind the stove. Neville gulped and closed his eyes before he could look too closely at the rounded posterior presented to him.

"Fiona!" Seamus shouted angrily.

Fiona jumped and banged her head on a pipe. Cursing, she rubbed her head, not bothering to pull back to see what he wanted.

"Get your silly arse out of there!" Seamus demanded, shooting Neville a furious look that said he'd seen far more than was good for him.

"Curse your dratted hide, Seamus, what are you after scaring me half to death like that?" Backing out, still rubbing her sore head, Fiona turned and glared at her brother.

Cobwebs formed a silver halo in her hair, and soot blackened her forehead as much as her scowl. Neville stifled a grin. Looking like that, the stubborn chit could almost be classified as adorable.

Seamus grabbed the back of her shirt, hauled her up, and shoved her toward the door. "Go put on something decent for a change and ask the Widow Blackthorne about the knife."

Catching the brat's upraised hand before she could land a blow, Neville planted himself between the siblings. "Your mother should have taught you it's easier to catch flies with honey," he addressed Fiona first. "I ought to send both of you to Blanche for training. She would have Seamus crawling on his knees and begging with just a few words."

Feeling the tension in the young man's muscles beneath his other hand, Neville glared at him. "It's a little late to complain about her appearance. And if it's my intentions you're questioning, I'm the one who will plant you a facer."

With satisfaction, Neville noted this last declaration startled Fiona. She was an obnoxious brat, but she was innocent of the way a man's thoughts strayed in her presence. Blanche would have her hands full.

Growling, Seamus jerked away. "Eamon warned me to keep my eye on her, and I mean to do that." The warning in his tone was unmistakable.

"The two of you are bloody damned fools if you think—"

At a loud thump on the ceiling, they craned their heads upward. Without a word, all three dashed for the front room and the staircase.


Neville signaled his two companions to halt their weary horses on a hill overlooking a bustling small town.

"I don't know why you couldn't have caught him before he got out the window," Fiona said crossly, glaring at the mob hiding their prey.

Hay wagons, farm carts, and mules cluttered the roads entering the town, shoving foot travelers to the muddy edges. The tents and crowds of trade day covered the town square—where once they'd hoped to buy looms.

"Sure, and I should have sprouted wings. I'm telling you, it's Colin. I'd know that black head of hair anywhere." Seamus reined in his mount. "He'll be at the Bull and Boar if he's paying off his debts. Can't think why else he'd head this way instead of making for a port."

"And it's not as if half the county and more doesn't have black hair," Fiona replied scornfully, easing her horse down the dirt path. "He was too small for Colin, but I'd know the coat if I saw it again. There's not many who wear a tweed that ugly, and the left pocket was torn."

The argument ceased as they guided their horses down the rocky hill. Not until they'd worked their way into the steady stream of carts and animals did anyone speak again.

"I cannot think why the murderer would have returned if he already has the money." Riding a blooded thoroughbred twice the size of most of the animals around him, Neville sought their prey amidst the flux and flow of traffic. The man had escaped on a fine-boned mare of Arabian descent, but no such creature appeared in this motley lot.

His comment silenced the squabbling siblings, Neville noted with thanksgiving. He'd once regretted not having brothers or sisters. He was rethinking that regret now.

"Do you think it's possible he *didn't* find the money?" Fiona asked.

That she actually asked a reasonable question, treating his comment with respect, almost prompted a smile. He possessed one of the highest titles in the realm, was respected by his peers, sought after by his superiors, and none of that gave him half so much pleasure as knowing he was winning the respect of this annoying Irish female. Unconsciously, Neville rubbed the back of his head where his attackers had cudgeled him.

"It's possible, I suppose," he answered. "Or it could have been someone out for what they could find. We could be on a goose chase."

"If it's not Colin, we'll never find him in this mob," Seamus predicted. "We might as well check the Bull and Boar and go home if he's not there."

Neville caught the fleeting look of disappointment in Fiona's eyes. Had she truly thought to catch the murderer so easily? Or was there something else behind the excitement she'd displayed earlier when it became evident the town was their destination?

"As long as we're here, we may as well look around. We certainly don't have any other direction to follow." Neville let his horse fall back beside Fiona, giving Seamus room to lead.

Fiona seemed relieved by his decision, although she offered no thanks. Neville considered needling her just to watch the fire of anger rise in her cheeks but decided that was beneath him.

When they finally worked their way through to the tavern, Fiona started to climb from her horse as the men did. Neville caught her reins. "It's not proper for a lady to frequent such a place. Stay here and make certain our scoundrel does not escape some other way."

She appeared on the point of protest, then thought better of it and returned to her saddle. "You'd best hurry. I'm that hungry, I am, I could eat your horses while you're gone."

Neville didn't trust that obliging tone. With sudden decision, he tied his horse's reins to a post and nodded at Seamus. "It only takes one of us to look. I'll fetch meat pies from that vendor over there."

The scowl Fiona threw him justified Neville's decision. Seamus tipped his hat and sauntered inside. Fiona sat her horse and glared.

"You might as well tell me what you plan," Neville told her, taking her reins. "It will only make me angrier if I have to find out the hard way."

"It's none of your concern what I do, my lord duke," she informed him arrogantly. "But if you intend to buy those pies, you should hurry before they're all gone."

Neville smothered another smile. She sat her horse in boy's breeches and shirt, her hair tousled in thick auburn curls down her back, her cheeks still smudged with soot, yet she possessed the temerity to order him around as if she were a duchess and he a mere commoner at her feet. It was ludicrous to the extreme, and so captivating he couldn't help being charmed.

"I fail to see humor in starvation," she said icily. "Would you care to share the jest?"

"Nothing of moment, my queen, absolutely nothing, just a momentary lapse. I'll fetch your pies if you promise to stay put."

Fiona shot him a suspicious look at his easy capitulation. "I'm not likely to go anywhere in this mob," she assured him. "Besides, I'm watching for a murderer."

"Sure, and I'm an Irishman," Neville mocked. "One foot off that horse, and I'll have you on a ship to London faster than you'll know what's happened."

# Seven

Neville tightened his lips in exasperation as he caught Fiona easing her mount through the crowd and down the cobbled street. He'd known damned well she was up to something. He never should have turned his back on her for even ten seconds.

Forgetting the meat pies, he strode toward his horse. He'd be damned if he let the brat roam loose in a rowdy crowd like this.

Neville caught up with her in front of a pawn shop where Fiona leaned from her horse to converse with a merchant in a leather apron. The dratted brat had taken him literally. She hadn't set her foot to earth, as promised. She must have sent someone in the shop to fetch the pawn broker.

Her ferocious scowl at being caught struck Neville as immensely funny, but people seldom appreciated his sense of humor.

"I'll give you fair trade for whatever the lady is pawning," Neville addressed the startled merchant. He prayed it wasn't too costly. He had not brought funds for more than a brief stay in this godforsaken place.

The man beamed. "A pound, my lord, and you may have this fine silver bracelet." He held up a slim band that caught the sunlight.

"He only gave me three crowns," Fiona grumbled. "And this is none of your concern, as usual, my lord duke. Keep your coins. They'll have better use elsewhere."

"The man deserves a commission for trading on the street." Neville flipped the broker a sovereign and claimed the bauble. He didn't know a great deal about jewelry, but the scrollwork on this piece looked old. He sent sulky Fiona a quick look. "Family heirloom?"

"As I said, it's none of your concern."

She abruptly steered her horse back to the street. For the life of him, he couldn't figure out why he bothered following. The first time he'd seen Fiona, she'd been a grimy urchin on the streets of London, searching for her brother, hiding from Michael, and creating chaos and anarchy all around her in the process. Two years had made a hell of a lot of difference in her appearance, if not her manners.

He'd scarcely reached her side before she grabbed his sleeve, and pointed down a side street. "There he is! That's the coat."

Neville glanced where she pointed, spotting the Arabian mare and the coat at the same time. "Get Seamus," he ordered before spurring his gelding in the intruder's direction.

Fiona watched in amazement as the proper duke sent his mount sailing over a hedge and across the emerald lawn of some well-to-do cit, evidently aiming to cut off his prey at the alley as he would a fox on a hunt. Instead of obeying the duke's orders, Fiona stayed behind her quarry, working her way through the crowd as quickly as possible to keep him in sight.

A tent cut her off from the fancy mare for only a moment. By the time she passed a mob laughing uproariously at a Punch and Judy show, both mare and man had disappeared. And the duke had long since departed down the alley. Gritting her teeth, Fiona took the only path that seemed logical, following the main road as it curved around a block of shops, hoping to catch sight of either the duke or their prey.

She found the duke first. Hat gone, golden-brown hair disheveled, he stood in his stirrups trying to see down a narrow, winding road past gaudy banners and shop signs, barrel wagons and cows.

"He had to have gone this way," she said as she rode up beside him. "I don't see any other alleys."

Rather than point out her disobedience, the duke reined his horse into the melee. "We'll follow the road out of town. Perhaps we can see easier there."

That suited her just fine. It's what she would have done. The duke might irritate her beyond redemption, but he did have a habit of making the right decisions — most of the time.

She wondered what he'd done with her bracelet. Aileen's orphans could have used the coin he'd given that broker. They couldn't eat jewelry. Buying the bracelet was not one of the duke's better decisions, but then, she hadn't explained the problem to him. She'd not let him know how much her grandmother's bracelet meant to her.

The crowd thinned as they wove their way out of town. Briefly, Fiona considered Seamus' concern when he found them gone, but he'd find something to occupy his time. He could look for Colin. She knew the man ahead of them wasn't Colin. That didn't mean he was the thief or murderer, but he wasn't Colin.

She watched the duke scan the road. His gelding was taller than her mare, and the duke towered another head taller than she, so his view was less obscured than hers. From his expression, she'd judge that he hadn't found their quarry. Although why she thought she could judge the expression of a man who never showed emotion was beyond her.

She thought she discerned annoyance in his posture now, but she could just be transferring her own feelings to him. "There's an inn ahead. We can make inquiries, and perhaps find something to eat that's bound to taste better than street fare."

His Grace dismounted and tied their horses to a hitching post. His effortless strength as he lifted her from her saddle nearly took Fiona's breath away. His hands lingered just a moment too long at her waist. His intent gaze made butterflies take wing in her stomach. She stepped away so quickly she almost tripped over her horse.

What was going on in his inscrutable mind now? He didn't want her going inside a roadside inn but couldn't leave her alone outside? She could tell him she'd been inside far worse, but she would only irritate him more.

Without comment, she climbed the inn steps, pushing open the door as if she'd done it all her life. Vaguely, she realized a lady didn't open doors for herself, but if she sat around waiting for men to do things for her, she'd still be sleeping in a cradle.

Behind her, Neville closed his eyes against the sight of swinging hips and long legs. For the first time in his life, he considered prayer as a resource against temptation. Perhaps she'd run about the village in those clothes all her life and the men there had come to accept it. But she was on strange territory now. Someone should have shaken some sense into her long ago.

It wasn't his place to do so. Duty dictated that he protect her until she was back in her brother's care again. That was all.

But stepping inside the lowly inn, Neville had a sinking feeling that he stepped outside all propriety now. A gentleman did not escort an unmarried lady into a disreputable roadside inn. He was only thankful that he was far from London and anyone who might recognize him.

The sounds of riot emanating from the tavern erased even that small prayer. The realization that Fiona was nowhere in sight sent him flying across the wooden lobby.


Leaning his shoulders against the doorjamb, crossing his booted feet, Michael MacDermot, the Earl of Aberdare, stared at the letter in his hand as if expecting images to appear beyond the hastily scratched words.

"What does he mean, they're searching for clues? That's what William's there for. Dukes don't grub around village streets looking for criminals. He's just supposed to bring Fiona back."

His adopted brother, the Marquess of Effingham, shrugged and contemplated a crystal paper weight that changed colors when he moved it. "I think that crack on the noggin warped Neville's thinking, not that I ever understood the way his head works, mind you."

"Simple," Michael replied. "Duty comes first. Neville would place his vote in the Lords before his own funeral."

Effingham grinned. "I can see it now, the ghost of Anglesey standing up to be counted and the whole bench fainting dead away. I should live so long."

Michael scowled. "I'd better go see what this is about. I can't have murderers running free around my estate." He levered his slender frame from the doorjamb and dropped the letter on Effingham's desk.

"Ahem," the marquess cleared his throat politely. "If my wife is to be believed, Blanche is in the family way again. You might want to rethink that decision. Ladies in their first months are notoriously unreliable."

Michael groaned and jammed his hands through his hair. "Oh, damn, so that's why she demanded peaches with her dinner last night. Devil take it, this town's put me off stride for certain."

Without further explanation, he dashed from the room, leaving Neville's letter behind.

Since his younger brother never cursed except in moments of high excitement—usually involving his wife—Effingham forgave his lapse. Picking up the letter, he read it over again.

It seemed curiously coincidental that a man just viciously attacked and left for dead would stumble across another crime in a sleepy Irish village where he'd gone for rest and relaxation. Michael's bookish Uncle William was *not* the man to look into the matter.

Tapping a pen against his lips, Effingham considered the alternatives. The bloody proper Duke of Anglesey had his annoying moments, but he was a man who could be swayed by reason. Too few of those existed in the archaic halls of British Parliament. Perhaps His Grace had annoyed one too many people this past year or so. Perhaps it was meaningless coincidence.

In either case, someone should look into the matter. Applying pen to paper, Effingham set in operation the rather formidable network of informants he'd established since coming to this country.

It never hurt to be prepared.


Dodging between two stocky farmers, Fiona grabbed a chair, swung on her heels, and slammed it against the skull of the first man crossing her path. The man groaned and collapsed to the floor with a satisfying thud. That would teach the lousy bastard to lay his molesting hands on her.

Fiona thought she caught a grimace of disapproval from the duke, but his fists were otherwise engaged in breaking a man's jaw, judging by the sound of the crack resonating through the room. They were overpowered five to two, but she thought they stood a fair chance of beating these drunken fools.

Grabbing a pewter pitcher from the table, she flung its contents at the attacker lunging toward her. He scarcely halted his lumbering progress. Fiona darted to one side, thinking to bring the pitcher down over his head, but with more luck than strategy, her assailant grabbed her wrist before she could strike. The pitcher clattered to the floor as he twisted her arm.

With lightning speed, a sword point notched the man's Adam's apple. The farmer gulped, dropped Fiona's wrist, and backed away.

In amazement, Fiona glanced around at the wreckage of the tavern. Four men lay groaning on the floor, clutching bruised and broken parts. She'd brought down only one. The fifth stood at sword point. Fiona's gaze traced the long black handle of the duke's walking stick to its source.

With barely concealed jubilation, the haughty Duke of Anglesey twisted the sword cane a little tighter against her assailant's neck. "How do you like your scoundrels served, my dear? Skewered and roasted over an open fire? Or slashed and stomped into the dust?"

Speechless, Fiona just stared. The duke didn't look as if he had a hair out of place. His immaculate linen remained properly unrumpled, and he was *smiling*. He had just laid flat three rogues and cornered a fourth, and he was smiling as if he'd made a particularly clever wager. And he'd called her "my dear." He must have cracked his noble head in the brawl.

His Grace lifted one arrogant brow and awaited her reply.

"Just let him go," Fiona whispered. "They're drunk. They don't deserve to die for stupidity."

Taking advantage of the duke's distraction, his captive backed away, spun around, and ran out the door faster than his squat legs should have carried him.

The duke looked mildly disappointed but now that his regard returned to her, he apparently lost interest in his victory. Fiona squirmed beneath his gray-eyed stare and wished for the triumphant knight of a moment ago.

"That's fair of you," he said, "since it's your own stupidity that started this. I suggest we do without your nuncheon and leave this place while we still have our skin."

Something about the way he said "skin" distracted her from the iciness of his voice. Aware of the flesh exposed by her torn shirt sleeve, Fiona called upon the well of defiance that had sustained her all these years. Grabbing a roasted chicken from a platter on the table, she stalked past her adversary with shoulders thrown back. She'd be damned if she let any bloody Englishman intimidate her.

# Eight

Bracing himself for the noise and the filth, Neville halted in the doorway of the orphans' cottage. Now that he had some understanding of Fiona's habits, he didn't have to follow her when she fled the castle.

The brawl at the inn—oddly enough—had given them each a new respect for each other. She still defiantly displayed her figure in the boys' clothes, but he could almost understand the practicality of them. Actually, he had begun to wonder if the brawl hadn't been a diversion created by their wily intruder.

He watched as Fiona lifted a heavy kettle from the fire and set it on the hearth. She didn't seem strong enough for such work, but the brat had qualities beyond the obvious.

Six small heads bent over the trestle table, slurping at porridge. In the corner, the grandmother rocked a sleeping babe. Domestic contentment reigned, for the moment. Neville had already learned how easily the room could erupt in chaos. He'd prefer not disturbing the peace, but Fiona had to face facts sometime.

She must have used the coins from the sale of her jewelry to provide food for the children, but surely she must see that she couldn't feed them forever. A household of eight needed far more than food. Besides a roof over their heads and beds to sleep in, they needed someone who could watch after them day and night. Their grandmother would die of exhaustion just trying.

Fiona stiffened as she noticed him. Her hair had recently been brushed and pulled back in a braid, so only a few unruly tendrils fell about her forehead. Glancing at the hungry children, she hesitated. Evidently his entrance would distract the quiet, as he had feared.

Neville returned to the yard, and she joined him there. In the sunlight, her cheeks had the same soft radiance as the orchids in his conservatory.

He had meant to restore her bracelet when they'd returned, but for some reason, he again ignored it as he sought the coins in his pocket. Catching her hand, he dropped the shillings in her palm.

"I have little enough to get us back to London. If you don't mind doing without, you can give them to the children. It still won't be enough, Fiona."

Black circles beneath her eyes gave indication of her sleepless night. For the first time since Neville had known her, Fiona exhibited none of her usual restless energy. He missed that vitality.

She glanced at the tiny stone cottages of the village leaning one against another, the dirt in the street, the pig rooting through garbage, the bright patch of Michaelmas daisies against a gray wall. She returned her gaze to him, her expression resigned.

"Colin's gone. There's those that think he did it."

"But not you," Neville supplied for her. He felt a twinge of envy for her loyalty to her old love, but Fiona was meant for finer things than a black Irishman who would drink her life away. But they had no other suspects, and there was little else they could do.

She shrugged. "It does not matter what I think. Burke's dead; the money is gone. I have no way of providing for even these wee ones and certainly not for an entire village. Perhaps if I talk to him in person, I can persuade Michael to buy the looms."

Neville breathed a sigh of relief. He wouldn't have to carry her to London in a sack then. "It's not Michael's money," he reminded her cautiously.

Her aura of weariness intensified. He preferred it when she threw him looks of defiance and called him names.

"I know, but Blanche is such a soft touch that it seems a sin to ask it of her. She would give away everything she owned and leave her own family without. We'd not thought to ask it of her. We'd meant to do it all ourselves."

"We've given your uncle a few leads to follow. Perhaps he'll find the thief." Neville curled his fingers into his palms and hardened himself against the hurt emanating from her. She was Michael's problem, not his. "You've done all you can, Fiona. You know that."

Defiance flared. "Not all." With that enigmatic statement, she marched off.

Neville didn't bother following her. He knew where to find her if he needed. In the morning, they sailed for London, and he would have accomplished his duty.

In London at last, Neville still wasn't ready to settle into those duties.

"Blanche, you must be out of your mind to think you can take an uncivilized hellion like Fiona and turn her into a proper lady. Do you know I actually found her on the top mast one day? She was looking for London, she said. In front of an entire yacht filled with sailors, she climbed those ropes and made a spectacle of herself!"

Reliving that moment, Neville scowled and upended his cup of tea, wishing it were something stronger. He knew he'd aged ten years since delivering Fiona and her brother to their respective destinations.

Blanche smiled serenely and poured more tea. "She is a breath of fresh air. You know how Michael despises taking his seat in the Lords. He's been pacing like a caged tiger for weeks. But if they're to pass the Catholic emancipation bill, he has to be here. I was afraid he would turn the townhouse into a carnival tent and invite the circus if I didn't do something. Fiona will provide the distraction he needs."

Neville rose to pace the carpet in much the same manner as Blanche had accused her husband of doing. "Then let her distract Michael with her antics and keep her out of society. She's a heathen, I'm telling you. She'll never take."

He'd debated the problem long and hard. Fiona couldn't be unleashed on London. Perhaps he could quietly introduce the chit to a respectable man or two without introducing her to society at large. He couldn't think of anyone he hated enough to wish that fate upon, but he hadn't had time enough to consider the dilemma thoroughly. "Save yourself a lot of trouble and let her play in the nursery with the children and see the sights, then send her home when the session is over."

"She does have a way with children," Blanche admitted. "She's taught Mary to jump up and down on the beds, and of course, Nicholas must do so too. It's excellent exercise for Mary's leg, and if she falls, it's all part of the game. I really can't ask Nicholas not to do what Mary does."

Neville gestured in triumph. "See? What did I tell you? It will be anarchy within weeks. You'd think she was eleven instead of one and twenty."

Fiona hesitated just outside the doorway to the salon, a flush staining her cheeks. She didn't know why the humiliation stung now when she'd never cared about anyone's opinion before. That's what she got for eavesdropping.

She hadn't realized how childish a grown woman teaching children to jump on beds must seem. She'd always unleashed her exuberance as she liked because no one had ever told her she couldn't. It had seemed simple enough when growing up. She had a mind of her own, and though it lacked the education she would have liked, it worked fairly well in her opinion. But the duke's acid declaration that she behaved like a child shamed her.

Cheeks burning, Fiona checked the gauzy neckerchief she could never keep tucked neatly in her bodice. Straightening it and refastening her brooch, she shook out her skirt, hoping the wrinkles would disappear. They didn't. She gave them a frown, took a deep breath to screw up her courage, and entered the salon. She wasn't one for hiding.

The duke's features remained impassive. Fiona decided if he raised his quizzing glass to inspect her any closer, she'd spit in his other eye. There briefly she'd thought him almost human, but the journey to London had returned his frosty self. And since he merely sipped from his cup without greeting her, she didn't bother curtsying for him.

Pretending he didn't exist, Fiona smiled at her hostess and settled on the settee. "I'm sorry I'm late. Mary insisted on a story before her nap, and I forgot the time."

"You will spoil the child. She's perfectly capable of reading every one of her storybooks on her own. I think she has them memorized. Do not let her take advantage of you. Just because her one leg does not work so well does not mean she's not a little demon like any other child."

The laughter in Blanche's voice indicated she thought otherwise, and Fiona didn't take her comments as criticism. Blanche loved her adopted daughter as much as she loved her son, as she would probably love any child. Fiona admired the countess and wished she could be a little more like her. But she was cursed with a cynical mind and sharp tongue and could not be content with babies and nesting, not when there were so many starving children and unhappy people in the world.

"They're beautiful children," she replied, but her mind traveled to Aileen's orphans. They didn't have beds for romping on, or storybooks for reading. She knew Blanche would shower them with gifts should she ask, but she couldn't ask. It was charity enough that the earl and countess took her into their home.

That bitter thought turned Fiona's head in the duke's direction. He was studying her as if she were some curious insect he'd never seen before. With a defiant tilt of her chin, Fiona allowed his inspection. "Well, sir duke, does this attire meet with your approval?"

His thin lips quirked upward for just a moment before he sipped his tea again. That she might possibly have amused him caused an unexpected tightening in her midsection. Back there in that tavern, when they'd fought side by side, she'd almost admired him.

The duke set the china back in its saucer. "At least it's a gown and not breeches," he replied. "And you're sitting in a chair and not a top mast. I'd have to say that's an improvement. How long does it last?"

Ignoring the deliberately baiting question, she turned to Blanche. "Must a lady always be polite when provoked?" she asked.

Blanche shook her golden curls. "Not with family. Neville's family. You may shoot him down any way you wish. He needs it. All the bootlicking goes to his head elsewise."

Fiona grinned, sank back in the chair, and flung the duke a triumphant grin. "So, my lord duke, when do you mean to introduce me to swarms of eligible men so you might marry me off and pry me out of your hair?"

The duke's magnificent eyebrows drew together in a warning frown that should have shaken her to her toes, but Fiona knew perfectly well she had nothing to fear from Neville. He towered over her by a foot and probably carried twice her weight, but he was a gentleman born and bred. She need only fear his caustic tongue, and she had ample shield against that.

"I've purchased boxes at the opera," he replied, fixing her with his implacable glare. "You'll attend with Blanche and myself this evening. If I hear anything more than 'Yes, Your Grace,' or 'No, Your Grace,' out of you, I'll throw you over the rail and into the pit."

# Nine

"McGonigle is undoubtedly leading one of the Whiteboy factions in your district, but much as I would like to pin the crime on him, it does not seem likely." In the foyer of the Earl of Aberdare's townhouse, Neville watched the earl absent-mindedly juggle coins. Michael's odd habits had ceased annoying Neville long ago. His impatience now had more to do with Blanche and Fiona dallying upstairs, while he waited to escort Fiona to her first social event.

"Someone needs to steer all that rebellious anger into more productive channels," Michael responded, not entirely off the subject but far enough for Neville to take several seconds to follow. For a moment, he almost thought the earl spoke of Fiona.

"You're a fair landlord, more so than any I've seen," Neville replied. "Your tenants have no reason for complaint. The man who murdered Burke is a common thief. I doubt that he has any connection to anything so organized as a band of ruffians."

Michael dropped the coins into his pockets as voices sounded on the landing above. "William isn't much good at anything but following orders. I'll have to find someone who can use his head a little more. No matter how bad the times are, there's no excuse for murder."

Neville scarcely heard him. He fastened his gaze on the staircase where the two women slowly descended. He had grown up with Blanche, and though she was a beautiful woman in her own way, he barely noticed her blond fairness beside Fiona's vivid coloring.

A tumble of auburn curls crowned their guest's high forehead and whispered around a slim white throat. Flashing green eyes dared comment. That she actually met his gaze without a hint of coyness caught his breath, but her defiance stirred something considerably lower.

Striving for his usual cool demeanor, Neville let his gaze drift from Fiona's face to the gown Blanche had chosen for her. The sight of full white curves rising above the flimsy gold bodice nearly undid him. A swift glance assured him that all her curves were equally spectacular, and his mind slipped from its lofty plateau straight into the gutter.

The vicious pounding in his head returned, and Neville dragged his gaze from the chit in her low-cut gown and back to the earl. "You're not letting her out looking like that, are you?"

Michael only grinned.

~

"By Jove, Duke, you've acquired a diamond of the first water there. Why haven't you snatched her up before half of London's slavering beasts descend upon her?"

Since Morton was close to slavering as he spoke, Neville seriously considered dropping his friend over the railing as he had threatened to do to Fiona. Morton's gaze scarcely wavered from the bosom rising above that blasted gold bodice. Rationally, Neville supposed the ladies in the other boxes wore gowns much lower, but he did not think they had quite so much to display as Fiona.

"Her dowry is modest," Neville responded curtly. "As is her lineage. She has need of a man with more wealth than I can provide her."

Morton gave him a shrewd look. "Then it's Gwyneth you've set your sights on. I warn you, old man, she's not what she seems. She'll give you a run for your money."

Neville could have told him the same about Fiona, but he refrained. To his surprise, the brat was actually living up to their agreement and behaving the perfect lady — for the moment. He'd have to aid her search for a wealthy husband. Morton didn't have a title, but he had funds enough. He had horses on the brains, Neville supposed, but that shouldn't matter for the minx's purpose. She could do far worse.

Fiona smiled a polite greeting as Neville introduced her. He resisted yanking Morton up by the cravat as his friend's gaze continued wandering downward. Neville wished Fiona would smile with a little more welcome and a little less coldness, but he couldn't very well correct her behavior.

Weren't women supposed to know these things? She possessed a smile that could shame the blazing sun. A smile like that could make a man her slave forever. Foolish chit, not using all her artillery up front. Disgruntled and not fully understanding why, Neville leaned against the back of the box and watched the couple with cynicism.

When the recess ended and Morton reluctantly departed, Neville returned to his chair beside Fiona. She kept her gaze fixed on the caterwauling soprano on the stage, but he knew from the way she fingered her fan that she wasn't paying attention.

"Why the devil did you freeze Morton out like that?" he whispered peevishly, blaming his irritation on his pounding headache. "He's got wealth and a pretty face and he drooled all over you. I thought you'd be pleased."

"He drooled all over me," she whispered with distaste, still staring at the stage. "How charming. And I thought you were introducing me to civilized society."

"Morton is civilized," Neville protested. "He's a scion of two earls and a marquess; his family dates back to Elizabeth's reign. He has bottomless pockets. You had only to smile, and he would have fallen at your feet."

She shot him a venomous glare. "You want me to marry a carpet?"

A carpet. Neville covered his eyes and sank back in his chair. A carpet. A descendant of nobility, a Corinthian to the bone, a member of every fashionable club in St. James, and she calls him a "carpet." What did he have to do, present her with a lion on a leash?

A man couldn't argue with the illogical meanderings of the female mind. He would simply produce every wealthy man in all of London and let her choose as she saw fit. It made no difference to him whom she chose so much as how quickly she chose.

The dreadful performance finally ended, and they escaped into the cool air. Fiona watched with irritation as the duke stalked off with scarcely a fare-thee-well. Did the ridiculous man think she was a piece of meat he need only display for some golden-coined buyer to snap her up?

Not hearing Blanche's concerned question, Fiona lifted the dratted tight skirt and stepped into the waiting carriage. She felt exposed, shamed, and furious all at the same time. Is this what she had bargained for when she agreed to come to London?

"Fiona? Is something wrong? Didn't you like the performance? I'll admit, I don't understand the Italian very well, but the music was quite good, don't you think?"

Fiona sighed and collapsed against the carriage squabs. She couldn't hurt Blanche's feelings. Keeping her thoughts to herself, she gave the easy answer. "I have a small megrim, nothing a good night's sleep won't fix."

Blanche laughed. "Enjoy a good night's sleep while you can. After tonight, you'll be on every invitation we receive. We'll only give a small ball for your come-out since there's so few in town this time of year, but you needn't worry. Morton will have your name on every man's tongue by morning."

*Oh, charming.* She couldn't wait to parade before an entire room full of panting animals. Why didn't they just auction her off to the highest bidder?

For the first time, Fiona doubted the wisdom of her plan. Maybe she should have accepted Eamon's offer after all. She would never feel comfortable in glittering society. How could she possibly marry some old man who simply wanted to show her off? Why had she thought she could do this?

Perhaps because—until tonight—she hadn't realized how men looked at her.

Skin crawling, Fiona wished for her boy's clothes back. She should never have been born female. She didn't have the right sort of mind. She'd hated the way Morton had kept staring at her bosom. What on earth did he see that every woman in the room didn't possess and probably displayed more elegantly?

Still, remembering the duke's stunned reaction as she had walked down the steps, Fiona knew a niggle of satisfaction. For that moment, she had known a woman's power. If she must continue on this ghastly path, she could at least amuse herself by practicing her wiles on the arrogant, inscrutable duke. It would warm her soul to see him panting as Morton had tonight.

"Didn't expect to see you here, old boy." Lord Bennet stopped beside Neville to study the ballroom. "Thought the session would last into the night. Slipped out early, myself. Couldn't see any point in staying. The Catholic Emancipation bill hasn't a chance. Don't know why you even bothered introducing it."

Neville scowled at the older man's comment. "I introduced it because we'll have a revolution in Ireland if something isn't done. The conditions there are deplorable."

His companion laughed. "The Irish have been threatening revolution for centuries. It's all they're good for. That and fine horseflesh," he amended. "And maybe I should have taken a longer look at their women when I was younger." He chuckled, and his gaze drifted toward the auburn tresses proceeding toward them. "Aberdare's young cousin is a fine piece of womanhood. If it weren't for the crowd of suitors around her, I might just consider getting myself leg-shackled again."

Since the speaker was nigh on sixty and rotund as he was tall, Neville didn't think his chances exceedingly high, but he had the distinct feeling that the old lecher expected an introduction. With cynicism, Neville gestured at Fiona as she emerged from the crowd. Mayhap the chit could put her charm to good use and sway the old man on the Catholic bill.

"Your Grace." Fiona curtsied and actually used the proper title, but Neville caught a distinct gleam behind lowered lashes. She even made a mockery out of politeness.

"The Viscount Bennet, Miss Fiona MacDermot." Neville made the introduction curtly. He'd considered seeking another mistress to relieve some of his physical frustration, but the necessity of providing an heir soon had been impressed upon him with that blow to his head. He couldn't in all good conscience set up a mistress while courting Gwyneth.

"My lord, a pleasure to meet you." The impish smile on Fiona's tempting lips made Neville grit his teeth. He hadn't even explained the necessity of twisting the viscount to their side in the upcoming vote, and she was still batting her eyelashes at him. He should never have reprimanded her for turning Morton off cold. She'd gone to the other extreme with every other man since.

Caught in his own thoughts, Neville lost track of the conversation until he discovered Fiona slipping her slender fingers around the viscount's pudgy arm. He jerked back to alertness just in time to catch Bennet's satisfied grin.

"Just saw the Lady Gwyneth arrive. You'll be wanting to fix her interest, I suspect, so I'll take this little charmer off your hands."

Neville wanted to shout that the viscount couldn't take Fiona any farther than Blanche, but the pair had already merged with the surging crowd.

Neville swerved his attention to the arriving guests and his goal for the evening. He'd concluded he didn't have time to search for a more suitable heiress than Gwyneth. Gwyneth was accessible, she was rich, and she would make a good duchess. If she didn't arouse his lust in the same manner as a wench like Fiona, that was all to the good. He didn't have time for adolescent cravings. He simply needed an heir, and Gwyneth could give him that.

Neville worked his way through the crowd, shaking a hand here, exchanging a piece of political gossip there, never losing sight of his goal. She'd already slipped to the edge of the crowd behind a potted plant. The child would have to learn confidence, but that came with age.

The image of Fiona chatting and flirting without a hint of shyness flitted through his mind, but Neville dismissed it. Fiona was a born flirt. He preferred his women shy and retiring.

He detoured long enough to acquire a glass of punch before approaching Gwyneth's hiding place.

"We cannot continue meeting like this," Neville said with a gentle smile as he handed her the glass. Cosseting her seemed the best approach.

She gave a nervous start even though she had to have known he headed in her direction. She accepted the glass without meeting his eyes. "Your Grace is too kind." she murmured.

"I don't suppose you could see fit to call me Neville," he asked wryly. "Miss MacDermot has mangled my title so many times that I'm not certain if I should respond to it any longer."

That elicited a smile from the lady. "She's quite spirited, isn't she? I admire her confidence."

Usually Gwyneth found a seat so she didn't tower over the company, but she had apparently arrived too late to claim one. Neville found it a trifle strange looking up at her. Perhaps these weeks of Fiona's company had twisted his perceptions. If he must compare, Gwyneth was actually the fairer of the two. Fiona's features were far too angular for beauty. Gwyneth's quiet demeanor simply didn't demand the attention that Fiona's vivacity attracted.

"Spirited is one word for Miss MacDermot," he agreed dryly. "But I did not come here to speak of her. I'm sorry we did not have our opportunity for a ride through the park last month. Would you by any chance be interested in trying it again?"

She seemed uncommonly nervous about the suggestion, but as Neville suspected, she didn't refuse.

"I would like that, thank you very much," she whispered.

Well, there were some advantages to his title, Neville thought after he'd made the arrangements and left his retiring intended to her mother's company. Marriageable females simply couldn't say "no" to a duke of the realm. He didn't like the notion that Gwyneth accepted his invitation simply because her family required it of her. Perhaps he should sound her out a little more when they were less closely watched.

Noting Blanche searching the crowded ballroom, Neville scowled and used his greater height to follow the path of her gaze. Fiona had the art of disappearing almost down to the same perfection as Michael, who wasn't anywhere to be seen either.

Not seeing either the earl or Fiona, Neville pushed his way through the crowd to Blanche's side. "Where's Michael?" he demanded.

"Oh, the library here has a collection of ships in bottles and he's studying how it's done." She flashed him a brief smile. "It's the only reason he agreed to come tonight."

Neville rolled his eyes in understanding. Michael's eccentric propensities were well known both inside and outside his family. Anyone hoping to attract the Earl of Aberdare to their homes had to provide suitable entertainment, and a violin player didn't count.

"So Fiona has escaped her leash?" he asked without need of further explanation.

"I'm afraid so. She was with the Lord Bennet just moments ago. I'm certain she's perfectly safe with him. But the round has ended, and he hasn't returned her here. I'm afraid she may have found someone more interesting. She doesn't quite understand the proprieties yet, I'm afraid."

That was stating it mildly. Neville handed his almost empty glass to Blanche. "Stay here. I'll find her. I need only look for a large throng of men."

Oddly enough, he saw no such gathering except in the gaming room, and Fiona wasn't there. Beginning to worry, Neville systematically searched all the adjacent chambers. He found her in the last place expected — the library with Michael.

Fiona looked up as Neville entered, wrinkled her nose, and returned to examining a large text spread out on the library table. Neville didn't think Michael even knew she was there. The earl had apparently discovered the technique of collapsing the fragile wooden ships and had dismantled one and pulled it from its bottle. The pieces lay on the mantel before him.

"Blanche is looking for you." Not wishing to disturb Michael lest he forget how to put the ship back together, Neville whispered the warning.

"I thought she was having a good time and didn't want to disturb her." She closed the text with a sigh. "I don't suppose we could leave yet?"

Surprised, still wary of his reaction to her physical presence, Neville kept a safe distance. "You seemed to be enjoying yourself. Did Bennet say something to disturb you?"

"The viscount? Scarcely."

She waved a dismissive hand, a gesture that drew his attention to her bosom. He thought he detected a small beauty mark just to one side... Catching himself, Neville shook off his reverie and applied his attention to her petulant expression. Most young misses marking such a triumphant debut as she had made tonight would be preening with happiness. Fiona appeared distinctly bored.

"You have captured the interest of half London's eligible bachelors tonight. You should be ecstatic. Or do none of them suit your discriminating tastes?"

She gave him a wry look and gestured again, this time deliberately drawing his attention to her breasts. "They are not seeing me, Your Grace. They are seeing these. I do believe if you'd lend me the use of some jewels, their eyes would cross and they would trip over their tongues and fall flat on their faces. Then I could have a veritable carpet of suitors to walk upon."

A choking noise from the mantel indicated Michael wasn't quite so oblivious as he seemed. Neville scowled as the earl turned and gave him a beatific grin.

"Well, your noble lordship," Aberdare said cheerfully into the silence left by Fiona's declaration, "shall we find her some jewels and acquire a most unique carpet for our ballroom?"

# Ten

"I understand you and His Grace are cousins of a sort," Lady Gwyneth commented the next day. She and Fiona strolled down a grassy hill toward their companions, who watered their horses at a stream.

Fiona liked Lady Gwyneth, but she never felt quite comfortable being dwarfed by a woman. Some other undercurrent bothered her also. Mayhap it had to do with the lady's interest in the duke.

Fiona scowled at that wayward thought and glanced toward Morton and the duke laughing over some jest. The late autumn light caught the gold in the duke's hair and gave his pale features a sun-kissed color much more pleasing to the eye than Morton's uninspired dark coloring. Fiona hoped they did not laugh over her, but she had the uneasy feeling that all London laughed behind her back. She imagined she and Gwyneth made a laughable picture when they strolled together. But Gwyneth was the only lady her own age who would condescend to speak more than two words to her, and they ended up in each other's company more often than not.

"We're cousins by marriage only," Fiona answered. "I'm quite certain the duke would denounce the relationship entirely were it his choice."

"He's a proud man, and not a bad one, I think," Gwyneth responded, halting before they reached the men.

Remembering Blanche's hint that Neville courted this woman, Fiona sought placating words. "He means well," she agreed. In truth, she knew little enough about the man other than that he forced her to face what she didn't want to face.

Gwyneth smiled. "You mean he's so conservative he makes you want to scream and knock his head against a wall. I've heard you too well on your theories of the British Parliament, and the duke is a staunch supporter of the forces controlling government now."

Fiona had the grace to blush. She'd said entirely too much, but she had no more control over her tongue than the trees had over the wind. Politics were not an acceptable social conversation, particularly for women, but they were the only topic of particular interest to her. "He means well," she repeated.

And she meant it. From what little bits she'd skimmed from dinner discussions, she understood the duke's position. She just didn't agree with it. Reform was needed now, not in some distant future.

"It's all right. I understand. He's a good man, but it's only natural to protect one's own interests first. Until Parliament consists of men who represent all the population instead of just the wealthy landowners, we'll never have fair legislation. I don't suppose you'd be interested in joining a small group of mine who share similar interests in changing the way things are?"

Fiona immediately went on the alert. Seamus had once belonged to a group of men who wanted to change things, but their means had been violent, and he'd almost hanged for his flapping tongue. She saw no peaceful means of accomplishing change, and she threw the lady beside her a wary look. "By what means?" she asked bluntly.

Gwyneth waved a placating hand. "Oh, peaceful ones, to be certain. We're just women, after all."

"Does the duke know you belong to such a group?" Fiona sent an anxious look to the two men waiting for them. She'd rather they didn't hear this exchange.

As if reading her thoughts, Gwyneth resumed their stroll. "Oh, he thinks we're a bluestocking group who have scholarly speakers and literary interests. That's what they all think. They don't expect women to have minds."

"And that's for certain," Fiona muttered as they came within hearing of the men. Unable to respond elsewise, she threw Mr. Morton a smile that left his jaw hanging open. She knew from her mirror that she wasn't particularly pretty, not in the vapid flower petal way of most of society's acclaimed beauties. Her forehead was too high, her hair too red, her chin too small. The list was endless. But she need only stick out her chest and smile, and men stumbled over their feet and fell.

She knew the duke favored Morton as a suitable husband for her. The man had money enough, she supposed, and they had a common interest in horses, but she wasn't foolish enough to believe that would persuade him to support an Irish village. No, she needed a doddering old man who didn't care about anything except pleasing her. The Viscount Bennet seemed best suited to that cause.

Neville watched the two women saunter down the path, their contrasting appearances capturing all the afternoon's light. He tried focusing on Gwyneth with her gleaming blond hair capped by an enormously expensive hat adorned with an egret feather. She walked with studied grace, carrying her height with ease now that she had an audience of only two. Yet his gaze persisted in drifting to the smaller figure beside her.

Fiona had actually acquiesced to wearing a suitable riding habit and using a sidesaddle, but her defiance crept out in small ways. She didn't wear feminine velvet in pretty colors and adorned with frills. Her habit had been cut to resemble a man's tailored riding coat. She'd even used the bottle green kerseymere that was so popular in men's fashion. Only the full skirt that she constantly kicked out of her way gave the gown a feminine touch. And she'd topped it all off with a high-crowned hat resembling a man's beaver. She ought to look ridiculous. Instead, she looked fetchingly dainty, like a sugary confection.

Gad! He had taken leave of his senses again. If there was any woman less dainty and sugary than Fiona MacDermot, he didn't know who it was. Her tart tongue could curdle milk. Neville glared at her, and she turned her haughty little nose up in the air and took Morton's arm as if he were the only man in the world for her.

Neville forced a smile and offered his arm to Gwyneth. She gave him a considering look. He didn't have the time nor the pretty words to turn a woman's head. Gwyneth would just have to accept him for what he was, a duke and naught else.

"I've asked Miss MacDermot to join my Thursday gatherings," Gwyneth said shyly, taking his arm. "You don't object, do you?"

Neville sighed in relief and patted her hand. "Of course not. I'm certain she'll enjoy the company." If nothing else, it would give the little hothead a safe place to apply her sharp mind and even sharper tongue. He'd much rather Fiona applied them to Gwyneth's literary afternoons and nothing more dangerous.


"If women could vote, we'd not have poverty. That would end the crime problem and open the doors for better education, which would relieve the suffering of those poor unfortunate laborers in the factories. It's all related."

Fiona listened to Mr. Bolingbrooke's speech with amazement, not just at the topic of women's suffrage, but at his raving raw naiveté. She wanted to stand up and scream that three-quarters of the men couldn't vote, and even if they could, they'd never agree on the means of ending poverty, but new to this group, she bit her lip and kept quiet. Lady Gwyneth's literary afternoon hadn't been quite what she'd expected.

Glancing around at the expensive silk gowns, the hair coifed by personal maids, the jewels provided by wealthy husbands and fathers, Fiona could tell these women knew nothing at all about poverty. She could explain it to them, but they wouldn't listen. They liked talking to show their humanity, but they didn't much like listening or doing.

If they really wanted to help, they could sell their jewels and fancy carriages and give the funds to orphanages. They could persuade their stiff-rumped husbands to pass bills for decent wages and working conditions and to eliminate the unfair trade laws that kept the poor, poor, and the rich, richer still. But they listened to long-winded speakers instead.

Sighing, Fiona let her mind wander. Lady Gwyneth seemed absorbed in conversation with an older man seated next to her. It had surprised her that men attended these afternoons also. Fiona thought it rather rude of their hostess to engage in discourse while the speaker lectured, but she supposed the rules of polite society bent for the truly wealthy.

She studied the man to whom Gwyneth spoke, but she didn't recognize him as one of the society beaus who congregated in the ballrooms she'd frequented these past weeks. Actually, he seemed vaguely shabby. He was too old to be a student as many of this crowd were.

The audience applauded and began breaking into small discussion groups. Fiona made her way across the room to the only person she knew. By the time she reached Gwyneth, the lady's mysterious companion had dissolved into the crowd.

"Isn't he a wonderful speaker?" Gwyneth asked as Fiona reached her.

"He speaks well," Fiona admitted grudgingly. "Now, if he only had something sensible to say..."

Gwyneth laughed and tucked her hand into the crook of Fiona's elbow, leading her toward the refreshment table. "You don't believe in female suffrage?"

"I'd see Catholic emancipation and voting reform first," Fiona answered wryly. "And even then I'd not believe in any glorious revolution."

"You're a cynic," Gwyneth declared. "Surely you believe in change?"

"Of course I believe in change. I also believe money speaks louder than words. Money will end poverty faster than all the speech-making in the world."

Gwyneth looked at her consideringly. "And you would marry a rich man like Mr. Morton so you might give away his money?"

Fiona laughed. "I'm not that foolish. Mr. Morton would not give me sufficient funds to pay a boot black." Deciding she'd said quite enough, she shifted the questioning to Gwyneth. "Would you marry a man who would give away all your wealth?"

"I don't believe much in charity," Gwyneth replied thoughtfully. "I'd prefer working for economic change, but I know of no man who would allow me to keep my dowry for such things."

Fiona had a vague suspicion that the lady wronged the duke with that notion, but she had no right to say it quite so blatantly. "I don't know," she replied, searching for words she hadn't quite thought about before. "If His Grace is anything like his cousin Blanche, then I would think his inclinations leaned toward helping others help themselves."

There, perhaps she'd done the duke a favor and forwarded his suit, although for the life of her, she couldn't imagine why the haughty duke sought this bluestocking Amazon for wife. Surely he had his choice of all the beautiful women in London. Why choose one who despised his conservative policies?

Gwyneth raised her eyebrows in surprise, but before she could comment further, someone caught her attention from her other side, and she was drawn away.

Fiona wandered about the crowded drawing room, admiring the bas reliefs on the walls. She wondered how much brocade draperies of such extensiveness cost while amusing herself with snippets of overheard conversation. Few even noticed her presence other than to include her in their audience when they commenced upon their favorite diatribes. She wasn't much inclined toward listening to nonsense. Bored, she took a position near a doorway leading to the escape of the front hall and wondered when she might send for her maid and the earl's carriage.

"You're certain it's Townsend behind the problem?" a voice whispered from the other side of the wall.

Fiona thought little of it. Conversations drifted past her from several directions. She might as well listen to one as another.

"It seems most likely," a feminine voice responded. "He and the duke are at loggerheads over the crime and Catholic bills. Townsend fancies himself as the next PM. He'll not let anyone stand in his way."

The mention of the "duke" could mean anyone of that title, but Fiona recognized the second voice as Gwyneth's. She'd known the lady was interested in politics, but this conversation seemed a little more intense than usual.

"I could have Townsend eliminated, but there's too many more Tories like him."

Eyes widening, Fiona bit her lip and waited for Gwyneth's reply. Perhaps she hadn't understood the expression "eliminated" correctly. The

English used odd phrases.

"I abhor violence," Gwyneth remonstrated, confirming Fiona's understanding while relieving some of her fear. "And as you said, there are too many more like him. We must simply protect the duke for now. There are far too few on his side willing to listen to reason as he does. We will need his support when the time comes."

"Miss MacDermot!" a cheerful voice called, startling Fiona. The voices on the other side of the wall suddenly quieted, and Fiona forced back a scowl as she greeted a sturdy young man she'd met somewhere during the past hectic week.

Unable to remember his name, she made a slight curtsy and inwardly cursed his intrusion. The Lady Gwyneth was involved in something far beyond these sedate lectures, she surmised, and she might never have a chance to determine what.

Should she warn the duke? And what could she possibly warn him of? She'd not heard enough to have any understanding.

As Gwyneth sailed through the doorway, pinning Fiona with a fierce gaze, she had a sinking feeling that the lady didn't know how little she'd heard. Somehow, she'd floundered into a mire from which she might not extract herself easily.

# Eleven

"Fiona, stop fidgeting!" Michael said crossly from the opposite carriage seat.

Blanche blinked in disbelief, but Fiona scarcely noticed. Clasping her gloved hands, she tried not to tap her toes. She hadn't seen the duke in days. She still didn't know what to tell him. Heaven only knew, she'd heard enough conspiracy in her lifetime. The Irish had a talent for secret societies. Still, she couldn't imagine a wealthy lady like Gwyneth becoming involved in one.

"She's going to explode," Michael pointed out to his wife. "Why haven't you removed her cork by now?"

Beside Fiona, Blanche giggled. "It's so much more fun to watch it pop," she admitted. "Now that you've become a staid old man, I must find my amusement elsewhere."

Fiona looked from one to the other, trying to follow their inane dialogue, but her thoughts were elsewhere. Michael and Blanche often spoke a language of their own. She couldn't think of another couple so thoroughly delighted with each other. She envied them their relationship.

Of course, they were both insane, so perhaps that made it easier for them.

Deciding she wouldn't surrender her sanity for whatever it was that kept two such disparate characters as Michael and Blanche from killing each other, Fiona glanced out the carriage window. She wasn't in the mood for another glittering ball.

Despite all the smiles and secret leers, none of her suitors had consulted her cousin about their chances. Of course, it had only been a few weeks. None of them were precisely in a hurry to get leg-shackled to a penniless Irish Catholic female. But she didn't have time to wait. Winter was approaching and the orphans would starve. The village needed work. She'd approached Michael about the looms, but he had a dozen projects on his plate.

"Do you think Neville has fully recovered from that blow to his head?" Blanche asked, apropos of nothing. "He's been behaving rather oddly lately."

Fiona's head jerked up. Blow to his head?

"Neville always behaves oddly," Michael replied dismissively. "I should imagine a man who has come that close to death might behave differently. I think he's decided it's time to settle down and produce an heir. You've said yourself he's taken an interest in Lady Gwyneth."

His Grace had nearly died? From a blow to his head. Acquired how?

"Yes, but Gwyneth is all wrong for him." Blanche twisted at her gloves. "I wish..." She sighed and started over. "He's too proud. We need a good fairy to bat him over the head with her magic wand."

Fiona smirked at the idea of some blonde, blue-eyed fairy batting the duke over his hard head. Perhaps one had coshed him over the noggin. Not everything had to be a conspiracy.

"Perhaps our Fiona could act the part," Michael asked with a grin in his voice. "Did you bring a leprechaun or two with you, lass? They're what our duke needs right about now."

"Little men in green?" she asked scornfully. "No, it's big men with a shillelagh he needs. Did they catch whoever hit him?"

Silence fell. Then both Michael and Blanche tried speaking at once. When that failed, Michael held up his hand and Blanche quieted.

"We're not letting that get about, Fiona. Neville has his pride and would rather it not be known." He hesitated, then continued. "The men were never caught. We're still looking for them, but there's few enough clues."

"Stupid pride," Blanche scoffed. "From the sounds of it, there must have been half a dozen of them, and he still managed to injure all but the one with the cudgel. I can't imagine Neville fighting like that. He was always the studious sort."

Fiona had *seen* him fight like that, and he'd appeared remarkably unstudious at the time. Actually, she'd thought him highly triumphant at his prowess. Men were like that.

"They robbed him then?" she asked, still not quite understanding what she wasn't being told.

Again, that hesitation. Fiona knew full well her noble cousin lied blithely and without compunction whenever he felt inclined. She was just as grateful that the carriage stopped in front of their destination so she needn't hear what ingenious bit of untruth the Earl of Aberdare spun now. Neville hadn't been robbed, she concluded. So someone had tried to kill him for a reason.

She still didn't have enough pieces. She didn't even know if the pieces she had came from the same puzzle. Perhaps she should have told Michael what she'd overheard, but then he would have taken the information and gone on one of his mysterious jaunts, and she'd never hear what happened. No, she'd wait until she knew more.

~

"Your cheeks are like roses this evening, Miss MacDermot." Viscount Bennet simpered as he led her toward the refreshment table.

And her skin was like pearls and her lips were bright rubies, Fiona sniped to herself. All in all, she preferred the pearls and rubies. Perhaps she could cash them in. She smiled as if the viscount had just blinded her with his wit and charm. "You flatter me, I'm sure, sir."

"Won't you take a seat while I find some refreshment? Would you care for punch or lemonade?"

The viscount looked inordinately pleased with himself. He wasn't a bad man. Fiona supposed she shouldn't be so cruel in her judgments. It would be nice if she could find a wiser, more kindly man instead of one looking to relive his youth, but she of all people knew life wasn't fair or kind. The viscount could give her what she wanted, and she supposed she possessed what he needed. It would work out.

Not up to smiling and chatting meaningless phrases, she took a seat behind a potted palm and watched his bald head disappear into the crowd around the table.

She'd scarcely seen the duke all evening. Apparently there had been some sort of violent discord in the Lords that evening, and he circulated now, consolidating his position and swinging votes to his side. She suspected he was quite good at what he did. Fiona sought other means of entertainment rather than the duke.

"The Irish are no more than savages," a voice on the other side of the palms said. "We gave Irish the vote back in '93, and what have they done with it? Nothing! They wallow in their fields with their pigs and potatoes. We listen to enough of the drunken Irish in the House without allowing Catholics too."

"It costs us enough to buy their votes as it is. There's no sense in depositing the gilt into the pockets of papists," another voice agreed laughingly.

Fiona knew better than to intrude. She'd learned some control over her temper these last years. But she simply couldn't let these ninnyhammers continue uneducated. Since no other appeared ready to play the part of teacher, she would have to do the honors.

Twisting her lips into a semblance of a smile, she stepped from behind the palm. The guilt on the faces of the two men before her immediately pinpointed the speakers. They knew who she was. Her smile grew a little broader.

"Most of the population of Ireland has no pigs," she informed them politely. "They ate them long ago. And the blight has taken the potatoes, so if we must wallow anywhere, it's in the stones of our fields. Admittedly, it's rather easy to buy the vote of a man whose family is starving, and if we send drunks to stand in Parliament, it's only because we can't send Catholics. When was the last time you visited Ireland, sir?"

Fiona thought she'd been quite reasonable in her approach, but both gentlemen turned purple with rage. She couldn't precisely place their names. She seldom bothered unless they were eligible bachelors.

"Now, see here, miss, I should think we have a good deal more experience in these matters than a young uneducated female. You're intruding where you don't belong."

The man saying this had gray hairs sprouting from his ears, Fiona noted. She really should concentrate on what she said, but she'd rather pull the gray hairs from his ears. "You have experience in pig wallows?" she asked innocently. "I must admit, I've never educated myself in the matter of pigs other than to know one when I see one. They're a greedy lot, you know, want to have everything to themselves."

Fiona heard a chuckle behind her and knew an audience had gathered, but she was beyond caring. She'd had enough slights and snubs these last weeks, heard enough of the whispers behind her back. She'd fight back, and to hell with them all.

The man with the hairy ears wasn't so insensible as not to recognize the insult. He spluttered in his drink while his skinny, bespectacled companion looked down his long nose at her as if he smelled something rotten. Fiona gave him a blazing smile and set him back a foot.

"I'm certain we're talking at cross purposes, Miss MacDermot," the bespectacled man said carefully. "Why, I consider the Earl of Aberdare one of my best friends, and he's Irish, you know."

A carillon of laughter escaped Fiona's throat at this imbecility. She couldn't help it, she really couldn't. They'd be patting her on the head any minute now. Clasping her hand to her throat to catch her breath, she replied between gasps for air. "And so is your dog, I daresay, but that doesn't mean you'd allow him a vote." A giggle escaped her before she could stop it, but she continued remorselessly. "So if my cousin were Catholic instead of an eccentric, would you still allow him to sit in government?"

"Bloody ignorant papists have no business in British Parliament!" a third voice joined in. "They're rabble who would have us all worshipping statues. The entire city of London would rise and overthrow us before that would happen!"

"Bloody ignorant people of any sort have no business in Parliament!" Fiona threw back at him. "And if you're not careful, the entire country of England *will* rise and overthrow the lot of you!"

Gasps of outrage rose. Angry murmurs drew Fiona's attention to the crowd they'd gathered. Realizing she'd become the center of their attention, her heart sank to her feet, but it was far too late to back down.

"That's sedition!" someone yelled.

"That's the truth," a familiar calm voice said from behind her, before a hard hand gripped her elbow and yanked her backward. "But the lady should know better than to believe anyone would listen. Make your curtsies, Fiona."

The duke said her name softly, but the softness didn't fool her. She heard the anger behind it, felt his fingers gripping her arm as if he'd break it, and knew she was surely sunk this time. Throwing him a defiant glare over her shoulder, not heeding the warning in his icy eyes, Fiona dipped a quick curtsy. Then she lifted her chin and pulled away from the duke's grip to march away from the crowd.

She did so blindly, having no idea of where she went. Her teeth all but chattered, and the moisture in her eyes warned of the necessity of escape. She'd ruined everything. She'd let her hasty tongue loose and stolen the future of the village, of Aileen's orphans, of everything she'd hoped and schemed for. She knew she'd done it. The lashing of the duke's scorn wasn't necessary to complete her punishment.

But he wouldn't leave her alone. Catching her elbow again, he all but threw her through a doorway she hadn't seen as she made her escape. She blinked as the light of the glittering ballroom dimmed to the dancing firelight of a small study. The sturdy wood and books lining the walls returned some of her equilibrium. She'd give half her life for a room of books like these. Her uncle's musty tomes of Irish history couldn't compare.

Taking a deep breath, she swung around just as the duke slammed the door behind them. The firelight played off the gold in his thick eyebrows and glinted on the quizzing glass he still wore. She wanted to smack the damned thing from his face, but the coldness of his set features warned she'd best keep her distance.

Not liking the feeling of intimidation the duke's icy calm invoked,

Fiona took the offensive. "Your interference was neither warranted nor appreciated."

"*Your* behavior wasn't warranted or appreciated," he responded, taking a step closer. "I warned you I would not have you embarrassing Blanche. How do you think this evening's debacle will make her feel?"

She hadn't thought. Fighting back tears of anger and regret, Fiona curled her fingers into fists and faced him with every shred of dignity she could summon. "I will apologize to her, but I cannot apologize to those pigheads out there. They are a disgrace to humankind. How can you let such ignorance go uneducated?"

"Apologies will not wipe away Blanche's humiliation. What the devil do you use that head on your shoulders for? Or is it just there to attract bees like a pretty flower, with no sense behind it at all?"

He stood too close. Fiona could smell his shaving lotion and the lingering odor of cigars from whatever smoky room he'd been called from. Her eyes were on a level with his linen cravat. He wore a gold stickpin that blinked in the uncertain light and blended with the gold threads of his single-breasted white waistcoat. Unlike her, he was always elegantly tailored.

She did what any trapped animal would do. She raised her fist and aimed for his flat stomach.

In one swift motion, Neville caught her fist, twisted her arm behind her back, and brought them altogether too close for comfort. Desperate, Fiona flung back her head and glared at him, not giving him the pleasure of a struggle. Immediately, she knew her mistake.

The Duke of Anglesey wasn't watching her expression. The position he held her in pushed her nearly exposed breasts into his face. He raised his gaze from the expanse of flesh above her bodice, but the heat in his eyes blazed a path straight through her middle, rendering her helpless. She'd seen hunger in the looks of other men before. She'd never seen it in this man's face.

And she hadn't known until now how she craved it.

# Twelve

Even the pounding at the back of his head didn't excuse what he was doing. Neville knew this was Fiona, his own personal demon, in his arms. He knew he courted disaster. Had she fought him, he would have halted immediately. But she didn't, and he didn't, and thus he brought about his own downfall.

His palm burned where it rested at the hollow of her back. He wanted her breasts pressed against his coat. He urged her so close into him that only his arm supported her. He could easily lift her into the position his body demanded, but some lingering sense of survival kept him from obeying that particular command.

Instead, Neville focused on moist red lips parted with surprise and perhaps something a little more. Mayhap she knew more of this game than he'd surmised. Giving himself permission to test that theory, he bent his head and covered her mouth with his.

The power of her kiss exploded inside his brain. The thin thread holding him back dissolved. He yanked Fiona closer still, lifting her so she fit more comfortably against him, reveling in the pressure of those full breasts against the linen of his shirt. Neville cupped Fiona's hips in his hands and drew more deeply from the nectar of her lips.

He recognized the inexperience of her first tentative response, but he was beyond caring. She kissed him with the ardency of an eager student. Nothing else mattered.

He'd never known anything like this in his life. His blood heated and his head spun as he probed deeper, demanding more, and she gave him everything he asked. Like a bud blossoming, her lips parted, and he tasted the sweet lemonade of her breath. Neville inhaled deeply, tested her tongue, exhilarated in her response as her lips pressed tighter and her tongue met his. Agony and ecstasy raced through him, warring over the next step, demanding the solace her reaction promised.

As his arm accidentally brushed her breast, Fiona quaked in his arms. Neville lost even a modicum of rationality.


From her position behind another potted palm, Gwyneth had watched Miss MacDermot's altercation with the politicians with disapproval and disappointment. Miss MacDermot was a little too spirited for her purposes. One couldn't think rationally while in a temper.

The arrival of the Duke of Anglesey to remove Miss MacDermot from the scene had been a relief, but the look in his eyes was puzzling.

Out of curiosity more than anything else, Gwyneth followed them. She raised her eyebrows as the duke hauled his cousin's protégée into the darkened study. That wasn't at all like His Grace. He'd always been the soul of propriety around her.

It was only when they lingered in the study that she recognized the impropriety. Gwyneth knew nothing of what happened between men and women, and she'd never thought of the dispassionate duke in those terms, but a firebrand like Fiona...

If she could put herself forward just a little, she might kill two birds with one stone. Tying the Tory to the Whigs would be an excellent piece of work. Gwyneth glanced around her. Several people had noticed the altercation, but she didn't think anyone had noticed the couple's departure. As was his habit, Fiona's cousin, the earl, had disappeared. Lady Blanche had gone to the lady's withdrawing room before the altercation began.

With satisfaction, Gwyneth noted the countess descending the stairs. Naturally, London's biggest gossip was making a beeline in Lady Blanche's direction to dramatize Fiona's transgressions. Perfect. Absolutely perfect. If she had any luck at all, someone would have notified the earl by now, and he'd be heading this way also.

She had everything to gain and nothing to lose. Carefully skirting the edges of the crowd, Gwyneth started in Lady Blanche's direction.

The duke's mouth intoxicated Fiona to a fever that inflamed her brain and rendered her thoughtless. She coaxed her fingers through his thick hair, drank in the manly scent of his skin, fell victim to the stimulating intimacy of his tongue probing hers.

He lowered them onto a sofa and seated her on his powerful thighs. The new position only made it easier for her to caress the fascinating whiskers on his jaw. She reveled in the strong arms holding her tight and the ability to explore the heady sensations he instigated. She supposed she should put a halt to this insidious temptation, but at the moment, she couldn't rightly remember why. She'd never known a man's caresses before, had never realized what so simple a thing as a touch and a kiss could do. She wasn't one to reject a lesson for the sake of propriety, particularly not a lesson as compelling as this one.

The gentleness of the duke's strength surprised her. The brush of his fingers against the side of her breast stole the breath from her lungs. The probe of his kiss created a longing for more, much more. She didn't recognize the sound of the door opening, nor hear the gasps that followed.

She did, however, hear Michael's roar of outrage.

"Fey-onah MacDermot, get your foolish self over here this instant!"

Neville practically dropped her. Hastening to right herself, Fiona landed on her feet before she'd gathered her lost wits. Amazed that her skirt had risen so high, she adjusted it, not looking up until the silence grew so thick that it could have broken if dropped.

Her head spinning too rapidly to think clearly, she noted the furious clenching of Michael's jaw, Blanche's worried expression, and the malicious twinkle of eyes she didn't recognize. Michael slammed the door on any further audience, but Fiona had a sense of more people outside the door. She gulped and stepped away from the man behind her. She couldn't look at the duke right now.

It didn't matter. He and Michael addressed each other as if she were no longer present.

"I'll expect your call in the morning," Michael said coldly, over Fiona's head.

"Expect me at eleven." The stiffness wasn't just in the duke's voice, but in his whole stance. He didn't touch her, didn't acknowledge her, gave no indication of what they had just done together.

Crumbling a little inside, feeling a cold wind blowing through the cracks of her soul, Fiona stumbled across the carpet in sympathetic Blanche's direction. If she didn't think about it, she could imagine this wasn't happening. She just wanted to go home, away from all the staring eyes.

Someone threw a cloak around her. Someone else led her out a side door, away from the audience hovering in the main hall.

Fiona never looked at Neville. But she saw him just the same, standing proud and aloof, waiting for the door to close and the world to leave him alone.

His noble gut roiled in protest at the humiliation, but Neville presented himself at the appointed time and place the next day. He stared beyond Michael's shoulder rather than acknowledge the earl's quizzical look.

"I never saw myself playing the part of furious father," Michael said uncomfortably. He stood beside the mantel, juggling two brass candlesticks and a delicate figurine. "But she's the only female relation I have. I have to look after her. Gossip is flying."

Neville winced as the expensive china figurine barely missed landing on the tile hearth. Michael hadn't fully recovered his talents after damaging his hands in a fire, but the earl never let that stop him. Michael might seem absent-minded and eccentric to the world at large, but he had a formidable mind and a tenacity that could kill any ordinary man. Neville knew better than to fall victim to the earl's ire.

"I understand. I'm fully at fault. With your permission, I'll have the announcement placed in the papers today."

Nonchalantly swinging his walking stick, Neville examined a drawing one of the children had tacked to a bookshelf, but his gut twisted tighter. He loathed impropriety and had little experience at mortification. He wanted to hide in shame, flog himself for stupidity, and curse the heavens for not allowing him this one small mistake. But beneath the shame — anticipation raised its insidious head.

He was out of his mind. He'd had an entire night to toss and turn and recognize his madness. But if he was losing his mind, he was gaining senses he'd never known he'd possessed. At the moment, insanity seemed a fair trade for more of Fiona's kisses. He might have spent half the night castigating himself, but with dawn's arrival, lust had won the argument.

A noise too much like a chuckle jerked Neville's attention to the earl. He glared at Michael, who now innocently balanced the candlesticks and figurines in a swaying tower.

"I'd wait on that announcement until you speak with Fiona. In case that blow to your head robbed you of all brains, I'll remind you she's a mind of her own. I'm depending on you to turn her mind in the right direction, but I'm not believin' it will be easy."

When the earl slipped into his Irish act, it was time to leave. Bowing coldly, Neville walked out, grimacing at the sound of a tinkling crash behind him. The figurine had been nearly a hundred years old, a mere infant compared to the other antiquities in this mausoleum. He would have preferred throwing the porcelain against the wall if it had to be broken, but even that wouldn't sufficiently express his sentiments.

Neville sent a footman in search of Fiona and idled his time in the front parlor, admiring the colors of the trees in the park across the street. He couldn't remember the last time he'd admired the color of trees. An image of Fiona in her tight-fitting green habit, her long auburn hair streaming behind her as she raced her mare beneath those trees, rose in his mind's eye and so captivated him that he barely heard her enter the room.

"You sent for me?" Fiona asked coldly, forcing Neville to swing around and greet his mental vision in the cold light of day.

She exceeded even his wildest dreams. Apparently prepared for this visit, she wore her copper curls in a tight knot at the back of her head, but wisps still escaped about her face, softening the severe image she meant to present. Nothing could disguise the long-lashed wide eyes glaring at him from behind rose-tinted cheekbones, or the determined jut of her little chin. A ribbon of amusement curled through him as he realized she had prepared her defense before he'd said a word.

In the interest of scientific experiment, Neville dropped his gaze to the high-necked bodice of her woolen gown. Even the ghastly brown and the loose design couldn't disguise the magnificence of her feminine curves. He'd had women of all shapes and sizes, yet had never much noted their differences before now. It was Fiona who held his fascination, but she wouldn't understand that. So he ogled her blatantly and waited for her temper to strike.

As predictable as the sun rising in the morn, her hand swung up to slap him, and he had her. Capturing those long, slender fingers, Neville brought them to his lips and kissed them.

Startled, she froze.

He had little knowledge of the gallantries that wooed and won women, but he instinctively understood Fiona. He had to stay one step ahead of her at all times, know her responses, and keep her off balance. That didn't mean he would come out ahead, but it at least gave him a fair chance.

"I've come to apologize for embarrassing you," he murmured, keeping her hand in his, relying on their proximity to have the same effect as it had last night. He was almost ten years older than Fiona and gave himself credit for a little more experience. He didn't think he'd mistaken her passionate response. If he had, now was the time to discover it. They had naught else in common but this physical attraction and must build a marriage from some foundation. "I shan't apologize for what I did," he added tauntingly.

Some women might have wide green pools for eyes, but Fiona's leapt with flames that would consume him. Neville wanted to pull her into his arms again, but his hastiness had led to disaster last night.

Dark lashes fell, and she looked away, attempting to shake his hand in an effort to escape. "I understand. It's quite all right."

Neville couldn't recall ever seeing her embarrassed before. "Was it? Quite all right, I mean." Amused, he couldn't resist asking.

She sent him an uncertain, vaguely rebellious look. "Was what quite all right?"

"My kisses," he persisted. "How did they compare to those of others?"

He relaxed as he saw her uncertainty begin to fade. He didn't want her uncertain. He wanted his fiery fairy with him in the room.

"It's not quite the same compared with stolen kisses from grimy little boys behind the hedgerows, my lord duke," she protested.

Pleased that she was as inexperienced as he'd thought, Neville goaded her further. "Might I presume my kisses were better?"

She curled her fingers into fists and stamped her foot. "Quit playing cat and mouse with me, sir. If you have some reason for this game, spit it out and have done with it. It wasn't my fault that you were humiliated last night, so you needn't torture me to get even."

"No, I'd not torture you." He ran his finger across her cheek, finding it as soft as the orchids he raised, yet blooming in a more magnificent color. He wasn't one for complaining about his plight. She would have made a marvelous mistress. She would make a terrible wife. Still, he'd spent all his life accepting responsibility. He'd live with what he'd done. "Or perhaps, I will, just a little. Marriage to a dry stick like me will not be so interesting as racing about the Irish countryside, but will surely be better than marriage to an old man like Bennet, won't it?"

Neville thought she stopped breathing. With interest, he lowered his gaze to see if her bosom continued rising and falling. He wanted to unbutton all those damned tiny jet buttons and explore more thoroughly, but that could wait. Not for long, perhaps, given his body's response to his mental images, but for a while.

"I'm not a piece of legislation you may examine and take apart and do with as you will," Fiona said coldly.

"And I'm not blind, deaf, or stupid, either," Neville said without ire. "I know you're a hoyden who will turn me gray before my time, but we must be practical about this, and admit that neither of us would disappoint Michael or Blanche. We could do far worse than each other."

That stopped her tongue, and he chalked a point in his favor. Maybe several points. He didn't think he'd ever heard anyone stop Fiona's tongue before. "I'm not a rich man, but I know where I can find a loom at a decent price. I cannot think your orphans will fare well with only an elderly grandmother to look after them, but if you can find someone willing to take them, I'll see that they're fed and clothed. I cannot promise more than that, but that's more than you would have out of any other husband you found."

"And what do you expect of me in return?" Fiona asked with the uncertainty he'd heard in her voice earlier.

"Heirs," Neville said bluntly. "I want heirs aplenty, and a wife in my bed whenever I want."

He knew he would have shocked any other woman, but not Fiona. He read the blaze of interest in her eyes, knew the devious workings of her mind, and bent them to his own purposes. He rather liked being in control of the situation for once. He more than liked not having to wield foolish romantic phrases to get what he wanted.

Without waiting for an answer, Neville pulled Fiona into his arms as he'd wanted to do from the moment she'd walked into the room. Instead of the finality of a parson's trap, the sweet bliss of freedom wrapped around him with the slide of her arms around his shoulders and the return of his kiss with the same reckless hunger that rocked him.

Just for once in his life, Neville damned duty to hell and took his pleasure where he could.

The sensation of freedom swept through Neville as he cupped Fiona's breast in his palm. He nearly came undone when she rewarded him with her moan of pleasure. He might have taken her there and then, putting the seal of certainty on their union, had a knock on the door not jarred him to his senses.

Michael's wry expression when he came upon them tumbled and breathing hard sealed their promise just as certainly.

"Dare I suggest a short betrothal?"

Catching Fiona's hand before she could twist away, Neville agreed with alacrity. "I'll have the license in the morning. Name the date."

Beside him, Fiona moaned and covered her mouth with her hand. Neville would have her well shackled before she realized what she did. He wouldn't give her time to regret her decision. He'd waited years to choose a wife. Now that the choice was made for him, he wouldn't wait a day longer than necessary.

He'd found his duchess. She wasn't an heiress, but she was the woman he wanted. For the first time in a long time, his duty took him down a path that matched his desires.

# Thirteen

Now that some distance separated her from the duke, Fiona almost wished she were back in his arms again, blinded with lust so she needn't think about what they'd just done. What in the name of the Holy Mother was she thinking? She despised Englishmen. She despised this particular Englishman. She despised his arrogance, his title, everything for which he stood.

But he had kissed her into senselessness. Like a silly infatuated girl, she'd let him lead her down the proverbial garden path. Her stomach quaked as she realized the duke and Michael and Blanche were even now discussing her *wedding* date.

Neville sent her another one of his blasted amused looks that melted her knees. She'd heard other people accuse him of being a dry stick, but they obviously didn't understand his warped sense of humor. He was laughing at them all right now, laughing at the whole humiliating situation, laughing as he stuck his head through the noose. Damn the man and his laughing eyes to hell.

"I...I thought a Christmas wedding would be nicer," Fiona said tentatively into a momentary pause in the conversation. She'd never said anything tentatively in her life. Already he was sapping her will and independence.

Blanche looked interested, but Michael and Neville grinned and shook their heads.

"She's panicking already," Neville said, catching Fiona's hand and drawing her closer. "We must do the deed quickly, before she realizes what she's done."

Fiona tried to jerk her hand away, but Neville's fingers simply tightened their hold. Under other circumstances, she might have found his strength reassuring. Right now, panic held her in thrall. She'd barely even considered *marriage*. She'd certainly never considered marriage to a duke. A duke! A bloody duke! She'd be a *duchess*.

The unholy incongruity spun Fiona's head. As if recognizing her sudden weakness, Neville led her to a nearby chair—a gold silk chair with delicately carved arms sitting in a pool of sunlight on a beautiful blue and gold woven carpet of exquisite design, all of which belonged to the duke. He owned this house where Blanche and Michael lived. She pressed her fingers to her temple.

"Perhaps I shouldn't take her to Anglesey until after the wedding,"

Neville was saying with amusement still lacing his voice.

"Oh, she's already seen it," Blanche replied blithely. "Michael brought her there when we first met."

Fiona tried to shut out the conversation. Anglesey, the duke's family seat. She didn't want to remember when she'd first met Blanche. She'd been garbed in boy's breeches and looked a grimy urchin. And Anglesey had been a palace. It had frightened her half to death at the time.

"I can't do it," she whispered. "I couldn't even be the scullery maid."

They ignored her. Plans for the wedding continued without her. Didn't anyone understand? She'd grown up in a farmhouse, for heaven's sake! A farmhouse with a muddy front yard and potatoes at every meal. She knew nothing of dukes and duchesses and palaces crawling with servants. What in the name of the devil would she do with herself?

Carry the duke's heirs. Heat crawled up her scalp, and Fiona buried her face in her hands. She'd sold her soul to become a brood mare.

"Uh oh," she heard the duke say. "We're about to experience either a fit or a whirlwind. Blanche, I think you'd better take her upstairs. Michael and I will handle the rest."

A fit. She would throw a fit just as soon as she recovered enough strength to remember how. And then she would run away.

Fiona looked up and caught the duke's implacable gaze and knew she was well and truly trapped. He would follow her to the ends of the earth if she ran. The oh-so-proper duke would never allow their indiscretion to go uncorrected. Propriety required marriage, and he would keep his honor at the expense of all else. Devil bother it. Someone should teach him that propriety was meaningless.

It seemed she would have to be the one to do so.

"I saw the announcement in the paper," a shy voice said.

Lingering on the edge of the rout that she hadn't wanted to attend, Fiona glanced around for the source of the voice.

"I think the two of you will make a lovely couple."

Fiona pushed aside the leaves of a preposterous tree. Gwyneth sat sipping tea on a sofa hidden by the plant. Slipping through the foliage, Fiona took the space beside her, feeling dwarfed by the other woman now that they were on the same level.

Vaguely remembering the hints that the duke had courted this woman, Fiona wrinkled her brow in puzzlement. "You do? Why?"

Gwyneth smiled shyly. "You're so vivacious and spirited, you'll add the part of him that's missing. I think that's the way the best marriages are founded."

Fiona contemplated the notion a moment, discovered the converse side, and would have laughed, if the topic didn't make her so nervous. "And he's so stolid and dependable, he'll add the part of me that's missing," she supplied without insult. "I'm not at all certain it works that way."

She looked at Gwyneth quizzically. "You're not sorry? I thought you and…"

Gwyneth shook her head vigorously. "I'll never marry. They only want me for my wealth, and I'd rather keep it for my own projects. Are you still interested in joining our Thursday afternoon gatherings?"

Not if heaven opened up and shot a bolt of lightning down, Fiona vowed, but she hated to insult this awkwardly backward girl.

"It's not all silly speechifying," Gwyneth hastily explained, as if understanding Fiona's hesitation. "We do accomplish a great deal. We've set up a foundation for foundlings, you know, and there are those of us working for better living conditions in the tenement slums."

Fiona didn't know if the wives of dukes involved themselves in such, but if she must stay in England, she would prefer saving orphans to having teas. She wasn't convinced that marriage to the duke was inevitable, but until she discovered a means of escape, she would have to behave as if she were truly affianced. She wondered if she could persuade the loom out of Neville before she discovered a bolt hole.

"I'd be interested in helping with worthwhile projects," Fiona hedged. "But I cannot say how long I'll be in London. My family is talking of retiring early to the country for the holidays."

"The duke, too?"

Suspicious of the question but unable to find a way around it, Fiona nodded. "He wishes to show me Anglesey. We're to be wed there."

Gwyneth almost seemed to sigh with relief. "Excellent," she said, before recovering herself and continuing politely, "You must be looking forward to the wedding."

That was the last thing on earth she was looking forward to, but Fiona held her tongue for a change. A lady who casually discussed murder, if that's what she'd overheard, was not someone she might confide in. "The duke is like family. I'm certain we'll rub along well enough."

Gwyneth smiled knowingly. "I'm certain. And speaking of family, here he comes now."

Through the leaves of the plant, Fiona glanced up to see the duke approaching, nothing more than polite interest on his face. She didn't know how he could possibly know their hiding place, but she'd learned enough about the set of his jaw to realize he sought her. He could spend the rest of his life looking for her, she thought idly. She'd never been much good at staying where she was put.

"Good evening, Lady Gwyneth." The duke bowed as he pushed aside the branches. "I thought I might find you here. And Fiona. I'm glad you've chosen to continue the friendship. Lady Gwyneth will make an excellent guide."

Fiona wrinkled up her nose. "Shall I tip her two shillings, do you think? One doesn't know precisely how these things are done in the city."

Beside her, Gwyneth giggled. Satisfied she'd set the pompous duke back a step, Fiona rose to leave the lady to her hiding place. Neville captured her arm and steered her toward the crowded room.

"Hiding won't do either of us any good," he remonstrated as heads turned in their direction. "We must smile and make all the world think we're delighted with this match."

Fiona flashed a smile at the first curious gaze she met. "And are we?" she asked through gritted teeth.

"Of course we are," the duke replied, nodding his head to an acquaintance while removing her from his path. "If we don't kill each other in the first six months, we should do just fine."

"Because by that time I should be plump with your heir and unable to do anything but sit and brood," Fiona answered with unexpected bitterness.

He shot her a look of surprise. "That's the very last thing I expect you to do."

He seemed sincere. Startled at the realization that she knew nothing at all about this man, Fiona studied him, but she saw only the polite facade of the politician as he accepted someone's congratulations and shook hands all around.

She couldn't reconcile the civilized gentleman of society with the hungry man who nearly devoured her behind closed doors. Or now that she thought about it, with the furious animal who could lay flat half a dozen attackers all on his own.

And she intended to marry an enigma like that?

~

"I want you to be comfortable here," the duke said as they traversed the magnificent front hallway of Anglesey, with Michael and Blanche following behind. The rest of their retinue—children and nursemaids, valets and maids—had all been dispersed throughout the mansion some hours earlier. The servants who had lined up on the front steps to greet the duke's intended had scattered about their various duties, leaving the family party alone to explore the wonders of this rambling, palatial residence. Fiona was too terrified to see any of it clearly.

Comfortable? She glanced around at towering cabinets packed with china and crystal dating back centuries, polished silver tureens casually used as vases, windows so high she couldn't imagine cleaning them, and wondered how anyone could be comfortable in all this wealth and magnificence. Soft carpets padded their steps over stones that had been traversed by dukes and nobility since the sixteenth century, maybe even longer. She'd not paid much attention to the duke's history lessons.

And he wanted her to live here? Unable to quell the panic that lived with her every minute of the day now, Fiona glanced up at the duke—Neville, he'd said she should call him. He walked these halls with the serenity and confidence of one who belonged in such surroundings. And she could see that he did. He was every inch a duke, exuding authority, assurance, and the knowledge that his roots grew deep in English nobility. How would she survive without being crushed beneath the weight of it all?

Her panic must have surfaced sufficiently for Neville to notice. Clasping her fingers against his coat sleeve, he turned to their chaperones. "Why don't you two go upstairs and make yourselves comfortable? I want to show Fiona the conservatory."

They weren't married yet. It was highly improper for them to wander off alone. Not that being among a houseful of servants could be called "alone," but they wouldn't intrude. Yet Michael and Blanche didn't hesitate, and even Fiona felt no wariness. Everyone knew the Duke of Anglesey obeyed all the rules of society and would never harm a lady under his protection.

"If you turn any paler, I'll have to set you out in the sun in a manure patch as I do my plants," Neville said as he opened the door to the conservatory.

A blast of moist, warm air hit her as they entered the glass-enclosed room. Fiona inhaled the aroma of greenery and soil and realized how much she'd missed the countryside. Whirling around in delight, she threw her head back to admire the exotic jungle of blooms climbing to the vaulted glass ceiling.

"I've never seen anything like it! It's heaven! How do you keep it like this? Look at those ferns! And the flowers! What kind of flowers are they that bloom this time of year?"

"Orchids." The duke crossed his arms and leaned against the door.

Fiona gently touched the brilliant purple lower lip of a huge blossom. "I've never seen the like," she repeated. "It's like something out of a fairy tale. Could I paint them sometime?"

"You paint?" His mobile eyebrows lifted in what was definitely surprise.

Fiona sent him a mischievous look. "A little. Among other things. Are you certain you have any notion at all of what you're getting into?"

Neville's stare took on new meaning as he looked her up and down, making her entirely too aware of the way her fashionable gown clung in all the wrong places. Or right ones.

"A very good notion, actually," he replied with the dryness that she recognized as humor. "You seem to believe that I'm blind."

Fiona hid behind a giant banana tree where the duke's knowing eyes couldn't strip her naked. "You *are* blind, Your Grace, when you see only what you want to see. This won't work, you know. I'm more than a pair of breasts."

Her bold statement obviously startled him into silence. Good. Let him really realize that she was no shy Lady Gwyneth.

Fiona gasped as bold hands slid around her waist from behind. Strong thumbs drew wickedly up and down her abdomen, creating shocking sensations in the lower part of her body.

"Granted, you're a good deal more than a pair of breasts," he whispered in her ear. "You've a naughty tongue, wicked lips, and long legs that could wrap around a man and hold him forever. And if I do not mistake, you've a creative mind that knows how to apply all that you possess. We may not know each other well in some ways, Fiona, my love, but in others, we're well matched."

Shocked to the core that the stiffly proper duke could say such things, Fiona did no more than gasp as his hand circled her breast.

"Let's put an end to your uncertainty, shall we?" he murmured, as his fingers did unspeakably wicked, magical things that melted her bones. "You seemed to enjoy this the other night, until we were so rudely interrupted."

Fiona didn't reply. *Couldn't* reply. Neville turned her around so their eyes met and the knowledge of his intentions pierced her with the force of an arrow bolt. He couldn't. He wouldn't.

But his head bent and his mouth covered hers, and somehow, any protest spiraled out of sight in the maelstrom of his kiss.

# Fourteen

Neville had never seduced a woman in his life. All his liaisons had been with experienced women who'd offered their favors. But Fiona was a fascinating combination of innocence and boldness, a sexual creature who knew nothing of her sexuality. With her, he could be the leader.

Briefly, Neville debated the wisdom of what he did, but he'd argued the point long and hard for days. He wouldn't change his mind now that he had Fiona exactly where he'd imagined her. The fragrance of her skin tantalized, the moist heat of her tongue intoxicated, and the lithe pressure of her body fueled his intent.

He would have her here, now, before she could panic and pull one of the disappearing tricks for which she was so famous. Once she learned how good it could be between them, she would accept the inevitable.

Lifting her, he carried her to a chaise longue beneath the bower of orchids. Fear flickered in her eyes as her head fell back against the pillows, but he kissed it away.

She responded to his touch so easily, he felt as if he could do anything — move mountains, swim seas, reach the stars. Her breast swelled into his palm as he touched her there.

"I would have our wedding day be joyous," he whispered, caressing her breast and silently cursing the myriad hooks protecting her from his invasion.

Fiona's hand hovered, not quite touching his jaw. Smiling, Neville caught and pressed her palm against his skin. She explored his whiskered jaw with interest.

"I don't want your fear of our wedding night to mar the occasion," he continued, returning to the hooks of her bodice.

"Michael will kill us," she whispered.

Just her voice created vibrations that spurred his hunger. He wanted to do this carefully, to make her want this mating as much as he did. If this was all they had between them, he wanted to nurture her passion. If he couldn't provide Anglesey with wealth, he could provide the heirs that would return its magnificence in time. A woman like Fiona in his bed was almost worth giving up dreams of restoring his heritage.

"It's only a week to the wedding. There's none to know if we anticipate our vows by a few days. Michael would be the first to understand." Finally releasing the bodice flap, Neville slid his hand inside and stroked her nipple through the silk of her chemise.

Fiona rewarded him with a gasp of surprise. "Neville, we can't do this. We really can't," she whispered, the wonderment in her voice belying her protest as he lay down beside her.

"It's quite simple, Fiona, my love. Let me show you." Smiling, he kissed her as she clung to his shoulders as if he were all that stood between her and hell.

He took her mouth more hungrily, preventing any immediate protest. Parting the ties of her chemise, Neville cupped her bare breast with his palm, and pressed his thigh between her legs.

Fiona drowned in sensation as her nipple puckered against his palm and an ache opened at the brush of his leg against a sensitive junction.

Neville's mouth suckled her breast through the thin silk, and Fiona cried out with the exquisite torment. Any form of intelligent protest died in the floodtide of passion. She'd never experienced the like before and had no defenses against it.

Neville's tongue bathed her flesh. The rough skin of his palm slid down her side as he pushed away her bodice. He cupped her hip and pulled her closer to the hard heat of him searing her through layers of clothing. Her hips lifted into his in unconscious response. With a will of their own, her fingers captured his hair. She cried out in protest as Neville lifted his head, then cried out again in wanton pleasure as he took her other breast into his mouth. *So that's what they were there for*, she mused idiotically as heat fueled a fire in the place where his thigh rubbed.

It was but the work of moments actually. Had they explored the entire conservatory, it would not have taken longer. She'd waited twenty-one years for someone to ignite the needs inside her, and she couldn't stop the wildfire once it began.

The warm, moist air of the conservatory lavished Fiona's skin as Neville slid her skirts upward. Golden pollen from the blossoms dangling over her head dusted her face as his fingers probed gently, releasing the pent-up moisture that would ease his entrance. Fiona opened her eyes in panic as Neville covered her with his heavy length. She saw the heat turn his eyes to molten silver, admired and feared the intensity in the set of his jaw. She loved the way his golden hair fell across his brow while the orchids danced in a sultry breeze above his head. She would remember this moment always.

Panic subsiding, she smiled her acceptance, and wrapped her arms around his shoulders to pull him down for one last kiss.

She had no idea at what point he unfastened his trousers, had no thought of such an occurrence. Her head spun deliciously with his kisses and the wicked play of his fingers. It felt too right to be wrong — until the urgency built inside her. Not understanding why, she frantically pumped against him, demanding something she knew he denied her.

That's when she discovered — too late — how far they had gone.

Pain seared through Fiona's pleasure as the hard thickness of Neville's male equipment pushed inside her. She hadn't known...

They didn't fit. She couldn't accommodate him. She couldn't...

Fiona cried out at the thick heat invading her body. Neville swallowed her cry in a hungry kiss as he braced his weight above her. Through her pain, Fiona sensed the strength of will holding him back, but even his kiss couldn't disguise the frightening intrusion of his maleness. She knew that was how flowers made seeds, but she hadn't know it would hurt, she thought insensibly as Neville pushed past all barriers and embedded himself deeper. She would swell up and give birth just as the flowers did, all because this man put a part of himself inside her. This man. The duke.

It didn't seem quite real. The thick fog of lust had parted with that first piercing pain. Fiona knew what she did now. And still, she couldn't stop. Her muscles contracted around his hardness, arousing an irritating tension that needed relief.

The pain transformed into a sensation she couldn't define as her hips rose to accept his driving thrust. She bit his frock coat to muffle her cry as his thickness slid deep beneath her belly. Her body seemed to require an attention only Neville could give. He hadn't even undressed. They were almost fully clothed. And still, their bodies grew moist with the accelerated heat of their mating.

Neville stroked her bare thighs, and Fiona wrapped them around him, just as he'd said she would. He touched her in a place that ached unbearably. His coaxing fingers had her bucking under him, searching for a release only he could provide. In a matter of moments, pain was forgotten in wonderment as she shattered into a million pieces.

Lost among the stars, she wept in joy as he filled her again. Murmuring soft promises in her ear, he drove them both over the moon until he planted his seed deep inside her.

Gasping for breath, drenched in perspiration, Fiona slipped into the languor of satiation as Neville slid off of her. She would regret what they'd done in a few minutes, but not now. Right now, she just wanted Neville's strong arm around her, reassuring her that the world still spun properly on its axis, and she wouldn't fall off.

"I knew you were the one," he whispered, smoothing tendrils of damp hair from her face. "This is as close to perfect as life can get, Fiona."

He lied, she thought vaguely. Maybe he didn't know he lied. This wasn't perfect, far from it. But it was good. Incredibly good. And if they didn't know what they missed, then they couldn't regret it. She knew more was out there. She was sorry they would never know it. But it didn't matter. She'd slipped and fallen and she would never find that bolt hole now.

He kissed her, and she could only remember how incredibly good it had been.

Anticipation replaced any lingering notion of regret.

"I think it's a damned good thing we set the date early," Michael said gruffly, watching the couple scuffling through the colorful leaves covering the lawn.

Blanche pulled his hand down to her abdomen and smiled. "Perhaps this new babe will have a second cousin of the same age. They can play together."

"They'll have the same birth date if we don't keep those two apart," Michael warned. "I want to punch him every time he looks at Fiona that way."

Blanche chuckled. "And you wonder why Neville raged when he'd found what we'd done before we married? I'd say he's getting even, but he never thinks like the rest of us. I'm utterly amazed that he's thrown over any chance of marrying money in favor of love. I never would have believed it of him."

"Then don't believe it now," Michael said crossly. "Your high and mighty cousin's just inflicted with a bad case of lust. And Fiona is no better than a mare in heat. I foresee only ruin and disaster when they both snap out of it."

Blanche smacked his arm and shoved his hand away. "I've never heard you so pessimistic. When they 'snap out of it,' as you so crudely put it, they'll discover they're in love. Sometimes the first flush of heat gets in the way of that fact."

"Blanche, my dear optimist," Michael sighed, kissing her hair, "That's what happened to us. That is not necessarily what happens to everyone."

"It wasn't lust," she said petulantly. "We loved each other from the start. Other things just got in the way."

"Well, other things will stand in the way of love in this case. This is a match made in hell if ever I saw one. I wish I'd never sanctioned it."

"You thought Fiona would turn him down." Blanche gave him a knowing glance and hastened her steps in the direction of the courting couple who had disappeared amongst the trees while they watched.

With a rueful grimace, Michael followed her. "You're right at that. It hadn't occurred to me that lust blinds even intelligent women."

Blanche stuck her tongue out at him, picked up her skirts, and ran across the lawn, laughing, as he chased her.

"Aye, and I hear yer a papist," the nearly toothless man in the stable said as Fiona called for a horse. He said it so Blanche couldn't hear. Considering the source, Fiona ignored him, taking the reins and leading the mount into the yard without his aid.

"She's one of them heathen Irish," a voice whispered as Fiona entered the mercantile a little later. Blanche had stopped outside to talk with a neighbor and didn't hear this either.

"She's bewitched His Grace," another voice agreed knowingly. "I saw crows perched on the fence. The crops will all rot in the barns."

Searching the gloom of the crowded store, Fiona discovered the whisperers behind bolts of cloth — two old crones who glared at her with malicious eyes. Back home, the villagers might occasionally disagree with her ways, but they respected her. She didn't know how to deal with this blatant fear and superstition.

She could only ignore it. Surely time would cure their fears. Fiona returned to the doorway to wait for Blanche.

"She's no one," a well-dressed woman passing by on the street said to her companion, both oblivious to Fiona's presence. "Irish rabble. Were it not for our dear duke, I'd cut her dead in the street. The Irish are such drunken heathens. I don't know how we shall ever face her politely."

Anger surged. She could endure ignorance and superstition, but these women should know better. Had she not seen Blanche hurrying in her direction, Fiona would have stepped outside and taught the biddy a lesson in humiliation. But she couldn't do that to Blanche. Neville's cousin had grown up here, knew the entire populace, and they all adored her. The two women looked up and smiled at Blanche as she approached.

"Honoria! Loyolla! How lovely to see you again. It's been so long..." Blanche saw Fiona standing in the doorway and a worried frown marred her brow. Hastily, she made introductions. "Have you met my husband's cousin, Miss MacDermot? You'll love her. I'm sure she'll have Anglesey ringing with gaiety once again."

Reluctantly, Fiona joined them. She wanted to scratch out the eyes of the two biddies instead of nodding politely, but she owed Blanche her allegiance. She would behave. For now.

The women twittered and fluttered, nervously waving handkerchiefs, reticules, and parasols. Fiona wished she were a foot taller so she could look down on them. Instead, she maintained the distant composure Neville used and refused to offer her hand.

"I'm not certain if the duke wishes to do much entertaining while in the country," Fiona said coldly when it came her turn to speak. "I'll be certain to mention your names should he do so, though."

She smiled inwardly as both women twitched. They had to have realized by now that she had been standing in the doorway and overheard their conversation. If they'd had visions of vast entertainments in the grand Anglesey palace, they could watch their dreams crumble to dust. The only way in hell Fiona would mention their names to Neville was as people she wouldn't greet if she lived to be a hundred. She gave them a wicked smile so they fully understood their fate.

"I've never seen Honoria and Loyolla so nervous," Blanche whispered as they parted company with the sisters and returned to the mercantile. "They organize the church's Easter fete so marvelously every year, I cannot imagine them flustered. Anglesey has apparently gone entirely too long without a duchess."

And it should probably go on a good deal longer without one. Even Lady Gwyneth would have handled the sisters better than Fiona had. She simply didn't have the temperament for niceness.

Fiona scarcely heard Blanche's chatter as they progressed through town. Obviously warned by the sisters, the villagers were on their best behavior, bobbing and curtsying whenever Fiona came in sight. But she saw no smiles or any genuine welcome. She sensed only resentment.

As they rode in the carriage back to the house, Fiona finally caught one of the comments Blanche threw into the one-sided conversation.

"I'm sorry, what did you say?" Fiona asked.

Blanche threw her a nervous look. "It's of no moment. I'm prattling, as usual."

"You said something about Neville being unable to fix those roofs another year." The roofs in question had solid slate instead of thatch, but

Fiona could see the gaps where the tiles had broken or slid off. They needed replacing.

"It's nothing. Do you think your Uncle William will arrive in time for the wedding? Neville has sent his yacht, you know."

Fiona knew nothing of yachts or sea travel, but she knew about leaky roofs. With some of the haze of panic out of the way, she could survey her surroundings a little more clearly. She should have paid attention much sooner.

As the horses clattered down the rutted road, Fiona opened her eyes.

Some of the tenant cottages were little better than whitewashed mud. The cottages she'd first noticed with tidy slate roofs were the exception. Most had thatch, and badly rotted thatch at that. Enclosed fields gave the tenants no garden plots of their own, and the only animals she saw were the sleek, well-fed cows inside the fences. The hedgerows were as poorly tended as the cottages, yet the fields showed signs of a wealthy harvest. Someone lived well off this land, but returned nothing to the people who lived here.

The towering spires and turrets of the sprawling Anglesey seat appeared on the hill ahead. The tall flagpole proudly waved the Anglesey flag, showing the duke was in residence. From her first visit, Fiona remembered the sprawling lawns divided by the ha-ha to keep the cattle from the drive. She remembered the wealth she'd seen in the vast expanse of rolling hill and field. But now she saw the little details, the unscythed grass where the cattle didn't roam, the untrimmed branches of a tree killed in some storm, the pitted drive in need of reworking. None of it was major. Perhaps Neville simply had a bad estate manager.

Surely an estate as vast as Anglesey had the funds for repairs. Didn't it?

# Fifteen

"Did you realize some of your tenant cottages are in sad need of repair?" Fiona paced the lovely navy and burgundy carpet of the informal withdrawing room where they'd retired after dinner. Unlike at Aberdare, there was a lovely warm fire, but she wasn't at all certain that it was the fire's heat warming her as Neville came closer.

"I will speak with my steward," he replied, catching her arm and halting her pacing. "How long do you think Blanche and Michael will take to say good night to the children?"

"Not long enough for what you're thinking." Fiona held him at arm's length as he bent to steal a kiss. "Really, we must talk, Your Grace."

"Back to 'your grace,' are we? Blanche shouldn't have stationed her maid in your room. I think I'll bribe her. We have better things to do than talk."

She wore a puff-sleeved evening dress and had not donned her gloves after dinner. Neville did unholy things to her flesh as he ran his hands up and down her bare arm. Just his proximity had the power to distract any intelligent thought. She pressed her palm against his cravat, knowing only too well the strength concealed beneath his deceptive clothing.

"Your mind is stuck in a narrow rut, Your Grace," she said bitterly. "Can we not ever converse on a different level?"

Neville tickled her cheek with a tendril of her hair. Every nerve in her body screamed to be closer, to steal his kisses again, to feel his arms around her, to feel the blood pounding recklessly through her veins, making her so alive that she could hear the birds sing in the dark. But she wasn't entirely an infatuated child. Part of her mind still functioned with maturity.

He chuckled, removed her hand from his chest, and kissed it. With that barrier removed, he leaned over to brush his lips against her cheek. He gave her a knowing grin as Fiona shivered in delight despite herself. "In a few months or so we might try intelligent discourse," he agreed. "I'll grant, there are other things on my mind right now."

Fiona shoved him away. "What will be different in a few months' time? How will we ever know each other if we never talk?"

Neville caught her waist, spreading one hand over the small of her back while the other lightly explored. Fiona shivered again but didn't move away. Couldn't.

"I think, for us, it might be best if we did our talking between the sheets." For once, he didn't look at her with amusement as he twisted a strand of her hair. "Anger comes a little less quickly when we can touch and remember the good things between us."

"You never get angry." Fiona slapped his hand away and turned around, forcing herself to walk away from his addictive touch.

"Don't I?" he asked in that annoyingly impassive voice.

She'd seen what he'd done to those drunks who had dared attack her, but she didn't think he'd been angry then. She had the distinct perception that he'd enjoyed himself. She swung around and faced him. "No, you don't. You watch the rest of the human race as if we're amusing creatures placed here for your entertainment. Well, I don't wish to be part of your entertainment. If we marry, I want to be part of your *life*. That means we must talk. That means you must explain why an estate as wealthy as this allows its tenants to suffer every time it rains. That means you must accept that we will disagree on almost every subject under the sun and we must come to some means of solving those disagreements." As Neville started forward, Fiona stepped away. "And going to bed is not the solution."

"That's a relief to hear," a dry voice said from the doorway. "If you're already disagreeing, I don't think bed the adequate solution before marriage."

Neville scowled and turned on the intruder. "I'm going to put a bell around your neck, Aberdare. Why can't you make noise like normal people?"

Michael shrugged and strode into the room. "For the same reason Fiona doesn't, if you haven't noticed. If I annoy you, Fiona will drive you insane. Are you quite certain that you're prepared for this marriage? I would not have her miserable for the rest of her life."

The duke seemed to grow half a foot taller and three stone heavier as he assumed a fighting stance, fists clenched, legs spread. Fiona marveled at the way he did that. At the same time, she wanted to smack him silly.

"I have no intention of making her miserable," Neville said coldly.

"But you will, and I'll return the favor." Fiona stepped out from behind Neville's back to stand between the men.

Looking down at her, Neville wished he could release her hair so it would gleam red in the fire's light. He'd seen it in a braid, knew it came nearly to her hips, and longed to see it loose and flowing—preferably across his pillow. But now her petal soft skin held his interest. It glowed with health and passion, just as the light in her eyes leapt and danced beneath the dark fringe of her lashes. His bride exuded passion just standing there, and he kept his hands in fists just to refrain from touching her.

"I'd not intentionally hurt you in any way," he said, ignoring the earl, focusing only on her.

"I know you wouldn't, but I'm perverse enough to wish you would because then I'd have the right to fight back. I bring nothing to this marriage. It makes me feel lowlier than any servant."

"Lower than a carpet?" Michael asked with amusement from behind her.

"Be quiet, Michael." Fiona didn't even turn around. She knew her cousin sought to soften the tension. But she didn't want it softened. She wanted it exploded. "Can you not see how wrong this is?"

"Michael has agreed to a very generous settlement. You do not come to me empty-handed, Fiona." Neville scowled over her head at Michael. "I am not marrying you for your dowry, however. I think you know very well why I want you as my wife."

"Is that enough?" she asked. "Can we base our entire lives on that? I'm Catholic, Neville. I'm Irish. I'm a farmer's daughter. Do you not think your people will despise you for making a duchess of such as that?"

"The Duke of Norfolk is Catholic, and it hasn't ruined him that I can see. You're making mountains out of molehills, Fiona. If we disagree, it won't be over your religion or your origins, I can promise you."

No, it would be over the roofs of tenant cottages and superstitious old biddies and the time he spent in London when she would prefer staying at Anglesey. It would be over her wish to see her home again and her refusal to entertain in the manner he needed and any of a half million other subjects. She knew this, yet she had condemned herself to it from the first moment she'd allowed his kisses. Why?

Neville caught her chin and lifted her face so their eyes met. "Don't, Fiona. Don't build walls before we find ways to breach them. I'm nearing thirty years of age. Give me some credit for knowing the woman I want when I see her."

Oh, Mary, Mother of Jesus, when he looked at her like that, said things in that intimate lover's voice, chills ran up and down her spine—more correctly, the juices spilled to her lower parts and she wanted him so much that she couldn't hear herself think.

"I'm trying, I really am," she whispered. "But it's not what I ever wanted, and the strangeness frightens me. We won't even be married in the eyes of my church."

"You're too wise to believe religion separates us and too brave to be frightened long, Fiona." He smiled and released her chin. "You'll hit me over the head with a chair if I don't behave, and I'm thinking it's my tenants who should be afraid."

She smiled weakly at his imitation of her accent. "Will my dowry buy the looms then?" she asked, returning to mundane matters until her knees could hold her without shaking.

"The looms and more, my dear. If you can wait until the session ends, I'll take you home to see for yourself."

That made matters less bleak. She curtsied and bestowed on him a mocking look. "I'll be holdin' you to that, my lord duke."

As she flitted from the room, Neville reluctantly turned to meet the earl's concerned gaze. Michael was the most intuitive man he'd ever known. Nothing got past him.

Michael sat slumped in a high-backed chair by the fire, studying Neville. "She's not a simple child, Neville. She's a strong-minded woman, although I'm not certain she fully recognizes that yet. I don't think hiding things from her is the best way of handling the situation."

Neville breathed a little easier. He didn't want the earl changing his mind and sending Fiona away, especially not after what they'd done together. And he damned well didn't want to tell her cousin what they'd done.

"I'm making ends meet now," he said cautiously. "You know how hard I've worked to make the entailed properties profitable. I'll let her use the dowry to fix those things she sees. That will keep her busy for a little while. I don't see why she should have to know more than that."

"And the year the harvest fails and your investments lose money? What will you tell her then when you have to turn off staff and let the cottages fall into complete disrepair?"

Michael knew Neville's financial straits were difficult—he didn't know the extent of the difficulty. He was sounding him out now, but Neville knew how to bluff. He'd been doing it the better part of his life.

"Every year I invest a little more and the profits are a little higher. I don't gamble, I don't drink, I don't frivol money away. I don't think Fiona will be nearly half so expensive to keep as most of the women of London. You don't have to worry about her starving or going shoeless."

Michael chuckled and relaxed. "No, but *you* will. Fiona hates shoes."

~

Having spent a frustrating day perusing the estate books, scratching for places where he could cut expenses so he could apply the money elsewhere, Neville decided he deserved some reward for his diligence. Inquiries of the footmen gave him the direction, and smiling at the aptitude of Fiona's choice, he hurried toward the conservatory.

Gladness swelled his heart, not to mention other parts of him, as he saw her slender back bent toward an easel while she colored in a sketch of one of the more delicate branches of miniature orchids in his collection. His scowl threatened to break his brow as a childish voice intruded upon his plans.

"Cousin Fiona, can I use that color there for my picture?"

He didn't walk so softly as Michael, and Fiona must have heard him enter, yet she merely handed her watercolor box to the child instead of greeting him. Even disguised in rich velvet, the girl's lame leg was evident from the way she sat in the chair.

"Do you think after we're married we'll be so hampered?" Neville growled with rare irascibility. Frustration would make a crotchety old man of him yet.

Fiona's amused look of understanding didn't help.

"That herd of heirs you require will hamper us greatly, Your Grace, but by then, perhaps it will not matter."

Herd of heirs. Neville groaned at the grammar and the image of producing that herd. And then he groaned at the thought of a half dozen Fionas racing about his feet. "Perhaps we ought to rethink the whole idea, then."

She looked startled, and Neville regretted speaking his thoughts aloud. He hadn't meant them as more than a jest, but they didn't have the kind of understanding yet. He offered a wry smile as he tried to explain.

"What if the Aberdare strain runs true? I will have a herd of heirs with red hair, whooping like wild Indians through the parlors, and a pride of princesses cutting them off at the pass with ropes slung across the hallways."

Fiona's smile broadened until it lit her face, and as he caught her imagination, she giggled. Beside her, little Mary looked at them both as if they'd lost their minds.

"A frightening thought, Your Grace," she replied with all solemnity when she'd sufficiently recovered herself. "But even more frightening is the idea of a line of studious little potential dukes, scrubbed and gleaming and not a wrinkle out of place, standing back and watching the herd of heirs and pride of princesses."

Neville narrowed his eyes, then turned to their miniature guardian. "I do believe there are cherry tarts for tea, Miss Mary. Why don't you run on and see?"

Delighted at this treat, Mary grabbed her cane, dipped a clumsy curtsy, and limped for the door. Satisfied that they were without an audience for the first time in days, Neville moved toward the reward he'd promised himself.

Fiona jumped up at almost the same time as Mary. But he knew she didn't retreat in fear of him. She was only worried about getting caught.

"I calculate we have exactly fifteen minutes before Mary reaches the parlor, Blanche realizes we're alone, and sends someone after us. Want to see how far I can go in fifteen minutes?"

"Are you counting, Your Grace?" She'd backed up against a table and couldn't retreat any farther.

"One thousand and one," Neville whispered as he planted his hands securely on the table on either side of her. "One thousand and two." He bent and captured her lips with his own, and all thought of numbers evaporated in steam.

She was so light he could lift her without trying, her waist so small that he could encompass it with his hands. Neville did both, setting Fiona on the table's edge so he could find better purchase. He cupped both her breasts in his palms, and filled his mouth with her moan of pleasure. The sound vibrated deep inside him, awakening needs and desires long dormant. He'd never been a man of passion, but Fiona drove him to the brink of it and beyond.

"The red-haired heirs can wait," he muttered against her lips. "It's a red-haired wife I want right now. Let me come to you tonight, Fiona. Send the maid away."

"I can't. I can't," she moaned again when he nibbled her lip. "She'll tell Blanche."

She shuddered in his arms and slid her fingers beneath his cravat, searching for his bare flesh. Neville took a deep breath and settled his disappointment. She was right, of course. He would have to make do with these hasty caresses for a few days more. And then he would keep her in his bed until they both died of exhaustion.

To hell with Parliament and reform bills.

He dipped his fingers beneath the neckline of her bodice and stroked the sensitive tips of her breasts. Behind them the door opened and the butler gave a polite cough.

Neville pulled away, reassured by Fiona's suppressed gasp that her desire remained as strong as his own.

Unable to turn lest whoever entered see the noticeable bulge in his trousers, Neville lifted Fiona from her perch and straightened her gown. "Two more nights, Fiona. Are you sure you're ready?" he whispered so only she could hear him.

He chortled at the challenge in her eyes as she lifted them to meet his. Fiona had never resisted a challenge in her life, he'd wager.

"I'm ready, Your Grace. The question is, are you?"

And a very good question it was, he mused as she walked out.

# Sixteen

"One more night, my love," Neville whispered, catching Fiona by surprise as she hid in the darkened library.

He'd spent the entire day about estate business, never once seeking her out, but now that she had reason not to face him, he located her faster than any vulture with its prey.

Fiona tried shrugging him off, but the duke merely shifted his hands on her shoulders. Embarrassment stifled the desire his presence usually stirred. She had to tell him sometime. She wished she'd had a mother to tell her how one went about these things. But she'd grown up in a household of men and knew only their language, not a woman's. "We can't," she whispered.

His fingers tightened, biting into her shoulders.

"Can't what?" he asked.

"We can't do it tomorrow." Tomorrow was their wedding day, the day they'd waited for all week. Her Uncle William and Seamus had arrived just hours ago. She and Neville would speak their vows in the morning, and then the duke would think he had every right to take her up to his bed and do what they'd done before. And she couldn't.

Neville's silence terrified her more than angry words. He could be so cold, so remote, so obtuse sometimes.

"I see." Releasing her, he leaned against the mahogany library table, every inch the noble duke. The lamp threw his sculpted cheekbones into relief. He didn't look at her, but at the slightly worn carpet beneath his feet. "May I ask if this is a temporary aberration?"

Fiona held her breath and nodded. Realizing he probably couldn't see her in the shadows, she spoke aloud. "Yes, only temporary," she said so softly, it was scarcely better than a nod.

The shoulders beneath his tightly tailored coat relaxed. "You mean that we may consider our red-haired heir postponed for another month?"

She could hear the grin in his voice, damn him. She'd spent the entire day pacing and worrying about a wedding night, and he just grinned and accepted that she was a failure as a brood mare. "You have an exceedingly narrow point of view, Your Grace," she answered coldly.

"Yes, well I have to, you realize. Otherwise I'd be running about like a chicken with its head cut off." He leaned over and cupped her chin, brushing her cheek with a feather-light kiss. "But I can focus equally well on you when necessary. What should you like to do with our temporary reprieve? I suppose I should have asked you earlier if there was any place you would like to go for our wedding trip. Brighton and Bath are a trifle out of season, but if you're interested..."

"I suppose it's too far to Ireland?" Fiona asked, doing her best to hide the wistfulness in her voice.

He gave her a look of genuine regret. "The session is not yet over. I have two bills that I have not given up on. I might stay away a week or two, but no longer. We'll go to Aberdare for Christmas, if you like."

He'd offered her more understanding than Fiona had dared hope for. She knew the importance of his work, even though she didn't believe government could ever accomplish anything except make the rich, richer. Still, she couldn't fault him for trying. She offered the only olive branch she possessed. "I suppose we could stay here. You could go into London for your sessions. Perhaps that would hurry up the process and Christmas will come early."

Neville appeared startled at the suggestion. But then he smiled, a genuine smile that had her heart pounding all over again, and she wished for the confidence to brush a fallen strand of hair from his brow. She wrapped her fingers around the edge of the library table instead.

"All right. Perhaps that's best. It will give you time to adjust to the estate at your own pace, without the burden of my attentions for a while. But stand forewarned, I will return before the week is out. I've waited too long for a wife and a marriage bed to forget them now."

She understood that completely. If he stayed here after the ceremony, unable to bed her, they would kill each other in frustration. She didn't know what she would do in this place with Michael and Blanche gone, but she would have to find some way to occupy herself. She had made a commitment for the rest of her life.

"The orphans?" she murmured, drawing him away from ticklish subjects.

"I've already made arrangements. Your uncle will see to them when he returns."

Fiona nodded. He'd done his part. She would do hers.


"We need to make some decision about purchasing that mine in Cornwall. Prices are down, but the men will go without work if we don't find another seam soon," Michael said, pacing the rug much as Fiona had earlier, Neville observed.

The pair of them had more energy than any ten people he knew. Scribbling his name across a document Michael had brought for his signature, Neville nodded. "I'll go down to Cornwall after Christmas."

Michael sent him a disgruntled look. "Don't be foolish. You'll be a newly married man. You can't leave Fiona to look after herself so early in the game."

Neville wondered what Michael would think should he learn of his earlier discussion with Fiona. Without glancing up from the papers, he dismissed the problem. "As long as Blanche is paying the staff at Anglesey, I'll earn my keep. She doesn't like you traveling too far, and with the child coming, she'll need you close to home. I can go to Cornwall."

Michael snorted. "You're not thinking like a married man yet, Duke. Fiona might have an opinion on that."

Neville finally glanced up at the man he had once considered his nemesis. For a change, he knew something better than Michael did. "By the first of the year Fiona will have had time to settle in. She'll have her own pursuits and won't miss me in the least, I promise."

Michael stopped his pacing and picked up several brass ornaments Neville had deliberately requested to replace the porcelain figurines usually there. The earl tossed the ornaments back and forth as he studied Neville. "Does Fiona know how much time you spend away from home?"

"Michael, you'll have to understand that what's between us isn't the same as for you and Blanche. One of the reasons Fiona will make a perfect wife for me is that she is completely independent and capable of entertaining herself. I won't have to spend every waking moment worrying over a clinging female." Remembering the scene with his mistress when she'd flung all his gifts back in his face, Neville gave thanks to God all over again for letting him see the light. He didn't have the temperament for demanding females.

"If you'd married Gwyneth as we all expected, you could have restored Anglesey's empty coffers immediately. Are you certain you'll not regret this?"

Neville heard the concern in Michael's question and didn't take umbrage. As Fiona's cousin, Michael had a right for concern. He set his pen down and shook his head. "Pour some brandy and let us celebrate our double cousinship. Anglesey has survived for centuries. Bankruptcy won't stop us now."

Lingering in the shadows, Fiona covered her gasp with her hand. She wished she'd entered without eavesdropping. She had only meant to wait for a break in the conversation. Now she knew entirely too much, and anger as well as fear shook her. *Bankruptcy.* No wonder the tenant cottages hadn't been repaired. She knew poverty well.

He should have told her he needed Gwyneth's money. He should have told her marriage between them was out of the question. He couldn't let his tenants suffer because of her, because of their lust and selfishness. It wasn't right.

Confused, appalled, and frightened, Fiona grabbed a shawl and fled out a side door. She would have an entire lifetime in which to repent if she didn't do the right thing now.

There was no child. She'd been given a reprieve from her foolishness. God had given her time to think this through.

She didn't place much consequence on the knowledge that she was no longer a virgin. She had never particularly expected to marry.

She had entered into this agreement in hopes of relieving the people of her village and saving the orphans. She hadn't realized that she might cause the suffering of others in return.

Fiona shivered and gazed up at the stormy night sky. Her shawl did little to keep the autumn wind from freezing her bare arms. Clouds scudded across what few stars dared show their faces. The wind had stripped the trees, and their naked branches tossed and turned against the sky. It seemed only fitting that she must make a difficult decision on a night such as this.

Michael and Blanche would never forgive her if she bolted. The duke would resent her for the rest of her life, and the notion brought tears to her eyes. She didn't want him hating her.

Disturbed by the realization that she truly cared what he thought of her, she had no choice but to admit that she didn't want to give him up. If she gave up the duke, she would never again know a man's touch or feel a child's suckle. She would condemn herself to a life of loneliness.

She didn't normally cry. She'd railed against the fates, shaken her fist at the stars, raced her horse across the countryside until she worked out her tears and anger. But none of those methods would work now. For just a little while, for a very little while, she'd felt needed. She hadn't realized how much she'd wanted that.

Of course, Neville didn't really need her. He could have any mistress he wanted, any wife he chose. Yet despite what she had done to his hopes for the future, he had treated her like a queen. He'd led her to believe she could truly be his wife, that he wanted her and only her.

And so, for his sake, she must be equally kind. He'd been forced to offer marriage. She would relieve him of the burden of marrying a penniless thorn in his side.

That decision formed, Fiona considered the consequences. Aberdare would suffer for it. There would be no dowry to buy the looms, though Michael might be persuaded to buy them after he quit being angry with her. The village would have to struggle along until then. The fate of the orphans was most pressing. She must hurry back to Aileen's children, find some way of providing for them.

She was good with horses. She'd trained the yearlings that kept Aberdare from bankruptcy. She could hire herself out, if she could disguise herself as a man. Something better might occur once she returned home.

Home. She needed the funds to return. She'd made that horrible journey alone once before. She wouldn't do it again without money. Blanche had given her a small allowance, but that wasn't sufficient. She hated stealing, but she had naught else. The duke hadn't even given her a betrothal gift. Everything had happened too quickly.

She would wait until Michael and Blanche had retired to their bed. Michael would have coins somewhere about. She didn't want to steal from Neville. She wasn't his responsibility any longer.

She wandered toward the warmth of the stable. The huge stone building broke some of the wind, and she brushed strands of hair back from her face as she paced beside it.

She didn't want to hurt Neville.

That idea struck her so forcefully that Fiona deliberately attempted to avoid it by listening to the wind. Instead, she thought she heard horses and voices. On a night like this? Shaking her head, she turned the corner, seeking the stable door and the warmth of the animals within.

She *did* hear voices.

Glancing up, Fiona saw the silhouette of a horse rearing a protest against the night sky. A groom fought to hold the animal down. None of Anglesey's horses behaved so badly. They'd all been properly trained and had no reason to fear their grooms. Had the duke possessed an animal like this one in his stables, she would have thought twice or more about marrying the man.

The groom led the horse inside the stable. The clouds had completely covered the sky now, and Fiona saw two men in the yard, their figures silhouetted by lights from the house beyond. They couldn't see her, thank goodness. She must look a fright. She slipped closer to the towering stone wall and out of anyone's sight.

"The announcement said he's to wed tomorrow. You'll not pry him away until he's bedded his bride," a stranger's voice warned.

"She's an Irish nobody. He's probably already bedded and bred her. There's no other reason he's given up his pursuit of wealth unless Aberdare threatened to close his purse strings. I think our duke will be willing enough to postpone the nuptials once I give him excuse."

The second voice had a ring of familiarity, but Fiona couldn't quite place it. She was torn between wanting to slap the man's face and the need to hear more. Instinct told her to be patient for a change.

"Claiming the chit is part of a conspiracy against the crown won't work without evidence, especially if she's carrying his heir."

Fiona bit back a gasp of outrage.

"I have evidence enough to send him hastening into London to confirm it. Quit worrying. We just need to stop this marriage before it consolidates Anglesey's name and power behind Aberdare and Effingham. Once we remove the duke's name from the bill, no one will listen to those two radical hotheads. They didn't go to school here, their ways are too foreign. The reform bills will disappear, never to return. We're doing this for the good of the country."

"I still don't like it," the unfamiliar voice muttered as the two men strolled in the direction of the house. "There's no guarantee that removing the girl will prevent Anglesey from supporting the bill."

The familiar voice held a hint of exasperation. "Don't push me too far, Durham. I'll handle the problem myself this time, rather than leave it to hired thugs."

Their voices faded into the night. Fiona sought some way of following them without being seen, but only the open stable yard stood between her and the house.

Swallowing her terror and confusion, she slipped along the wall of the stable toward the kitchen and the rear entrance. The men would be admitted at the front. She could discover who they were easily enough, but could she stop their lies as easily?

She didn't entirely understand their plans. Neville was aware of her brother's connections with Irish rebels. If these men had contrived some evidence against her, duty would require he look into the matter. She didn't like it, but since she'd planned on leaving anyway, their plan didn't affect her drastically as yet.

The things she hadn't quite heard or that had gone unsaid and the part about hired thugs worried her the most.

Anyone who knew Neville would know that if he'd made up his mind to support the reform bill, he wouldn't change it simply because his affianced wife betrayed him. Even with Fiona out of the picture, Neville would swing his whole support behind Effingham's bill. And these men meant to stop him.

These men had already hired thugs to stop him? They may have been responsible for the attack that had left Neville near death! He had to be warned of the possibility.

Reaching the cover of the trees at the side of the house, Fiona scampered across the courtyard, up the steps, and into the back hall. Breath rasping raggedly, she raced up the back stairs. She would tell Michael.

She found Blanche in the sitting room of her bedchamber. She glanced up from her knitting in surprise as Fiona burst in.

Fiona glanced at the baby cap forming beneath Blanche's talented fingers and closed her eyes against the sharp blow of realization. She'd forgotten Blanche's pregnancy. That's why Michael was so concerned about who would go to Cornwall. Blanche had a strong mind and character, but a weak constitution.

"Fiona, what's wrong? You look as if you've just ridden in on a broom." Blanche smiled to take any sting from her words.

"Where's Michael? I need to ask him something." Frantic, Fiona tried to think of some way of warning Blanche, some way of telling someone, but she didn't know how without worrying her.

"Oh, some gentlemen just came in from London. He and Neville are meeting with them in the study, something about the bill they're sponsoring, I suppose. I do wish people would be a little more sensible. We cannot live in the past forever. But no, they must stick their heads in the sand until someone shoots them in the rear."

At any other time, Fiona would have laughed at this lovely lady's prosaic description of most of British Parliament, but she didn't have a laugh left in her. Panic seeped in as time grew shorter. Should she run down to the study and accuse the visitors of wickedness?

Who would believe her? Making some flimsy excuse, Fiona bowed out of the sitting room.

Michael might believe her, but she couldn't speak with him alone. Neville would have to investigate. He was too dutiful not to. If they'd had a love match, it might have been different, but there was no chance of that. He'd investigate.

*And if he didn't change his mind about the bill, something terrible would happen to Neville.* She knew it. She'd heard it in their voices. *Once we remove the duke's name from the bill...* How? With hired thugs? More lies?

They intended to stop her marriage, condemn any child she bore to bastardy, and discredit Neville in such a way that he couldn't support the reform bills now or in the future. Damn good thing there was no bastard apparent.

Fury blending with fear, Fiona raced to her room, seeking some means of protecting Neville until Michael could investigate. Neville wouldn't necessarily believe her if she warned him of what she'd heard. Once those men gave him evidence condemning her as a traitor, he wouldn't believe anything she said.

She couldn't let him go to London into whatever trap those two planned.

But if she wasn't here, his damned pride would force him to come after her.

# Seventeen

Neville snarled at the documents littering his desk, the ones Townsend and his sniveling son-in-law had delivered the prior night. He already knew about the seditious behavior of Fiona's friends and family — hell, all of Aberdare. That didn't make Fiona a traitor, as these papers declared. If she had any link to the violent White Boy factions disrupting the Irish countryside, he'd personally eat Townsend's hat.

He already knew of the failed attempt by Irish factions to blow up the heads of government a few years back. Fiona had been involved in that, admittedly. She'd been the one who'd warned Michael.

He didn't trust Townsend and his cohorts for a bleeding minute. They were up to something by rehashing this old news. They didn't come all the way out here to stop his marriage purely on an altruistic basis. If anything, he would have expected them to let him marry a traitor, then turn Fiona over to the government out of spite.

But Fiona's disappearance on the same night that they brought this filthy "evidence" was suspicious in the extreme. Michael was out looking for her, but that was only an excuse to avoid Neville. They both knew where she'd gone.

Cursing, Neville picked up a piece of his own stationery. Fiona's bold handwriting leapt from the page, and he covered his eyes against the accusing glare of her words, blaming weariness for the moisture pooling behind his eyelids. The raw pain slicing through his insides had nothing to do with her note. One didn't feel pain when jilted by a mistress or an object of lust. His pride hurt, that's all. He slapped the paper onto the desk.

His head pounded as if a dozen tiny imps beat upon it with steel hammers. Neville rubbed his eyes to clear them again, then took another sip of stale brandy. He still couldn't believe it.

She'd left him.

He couldn't believe any woman would walk away from marriage with a Duke of Anglesey. Worse, he couldn't believe the anguish her desertion caused. Neville knew Fiona didn't love him. But he'd thought they'd worked out an understanding. Why hadn't she said something? Why couldn't they have talked about it?

*Talked about it.* She'd told him she wanted to talk, but he kept putting her off. He hadn't wanted her discovering all the pitfalls awaiting them. He'd wanted her in his bed and breeding his heirs before she had any notion of the depths of the problems before them. He'd been blinded by lust, crazed with a need to perpetuate the line, driven to desperation by a crack on the head. Maybe he should consider Bedlam.

Neville finally surrendered to the need to hold her letter again. He picked it up, read the characteristically bold handwriting, and searched desperately for the truth between the lines.

*It's for your own good I do this* the note began.

It sounded just like Fiona. He wanted to hear her speak the words. He wanted to watch her eyes light with desire when he reached for her. With a groan of dismay, he flung the paper aside.

Maybe fools would take her flight as admission of guilt, but they didn't know Fiona as he did. Neville groaned again as he realized how exceedingly well he knew his beautiful, passionate Fiona. No matter how much she believed in the rebel cause, he knew she would never hurt Michael or Blanche—or himself, for all that mattered. Fiona's generosity spilled over on everyone, even an arrogant English lord.

Michael slammed into the study, providing needed relief from Neville's painful thoughts.

"She's gone," Michael said grimly, his eyes gray from lack of sleep as he reached for a piece of brass statuary on the mantel. They had been up all night arguing with Townsend, and Neville supposed he didn't look any better than the earl.

"She lifted coins from my dresser and took your mare as far as the coaching inn," Michael continued, confirming their fears. "The groom's returning it to the stable now. She passed herself off as a governess at the inn. The maid said she borrowed one of her old Sunday dresses. There's no guarantee she'll continue traveling in that disguise. She prefers boy's clothes."

Neville knew that. If Fiona was innocent, then she simply ran from him and the bankruptcy their marriage would cause, as her letter stated. She'd explained her position, and he had no reason to doubt her.

Neville rested his head against the back of his leather chair so he could study Michael without expending the energy of holding up his aching head. "She wrote a letter to you too, didn't she? Why won't you let me see it?"

Michael scowled and danced the brass ornaments from the mantel between his fingers. "She merely apologized to me and Blanche. There are some personal things in there Blanche would prefer not revealed, none of them of concerning you. I've told you what she said. It's nothing more than what's in the letter she wrote you."

"Then let me see it!" To his own astonishment, Neville slammed his fist into the desk, sending papers flying. He never lost his temper. Never.

"Why don't you take that so-called 'evidence' Townsend brought you and have a warrant sworn out for her arrest? I'm sure the military will take care of the matter and you needn't concern yourself any further." Michael's voice dripped scorn.

Neville wadded up the papers beneath his hand and flung them at the fireplace. "You see to Townsend's shit. It's more up your alley than mine. I want to hear Fiona say to my face that she doesn't want this marriage. Something is wrong, and I want to know what it is!"

Furious with himself for raising his voice, Neville staggered from the desk chair. He'd emptied the brandy decanter almost entirely by himself since Michael didn't do more than sip liquor. Thankfully, the full effect of the alcohol hadn't hit him until now. He needed numbness for the next step.

"Then find her," Michael replied icily. "You're the reason she ran off."

"Damned right I will." He'd known all along that's what he'd have to do. Drinking himself into a stupor wouldn't return Fiona. Not that he wanted Fiona returned, Neville told himself. No, he wouldn't have the little demon now if hell froze over and heaven beckoned. But he wanted to know why she'd left him. And none of this rambling nonsense about not being good enough to be his duchess. His bold Fiona wouldn't let her orphans starve or her village go without its looms out of fear of his tenants. Or lions or tigers for all that mattered. Or dukes.

The worry that Townsend had done something to her turned Neville's mouth to dust. It wasn't a reasonable assumption. Townsend had evidence to throw her in prison. He didn't need to harm her. Fiona had written those letters and left of her own free will. There'd been no time for Townsend's interference.

But instinct said differently. Neville allowed his valet to dress him for traveling. He'd put his entire life in order, knew every step he must make from one day to the next to accomplish the enormous list of tasks his responsibilities required. Fiona had thrown all that into chaos the moment she'd walked into his life. Yet he couldn't let her go.

He glanced at the clock as it chimed — ten. The chapel bells should be ringing in his wedding guests right now. In a few more minutes, he would have been a married man. Instead, Seamus and William were repacking their bags, and the rest of their small guest list would be racing back to London with the wonderful tale of how the Duke of Anglesey had been stood up at the altar by a chit of an Irish girl. All England would have a good laugh at his expense. Let them. He wouldn't be there to enjoy it.

Neville stood at the helm of his yacht, letting the sea wind blow all thought from his mind. He had the force of His Majesty's Navy at his command if he wished. Fiona didn't stand a chance of escaping him.

William wandered up to stand beside him. The wind whipped his loose country clothing around his portly body and reddened his bulbous nose. "She'll be there, Your Grace, just wait and see. Fiona's a good girl. She just gets bees in her bonnet sometimes."

"Fiona is a rebellious force of nature," Neville said coldly. "Someone should have clipped her wings long ago."

William gave him a sidelong look. "I'm after thinkin' birds with their wings clipped are pretty baubles, but they're not birds anymore. Fiona is what she is and what God intended for her to be."

"Did you ever consider God made us naked and perhaps intended us to be that way? Does that mean you should run about bare assed?" Neville asked scornfully. "If children aren't taught manners and behavior, they turn into heathen savages."

"The girl knows what she's about," William replied confidently. "If she ran away, it's with good reason. And might there not be something you should be telling me about that reason, Your Grace?"

"I gave her no reason to run. You read her letter. It's all nonsense." A blast of cold air whipped Neville's hair around as land loomed closer, but he absorbed the blow as he did all others.

"Maybe nonsense is all she thought you needed." Without further pleasantries, William departed, leaving Neville to his own cold reflections.

They wasted a day in Dublin checking for ships that might have arrived from England in the last few days. Knowing Fiona traveled on little coin made him shiver. There was slim chance that she would arrive first. Neville sent William up the coast to leave word in every likely port. He'd left Michael in England checking for the ship she'd sailed on, but they both knew Fiona's talents for disguise. Neville assigned his yacht captain to wait for Michael's message. They would question the crews as the ships arrived.

In the meantime, Neville harnessed his restive gelding and set out for Aberdare.

The late October weather brought chilly winds and drenching

downpours. Neville stopped only long enough to steam his wet clothes in front of a roaring fire and quaff a mug of hot cider before hitting the road again. He would have Fiona's dratted orphans held hostage before she arrived.

He rode into the dreary little village a little past midnight. A dog howled at his approach, and a pig snorted in reply. With his horse picking its way down the muddy lane, Neville considered going to the castle and waiting for dawn, but instinct drove him to check on the orphans first. Fiona would go nowhere until she had seen to the children.

The forlorn hut showed no sign of light or smoke, although the temperature had dropped considerably the past few hours. Shivering in his greatcoat, Neville dismounted and considered his next move. He couldn't just walk into a house full of sleeping children.

He looked around for somewhere he could shelter his horse and mount guard until morning came.

Under better circumstances, he wouldn't deem the cottage fit shelter for his horse. Swearing at the ramshackle sheds, Neville tied the gelding inside the roofless walls of a crumbling stone barn. At least the walls cut off the wind, and the rain had stopped.

Gingerly, he picked his way across the mud. His valet would have a falling down, screaming fit when he saw his boots. Fortunately, he'd left the man behind, and he wouldn't see the boots for some days to come. This had better not take longer than days. The crime reform and emancipation bills required his presence in London.

He wanted to reassure himself that the children were still inside before settling down to watch the place for the rest of the night. William had said they were still there, scrabbling along with what the neighbors provided and on the coins Fiona had given them.

Peering in the back window, Neville could just make out several lumpy forms near the dying embers of the fire. They were still there. Relieved, he started to walk away.

Something hard and long smashed across the back of his head.

Thinking only *not again*, the mighty Duke of Anglesey splashed face forward into the muddy path between the cottage and the privy.


Burrowing his aching head between his arms in hopes of drowning out the drunken trio at the end of the bar harmonizing in an old folk song of ancient battles and dying Irishmen, Eamon O'Connor cursed his fate, cursed the liquor, and cursed all hymns to dying Irishmen. For once in their lives, couldn't they sing of victory and triumph?

Tilting his head and opening one bloodshot eye, he verified that the man he followed continued his intense conversation with the newly-arrived Englishman. The pair deserved each other, he thought maliciously.

He ought never to have taken this assignment. He owed Michael MacDermot a damned lot, but not enough to follow this scoundrel about. Ireland seethed with secret societies and terrorist organizations that believed their own narrow-minded points of view would solve the work of centuries. Once he'd been idealistic enough to believe their tales of outrage and to sympathize with the world of woe around him. Now, he just wanted them all to bugger off and leave him alone.

But he owed the earl and wouldn't see Fiona hurt, even if she had fallen into the treacherous snare of a damned English duke. That obnoxious weasel at the back table would harm anyone who stood in his way, and as best as Eamon could determine, the better part of the law stood in the rogue's way. Eamon thoroughly despised absentee landlords, but this particular landowner was deserving of his own special place in hell.

He really should report to Michael, Eamon knew, but there wasn't much he could report or that Michael could do. The ruffian he followed had money in his pocket, but Eamon couldn't determine of a certainty from what source—unless it was the English landowner who sat across from the cad now. Eamon didn't think it likely that either of them had been near the village when Burke died, but since then, the man he'd been following had talked to each of the suspects Michael had mentioned. And now he was talking to a wealthy man.

The question remained, what did a bloody English *nobleman* have to do with a lot of discontented Irish?

# Eighteen

Rain pouring down her face and hair snaking in damp tendrils beneath the neck of her shirt, Fiona gathered her cloak closer and stumbled down the lane toward the cottage.

She'd been mad to leave Anglesey. Who would dare harm someone as powerful as a duke? It all seemed some sort of bad dream now, with the cold Irish rain beating down her back and hunger eating at her belly. She hadn't remembered how miserable the cold and the wet could be. How in the name of the Holy Mother of Jesus would she keep Aileen's orphans warm and fed in this weather?

Wiping rivulets of water from her eyes, Fiona slogged up to the cottage, every inch of her caked with mud.

The door popped open before she could knock. Sean, Aileen's eldest, stood on the threshold, his narrow face drawn with anxiety. Fiona's empty stomach contracted.

"Sean? What is it?" She stepped into the cottage as the boy opened the door wider.

A blast of moist heat hit her. The fire was roaring, but how they'd paid for the peat was a mystery to her. She was too grateful for the warmth to care. Hanging her dripping cloak on a hook by the door, she scanned the interior, counting heads. Before she reached the requisite seven, her gaze stumbled over the long masculine figure stretched out on a pallet before the fire.

Neville.

*He'd followed her.* He'd heard Townsend's wild claims and followed her, as she'd hoped. Had he come to see her hanged as a traitor, or did his bedeviled pride bring him?

She panicked at his stillness. She had wanted to protect him, not kill him.

Blinking back moisture and hiding fear, Fiona kneeled beside the duke. He didn't stir. His eyes didn't open. Her pulse accelerating, she turned to Sean. "Is he sleeping?"

A rush of Irish poured from the terrified boy, interrupted occasionally by the old woman in the corner and one of the girls. As well versed in the old language as the new, Fiona still had difficulty comprehending.

"Mary, Jesus, and Joseph," she muttered as some of the problem sank in. She should have known the damned duke would arrive ahead of her. But she'd had no way of warning the children.

Sean had only thought to protect his family from thieves and murderers when he'd knocked the stranger over the head. Not until it was light had he recognized the Englishman.

She'd run here to keep him safe, and the children had done for him.

Fiona pried at the duke's eyelid, checked his pulse and breathing, and prayed. He lived, she could say that much.

"Mrs. Callaghan, have you sent for my Uncle William? Surely he arrived with the duke?"

The old lady rocked in her corner, cuddling the sleeping babe against her. "He's not arrived. The lads have asked."

There was no point in asking for a physician. There was none to be had, even had there been coins to bribe one into coming. And Fiona wasn't entirely certain it should be known that the Duke of Anglesey lay prone and helpless in this miserable hovel.

She didn't dare move him until he came around. Blows to the head weren't something one took lightly. She'd seen grown men permanently turned into helpless babes after a drunken brawl. Infants dropped on their heads were never quite the same. A man who'd been hit twice in the same place, causing unconsciousness in both cases, could easily have his brains scrambled.

At least the children had had the sense to keep him warm and dry. She didn't hear the pneumonia in his lungs, which was more than she could say for herself if she didn't strip out of these wet clothes.

"Have you paper and pen then, Sean? I'd send word around to the castle. They'll be looking for us. And the duke's horse? Where is it?"

After ascertaining which of the children could manage the horse, Fiona took a piece of brown sacking and a stub of charcoal Sean gave her. She scribbled a hasty letter to the castle housekeeper and sent the second eldest out into the rain to deliver the message and hide the horse.

"Now we should have some bread and a bit more shortly. Have you a potato I can eat until help arrives?"

Shyly, the children produced potatoes, a flea-ridden blanket, and a cup of rainwater from various dark corners of the cottage. Fiona sipped thirstily at the water, roasted the potato and ate it half raw, allowing her clothes to dry by the fire rather than undress and wrap in the blanket. In all that time, the duke never stirred.

Fiona studied the pallor of Neville's face, the strong bones and high brow, the thick eyebrows that accented his usually stern demeanor. He didn't seem quite so intimidating laid out flat and helpless, his lids closed over all-too-observant eyes. But she knew the passion he hid behind his stoic facade. And she admired the keen intelligence of his powerful mind.

Daringly, she caressed his brow, brushing his hair back from his face. The stubble of a beard roughened his jaw. Neville often shaved twice a day so as not to appear uncivilized. He would have failure of the heart did he see himself now. Smiling, she tested the texture of that dark growth over the hard curve of his jaw.

A strong hand captured her fingers. She stared into open gray eyes in surprise. Fiona hadn't realized how worried she'd been until relief almost inundated her. "Neville! Thank all that is holy, you're awake!" She blinked back tears, blaming them on joy.

Silvered eyes watched her with uncertainty. Neville never looked uncertain. When he said nothing, Fiona bit her lip to keep her teeth from chattering. Perhaps he was a bit confused.

"I'll have tea as soon as the boys come back with the makings. Will you take a drop of water then?" She tried helping him into a sitting position, but he didn't cooperate. He wouldn't release her hand. Fear twisting its augur deeper, Fiona touched his forehead in search of fever.

"Sean was simply protecting the babies. You should never have come here in the middle of the night. There's too much meanness afoot."

Neville closed his eyes again, but he continued clinging to her hand, the pressure of his fingers nearly cutting off the circulation in hers.

"It's all right, Neville. When you're feeling better, we'll take you to the castle. It's just a little bump on the head. If you could drink the water, I could give you something for the pain." She tried reassurance, but she wasn't certain she reached him. His fingers didn't unclench.

The door burst open and the boys tumbled in with sacks of food, followed by the closest thing the castle had to a major-domo.

"Miss Fiona! We've been that worried about you. And His Grace!" Doyle threw up age-spotted hands in dismay. "What's to become of us? We're destroyed, we are."

"Don't be ridiculous, Doyle. Did you bring me clothes? These will never dry out in this weather. His Grace is just a little unwell. We'll have him up and about directly."

The fingers clutching hers didn't relax, preventing her from standing to see what Doyle had brought. She supposed she should feel some relief that Neville still retained his strength. That he didn't speak caused more concern than any relief she might feel.

Doyle glanced nervously about at the cottage teeming with children, all staring at him. "I must speak with you privately, Miss Fiona. It's urgent."

Privately. Of course. They would retire to the master drawing room, she thought sarcastically. "Has the rain lessened?" When Doyle nodded, she gestured at the children with her free hand. "Go wash yourselves at the well. Sean, make certain the young ones are good and clean before you bring them back here. We'll have a feast shortly."

At Fiona's fierce look, Sean grabbed the toddlers and shooed the lot of them out. Only Mrs. Callaghan and the babe remained, and they slept in the far corner.

"All right, what is it, Doyle?" Was it her imagination, or did the pressure of the duke's fingers lessen?

The old man coughed uncertainly, and lowered his voice to a whisper. "It's McGonigle's men, Miss Fiona. Eamon has warned us that they mean to torch the castle. If they should hear His Grace has returned, there's no telling what they'll be doing."

*Oh, Lord God in heaven, deliver us from evil.* Fiona closed her eyes and drew closer to Neville's warmth. Reaching out to a barely conscious man for reassurance was the act of a fool, but Neville had strength, and she needed to borrow a little. The fingers wrapped around hers squeezed.

"No one knows the duke has arrived, do they?" she demanded. At Doyle's vigorous shake of his head, she thought quickly. The younger children couldn't be relied on to keep quiet once the village awoke. Word would be out shortly.

"Castle. Save." Neville's whisper startled her from those reflections.

Pain etched Neville's face, but Fiona knew his expressions well. Stubbornness and determination tightened his jaw. Stupid man, as if a castle meant anything. She supposed that was just one more example of the chasm between them.

"Doyle, have you sent for the authorities? I know Michael and the colonel are at odds, but the army ought to be of some use. They can guard the damned castle." There, that should reassure Neville. She wouldn't worry him with the unlikelihood of any army arriving in time to stop McGonigle's White Boys. The army moved on tortoise legs, while the ruffians struck like lightning.

"Eamon's passed the word, but who's to say—"

Fiona waved a hand to hush him. "Fine, then we must get the duke and the children out of here. If McGonigle is stopped from destroying the castle, he might take out his anger on Michael's tenants. I can't believe he'd be stupid enough to burn the new cottages, but he'll look for some target, and these old barns could qualify. Damn, I wish I could hang the man by his toes!"

Frustrated at the senseless violence that broke out across the countryside whenever tempers flared, Fiona gnashed her teeth and sought some solution to their current predicament. She couldn't do everything. She'd leave McGonigle for another time, after she had Neville and the orphans in safety. They really couldn't hide a duke in a hovel.

"The yacht! Neville, where did you leave the yacht? Sligo?" He didn't open his eyes, but they scrunched up as if in thought. "Sligo," he repeated uncertainly, with a slight nod of his head.

That was closer than Dublin. Breathing a sigh of relief, Fiona turned back to Doyle. "Bring us a wagon, blankets, food, whatever you can find quickly. I'm taking the duke and the children to Sligo. Get everyone else out of the castle and to safety until the army arrives. If the castle burns, it burns. It's not worth wasting lives over." Another thought prompted her to bend over Neville again. "Where's Uncle William, Neville? We must send word so he doesn't come near."

The children returned in a laughing, chattering explosion of noise as they carried in bundles of food from the castle larders. All hope of further conversation gone, Fiona sent Doyle on his errands, and set about making their meal as if the whole world did not crumble around her.

The nearly inert man beside her said nothing more.

The demons dancing in his head had voices now. They shrieked and twisted the pain into a living wire coiling through his brain, driving out all coherent thought. He sensed the fire baking one side of him, gradually realized his clothes were damp on the other side, and even recognized the itches of fleas from the pallet he lay on. But little else entered his consciousness except The Good Voice.

He waited attentively for every instance of the familiar, welcoming sound. That most of the words went right on past him mattered little. The Good Voice spoke with a reassurance and a boldness that drove out the demon voices. He occasionally opened his eyes to find the source of that magical sound. So far, he'd caught only the silhouette of long hair and slender curves before the demons shouted, and he shut his lids again. Somehow, he knew that hair blazed with the same fire as the peat in the hearth.

He didn't bother struggling to sit up at her urging. The effort wasn't worth the pain. He knew he needed to get beyond the pain, but he couldn't precisely remember why. It was just something he had to do.

And when he did, he would remember the beautiful creature behind The Voice. That blissful thought alone made the pain bearable.

He agreed with every question The Voice asked because it seemed the wisest thing to do. He wished he could remember what Sligo was for her sake. But already the reason for wanting to know was sliding away.

# Nineteen

Pain slammed through Neville as they lifted him into the back of the wagon. Groaning, he attempted protest, but he couldn't form the words. Childish chatter clamored, and he winced.

Cold air washed over him before someone tucked a soft blanket around him. The Good Voice returned, and he listened as closely as the demons would allow.

"Sean, where's the duke's purse? He wouldn't have traveled without one."

He caught the word "purse" and the questioning tone. The childish reply spoke in guilt and defiance. Odd, that he knew what they said without hearing the words.

The Voice scolded but equally reassured. He marveled at how the melodious sound could convey so many meanings at once. He sensed her presence, but he couldn't touch her, and frustrated, he fought against the wool binding him.

"Neville! It's all right, Your Grace, I'll make a pillow for your head. But first I must lift the children around you. There's so many of them, no one will know you're here. Just lie still and be quiet a while longer."

He understood "pillow... children... quiet." Absorbed with translating those clues, he didn't object when his only means of communication departed. He could hear The Voice not far away, cajoling, promising, laughing, comforting. Such a variety of sounds she made.

Small bodies giggled and wiggled around him. Becoming aware of his helplessness, he struggled against the confinement of the blanket again, without success.

"Mrs. Callaghan, sit up beside Sean with the babe. I'll sit back here with the children. With luck, we should reach Sligo before nightfall."

He knew the instant she returned to his side. Even the children sat still. He sensed a solemnity to the occasion but not the reason for it. As gentle hands lifted his head and created a pillow in a soft, warm lap, he sighed in deep contentment.

The wagon jerked into motion and the demons shrieked again. Pain hammered his skull as he fought to free his hands so he could hold his head. Instead, soft fingers stroked his brow.

"I'm sorry, Your Grace. I know it must hurt. I've a potion for you if you'll drink it. I don't dare give you the laudanum, but this should help a little."

"Hurt... potion... laudanum," registered in his scrambled brain. He didn't want laudanum. He wanted coherence. He jerked his head aside as she held something to his lips. "No... laudanum," he pushed past his unwieldy tongue.

"Not laudanum," she repeated carefully. "Herbs. Not sleep."

He sought the missing pieces for meaning. "Not laudanum," he understood. Warily, he tasted the liquid she dribbled between his lips. Not laudanum. Wearily, he drank it all.

The wagon jolted over muddy, rocky roads, listing from side to side, rocking its occupants who giggled at first, then whined. Caught in a quagmire of a pothole, the wagon stopped at one point. While a helpful farmer pulled them out, The Voice led the children in song. Childish voices piped unintelligible words, and Neville smiled. An image of a bird in a tree appeared in his head, and he imagined it warbling in harmony.

Light from the emerging sun filtered through his closed eyelids and lanced through his pounding brain. He almost wished they'd pull the blanket over his eyes, but he couldn't put the words together to request it.

As the wagon rattled down the road, he listened to The Voice exclaiming over apples. Laughter and eager crunching followed, and his belly rumbled. As if sensing his hunger, the gentle hands holding his head caressed his jaw.

"Would you have a slice, Your Grace? I've peeled it for the babes so they won't choke. Perhaps you could take a bite or two?"

The sweet juice of the fruit slid past his lips. Not entirely grasping her words but understanding the taste, Neville opened his mouth and allowed her to feed him the apple slice. The burst of flavor awoke his hunger with a vengeance. "Apple," he demanded.

Her laughter trilled as brilliantly as bird song. He discovered pleasure in the rocking motion beneath him, the softness of her lap, the juice trickling over his lips, and the sun beating down and warming him. He couldn't remember ever experiencing this kind of simple pleasure. Surely he'd known it at some time, but his mind wasn't quite up to the memory yet.

Feeding the duke on apples, entertaining the children on wild tales, Fiona tried to live in the moment and not worry about the next. She didn't like seeing Neville so still and speechless. It didn't bode well. But she'd long ago learned not to fret because she couldn't move the moon and stars.

So she imagined a picnic with the duke resting his head on her lap while she spun tales for the children they would never have together. If she'd thought their future could hold moments like this, she might have found a better way of handling the situation at Anglesey, but life was all about disappointment, and she knew better than to fool herself. So she borrowed this moment out of time.

The wagon dragged into Sligo at sunset. She was tempted to seek the duke's yacht, but uncertain of the danger, she directed Sean toward a respectable inn. If the duke had enemies, surely they knew where to find his yacht. It was best not to reveal his helplessness just yet.

"I don't have Doyle here to move you, Your Grace," she whispered, wishing the nearly comatose man in her lap could hear. "Could you see your way to walking?" She didn't expect an answer, and she certainly didn't expect him to sit up and walk away. She just needed someone to talk to, and the children weren't helpful.

"Walk," came the murmur from dry lips.

Startled, Fiona raised her eyebrows. Cool gray eyes stared back at her. He was awake!

Tamping down her excitement, she kept her voice low as she issued orders to the children to behave, and sent Sean to check on the availability of rooms. She didn't know how she would disguise the duke, walking or not walking. "Shall we try sitting you up first?"

His arms struggled at the cocoon of blankets. Hurriedly, Fiona unwrapped him. He still wore his frock coat, although it looked as if it had been thrown on the ground, rolled in the mud, and wadded up to dry. She shook out a blanket, draped it around his shoulders, and offered support as he struggled for a sitting position.

She could almost literally hear him fighting the pain as he leaned against her shoulder. The man she knew would never have leaned on anyone.

"All right, the end of the wagon is a few feet away. Do you think you can scoot over there?"

Fiona held her breath as he hesitated. She wasn't at all certain that he comprehended. So far, all he'd done was repeat what he heard.

"Neville?" she whispered. The name came much easier to her tongue now than it used to, when he was his usual authoritative self. When he didn't respond, she tried another tactic. "Move forward."

That simple command produced a better response. He nodded, winced, then edged toward the end of the wagon.

Sean ran out, followed by an aproned innkeeper. Hiding her fear, Fiona threw part of the blanket over Neville's head. He halted with his legs dangling half out of the wagon and grasped the wool so it didn't fall.

"He's got but two rooms."

Fiona thanked the boy's intelligence for stopping his tongue before he said her name. She gave him a grateful smile, then turned an anxious gaze to the rotund innkeeper. "My husband is injured, sir. We're seeking a physician. If you would, I've the coins to pay for the rooms in advance."

That news brought an immediate smile to the man's face. "Of course, missus. Allow me to help with the poor man. Was it a fall from his horse? Knew a man once, fell from his horse, near broke his head open, he did. Never the same again."

She didn't need that cheerful news, but she managed a grateful smile. "His horse, yes. Minding his own business, and the animal just up and throws him. Never saw the like. Here, let me take the other side. Granny, if you'd see to the children..."

In a thick cloud of confusion, they helped Neville inside while children toddled, skipped, and chattered in a whirling pattern around and between them. Mrs. Callaghan held the sleeping infant and occasionally shooed a straying tot ahead of her.

Once installed in their rooms with Neville's purse several coins lighter, Fiona sat on the edge of the bed, closed her eyes, and gave herself up to weariness. Tired children explored, climbed the furniture, and clawed through the sacks of food.

"Nanny."

Fiona smiled at the word from the man beside her. He'd actually said something on his own, so his brains weren't entirely scrambled. Leave it to a bloody rich duke to think of nursemaids. Not so rich, she amended, just spoiled.

"Not likely," she replied. She thought she heard him laugh. She probably imagined it. She so desperately wanted his help that she would imagine anything even resembling it.

"Food," he said succinctly.

That was the answer of course. The children couldn't shout and whine and cry with their mouths full of food. Clapping her hands, Fiona set the older ones to cutting bread and cheese. Mrs. Callaghan had already produced a pot for boiling water on the brazier. They'd have hot tea and toasted bread in their bellies shortly. Weary as they all were, surely they would sleep.

She propped pillows behind Neville so he could sit up, supported by the iron bedstead. His eyes were open more often now and seemed to observe the chaos. He carefully examined the cup of tea she offered, then took the handle. She guided his hand toward his mouth. As he sipped the brew, some of the tension slipped from his posture, and he closed his eyes and drank without further aid.

Doyle had only packed a few tin mug s, but the children knew how to share. The smallest needed the mugs held for them, and Fiona helped Mrs. Callaghan with that task while keeping her eye on the man in the bed. The blanket had fallen from his shoulders, revealing the rumpled, muddy mess of his clothing. She'd have to send to his yacht for clean ones if she could.

Sean had said Neville hadn't carried a bag with him. He must have been in quite a hurry to leave the ship without a change of clothing. If she considered the fit of fury Neville must have been in at the time, she could almost look at his current state as a welcome reprieve. Almost.

As the eldest took turns leading the youngest to the privy behind the inn, another thought increased her nervousness. Until now, Neville hadn't taken in enough liquids to need the use of a chamber pot, but he'd just drunk two mugs of tea. Unless his body was more damaged than she'd thought, he'd need the pot or a privy before long.

She'd cleaned and bandaged wounds for the village workers over the years. She'd given them herbal teas to ease their headaches after drunken sprees. She had little shyness of men's bodies. But somehow, even after what they had done together, the intimacy of tending the duke's needs overwhelmed her.

Mrs. Callaghan took the youngest and the oldest children into the adjoining room where they washed, and arranged pallets or shared the bed. Fiona tucked blankets around the three middle children and heard their prayers. When she returned to the high bed, she discovered Neville watching her gravely.

"You." He pointed at the door.

She understood, even if she wasn't certain she agreed. "You'll be all right?"

It took him an inordinate amount of time to understand the question, but finally, he repeated. "All right."

She tried not to let relief overwhelm her at this indication that some of his comprehension was returning. Not willing to consider what that second blow had done to the duke's fine mind, Fiona set the chamber pot near the bed and hastened out the door to the privy.

She knew this inn, had slept there before. She knew to avoid the tavern and to carry a candle through the darkened halls. She would have preferred company, but she could deal with most anything that came her way. Fortunately for her exhausted state of mind, nothing came her way.

Returning to her chamber, she found Neville had removed his constraining frock coat and hung it over a chair. She smiled at that tidy touch from a man who could barely hold his head upright. She'd taken the only candle, but the brazier gave off sufficient light to see that he lay in the bed, his golden head denting one of the pillows. The other pillow waited for her return.

Thanking the good Lord that Neville retained enough strength to look after himself to some extent, Fiona studied her current predicament. Doyle had packed a bag for her, so she had clean clothes and a nightgown. She thought Neville slept, but she hesitated at undressing in his presence. It was a stupid notion, and she resolved not to give in to that missishness.

Stripping to her chemise, she wriggled on the nightgown, then pulled back the covers on her side of the bed. A strong male hand politely lifted them for her, holding them up until she crawled between the sheets. Embarrassment flooded Fiona's cheeks, and she lay frozen on the far edge of the bed.

"Here," he whispered, letting the covers drop back and tapping the place beside him.

She couldn't hit him. She couldn't scold. For all she knew, he made demands like a child, wanting the comfort of her closeness. But she didn't have the excuse of a scrambled brain. She remembered quite distinctly the episode in the conservatory when he'd turned her mind to mush and her body into liquid fire.

She slid down in the bed a little more, edging just a few scant inches closer. "Sleep," she whispered.

"Mine," came the distinct reply as his hand reached out, caught her waist, and hauled her toward the center of the bed.

So much for scrambled brains. Fiona stiffened, resisting the urge to turn and flatten herself against him.

His hand stroked the cloth over her hip, then rose higher, his fingers finding purchase around her breast. She stopped breathing altogether.

Biting her tongue, she waited for what would happen next. Just the stroke of Neville's hand had set her insides aflame, even though she suspected he had no clue as to what he was doing. She couldn't risk pregnancy without the safety net of marriage, no matter how much she longed for the reassurance of his touch.

When he didn't move, she turned to see if his eyes were open.

He snored.

So much for sleeping this night. Mentally relieved but fighting a sharp disappointment, Fiona wrapped her fingers around his and studied the ceiling. Now what was she going to do?

# Twenty

He woke to the sound of childish whispers, the gray light of a rainy day, and the tempting warmth of a feminine body pressed against his side. He also woke to an erection that could have rammed stone walls, until he realized he didn't have the slightest idea where he was or who he was with. That eased one pounding ache sufficiently to recognize the other one in his head. So much for lust.

Gingerly, he tested his surroundings with his other senses rather than open his eyes just yet. His stiff, rumpled clothing had pressed a permanent wrinkle into his backside, he decided. He couldn't imagine going to bed fully dressed, especially if he shared the bed with a woman. And he was quite certain his companion was female. Her decidedly lush breasts pressed into his side, and a small hand curled trustingly in the middle of his chest. He thought he smelled lilacs.

The childish voices grew more argumentative, ending any thought of exploring soft curves. Prying open one eyelid, he glared in the direction of the noise. Three unknown children tussled over a pillow and a blanket. He glanced down at the woman tucked against his side. She slept, undisturbed by the noise.

He didn't have many means of silencing the hooligans, and he was oddly reluctant to wake the woman. Carefully, he slid the pillow from beneath his own head and heaved it in the direction of the commotion.

The children looked up in surprise. He held a finger to his lips and pointed at the sleeping female. They instantly silenced. Briefly.

They discovered the sacks of supplies next. He winced as one yelled over the discovery of some delicacy and another attempted to steal it. The woman beside him stirred. At the same time, he heard more childish voices piping from behind the wall. The pounding in his head intensified.

Giving up on quieting the children, he concentrated on the female. Dark hair streaked with red tumbled in profusion across her pillow. A thick fringe of dark lashes swept over high, flushed cheeks, and ripe lips parted in sleep. He smiled as he recognized the woman he'd claimed as wife. The smile lasted only long enough to realize he couldn't remember her name.

For all that mattered, he couldn't remember his own name.

Preoccupied by that discovery, he wasn't aware when she first awoke. Only her whisper startled his muddled thoughts back to the moment.

"Neville?"

Neville? That sounded right. Maybe. Lifting a hand to his pounding head, he tried focusing on a reply. No name came out. It was there, he was certain. It just didn't emerge. Frantically, he looked around the room, searching for anything familiar he could name. Nothing. His tongue stuck to the roof of his mouth, and pain lanced through his head.

The woman scrambled up beside him, looking as panicked as he felt. She touched his cheek, held a cool hand to his brow. Neville's gaze focused on the view she offered of unfettered breasts cloaked in thin linen. Panic subsided as he noted two of the tiny buttons had come unfastened and he could catch a glimpse of pearly skin.

"Lovely," he sighed.

She sat back on her heels and glared at him. "You scared me half to death, your worship. How's your head this morn?"

Musical bells and scolding tones didn't match. He glared back but again, couldn't find words of reply when he hadn't the faintest idea what she'd said. Rather than appear entirely addled, he nodded to the children arguing in the corner. "Noisy."

"Well, at least you've moved on to adjectives today," she said with a sigh, climbing from the bed. "You might make one word speeches all the rage in the Lords, and wouldn't that be a blessing."

He didn't bother trying to understand the string of words. He just smiled at her wry tones. Redheads had a temper, he remembered. At least, he thought he remembered. He didn't know where else the thought came from.

The youngest child bounced up to the bed. Wide dark eyes watched him, while sticky lips sucked on equally sticky fingers. Neville stared back. He didn't think he'd ever seen this creature in his life. Surely it didn't belong to him, but the woman did. He knew that of a certainty.

"Here, your lordship, wipe the little monster down."

A damp rag was shoved into his hands. Neville glared at the woman, then back at the child. He might not understand what she said, but he knew what to do with wet rags and sticky fingers. The child didn't protest as Neville cleaned him up.

He watched in amazement as another troop of midgets danced into the room a short time later. They emerged from the walls like cockroaches. He wanted to send them all away so he could concentrate on the lovely woman whose tempting curves were now wrapped in a hideous black shawl. But then he would have to concentrate on his communication problem, and that made his head hurt. So he followed the antics of the tribe of midgets instead.

He cleaned them off if they bounced on the bed. When one appeared half-naked and carrying a shirt, he pulled the garment over his head. Or her head. He wasn't entirely certain. The entire lot had hair of various and assorted colors curling about their ears, except for the one with stick straight hair that stood on end. It was a trifle difficult distinguishing gender until they were into dresses or trousers.

At some point one of the elder children brought him some steaming hot tea and a crumbly cake of bread. It scarcely filled his protesting stomach, but he had some sense that there was barely enough to go around. That didn't seem quite right. His memory had holes in it, large gaping holes that frightened him, but he did have some awareness of how things should have been. The visual image of groaning sideboards of assorted egg dishes, rashers, sausages, and muffins haunted his empty head.

Unable to voice his question, he sipped his tea and munched his bread. The woman he knew must be his wife disappeared into the adjoining room and returned fully dressed. To his utter relief, she ushered the children back to that room and closed the door on them, leaving the two of them alone.

Neville studied her quizzically. Among other things he remembered, one did not get dressed when interested in bedplay. And he was definitely interested. His mind might not be functioning fully, but the rest of him had no such problem.

He didn't like her high-necked gown, but he couldn't form the words to tell her. He just fastened his attention on the full curves of her bodice as she approached, and the lower part of his body tented the blankets.

"Damn you, Neville, I need your help. Sean aimed for the wrong part of your anatomy." She sat down beside him, wrapping her shawl tightly, blocking his view of the scenery. "I don't know if it's safe to go to your yacht, but I have to let them know where you are and find you some clean clothes. I lured you here to keep you from harm in England, but I've just muddled everything worse. What the devil am I supposed to do?"

His gaze instantly lifted to her face at the distress in her voice. Worry wrinkled her lovely eyes and twisted her lips into flat lines. He couldn't abide seeing her like that. Searching his addled brain, he sought some means of reaching her.

"One... word." There, he'd done it. Triumphant at this small accomplishment, he waited for her response.

She frowned and studied him. Reaching some decision, she nodded.

"Yacht."

That wasn't the response he wanted. He recognized the word, but couldn't put it together with any other. He shook his head. "Where?"

"Sligo." She waited expectantly.

Frustration began to build, accelerating the pounding in his head. He clenched his fists and tried again. "Home. Go home."

Her lips tightened. "Can't. Danger."

"Can," he answered stubbornly. "No danger." He wasn't certain what he demanded, yet he knew he didn't belong here. Neither did she. He had to get back to where he belonged.

She rubbed her brow as if it pained her as much as his did him. Then she leaned over and kissed his cheek, enveloping him in the scent of lilacs. Before he could grab her, she sat up again. "Rest. I'll be back."

She was gone before he could collect his befuddled senses and stop her. Frustrated, Neville slammed his fist against the bed again and again, swearing with the one curse word arising through the fog of his mind, one that seemed particularly apt considering the state of his aching loins.

Fighting a growing panic, Fiona searched up and down the harbor for the familiar sight of the duke's yacht. For the love of Mary, she'd sailed on the damned thing. She knew what it looked like.

The yacht wasn't there.

Being left alone with the burden of the duke's illness, the orphans, the danger to His Grace and to Michael's holdings, terrified her. She had to find help. She couldn't do it all alone.

Draping her shawl around her face, she stopped and talked with the harbor master, asking about private ships, but he'd not seen anything but the fishing boats that sailed out regularly. When he began to look at her with curiosity, she hurried away.

A physician. Perhaps she could find a physician who would know what to do. If only she could get word to Michael. But she didn't like worrying Blanche until she was certain they had cause to worry. Neville could come around. She'd seen it happen.

She hurried down what passed for a prosperous street in Sligo. The duke was her responsibility. She had known he would follow her. It was her fault he had come here and got his head bashed in. She scanned the swinging overhead signs for one that indicated a physician.

She still had a few of the duke's coins left. She'd spent them rather recklessly, believing she would have more on the yacht. But now she had a wagon load of children and nowhere to take them or any means of feeding them. She could look after herself, but seven children, an old woman, and an addled duke presented a burden beyond her abilities. Where was the damned yacht?

She finally gave in and asked for the physician's direction. He wasn't in, of course, and she left a message asking that he come to the inn. Until she knew his fee, she didn't dare spend any of the remaining coins.

Fiona almost cried in relief as a familiar face appeared in the crowded street. And then she remembered who he was and what he might have done, and she sought to hide, too late.

"Fey-onah, my love! What brings you to this gateway of hell?" The handsome features beamed in pleasure beneath a head full of dark curly hair.

"Colin." Nervously, Fiona kept walking in the direction of the inn, forcing Colin to turn and follow her. "I thought you'd gone to America."

"Patsy didn't want to part from her family while the babe's due. And what is yourself doing here? I thought I'd heard you'd gone to be a duchess."

Oh, damn. Did all the world know her business? "I'm looking for a place for Aileen's orphans. And yourself?" She avoided the issue as neatly as possible.

"Looking for work. The fishing is bad. Thought I'd go on to Belfast next. You wouldn't happen to have a coin or two about you, would you, Fiona? I hate asking, but it's that low I am, and with the babe coming... You know how it is."

Did that mean he'd not killed Burke for the money or that he'd gambled it all away already? Cursing the suspicion that Burke's death had thrown upon her childhood friend, Fiona shook her head. "You know better than to ask, Colin. I've no allowance from my cousin. If I did, I'd spend it on the orphans and not on your gambling."

"Arrah, and you've always been a hard woman, Fiona. You've a place to stay, then? Could I come up and share a drop of tea?"

Tea wasn't what he wanted. He hoped for whiskey. She knew his sort, and his handsome charm had never spun her head. Not in a long time, leastways. Clamping her lips, she shook her head. "The least one is ill. It could be the mumps. Have you had the mumps, Colin? It can kill a grown man. You don't want to come near if you're not after having them."

"And weren't you the one giving them to me when we were wee ones?

Don't begrudge an old friend a cup of tea, lass. Come along with you, then." Catching her hand, Colin placed it firmly in the crook of his elbow.

Damn. Damn, and double damn. Cursing furiously all the way up the street, Fiona sought some means of escaping Colin, and preventing him from seeing the duke in his helpless state. She could be walking on the arm of a murderer, for all she knew. She couldn't believe it of Colin, but Neville was right. Desperate men sometimes did desperate things.

Fighting the urge to scream in frustration, Fiona fumbled for her purse as they reached the lobby of the inn. She knew one certain way of diverting a man like Colin.

Producing a coin, she held it out. "Why don't you buy a pint while I check on the orphans? I'll be down directly."

Colin gave her a dark look of suspicion as he took the coin. "And who is it you're after keeping from me, *cailin*? You're not harboring a man up there, are ye? For Seamus's sake, I'd have to take the man apart."

"Don't be ridiculous. Have you ever been in a room filled with six children and one squalling babe? I'm doing you a favor, I am. Now go hoist your pint. You know that's all you're after."

"Fiona! Fiona MacDermot! I never thought—" A woman hurried across the floor and stopped abruptly as she caught sight of the handsome Irishman at Fiona's elbow. Her expression of welcome immediately turned to one of outrage. "Well, I never! And you with a wife and babe on the way, Colin Moriarity!"

The Widow Blackthorne. Groaning inwardly, Fiona steepled her fingers against her forehead and swore to worship the devil if God couldn't do better than this. What was the widow doing in Sligo? Catching a ship with poor murdered Burke's coins?

"And a pleasure it is to see you, too, Mrs. Blackthorne," she said dryly. "Won't you join Colin in a pint while I'm after seeing to the orphans? They'll have the room destroyed if I'm not lookin' in on them soon."

Not caring what glances the pair exchanged behind her back, Fiona hurried up the stairs and away from any witnesses. She didn't know how long she'd been gone, but she knew it was too long. Neville could have had a relapse. The hooligans could have tied their granny to a chair and let themselves out the bedroom window. Aileen had never been much for discipline.

She burst into the room to a wild shout of triumph from inside. Closing the door and leaning against it, she swiftly absorbed the scene before her.

Neville sat in a chair near the brazier. He bounced two of the youngest on his knees, teaching them to clap hands, while Sean burped the baby over his shoulder and the rest played some wild game involving twisting a blanket into a jump rope and alternately tugging or jumping at it. Terrified Mrs. Callaghan had died of exhaustion, Fiona gathered her strength and pushed off from the door.

"Miss Fiona! Miss Fiona! Can we play outside, can we? Can we see the ships? I'm hungry! Can we have more apples, please?"

Fiona scarcely acknowledged the voices attacking her from all sides. Taking up one toddler in her arms, she watched Neville. If he were strong and in his right mind, half her problems would be solved. But she saw only the glint of admiration in his eyes as he set the younger two on the floor and let them join the fray. She didn't need his damned admiration right now. She needed his help. His lack of welcoming speech told her all she needed to know.

"I'm sorry to take so long." She waited to see if he understood. He continued watching her, his expression one of pleasantness and no more.

"Doctor," she said succinctly.

He grimaced and rubbed the back of his head, nodding his understanding.

"No yacht."

He looked briefly puzzled, seemed to concentrate, then frowned. "Dublin?"

"Sligo," she countered. "Not Dublin." Talking in one word sentences made understanding hideously difficult, but at least she thought they were communicating to some extent.

Neville firmly shook his head, then winced. "Yacht. Dublin."

Oh, hell. "You told me Sligo!" she nearly screamed.

He gave her one of those ducal looks with one raised eyebrow. "Yacht. Dublin."

Someone rapped at the door behind her.

"Miss Fiona! We've a proposition for ye! May we come in?"

Oh, double hell. Colin.

Before Fiona could head him off, the door opened. One of these days, she'd learn to lock doors. In a panic, she glanced at Neville. He winked, and swiped another toddler from the floor.

Well, that certainly made for a domestic scene.

# Twenty-one

"William, what the divil do ye do here when they're after burnin' your house down back home!"

The portly man striding anxiously up and down Dublin's dock turned on his heels at the cry, his face taking on a deeper flush of fear. "Eamon! Don't frighten an old man like that."

The younger, lankier man hurried toward him. "I've notified the army, but the bastards are sitting on their rumps. You need to get back there now, warn them Lord Aberdare will have their heads if they let the castle burn."

"My genealogy! I can't let them burn my genealogy. If it's lyin' you are, Eamon O'Connor, it's your head that will roll." William hastened down the dock toward the cobbled street leading into the city.

"It's McGonigle stirring up the trouble. The earl has asked me to look after the matter of Burke's murder, but all I've seen are the English conniving with every blackguard in the county. It's after the earl, they are, and no mistake."

"Don't be ridiculous," William replied, already huffing at the pace the younger man set. "Michael never harmed a soul in his life. It's the duke they want, I'll be bound. Have you seen our Fiona?"

O'Connor jerked to a halt and stared at Fiona's uncle. "Our Fiona? Is she not on her honeymoon with the blasted duke?"

Gasping for breath, William willingly halted. "She ran away the night before the wedding. Michael's scouring the isles in search of her now."

O'Connor swore vividly and inventively in three languages. "The brat was born with greased heels, I swear." He suddenly looked alarmed. "She would not have gone back to Aberdare, would she? There's something afoot, and I'd not have her in the middle of it."

"We don't know where she's gone!" William exclaimed in exasperation. "Michael thinks she sailed from Portsmouth, and a ship arrived from there a day or so ago, but no one on board claims to have seen her." His expression became even more alarmed. "The duke's gone to Aberdare in search of her. If there's something afoot..."

O'Connor resumed hurrying up the street. "That explains it then," he said grimly. "That explains it all. The bastards think to kill the emancipation and crime bills with a single blow."

"Don't be foolish," William huffed, hurrying to keep up. "Michael does naught but vote yay or nay, then wander off with his head in the clouds.

There's naught to harm him for."

O'Connor grimaced. "Not Michael by himself, nor the duke, nor the marquess, but together, they're an unholy triumvirate. Michael has his wife's wealth, the marquess has his way with words and manner of twisting arms, and the duke has power and experience. The duke would never have signed those bills if Michael had not persuaded the marquess to sponsor them and the marquess had not twisted the duke's arm. That's the way of it, William, and if I know it, so do those who oppose them. You've sent your niece into a viper's nest."

"Fiona sent herself," William grumbled. "I don't have a blamed thing to do with anything she does."

O'Connor stopped at military headquarters and glared at the stone wall of the building rather than the old man beside him. "Her old beau, Colin Moriarity has been meeting with an English lord, so has McGonigle. And you know who lives in the lord's home?" He gave William a bedeviled look. "The Widow Blackthorne."

"Holy Mother of God, 'tis a zoo," Colin muttered almost reverently as his gaze encountered the romping children, one of whom tumbled at his feet.

Picking up the child before his whimpers could escalate, the widow gave him a look of disgust. "'Tis yerself you're seein' here, Colin Moriarity. Undisciplined and heathen as the beasts in the field." She patted the sobbing child on the back and glanced up at Fiona. "What do you mean to do with the lot?"

Then her gaze encountered the man in the chair beside the brazier, dangling a toddler on his knee, and she fell silent.

Colin, too, had discovered the stranger, and his brow drew down in a scowl. Glancing over her shoulder, Fiona read the command in Neville's expression well enough. The dratted man didn't need words. Just the lift of his expressive eyebrow could order armies about. His words might be scrambled, but she had the rather relieved suspicion that his brains weren't.

With a sigh, she set the child in her arms on the floor and sent him off to his brother. "Sean, take a coin from my purse and go fetch some apples for the lot. I'll see to tea in a little while."

The nine-year old proudly helped himself to the money, gave their visitors a look that would have rivaled the duke's, and marched out on his important errand.

Without any idea of what else to do, Fiona crossed the room and took the toddler from the duke. She feared he'd topple should he stand, so she pressed his shoulder, hoping he'd stay impolitely seated.

"Neville, this is Mrs. Blackthorne, from the village, and Colin Moriarity, an old friend of mine. Mrs. Blackthorne, Colin, this is my husband, Neville Perceval." She prayed they wouldn't recognize the name or that the duke wouldn't question her labeling of him as "husband." She didn't need any more complications.

She should have known better. The widow immediately dropped into an elaborate curtsy. "Your Grace," she whispered. "I never thought to make your acquaintance." She rose and aimed a look of irritation at Fiona. "You brought him to the village and let him carry packages about, but you never introduced him to anyone. Were you that ashamed of us?"

Well, at least she didn't have to worry about the townspeople treating her differently should she ever marry the duke.

"We were arguing at the time," she answered in clipped tones, hoping to hurry and end this debacle, or at least cover up the fact that Neville hadn't replied to the introductions. Maybe they would think him too arrogant to speak. "We'd hoped to find family for the orphans here. What was the proposition you came to tell us about?"

Prevented from advancing into the room by the tide of children ebbing and flowing at his feet, Colin stayed glued to the door. Fiona suspected that he'd noted the duke's lack of speech, but the English nobility weren't known for their friendliness in these parts. Besides, Neville was busily engaged in wiping the bloody nose of the three-year-old. Mayhap it was just awe that kept Colin silent.

Instead of answering Fiona's question, the widow continued watching the duke with fascination. "What happened to his clothes?" she whispered in bemusement, for Fiona's ears only. "I thought dukes had servants to keep them dressed grandly."

"We only meant to be here a short time, but we had an accident, and our bags were stolen. We've only just arrived, and it's after our business we must be. If you'd just tell us about your proposition..."

To Fiona's dismay, the duke set aside the quieted child. Removing her hand from his shoulder, he pushed up using the chair back, and limped crossed the room. He held out his hand to Colin. "Moriarity," he repeated in that damned authoritative tone that made people jump whether they willed or not. Turning to the widow, he gave a nod. "Mrs. Blackthorne."

Fiona thought for a moment they would go down on their hands and knees and bow and scrape, so awed were they by this man in rumpled linen and mud-coated trousers. She'd like to know how he did that. She frowned at him for good measure, but he only quirked his lips in return. She had the distinct impression that he laughed at her. Again. Whoever said this man had no sense of humor, lied.

"Proposition?" he inquired, drawing the word out carefully.

Colin stammered into the breach. "We wanted a proper memorial for Burke, for a man in the village what was killed."

Realizing he made little sense, Colin stopped, prepared to start at the beginning, but the widow intervened.

"Burke didn't get a proper wake. We thought a memorial service in the Great Hall at Aberdare might help the village to overcome its grief. Fiona, er, Lady..." She shuffled her thinking and sought the proper form of address while the duke waited.

"Just Fiona," Fiona filled in impatiently. "I'm not about to be Your Graced all the day. And as much as I'd like to see Burke honored, I don't see that it will do more than cost money for barrels of ale. I'd see the coins better spent."

The duke's warm hand caressed the nape of her neck, not lovingly, but with warning. And perhaps to steady himself. Fiona shot him a suspicious glare but shut up. She would like nothing more than for him to fish them from this mess, but how he was to do it without speech left even her agile brain stumped.

"Continue," Neville commanded.

He'd moved on to verbs now, Fiona thought sarcastically. How grand. Now he could really give orders.

Despite the sarcasm, she couldn't help admitting relief that he had the mental capability to take charge. The idea of that powerful mind lost forever in a fog of speechlessness had gnawed at her more than she cared to acknowledge.

Colin straightened his spine. "There's those who say the earl's forgotten them already. It's a hungry winter we'll have without the potatoes to keep us."

The widow interrupted, nervously smoothing Colin's harsh words. "We know the earl can't feed us all. We're just his tenants, after all. He's eased the rents and built us new houses, and we're eternally grateful, but we have to eat. We'd thought, if we had the service, all the village would come..."

Colin made a gesture of disgust. "It's no use, Mrs. Blackthorne. The duke won't be interested in the likes of us, and the earl's too busy. We're but making fools of ourselves. It was a daft plan, anyway."

The door behind them shoved open, scattering the little grouping as Sean dashed in with his bag of apples. The screams and shouts that ensued prevented further conversation, until the duke took matters in hand.

Frowning at the commotion, he released Fiona. Holding himself stiffly, as if still unsure of his balance, he waded into the fray. Shooing the lot toward the second room, he motioned for Sean to take the knife and peel the fruit for the youngest. Leaning a hand against the bed for support, he removed a stolen apple from one of the older children and handed it to one of the younger.

The children obeyed his every silent command with alacrity, although not without protest. He picked up the loudest complainer by the shirt, glared, then set him on his feet again, effectively silenced. Within minutes, the room had cleared of the disruption.

"My word," the widow whispered in astonishment. "He does have a way with children."

"He's used to giving orders and having them obeyed," Fiona replied in near giddy relief. "They're good children, they just need a strong hand. I wish we could have found a home for them. Neville has promised to pay for their support, but it's family they need."

At the mention of "support," Colin looked up with interest. "His Grace means to provide for all those hungry mouths?"

"You're offering to take the task?" Fiona asked wryly.

Colin looked properly horrified. "Not me! It's America bound I am as soon as Patsy has the babe. I was thinking of McGonigle. He and his wife never had children."

Neville limped up behind Fiona, circled her shoulders with his arm, and guided her toward the bed. He gestured for the widow to take the room's only chair, for all the world as if they conversed politely in his ducal drawing room.

Relieved to have him off his feet, still worried that Neville didn't understand a word being said, Fiona sent him an anxious glance. Sitting beside her, he smiled and placed his other hand proprietarily behind her. "Wife," he whispered in her ear as he leaned close.

Not at all certain that he didn't retain all his senses and merely teased her, Fiona glowered and returned to their interrupted discussion.

"I'd like to see McGonigle saddled with seven brats," she declared.

"That would curtail his rebellious activities considerably."

"That, or drive him to drink," Colin agreed.

"But don't you see?" the widow interrupted. "It's perfect. The duke can make McGonigle his magnanimous offer, McGonigle will puff up with pride, his wife will be thrilled to tears, the extra coins will make the butcher and baker happy... And once all the grousing and suspicion stops, we can reach some sensible solution to our problems."

"Looms?" Neville asked with deceptive simplicity.

He must have some understanding of the conversation. Fiona glared. If he had that much understanding, then he knew she wasn't his wife, and he didn't owe her looms or support for the orphans. Without her dowry, he could afford neither. But he might not be remembering the treason charges his enemies were holding over her head. She needed to learn to juggle problems like Michael juggled balls.

Both the widow and Colin turned their attention to the duke, hope so blatantly lighting their faces that Fiona absolved them of all suspicion in Burke's demise. Did that make McGonigle the murderer? Shuddering at the thought of putting the orphans into the hands of so evil a villain, she wasn't certain where to begin.

"We'd discussed buying the looms," she finally said into the growing silence. She cursed Neville for mentioning the topic. "It's nothing certain, you understand. Lord Aberdare must still be consulted. I've not even approached him yet about using the Great Hall until we can afford elsewhere."

"That's it, then," Colin said with finality. "We'll settle the children on McGonigle, hold the memorial, let everyone know about the looms, and we'll live on hope a while longer. It can work. Will you be starting back to Aberdare in the morning?"

Astounded at how quickly this ball started rolling, Fiona sat with her mouth open, unable to form a suitable reply. Beside her, the damned duke grinned and murmured, "Speechless?"

She wished. Aware that all attention now focused on her, Fiona raised a trembling hand to her temple and sought some argument to postpone any decision until she had time to think. She couldn't make quick decisions on such important matters.

"Well, Fiona, is it helping us you are?" Colin demanded. "Or are you too far above us now to care?"

That did it. Leaping to her feet, Fiona slammed open the door and gestured toward the hall. "Out, Colin. I've enough of your blather. I'll not be browbeaten into doing anything until I'm ready. Go back and see to your wife. I'll see you again when I'm ready, and not before."

The duke and the widow both stood up when Fiona did. Neville placed calming hands on her shoulders. He nodded as Mrs. Blackthorne curtsied and lifted a ducal eyebrow in Colin's direction.

"Later," the duke said ambiguously.

Colin immediately perked up, gave the duke a respectful salute, and offered his arm to the widow. "We'll come help with the children in the morning, shall we?" he said cheerfully. He closed the door before Fiona could tell him what she thought of his reply.

Before Fiona could vent her fury with a stream of invectives at the door, the duke pulled her around and lowered his head, capturing her mouth with his.

"Damn you," she whispered before succumbing to the temptation of losing herself in the spiraling heat of the moment. Sliding her arms around broad shoulders, she let her problems disappear behind the cloud of longing Neville's caresses inspired.

Later, she would worry about looms and orphans, dangers and dukedoms. Later, she would worry about the meaning of this overwhelming flood of relief she felt at his rapidly recovering memory. That he might never return to normal frightened her more than she could bear. For right now, she would bask in the worship of Neville's kiss and the promise of his embrace and give nothing else any consideration.

The adjoining door exploded open, blowing in a confusion of curls and giggles, carried on the wails of a babe.

Neville lifted his head and grinned at Fiona's dazed expression. Caressing her left breast with one hand, he murmured wickedly, "Heirs."

# Twenty-two

By the faint light of the coal brazier, Neville stripped off his wrinkled linen and washed in heated water, wishing he could dunk his aching head as well. He thought the children asleep, although an occasional wriggle kept him guessing. Still, it was dark, and he couldn't abide his stink much longer.

His wife had slipped into the other room to change and check on the children there. She would be back shortly, and he rushed through his ablutions in anticipation of sharing the bed with her. The pounding in his head had dwindled with the past day of idling, and his desire had escalated.

Some events shone clearer through the fog of his memories than others. He suspected his mind simply declined to recall those things for which he wasn't ready. The irritation of his speech problem prevented him from concentrating too hard on what he didn't wish to remember.

Their guests today had called him a duke, and he had a vague notion of mountains of responsibilities and torrents of tasks awaiting him. But no one pressed him to remember them, and his mind sought more pleasant occupations.

He had no memory whatsoever of caring for children, but with no other chore on his horizon, he found the task easy. Keeping sticky fingers and faces washed, making sufficient trips to the chamber pot, feeding and keeping them warm were chores he could accomplish without words. Providing the occasional hug, wiping away tears, and just giving them a little attention had worked miracles.

The simple-minded tasks gave him time to concentrate on the more important enigma of the woman he considered wife. He knew his memory was murky on the point, but he had a distinct recollection of a bower of orchids and welcoming arms to fortify his reasoning.

Pulling on the coarse cotton shirt Fiona had brought back from one of her forays, Neville noted its length, wrinkled his nose at the texture, and stripped off his muddy trousers. He didn't think he was accustomed to sleeping in his shirts, but he had little choice now.

Steadier on his feet with practice, he added more coal to the brazier, pulled a blanket around one of the more restless children, and climbed into the wide bed. His wife was taking an inordinately long time changing into her nightshift. He suspected she hoped to find him asleep. Not bloody likely in the state he was in.

At last, the door opened and a figure in white slipped through, her lovely hair in a thick braid down her back. While waiting for her, Neville occupied himself imagining untangling it. She crept around the room, checking on the children and the door lock, — as if he hadn't already done that.

Smiling, he waited until she slipped between the sheets. "Fey-onah," he murmured proudly. He'd practiced the name all the day, keeping it in his errant memory.

He couldn't name the children or their guests today. Those names had slipped back to wherever they'd come from. But he remembered *Fiona*.

She jumped nervously, easing away to turn on her side, facing him. "You're awake."

He stroked her cheek and remembered the petal softness of the flowers he grew. Pleasant memories were easier than the unpleasant ones. "Awake," he agreed.

"You need to rest. Tomorrow will be a long day."

He understood more and more of what was said, but he shrugged off the words as unimportant. A funny thing about blows to the head — they rearranged one's priorities. He'd learned he could function without words. But he couldn't function entirely without this woman. He supposed that would have annoyed him in another time or place. Right now, it seemed eminently sensible.

"Rest later." Grasping her arm so she could not escape, Neville leaned over and covered her mouth with his. He had no difficulty remembering what to do in this situation. Her lips were gloriously pliant and exciting as he tasted them.

She struggled briefly. He didn't want to fight her. Gently, he stroked her breast through the softness of her gown, and trailed his kisses along her jaw.

"Neville, we can't," she murmured in a tone he associated with panic.

"No?" He didn't stop what he was doing but merely asked because it seemed necessary to respond. She shivered as his tongue licked her ear lobe, and her nipple peaked beneath his caressing fingers. He slid his hand lower, urging her hips closer to his.

"No! Neville, stop, please." She pushed an entreating hand against his chest.

He understood those words too well. Frowning, he raised up on one elbow to look down at her. "Why?" he demanded, finding the word without even trying.

"We're not married," she whispered. "Not married," she repeated, in case he hadn't understood.

Not married? That didn't make sense. Collapsing back against his pillow, Neville stared at the ceiling and searched his aching brain. He knew what they had done together. That was the one distinct memory he possessed. He hadn't even unclothed her. They'd made love beneath a bower of orchids. They'd made love in heated passion, without a qualm of remorse. His memory might be fuzzy, but he didn't think he was the kind of man who would ravish virgins without vows being said.

Virgin. The recollection of her innocence prompted him to question the rest of the setting. Surely a newly wedded couple did not make love in a conservatory?

His head throbbed thinking about it. With decisiveness, he turned on his side again. "Marry tomorrow." He bent to take her mouth again, satisfied that he'd solved any further complaint.

"We can't." She shoved against his chest again, a little harder this time.

He didn't like being thwarted, he discovered. Irritation mixed with frustration. He was ready. She was ready. The children slept. What more could she ask? Besides, their sleeping in the same bed made the point moot. They had to marry. His inability to word the argument, however, gave him some understanding of her refusal. She didn't want an idiot for husband.

Growing angry, Neville glared down at her. "Not stupid," he announced distinctly. How could he find the words to say he could provide for her, even if he couldn't speak correctly? Or how could he ask if she thought him repulsive now that his tongue had gone astray?

"Stupid?" She seemed genuinely puzzled. "I've never accused you of stupidity." Her fingers wrapped in the cloth of his shirt instead of shoving him away. "You're the most intelligent man I know. We just can't marry."

He followed enough of that to let his anger recede. Stroking the soft tendrils that always escaped about her face, he returned to his original question. "Why?"

She struggled for an answer with as much difficulty as he phrased his questions. "I'm Catholic, you're Anglican," she finally said.

Those words meant little or nothing to him. Dropping back against the pillow, he sought a clearer explanation, but his thoughts traveled in circles. They'd made love. He remembered some discussion of heirs. If they hadn't been married, they'd planned it. Was this Catholic/Anglican argument something new? Why would it interfere now if not then?

It didn't matter. He knew beyond any doubt that he must marry this woman he'd made love to and slept with. He might not remember concrete events, but the proprieties were ingrained. He couldn't explain, but she wasn't stupid either. He would wait a little while, until his speech returned. By then, perhaps something would occur to make her understand.

As far as he was concerned, she was his wife.

His hand closed around hers as they lay silently, sharing the same bed. Neville discovered he liked the proximity. He could touch her when he liked, share her warmth, speak without the restraint he felt around others. He didn't know what obstruction prevented marriage, but he would overcome it. Either that, or they would share a bed without vows. He had no intention of letting her go. He wondered if possessiveness had always been a part of his character.


"Aberdare could be dangerous," Fiona protested as Neville picked up the last of their meager belongings and shoved it into a satchel.

She wanted to trounce him as he gave one of his lordly shrugs.

"Not hide," he replied with casual indifference.

She would give everything she possessed if she could know what wheel was spinning inside that impenetrable head of his. The physician she'd called had been of little or no help in telling her what to expect.

Rather than wait for Neville's speech to return, she'd tried explaining what had happened the night before their wedding. Neville had seemed to listen, but she couldn't tell how much he comprehended. She had suggested they find his yacht, but he had looked at her as if she were the crazed one. Of course, without any funds, reaching Dublin on the opposite coast would be a trifle difficult. Still, she didn't think Aberdare the safest place to be.

The castle might not even be there if McGonigle had his way.

Shivering at the thought of her ancient home in ashes, Fiona lifted the infant from Mrs. Callaghan's arms, took a toddler by the hand, and proceeded out of the inn room that she had shared as wife with a man she could scarcely claim to know. For a brief few days, she had felt very married. Had she been given sufficient time to think about it, she might say she enjoyed the experience. But her days had disintegrated into reacting to whatever disaster struck next. Right now, Neville was that disaster.

Gone was her brief reign of power. Neville commanded the troops. He'd settled the children in the wagon bed with more apples. Placing Mrs. Callaghan near the front of the wagon bed and Sean at the back, he'd assured a modicum of authority over the chaos.

Fiona looked at him skeptically as he reached for her hand to help her onto the bench beside the driver's seat. "You'll drive?" she asked in the circumscribed fashion they'd developed for communicating.

He gave her a lofty look that didn't need translation. Men! Scrambling into her place, Fiona reached down for the infant he'd held until she settled. She didn't have the fascination with children that Blanche possessed, but then, she'd grown up in the village, surrounded by hordes of children, and the birthing process had no mystery for her as it did for an isolated only child like Blanche. Fiona liked the creatures well enough, knew them as a natural result of living, but her mind sought higher goals than reproduction. Unfortunately, she was a female, and not in a position to expect more.

As Neville climbed up beside her, Fiona felt a strong awareness of his masculine presence. If he had his way, she would be breeding within weeks. The image robbed her of breath. Seeing pregnant women and contemplating that state for herself were worlds apart. She'd best not dwell on it. She'd not let Neville give up his authority in parliament because of her. Which meant the only way she'd ever carry the duke's child was as his mistress.

She didn't want to think about that just yet. Michael would be furious should he ever discover how they'd spent the last few days, and he'd surely find it out. Michael knew everything. She would depart for foreign ports once they'd settled all these other matters.

Neville drove the recalcitrant mules with ease, though Fiona knew he was more at home in an elegant carriage, behind four well-bred horses. The sun occasionally peeked out from behind the mist and gloom of early dawn. Apparently Colin and the Widow Blackthorne weren't early risers, thank the heavens. She supposed she should feel guilt at leaving them stranded in Sligo, but she honestly didn't think there was room left in the wagon.

"Cold?" Neville asked anxiously as she shivered inside her shawl.

He might be an impossible man, but he was a thoughtful one. Fiona had little experience with anyone paying attention to her comforts. She snuggled the sleeping child closer, and smiled at his inquiring look. "I'll survive. Next time we do this, though, let's wait for summer."

His frown of puzzlement gradually gave way to understanding, and he grinned back at her. "Summer. Brighton. Beach, sun." He waved his hand over his head. "Imagine."

Perhaps he hadn't entirely regained his command of language, but his comprehension had multiplied tremendously. She'd need to start watching what she said.

"I'd imagine it a lot easier if I were in front of a warm fire," she replied dryly.

That crack earned a look of concern. "Aberdare, big fire," he said, wrapping his free arm around her shoulders and pulling her into his warmth.

She didn't like the ambiguity of that remark. If McGonigle had his way, Aberdare would make one big bonfire all right. And she was thinking of giving the orphans over to him? She must have suffered the same blow to the head as Neville.


"Divil take it!" Eamon roared, watching from the castle's upper story window. "Look at who's after rolling up the hill, bold as brass, if you please."

The slight man in the corner of the library probing at the mangled remains of a ship inside a bottle didn't bother looking up. "Neville and Fiona," he replied without inflection. "It's about time."

Eamon glared. "Bloody damned sure of yerself, ain't ye?"

Michael lifted his head and grinned. "Bloody damned sure of Neville. The man never wavers from the straight and narrow."

Eamon tore at his hair with both hands. "How does your wife tolerate you? We've an armed camp surrounding us, a band of bloodthirsty rebels after our hides, traitors all in between, and you're sitting there like the Queen of May. I'd shoot you myself if it weren't a waste of bullets."

"Speaking the King's English for a change, are you?" Michael asked without anger.

The explosion of French and Irish invectives that followed didn't turn a hair. He poked around inside the bottle until the litany died to a grumble.

"Do they have the orphans? We'll need to warn the cook, if so."

Not bothering to reply, Eamon slammed out of the library. Not until then did Michael rise from his chair and check out the window to make certain the errant duo were alive and well. He had confidence in both of them, but enough respect for the fates to worry.

He frowned at the weariness he saw in their faces as the wagon rolled through the army camped on the castle grounds. The normally stoic duke had a crease across his brow that indicated pain. And Fiona, the buoyant grasshopper, was huddled inside her shawl like an old woman. For a moment, he wished he'd brought Blanche with him. She could get to the heart of the matter quickly enough.

But Blanche had no business in this hotbed of rebellion. And she wouldn't approve of what he intended to do next. She had this irritating habit of believing the end didn't always justify the means. He, on the other hand, did whatever was necessary to accomplish whatever needed doing. And from the looks of the pair in the wagon, someone had better take them in hand.

Whistling, Michael strolled down the massive front stairs toward the foyer. Unlike his adopted brother, the marquess, he had more faith in action than in the written word. That being the case, he'd best get busy arranging all the actors in their various places.

# Twenty-three

Fiona focused on the castle ahead rather than the soldiers scuffling, cooking, and lounging about her home's muddy courtyard. Apprehension rose at the whistles and catcalls following the wagon as it rolled past the encampment.

Even the children grew silent. The toddler in Fiona's lap squirmed and stuck her thumb in her mouth. They had good reason to fear soldiers.

Neville appeared unconcerned by the troops. Of course, as an Englishman, he thought of soldiers as brave lads who fought Napoleon. England had no standing army camped on every corner. Ireland did, and had known the misery of armed warfare for centuries.

Biting her lip, Fiona prayed the villagers looked on these men as protectors, but she knew that many of the village folk belonged to the secret society threatening the earl's holdings. If she looked beyond these soldiers going about their daily tasks, she'd see their guns and swords — weapons they would use against farmers armed only with pitchforks and spades. Violence hung only a child's cry away.

Shivering, she hugged the babe in her arms. Neville threw her a look of concern and tried to draw her closer against his warmth, but she resisted. Lifting her chin, she concentrated on the castle and home.

She almost cried in relief as Michael, the Earl of Aberdare, strolled through the open castle doors, followed by her Uncle William and Eamon.

There was nothing the least lordly about this earl, Fiona noted with a smile. His thick auburn locks were almost as tousled as her own, his smile of welcome almost as large. He wore a shabby green tweed coat and mud-splattered boots, indicating he'd been examining the drainage project before their arrival. As soon as Neville halted the wagon, Michael grabbed the toddler from Fiona, tickled her under the chin until she giggled, then handed her to Sean, who had already vaulted from the wagon bed.

"And it's a healthy, well-scrubbed lot ye seem to be," Michael declared, rubbing Sean's dark head. "I trust you were after enjoyin' your little sojourn in the city."

"Cut the blarney, my lord." Fiona scowled at her cousin, who grinned and stood with hands behind his back as Eamon helped her from the wagon. "Had I my way, we'd be in Dublin by now."

"And it's a good thing you didn't have your way, isn't it now?" Eamon said, lowering her none too gently to the ground.

William steadied the horses as Neville climbed down. The duke assisted Mrs. Callaghan from the wagon bed, then circled the wagon to remove Fiona from Eamon's company. Fiona scowled at the maneuver, but she had more important things on her mind than the juvenile competition between two grown men. "Have you talked to McGonigle yet?" she demanded.

Michael threw Neville an understanding look. "Nothing subtle about the lass, is there? And how do you find yourself, Your Grace? Underwhelmed by our Fiona's civility?"

Neville tapped her cheek and smiled as if all the world was his oyster. "Grasshopper," was his only response.

Michael greeted the reply with laughter, Eamon with a scowl.

"Well, I'm glad you found her. Now we'll arrange for a jar to keep her in." Turning his attention to the children milling about the yard, Michael collared two and led them away. "Come along, brats. There's food in the kitchen."

That caught their attention. Fiona watched as the children scampered after the earl, not in the least awed by their host's title or castle.

She returned her gaze to Eamon. "Why the divil did ye let him bring the troops?"

Neville squeezed the back of her neck in warning, but she would have none of his caution. She tossed him a glance of irritation, but he didn't back off.

"*I* ordered them out here," Eamon replied coldly. "What else was I to do when no one knew where you or the duke were to be found, and with McGonigle and his lads threatening to burn the place to perdition? Your uncle was half out of his mind with fear. You shouldn't have done that to him, Fiona."

"It's not myself you should be worrying about. It's the village and the—" She glanced at Neville as his grip tightened on her nape. "And you have a better idea, my lord duke?"

"Inside," he said pleasantly, lowering his hand to her back and steering her toward the door.

Hemmed in with Neville on one side, Eamon on the other, William bringing up the rear, and Michael ahead, Fiona knew how a hunted fox felt. She had bolt holes, if she could reach them. She just wasn't certain if bolting was the answer this time.

She pushed her worries aside while they dined on steaming bowls of lamb stew and shepherd's pie. For the first time in a week, Fiona felt full— and sleepy.

She couldn't give in to the exhaustion. Too many people, too many things, needed her attention. She tried to persuade Michael to send for McGonigle but he threw her a roll and continued discussing pasturage with Eamon.

Neville added his cryptic comments upon occasion, but no one found it strange that he concentrated on Fiona. At her frown of worry, Neville tapped her hand reassuringly.

Fiona drew her hand away. "I don't need coddling."

"Not coddling." He refilled her wine glass since the castle didn't have sufficient servants to do it. "Don't worry."

"Oh, and I should eat, drink, and be merry while the army sits on our doorstep and McGonigle wanders the night with his torches," she scoffed.

"Earl's problem, not yours," Neville said firmly. "Your problem..." He sought the phrasing, gave up, and pointed at himself. "Me."

"And am I not after knowing that?" she muttered. "One big, huge problem after another."

He grinned, held his hand flat to his head, then drew it across hers, indicating the difference in their heights. "Not big." He pointed at Eamon, who towered above them all. "Big."

Fiona couldn't help laughing at his antics. She'd never seen the reserved duke quite so outgoing. The blow to his head may have addled his speech, but it had certainly made him more personable. She dreaded the moment he regained all his faculties and remembered how she'd run off on the eve of their wedding.

But she couldn't wish him to stay addled forever either. As hard as she tried to distract others from the duke's lack of speech, sooner or later, one of his enemies would discover his disability. She didn't know what would happen then.

The inhabitants of Aberdare Castle had never stood on the formality of ladies withdrawing while the gentlemen enjoyed their brandy and cigars after a meal. Truth be told, the lengthy dining hall was too drafty for lingering. Tired of having her more pressing matters ignored while the men discussed farming, Fiona headed for the library with its roaring fire.

"Shouldn't you be lookin' after the children?" Eamon demanded as the other men rose, glasses in hand, and followed her.

Fiona didn't turn around as they joined her by the hearth. "And you could do as well as I can, Eamon O'Connor, if you're that worried about them. I've a thing or two to say and I'll not be leavin' until I do."

She heard Michael's chuckle and her uncle's sigh, but no sound from

Neville. Perhaps seeing her here, where she was more herself than in London luxury, he was having second thoughts about his nonsensical marriage demands. She had seen enough in London to know ladies did not behave as she did, and she had no intention of changing.

"Out with it, Fiona, my own," Michael said as he leaned against the mantel where an assortment of his juggling tools rested. "You'll burst at the seams if you don't have your say, but it's up to bed with you after. You look weary enough to fall asleep on your feet."

William took his favorite chair beside the fire and lit his pipe. Eamon pulled a chair into the shadows across from him, stretching his long legs so his feet rested on the hearth. They looked as if they'd settled in for a long winter's night.

Neville's hand rested on the high back of her chair, for all the world like a king with his queen, despite the lowly homespun garments she'd bought for him in Sligo. With his other hand, he swirled brandy in his glass, but he'd not drunk much of it. For a change, his attention seemed elsewhere than herself.

"We need to talk with McGonigle," she said.

"And so we will." Michael idly spun one of the brass balls on the mantel. "But he's not so foolish as to walk into an armed camp. I'll see him myself in a bit."

She hadn't thought it would be that easy. She proceeded hastily to her next demand. "You have to take me with you. I know the man. He's arrogant, narrow-minded, and bull-headed, but he's acted the part of leader here for years when there was none such. He means well, even if he is wrong-headed."

"Aye, and I've ascertained that much for myself, Fiona," Michael said kindly. "Why don't you go up and get some sleep and leave me to my problems? You've taken on enough of your own without adding mine to them."

Neville watched Fiona's shoulders slump, could almost feel her nervous energy evaporate, replaced by a peculiar vulnerability. These last days he'd seen her as a strong, competent woman, one who took responsibility for all within the circle of her command. And she was very good at it. But it appeared Michael's words had deprived her of something she needed. Neville puzzled over that as the argument continued.

"I'd be there, if you don't mind, Michael," Fiona said quietly. "I've things to ask of him."

"Ye've no business dealin' with the likes of that, Fiona MacDermot, and well you know it. You'd do well to study the role of duchess from now on." Eamon gave Neville a piercing glance. "Speak to her of her place, your honor."

Neville grimaced at this nagging thorn in his side and pressed Fiona back in her seat before she decided to slice him as well as the thorn. "Her place... beside me," he replied with as much studied concentration as he could summon with Fiona squirming beneath his fingers. To his relief, she stilled at his words. Frigid with fear, was more like it.

Neville sensed Michael's unnerving intelligence focused on him. If he had to face the earl alone, he would be stripped of the cover Fiona had provided him these last few days, and he knew he wasn't prepared for that. He didn't want it generally known that the Duke of Anglesey had lost part of his mind. And he didn't want Michael rescinding his permission for Fiona to marry now that he was a semi-idiot.

"I'll have a word with you about that," Michael said dryly. "But not now. The both of you look weary unto death. Fiona, if not for your own sake, then for the duke's, go to bed."

"Not until I've had my say," she said firmly.

Neville didn't want to let her go without him, but the proprieties stood in his way. The earl would have his head should he try to follow Fiona to her room.

To hell with the earl. Gripping Fiona's shoulders tightly, Neville spoke before the earl could. "The children," he said with as much authority as he could manage.

"McGonigle and his wife have no children of their own." Fiona stepped into the breach left by his disability.

Neville exhaled a small breath of relief. He didn't think he could have explained it in a million years, even with his speech intact.

"The McGonigles have the largest house in the village," she continued. "I want to persuade McGonigle to keep the orphans together. Don't you see? If he's busy feeding babes, he'll not have time to roam the night looking for trouble."

Silence descended upon the room, except for the crackle of the fire. His headache returning, Neville wanted nothing more than to take Fiona to bed and sleep, but he feared he would have to fight Michael, and possibly Eamon, if he wanted to accomplish that goal.

Defiantly, he took Fiona's hand. "Come, to bed." Neville squeezed her fingers and pried her from the chair.

"I don't think she needs your help, Your Grace," Michael said from near the mantel where he now juggled several balls. "I think we have a thing or three to discuss, and the orphans are just a small part of it."

"Not tonight." Neville thanked the heavens for the brevity and authority he'd wielded all these years. They served him well now. There were three men in this room who could easily kill him for leading Fiona out of the library, but not one of them stirred in protest. Perhaps they thought he'd return once seeing Fiona to her room. Not bloody damned likely. He wouldn't give her the opportunity to escape before he'd found a priest or vicar and sealed their vows.

"Is your memory returning, Your Grace?" Fiona asked quietly as they traversed the dark halls to the children's room.

He didn't know why she asked. He didn't know how to answer. To him, it seemed irrelevant. He knew who he was. He knew what he had done these last few days. He knew what needed doing in the immediate future. That was enough for now.

"Why ask?"

She threw him an enigmatic glance. In the light of the single candle, he could see only dark-lashed eyes, pale cheeks, and full lips posed in a thoughtful pout.

"Because you're behaving like a husband, my lord duke, and if you had a clear memory, you would know that cannot be."

Neville winced at the sudden pressure in the back of his head. He didn't want to hear this. He knew what he wanted. He wanted her. He didn't want to consider any objections. His memory of certain events might be a little hazy—he figured he could recall them if he truly wanted, but he didn't—only he knew himself quite well. He didn't take innocent young misses to bed without paying the price.

"Remember," he replied ambiguously. "Mine." He twirled his finger in a thick strand of hair at her nape.

She sighed heavily and entered the room to check on the children. They lay sprawled in every conceivable position about the nursery: across the bed, on the bed, before the brazier, on the rug. Apparently Mrs. Callaghan had taken the infant and the youngest toddler into the nursemaid's room adjoining this one. Neville shook his head in disbelief at the strength of the old woman. He'd see her relieved of this burden. She deserved peace at this time of her life.

Once reassured all was well, Fiona slipped from the room and stood uncertainly in the hall, avoiding his eyes. For the first time, Neville forced himself to acknowledge her reluctance. Had they pushed her into a marriage she did not want? Did she love someone else? Thinking of the tall Irishman downstairs, Neville fought an instant's panic. Surely not. They didn't act like lovers.

And then there was the alternative that loomed large in his mind. Did she fear he would remain a speechless idiot all his life? Any woman would think twice about marrying a man who looked like an idiot to all the world, even if he was a duke. And a strong assertive creature like Fiona would despise weakness of any kind.

Suddenly terrified and having no acquaintance with that emotion, Neville kept his hands to himself. "Explain," he demanded, just as if their conversation had never been interrupted.

She looked at him wearily and shook her head. "We will not suit, Your Grace. Let it be. I'll go to America and you may marry Lady Gwyneth, as you would have had our paths not crossed."

Gwyneth. That summoned an image of an Amazon that did not allay his fears in the least. Neville shook his head vehemently. "Never."

He couldn't read the look in her eyes before she turned away and started down the corridor.

"I'll show you to your room, Your Grace." She spoke quietly and politely.

Fiona never spoke quietly and politely. She exploded with joy or fear or rage. She insulted, praised, shouted, or cut men to ribbons with her tongue. Some men would consider her a virago. Others would call her worse. Neville called her the part of him he'd lost.

His heart pounded as he grabbed her shoulder and swung her around. He couldn't recall ever being this terrified in his life. He didn't want to ever be this terrified again. With Fiona by his side, everything would work out. Without her, he might as well dry up and blow away.

"Our room," he demanded. He couldn't let her see his fear.

"We can't," she whispered.

Did he hear the tiniest bit of desperation there? Was that just a flicker of longing behind her determined expression? It didn't matter. They had no choice.

Neville opened the door behind her and firmly pushed her into the room. Stepping in behind her, he shut the door. And locked it.

# Twenty-four

Fiona stood, shivering, on the castle ramparts, watching the army packing its gear in the courtyard below after the earl sent them on their way. Michael had vetoed Eamon's call to arms, agreeing with her that soldiers could only exacerbate their problems with the villagers.

Now that Michael had opened communications with the rebels, no one had come to burn them out. Yet. She tried mentally hastening the army on its way, but she couldn't summon the necessary concentration. Her thoughts kept creeping back to last night and the duke.

He hadn't taken her as wife. Somehow, she had known he wouldn't. They'd slept together as innocently as they had the prior nights with a room full of children as chaperones.

Perhaps not so innocently. He had held her all night, as if fearing her escape, and she'd wished his hands would slip elsewhere on her person besides her waist. She couldn't believe she'd slept a wink, but she'd awakened to the arousing sensation of his fingers circling her breast. Primeval needs rose at just the memory.

She'd wanted to linger in his embrace, to follow where the exciting sensations led, but Neville hadn't let her explore. He'd kissed her ear, run his hand down her side and over the curve of her hip, and then he'd climbed out of bed. Drat the man's self-control.

She didn't shiver with cold now, although the ramparts were a windy place. She shivered in anticipation. Only the duke's speech was muddled. The rest of the man remained fully intact. Perhaps he bent the rules by sleeping with her, but he wouldn't risk the chance of a child until vows were said. In that, he remained the proper man she remembered— humorless, autocratic, demanding, seeing no path but his own.

Yet he was down in the courtyard now, showing Sean how to hitch a mule. And he'd made no mention of his bills in Parliament or his estate in Anglesey since he'd arrived in Ireland—or leastways, since the boy had bopped him over the head.

Could she trust the man she'd seen the past few days, or would he revert to his old self as soon as he fully recovered? *If* he recovered.

She hated that she would be responsible if he was permanently disabled.

But Neville was making it compellingly obvious that even disability didn't deter him. He was far stronger than she dared hope or believe. Strong enough to endure bankruptcy and murder? Strong enough to understand that she was a danger and not a proper gracious duchess?

She had to find out before they both made the biggest mistake of their lives.

Spinning back toward the tower stairs, Fiona fled the ramparts.

From the courtyard below, Neville watched the slender figure on the roof hurrying toward the tower and breathed a sigh of relief. When she'd first appeared up there, he'd feared she'd gone there to throw herself off. He'd carried his heart in his throat until she'd started her familiar pacing. Pacing, he could deal with, though he was still relieved when she decided to come down.

As if he'd been watching too, Michael suddenly appeared in the courtyard, his uncovered hair gleaming in the wintry light. "Grasshoppers don't live well in glass jars," he stated without preamble. "We have to talk."

Talk. Just what he couldn't do. Neville cast a glance back to the boy merrily hitching up mule wagons, noted the steady parade of uniformed soldiers marching down the road, and saw no escape.

"Find priest," he said as forcefully as he could, but he knew he couldn't fool Michael.

"That's what we have to talk about." Michael shoved his hands in his pockets. "Are we going to do it out here in the cold or inside where it's comfortable?"

Neville released the animal he was working on and pressed his fingers to his temple. Damn his aching head anyway. Too many things depended on his unreliable brain. "Can't talk," he finally admitted through gritted teeth.

"Tell me something I don't know," Michael said grimly. "Why isn't Fiona down here covering up for you?"

Ignoring a question he couldn't answer, Neville stalked toward the door. "Find priest. Vicar. Banns, license."

Michael hurried after him. "For a man who can't talk, you get your point over quite excellently. How am I supposed to argue with you?"

Neville pointed at the slender figure flying down the massive stone stairs. "Don't," he said emphatically. "Pointless."

He thought Michael stifled laughter. He wished he felt like laughing himself. He wished Fiona was running down those stairs to lovingly rush into his arms. He might as well wish to be King of England.

"We must talk," Fiona said, before she'd reached the bottom step.

Michael did laugh then. Neville merely crossed his arms over his chest and waited impatiently for her latest attempt at evading the inevitable. Not only must he deal with his unruly brain, but with his unruly body every time she entered the room.

She wore her hair pulled back in a black ribbon, but the wind had tumbled it about her face and shoulders in a glorious disarray of shimmering copper strands. Neville's gaze lowered to the fullness of her bottom lip. He wanted the right to kiss her here and now.

Her blush satisfied him that she'd noticed the direction of his gaze and read his mind. Maybe she'd been thinking about this morning too. At least she'd put on a gown instead of trousers. Maybe her sojourn in London had taught her some feminine habits.

Amazed he'd remembered that much, Neville almost missed her first breathless words.

"Colin and Mrs. Blackthorn are coming. I've seen them just over the hill."

Neville didn't miss the significance of her statement. Perhaps the household hadn't realized where the two of them had slept last night. The castle halls rambled in a maze of rooms and chambers. There were few servants to gossip. But Colin and Mrs. Blackthorn knew exactly how they'd lived these last few days.

"Explain Michael," he commanded her.

Fiona glared at him, pouted out her luscious bottom lip, then with a toss of her head which tumbled silken hair down her back, she stalked into the Great Hall with grace, grandly confident he and Michael would follow. Which they did.

Succinctly, she explained the blow to Neville's head, the trip to Sligo, and their encounter with Colin and the widow. She neatly blurred the facts by mentioning the separate rooms at the inn. But there was no denying that Colin and Mrs. Blackthorn thought them husband and wife.

Finding nothing to juggle in the empty hall, Michael paced as Fiona spoke. When she finished, he spun around and contemplated them both.

"All right, then, that's easily handled." He gave Neville a quizzical look. "The blow's just addled your impeccable speech, Your Grace? You're quite certain you're still competent to look after our Fiona?"

"Perfectly competent."

Neville wished he felt as competent as he sounded. But mostly rooted deep inside him was the knowledge that he couldn't let Fiona go. He knew he wasn't an idiot. Fiona knew it too. He didn't think her capable of rejecting a man because of a minor speech impediment.

"I'll hide," she suggested. "Just tell them I've returned to Blanche in London."

Fiona appeared ready to bolt. Neville grabbed her hand and held on tight. "No."

Michael turned his penetrating gaze on his cousin. "You wouldn't wish to make a liar of yourself and the duke would you now, Fey-onah, my own?"

She paled. "Michael, be reasonable. We can tell them I'm off to America, if you prefer. Tell them anything. Don't do this to Neville. I explained in that letter—I'm a *danger* to him. Our marriage will ruin him. I thought he was your *friend*."

Neville easily read the laughter in Michael's expression. They hadn't always been friends. He remembered that much. If he admitted the truth to himself, their characters were too diametrically opposed—as his and Fiona's were. Yet he clearly remembered that he'd come to respect the intelligence and perceptivity of this eccentric Irishman. And he believed the earl had come to rely on Neville's knowledge of what was possible and what was not in the business world. It could work.

"Because Neville is my friend," Michael replied. "I trust his judgment, Fiona. If you would take him for husband, you should trust him too."

"But he doesn't *know*." Fiona stamped her foot, seeming ready to implode. "His head got bashed before I could explain."

Neville placed both hands on her shoulders to keep her from flying toward the rafters and lifted a questioning eyebrow.

She threw him a look of irritation. "Your friend Townsend seeks to destroy you through whatever means available. He brought you papers declaring me a rebel and a traitor so he could destroy any friendship between you and Michael. And from what I overheard, he may have hired those ruffians who hit you over the head the first time. It's likely he'll do anything to keep you out of power and sever the ties between us. I'm a *danger* to you!"

Neville briefly wished for the return of the fog in his brain, but Fiona's blunt speech had blown away the last few comforting remnants.

He *remembered* Townsend's appearance on the eve of his wedding to Fiona. He remembered the damning papers. And he remembered Fiona's disappearance. His headache returned with a vengeance.

He fixed her with a fierce gaze. "You ran away."

She turned and glared back at him. "What good can you do dead? Or married to a traitorous Irish Catholic?"

"*My* choice. My decision," he said emphatically, frustrated that the words still did not come easily.

"You wouldn't have believed me. You would have stayed there and let Townsend destroy you. What would you have me do?"

"*Trust* me." To his astonishment, Neville realized he was shouting. Clenching his fists, he glared at her in helplessness. He couldn't pull together the right string of words he needed. Finally, he just said, "Not a child."

Michael interfered before they could come to blows. "Fiona, lass, the point is moot. I've both a vicar and a priest on the way, and the entire village invited to see you repeat your vows. No one need know they weren't properly said the first time. See to your orphans, your gown, the festivities, and whatever else is necessary for a ceremony in the morning. Your betrothed and I will see to the other details. Can you do that?"

Astounded, Neville stared at the earl. Impaired as he was, he'd thought he had a battle on his hands keeping Fiona, but Michael simply brushed the handicap aside without question.

Never having experienced that amount of trust before, Neville didn't know how to respond.


Michael's words had a different effect on Fiona. Feeling more and more like a caged animal, Fiona mustered as much dignity as she could, and swept from the hall.

If she didn't find an escape soon, she'd be a brood mare for an Englishman with a death warrant on his head.

Or did she dare actually trust the damned duke, as he'd asked?

Fiona went about her tasks with an increasing sense of helpless confusion.

The kitchen was a chaos of activity. Every pot, pan, and bowl was in use, and at least half the women of the village turned to greet her with excitement and a merriment she hadn't seen on their faces in years. The castle had been abandoned for decades after her grandfather's death, and Michael had only visited it a few times in the two years since he'd inherited. There had been a celebration when his son was born, but not to this extent. The villagers had known little of the earl then; they'd known Fiona all their lives.

Of course, her marriage to a duke gave them even more reason for hope and gaiety. They thought she would bring them riches and power.

Colin and the Widow Blackthorn arrived at the same as one of the orphans crossed the kitchen cat the wrong way. As the scratched child wept, the other children scampered about underfoot, searching for their runaway kitty. The village women drove Fiona and the orphans out of the kitchen and into the arms of Mrs. Blackthorn.

The children scattered, but the widow insisted on finding Fiona a suitable gown in the castle's wardrobes. Resigned to chaos, still in a frenzy of confusion, Fiona marched upstairs.

They uncovered trunks of moldering material and moth-eaten, outdated garments, and finally retrieved an elegant emerald velvet that was still salvageable. Letting the widow force her into the heavy gown with its ancient train so she could pin and tuck for alterations, Fiona stewed over the decision she must make. Bolt, or trust the duke to take care of himself — and marry him.

From the window of her second story chamber she watched the men ride out, free as birds to go where they would. Trapped in the heavy gown, pinned to her stool while the widow kneeled at her feet, Fiona felt like a medieval lady watching her knights ride to war, leaving her alone with the thankless tasks of the household.

She despised housekeeping. She couldn't cook. She knew nothing of ordering servants, as evidenced by their bullying her out of the kitchen. When Fiona finally escaped the widow's ironclad hold to order the Great Hall cleaned for the company, she discovered the enormous chamber already filled with an army of laborers scrubbing and ripping down tattered tapestries. She was useless in her own home. How would she ever fit into the duke's well-ordered life?

Events were proceeding at a comet's pace. How could she *think* like this?

The men had taken the horses, so she had no escape there. It didn't matter. Each time she attempted to leave the castle, someone came between her and the door with another inane question or task for her to do. Fiona suspected a conspiracy.

Everyone had decided for her. How could they be so foolish as to think she could be a proper duchess?

They didn't care if Neville had the proper wife. Only *she* cared about Neville's future.

She had to trust Neville as much as she trusted herself. These last days had proved that marriage wasn't as simple as she'd expected. But it might be more wonderful than she'd thought.

As the afternoon waned and the priest arrived, giddy excitement and anticipation raced through the gloomy corridors and empty chambers. The village hadn't seen a priest in months. Through the general scurry for hot baths and Sunday clothes, Fiona had a devil of a time getting the poor man fed before he was forced into duty in the confessional.

Teeth clenched against nervousness, Fiona fought her own inner battle on the subject of religion. When they'd planned to marry in Neville's Anglican chapel, she'd known Neville would never accept her religion as his own, so she'd seen no sense in belaboring the topic. But a priest now... She took a deep breath for courage. A local priest was likely to raise a holy stink about an Englishman, much less an Anglican.

She avoided the man, hoping she could postpone the sermon he would read her about the purgatory she would face should she raise her children outside the church. She had already decided she would suffer the better part of hell right here on earth with this marriage, so what was a little purgatory? She just prayed the men would return before she suffered the brunt of the priest's wrath.

But the wretches had set the hornet's nest swarming and run for cover, leaving her to deal with the results.

Just as she snatched a few bites from the kitchen for her evening meal, the priest sent for her. With the dragging gait of one sentenced to eternal damnation, Fiona approached the antechamber the priest had commandeered for his confessional.

# Twenty-five

Neville had known frustration, disappointment, and fear in the past, but nothing to compare with his towering vexation with the smug, black-robed, crow of a priest.

Who refused to marry them.

Unable to strike a priest, he needed to beat his fists into yielding flesh at Jackson's boxing salon. Failing that, a sweaty round of fencing with an unshielded point might suffice.

He'd always vented his inner furies by such means before, gaining the release needed to maintain his public composure. He had no such outlet here, and more reason for rage than usual.

Like his very real terror that Fiona had run away again because of this self-righteous vulture.

Neville glared at the priest, and something popped inside his head. "Get out of my sight," he said, fury washing away his awareness of his words. "You have no idea what you've done," he shouted. "I've never laid hand on a man of the cloth before, but if you don't leave *instantly*, I'll not be responsible for my actions."

The priest didn't budge.

Michael returned from checking with the servants and stepped between them, raising his eyebrows at Neville's spate of words. "She's still here. I've had one of the women check. Eamon's found another bottle of whiskey. Go join him while I talk with the good father."

"I don't want him near Fiona again," Neville insisted. "Now I see why we've resisted the Catholic reform bill all these years. They're no more than a lot of narrow-minded pagan savages..."

Michael twisted his arm and shoved him in the direction of the library.

Instinctively, Neville raised his fists and swung, careless of his target or his reasoning. No one had shoved him since he'd come into his dukedom, and he'd had all he could take for one day.

Michael caught his fist in one hand, shoved harder, and blocked the second blow aimed at his stomach. "Stop it, Your Grace. It's not me you want to hit. Fiona's fine. She's as furious as you are, and if you proposed to run off to Gretna, she'd no doubt accept, if just to get even with the priest. It's a wonder his skin hasn't been flayed from his back by the lash of her tongue. It will take me a bit, but we'll have the wedding if you'll let me talk to the father. Go on with you now. Eamon will drain the bottle before we get there."

Robbed of his fight, Neville growled, scowled at the priest, and stalked off to the library. He had no quarrel with the drunken Eamon, but he tried to summon one. He needed something to hit, and with the priest removed from his reach, the Irishman seemed fair game.

"Got away again, has she?" Eamon asked caustically as Neville entered.

"Not this time, no thanks to you and your kind. The blithering priest refused his blessing. He won't marry us. And the damned vicar hasn't shown up yet." Neville poured a large measure of the golden liquor into a glass.

"Surprise that," Eamon replied lazily. "Imagine an Anglican priest roaming these parts. It'll be a wonder if he keeps his head attached long enough to get here."

Neville heaved the glass, whiskey and all, at the Irishman's head. It smashed into a thousand tiny splinters and sparkling drops against the paneled wall. "I'd see the lying lot of you hanged and left out to dry. See if I let Michael persuade me to your charity again." He headed out of the room.

"I see the cat's let loose of your tongue," Eamon called tauntingly as Neville walked out. "Do you think our Fiona will still take pity on your poor cracked head and marry you anyway?"

Michael caught Neville stalking the corridors, throwing open doors left and right in search of Fiona. "She's locked herself in her room but the Widow Blackthorn is with her. The staff knows Fiona's ways. They'll not let her fling herself from a window or climb to the parapets at a time like this."

Neville clenched his fists, trying to disguise his frustration. He didn't want the widow sleeping with her. That was *his* prerogative.

As if reading his mind, Michael frowned and walked toward the library. "There'll be none of that until after the ceremony, your worship."

Neville could see where Fiona had learned disrespect. With nowhere else to go, he followed Michael. "Will there be a ceremony?" he demanded.

Michael threw him a hooded look as he opened the library door. "Your speech seems to have made a remarkable recovery."

Now that the realization that he could talk sank in, Neville calmed to some extent. He could use his wits and tongue instead of his fists. He could go to Fiona whole. "Want to hit me over the head again?" he mocked.

"Yes," Michael answered bluntly, pouring a glass of whiskey from the nearly empty bottle, scarcely giving Eamon's drunken sprawl a second glance. "I've a plan to get the rebels talking to me. It will work much better if you're still an addled idiot instead of a threat."

"Thank you." Neville threw back a swallow of the liquor, relishing the raw burn sliding down his throat. Perhaps Eamon had the right idea after all. Drunkenness had a certain appeal. "First, tell me what you've done to the priest. Then tell me your plan."

"I've bribed the priest, of course. That's all he was after. There's not a clergyman in the country who can't find use for a few extra coins for his flock. Although it cost me a good deal more than usual to soothe his umbrage after Fiona called him a bilious boil on the face of the earth. I think you owe the priest for your bride's new loyalty."

Neville wanted to chuckle, but he knew Fiona well. Once her temper cooled, she'd be back to questioning his safety, her purpose in his life, and whether the moon followed the sun.

"She could still murder him in his sleep and take the next ship to Boston," he countered.

"As a precaution," Michael continued, ignoring the comment, "I have men looking for the vicar. McGonigle's probably holding him for hostage to get some of their own back. There's none hereabouts happy to pay their tithes to the government church while their own goes begging, so you'll understand their resentment."

Neville supposed he could understand a lot of things if he put his mind to it, but his mind wasn't on churches and priests and misbegotten Irish rebels right now. His thoughts were of a warm, soft woman and a tumble of auburn curls. He nearly groaned his need, and despised himself for it.

"All right, let's hear the plan then." With resignation, Neville dropped into a seat by the fire, prepared to wait out the long night before his nuptials by getting royally drunk.

The next day, still wound tighter than Effingham's eccentric floor clock, Neville waited at the makeshift altar in the far end of the Great Hall, his head pounding more from an excess of whiskey than any blows.

Everyone in the whole blamed castle had conspired to keep him from Fiona all night and morning. For all he knew, she'd resorted to her grasshopper ways, and they planned to leave him standing at the altar like a bloody offering to their pagan gods.

Beside him, Michael balanced a prayer book on his finger and spun it around. The earl's highly irreverent outlook on life applied equally to religion and government. Neville wished he could be a little more like him, but whereas Michael had spent nearly thirty years of his life wandering the world without a care to his name, Neville had spent those same years worrying first on how he would make a living, and then on how he could make a living not only for himself, but for the hundreds of tenants and servants he'd inherited. Somehow, in that mass of responsibilities, he'd lost any ability for careless impulse.

Someone produced a melodically angelic riff on a fiddle, and Neville's back stiffened. A mouth organ joined the melody, and he held his breath. His gaze skipped over both the priest and the rescued vicar and fastened on the fairy-figure stepping through the far doorway.

Candlelight from the hundreds of wall sconces danced patterns of light and shadow over his bride's pale features. The heavy velvet gown clung to a figure so slim, Neville feared a sudden draft would break her in two. A single emerald stone on a thick gold chain rested at her throat, drawing his attention to the expanse of creamy flesh swelling above her bodice.

Neville's mouth went dry. He wanted to cover her up so no other greedy eyes but his could see her. At the same time, he nearly burst with pride that Fiona came to him and no other man.

She was finally close enough that he could see her eyes. They looked shadowed and worried, but they fastened on him as if he were the last bastion of sanity in a world gone mad. With a lump lodged in his throat, Neville reached out to take her hand. Her fingers were icy as she grasped his.


With the priest speaking in Latin and the vicar reading from the prayer book, the room could have been the Tower of Babylon for all Fiona knew. The dozens of candles on the altar and the wintry light angling through the high slots in the walls cast a holy aura over the scene. If the priest's sonorous tones and the scent of incense were intended to impress the solemnity of the occasion upon her, she was suitably impressed. In fact, she was damned intimidated.

She took a deep breath to steady herself as she kneeled beside Neville at the makeshift altar to accept Communion. That the duke had endured this madness for her sake confirmed the decision she'd finally made. He was a good man, far better than most, one worth trusting, even if she wanted to rip out his hair for risking his life like this.

Perhaps *because* he was willing to risk his life for her.

Problems aplenty awaited them, but he was right. The strength of their characters and what they had between them might be enough. The infuriating priest had made her see clearly—she could not, would not hurt Neville anymore.

From beneath the lacy mantilla covering her hair, she glanced at the man who had claimed her hand and held it firmly now. The duke's expression of complete certainty reassured her. He was the one getting the wrong end of the bargain, yet he didn't express a single doubt. Perhaps the blow had addled his brain more than anyone knew.

Fiona's heart danced a reel in her chest at the light in Neville's eyes as he raised her up and held her with his intense gaze. Holy Mary, Mother of Christ, if he looked at her that way every day of their lives, he would not only have his herd of heirs, he would have her slavering at his feet.

Fiona returned her attention to the priest, but she heard nothing. This was her wedding day. Unlike other girls, she had never planned it. So she didn't know what she felt now as the words of the ceremony demanded her vow to love this man from this day forth. The "honor and obey" part went right past her head.

Neville's hand tightened around hers, and nervously, she met his gaze as she murmured "I do." His response was firmer than hers, but then, men thought "love" something one did in bed. Still, his confidence again bolstered her flagging nerves.

Fiona's eyes filled with tears as Neville completed his vow by sliding the silver bracelet she'd sold onto her wrist, before placing the ring on her finger. The bracelet was all she had of a grandmother she'd scarcely known. Her mother had passed it on to her the day she died. She'd hated selling it, but feeding the children had more priority than sentimentality. That Neville had guessed how much it meant to her shattered all her defenses. She scarcely noticed the gold band with which he formally claimed her. The bracelet said everything their words had not.

She hoped it was a sign that he respected her and her wishes.

The phrases pronouncing them man and wife reached her through a daze. The brush of Neville's lips reminded Fiona they had scarcely had time to learn even such a minor part of courtship as kissing. And now they were married, irrevocably tied for eternity.

At least, as Neville had promised, she need not spend her wedding day dreading the night to come. If nothing else good came of this entire fiasco, she knew she could anticipate the pleasure of her husband's bed.

Her husband. Gulping back her terror, Fiona clung to Neville's arm as the crowd swarmed around them, kissing, shouting congratulations, crying, patting them on the back. Her husband. His wife.

The moment someone called her Your Grace, the blood drained from her head, and Fiona shot Neville a look of panic. All those times she'd mocked his lordly title, and now she shared it with him.

Obviously reading her expression, the duke raised that damnable shaggy eyebrow of his and grinned. The grin did it. She wanted to smack it off his smug face. She finally let loose of his sleeve.

"Would you prefer Mrs. Perceval, or Lady Duchess?" he whispered, accepting a drink someone shoved into his hand.

"Mrs...." she spluttered, before her entire body stilled. "A complete sentence. You just said a complete sentence," she marveled.

He held a finger to his lips as someone barged between them, separating them at last.

Fiona scarcely had a moment to question him after that. Every woman in the village had to hug her and whisper words of advice, advice that became increasingly bawdy as the brew flowed and spirits rose. Young boys tried to kiss her cheek. Young girls stared at her gown in awe. The men maintained a wary distance, occasionally touching a forelock in respect, sending Neville a nervous look, or shaking Fiona's hand with cautious praise.

All except Colin and Eamon. With the kegs of ale flowing freely in one of the empty chambers set aside for refreshments, Colin and Eamon found reckless fortification in the brew and hovered at Fiona's side.

The fiddle and mouth organ began a reel that set feet tapping, and Fiona searched for Neville in the throng. He stood surrounded by men who argued vociferously with him as they would never do with her. He was still treating them with one word replies. She prayed they were forming a peaceful alliance.

"Let's have a dance, Fiona, my own," Eamon called when he noted the direction of her glance. "Let the asses bray while we enjoy the day."

She should be dancing with Neville. But her anxious glance told her he would be embroiled for a long time to come, and with a sigh, she accepted Eamon's offer. The day loomed forever long. She might as well make what she could of it.

She skipped up and down the hall with Eamon, spun in a reel with Michael, lifted her skirts and tapped out a jig to beat Colin at his best. The crowd roared with approval and gaiety. After a cup or two of punch to quench her thirst, Fiona's head spun with the noise, and her laughter flowed as freely as the music and the spirits.

McGonigle took his place in the line of dancers beside her. None of the men had bothered telling her the outcome of their confrontation with the rebel leader, but the fact that they hadn't thrown him from the castle said Neville had brought him to a truce. She didn't dislike the man so much as his methods, and for the sake of the orphans, she didn't object to his presence.

Eamon did, however. With drunken bravado, he lurched into the line beside Fiona, taking the place between her and McGonigle. "My turn, I believe." He hiccuped.

The burlier man tapped Eamon on the shoulder. "I've come to talk with the lady. Out of my way, you whiskey-laden sot."

Before Fiona could gather her spinning thoughts, Eamon's fist shot out, McGonigle retaliated, and a woman screamed.

The melee spread quickly. Someone attempting to separate the combatants got hit, roared with rage, and launched into the fracas. Another jumped in to help him. With blood riding high on liquor and the tension of the past days of army occupation, tempers frayed rapidly.

Accustomed to the swift degeneration of frivolity into violence, Fiona backed away. They'd all be weeping in their beer and singing mournful ballads together before the day ended, but she'd had enough violent emotion for one day. If she didn't escape soon, she might surrender to the temptation of smacking someone. Her missing husband might be a good one to start with.

She saw Colin fighting his way through the mob in her direction, but she would have none of the slippery bastard. He had a wife big with child at home. That's where he belonged. She wanted Neville, and if her husband didn't have sense enough to know that, she would take herself out of here.

She smacked off Colin's hand as he reached for her. "Leave off and let me by, Colin."

"Let me take you out of this, *cailin*. I'd have a word with you, if I might."

"Not with my wife, you won't."

Before Fiona's wondering gaze, Colin rose several inches into the air. Her eyes widened as she realized Neville held him by the back of his neckcloth. The duke appeared perfectly calm, but Colin's face was turning blue. Her already shredded nerves and temper gave way.

"If I'm supposed to be impressed by your prowess, my lord husband, let me assure you, I am not. But by all means, don't let me disturb the two of you. Go about your games without me."

She shoved past, lifting the nuisance of her heavy train and all but running from the room, her head pounding in fury, her eyes filled with tears. Nothing, but *nothing* was going right. The whole damned world was run by apes.

As his wife ran from the room, Neville exploded with the frustration that had been building within him for two days. Torn from her side by McGonigle and his demands, forced to watch every man in the room dance with his bride—while he grunted inane responses to political diatribes and Michael talked them into reason—Neville could no longer keep the volcano of his long dormant emotions from erupting.

Slamming Colin against the wall and letting him slide to the massive ebony table beneath, Neville clenched his fists and ran after his wife.

He'd be damned if he let Fiona escape again.

# Twenty-six

Neville found Fiona in her bedchamber, heaving clothes into a trunk. She looked up when he slammed the door behind him, then ignored him by defiantly flinging her mantilla into the trunk's rummage heap and reaching for another garment from the stack upon the bed.

Neville swept the entire stack from the bed and in the general direction of the trunk. Clothes tumbled in disarray all across the floor. "No more running away!" he yelled.

Not one to be caught off balance, she scowled again. "I'm not running!" she shouted back, kicking the trunk out of the mess he'd created and bending over to retrieve her scattered garments. The wooden trunk scraped against the wooden floor, but the rising noise of the fracas below drowned out the worst of it.

"Dammit, you just did." Neville finally gave in to the need to punch something by striking at a moldering tapestry on the wall. He choked on the clouds of dust billowing from the ancient cloth, then pounded it again in retaliation. The rusted chain holding it in place broke, and the heavy piece collapsed on the floor in another storm of dust.

"Look at what you've bloody well done!" Fiona screamed, heaving a crewel work pillow at the wall where the tapestry had been instead of the more obvious target of his head.

"I'll take the damned thing and wrap it around the clothheads downstairs." With a remarkably cleansing fury surging through his veins, Neville dug his fists into a matching tapestry and ripped it from the wall. The chain shrieked with protest before snapping. He heaved the heavy cloth toward its companion piece as if it weighed nothing. "If I ever see that piece of scum near you again, so help me I'll..." He kicked the entire stack of cloth toward the door, effectively barring exit or entrance.

"To which piece of scum do ye refer, yer lordship?" Fiona asked mockingly, grabbing a handful of clothes from a wardrobe and flinging them at the already overflowing trunk. "The ones who danced with me when my husband wouldn't? The ones who brought me punch when my throat grew dry explaining why I didn't dance with my own damned husband?"

"The ones who make demands of me on my wedding day!" Neville shouted back, sweeping his hand in an angry gesture. An assortment of ornaments from the mantel followed the path of his arm, crashing and bouncing across the stone hearth with metallic jangles. Momentarily astonished as a pewter mug rolled across his toe, he recovered and defiantly smacked the last tottering candlestick onto the hearth with the rest. He'd never had a tantrum before and found it heartily enlightening. "The ones who danced with you when I should have been the one at your side."

With wide-eyed amazement, she watched him strew candlesticks, tinderboxes, and flatirons to the hearth. "Why the divil I ever prayed you'd talk again, I'll never know. I forgot just how damned arrogant you are!" A half sob, half giggle emerged as she picked up her hairbrush and flung it at the far wall, apparently attempting to emulate the clatter he created. When that didn't work, she reached for another pillow and flung it directly at him.

Caught by surprise, not so much at the pillow striking him as by the almost helpless noise she'd made, Neville flung the pillow back at her. Resentment soared again as he remembered the remark Eamon had made. "I suppose now that you know my head's no longer cracked, you're sorry you married me."

"That I am!" she raged with more vigor. "I've no worth to you but as a brood mare. I cannot roof your tenants' houses nor buy your farm lands back. You should never have let Michael force us into this."

"So you know about that now." Neville jerked off his tailored coat and flung it toward the overflowing trunk, his blood still boiling but his interest taking another direction. "And are you sorry that I'll not have the coins to feed every orphan you find? Did you really think the likes of your doddering viscount would have done so?"

Fiona had only briefly entertained that notion, but she wouldn't give him the satisfaction of knowing that. Her heart skipped a beat at the sight of the duke standing there in starched shirt sleeves, his frilled cravat spilling over his white silk waistcoat. She gulped a little at the breadth of his shoulders as he stood arms akimbo, glaring at her. "If I cannot bring you money, then there's no point in any of this, is there now?" she demanded. The sight of Neville really, truly angry left her breathless, but she fought him for the sheer pleasure of watching his eyes flash with silver.

"Aye, but it's an excellent brood mare you're after being, aren't you now?" he mocked.

Fiona watched with wariness as he unfastened his waistcoat. "And if I'm not? There's enough penniless hungry children in this world without my bringing in more."

The waistcoat sailed across the room to join the growing jumble of clothing. Candlelight caught the golden gleam of Neville's hair as he stalked her. Fiona drew a deep breath of pleasure at the sight. Fired with anger, he was a magnificent beast.

"It's a little late to think of that now, isn't it, Fiona, my wife?" His eyes glittered molten fire as he reached for her.

Fiona dodged his grasping hands and clambered over the bed. "What if I don't want children?" she demanded. "Will you force me?"

Instead of following her over the bed, he placed his fists at his waist and studied her through narrowed eyes. Her pulse raced and her breath came in nervous gulps. She wasn't afraid, not of Neville. What she feared was the way she felt when he looked at her like that, seeing through every sham and pretense. She didn't want him seeing what she couldn't see herself.

"With any other woman, I would walk out of here right now," he said slowly, as if pondering every word.

Fiona halted her wild flight and watched him. Hope crashed against the walls of her heart like the tide against a flood wall. She said nothing.

"But not with you, Fiona," he said, his gaze holding her pinned. "I've held you in my arms. I don't think your kisses lie. You can deny it all you like, but there's something between us that won't go away as easily as you might wish."

Fiona shivered and the goosebumps rose on her arms. She stared, trying hard not to believe this marriage was more than a trap.

From below, over the crashing chairs and shouts of the brawl, emerged the sweet sound of a flute.

"Michael," Fiona whispered, still staring at Neville as if he'd gone mad. "They'll quiet now." Even as she said it, a fiddle joined the music of the flute.

Shoving aside the debris he'd created, Neville approached the chaos on her side of the room. "Dance?" he inquired politely.

Carefully, apparently unsure if she approached a madman or a lover, Fiona stepped over the remainder of her clothes. "Yes, please," she said as politely as he, as if they hadn't just raged and roared at each other seconds before.

She felt damned good in his arms. Closing his eyes in pure joy as his hands finally encompassed Fiona's slender waist and slid over her velvet bodice, Neville swayed to the haunting melody of the music below. He had no idea what kind of music it was, what kind of dance it involved. The steps were unimportant. What mattered was the living, breathing woman in his arms.

The fresh scents of heather and lilacs wafted from her hair. Someone had pinned all those gorgeous thick curls into an improbable creation at the crown of her head, but their handiwork had come partially undone with the heat of exertion. Dazedly, Neville dug his fingers into the heavy mass and sought the remaining pins. Fiona offered no objection as her hair tumbled free and loose about her shoulders.

Satisfied now that he could wrap his hands in her hair, Neville contented himself with gliding to the music while soaking up the pleasure of finally holding this will o'wisp in his arms.

The beat of the music increased, reminding Neville of his jealousy at the flash of slender ankles beneath heavy velvet as his wife danced in arms other than his. He swung her harder, watching with delight as Fiona grabbed at her skirt and lifted it out of her way.

Neville skipped her across the floor to the wild music of the fiddle, danced her over heaps of clothes and fallen candlesticks, swung her in a breathless reel, then danced her back again. Fiona rewarded him with a flash of ruby lips and white teeth. Fiery hair swung down her back as he spun her again.

It was a heady magic he couldn't resist. While the music played on below, Neville halted their wild cavorting to seek the promise of her laughing lips.

Her arms slid over his shoulders, and Fiona breasts pressed into his chest so tightly he could feel the hectic beat of her heart pounding with his. Breathing unevenly, Neville demanded more. Without protest, she opened her mouth, and he captured that moist sweetness with his tongue.

His bride moaned against him and dug her fingers deeper into his hair. Realizing that finally and at last he had the right to touch this woman as he pleased, Neville sought the laces of her old-fashioned gown and pulled them loose.

Fiona's cry of surprise scarcely matched his own groan of discovery that she wore nothing beneath the velvet. Cupping his hand over heated flesh, Neville smothered her in kisses of delight.

She grabbed his lapels to steady herself, nearly tumbling them into the bed before he caught his balance. Deliberately circling her swollen nipple with his thumb, Neville gazed down into Fiona's flushed and dazed features. "I want you now, Fiona. I want your skirts off and your bare flesh beneath mine. Will you accept me as your husband?"

Fiona could scarcely think the words, much less say them. The eyes she'd once thought cold and hard as stone watched her with the heat of molten silver. The studious duke had transformed into a man flushed with triumph and arousal. His normally combed locks fell in golden-brown disarray. His cravat had come unfastened—she had a vague memory of pulling at it—and she caught a glimpse of hard male chest beneath the frill of his open shirt. She'd not had a chance to see him unclothed last time. The realization that she now had the opportunity—and the right—to see the duke fully nude brought a flush to her cheeks as she met his gaze. Without any further hesitation, she sought the buttons of his shirt.

Before she could unfasten more than one, Neville lifted her and pushed her heavy wedding gown over her hips and to the floor.

Fiona defensively covered her breasts as he stared hungrily at her nakedness. "None of my chemises fit under that bodice," she muttered.

"I think I'll order all your gowns that way." He pushed aside her arms. "You are the most beautiful creature I've ever seen in my life."

Since she felt certain he'd had his share of London's beautiful courtesans, Fiona doubted that, but she liked the sound of it anyway. She had enough arrogance to enjoy the power of holding the attention of one of England's most influential men.

"Your turn, my lord duke," she whispered. "I would see you, too, this time."

He seemed reluctant to let her go even long enough to unfasten his shirt, so she resumed the task on her own. As soon as her fingers touched his flesh, however, he jerked the linen over his head.

Fiona stared in stunned fascination at the broad chest revealed as Neville's fingers nimbly worked the buttons of his trousers. She hadn't expected muscles on a man confined to a desk, but his shoulders and upper arms bulged as strongly as any laborer's. She daringly touched his flat male nipples.

"Fiona," he growled as she tested the springy light hairs on his chest. "I'm a man on the brink of destruction. Be careful what you do."

The urgency in his voice liquefied her insides. Curiosity forced her gaze upward. She just had time to note the way Neville's jaw clenched and his eyes smoldered before he bodily lifted her and threw her among the rumpled sheets of her bed.

Fiona sprang to her knees before he divested himself of his trousers and shoes, not yet ready to lie flat and subservient beneath him. But her first sight of Neville's full nudity robbed her of all defiance.

He climbed on the bed, kneeling before her, pulling her hair until she leaned into him. "Red-headed heirs, Fiona," he murmured. "Lots and lots of red-headed heirs."

The words traveled straight to her womb and burned like a hot poker. She gasped as his hands possessively pushed up her breasts. His lips fastening on her nipple melted all her remaining defenses.

He had her flat upon her back within minutes, writhing and moaning as he worked his kisses down her throat. The sheets twisted beneath her as the music in the room below changed to a manic Irish jig. Her hips rose and fell to the rhythm, to Neville's touch on magic places, to the music of her soul as he sipped at her lips and groaned with equal wildness.

"Now, Fiona," he muttered against her ear. "Let me have you now. I've waited too damn long as it is."

As the fiddle reached a frenetic crescendo, and the flute piped its wild melody, the music swept them away on a whirlwind. Fiona arched her hips upward in blatant invitation. She cried out in abandon as he accepted her invitation and surged into her.

They moved with the music, with the pounding of their hearts and blood, with the rhythm of their souls. Fiona's fingernails bit into Neville's back as he plunged so deep she thought herself mortally wounded. She spiraled upward so fast, she screamed as Neville finally pushed her over the whirlwind's edge.

The scream fell into a dead silence from below, but neither of them noticed as their own melody continued to play in their heads. Fiona quaked and trembled again as Neville found new momentum, and fell with her into the dizzying aftermath of passion.

Fiona woke some minutes later to Neville warming her breast with his hand. A heavy, masculine leg held her trapped against the wrinkled sheets, and the musky scent of their love-making was nearly as erotic as the play of his fingers against her skin.

She supposed she should feel shame and wickedness at the lack of restraint she'd just displayed. Instead, she felt a strong stirring in her lower parts as Neville raised up on one elbow and studied her with a look of intent that she read well.

"I like making you scream with passion," he said in a voice more harsh than gentle.

She drew her fingers down the line of his long jaw. "You will grow accustomed enough to my screaming, my lord husband, for I do it in anger as well as pleasure. Then how will you feel about your shrew of a wife?"

"I think I've found the key that turns your anger into pleasure, my lady wife," Neville replied mockingly. "I'll simply turn the key whenever the need be."

He plundered her mouth, stifling her irate protest. Capturing her with his greater weight, he claimed her thoroughly as she parted her legs in surrender.

She should have known a man who could command governments could command her too-willing body with impunity. She would never be fully herself again.

Instead of frightening her as it ought, the prospect excited Fiona beyond imagining. She had never been a part of anyone or anything before. Catching the wide shoulders of the man above her, she arched hungrily into his embrace, and took him deep between her thighs. As he moaned and lost control, she knew she owned a piece of him as well.

# Twenty-seven

Fiona ached in places she hadn't known existed, yet at every twinge, she shivered in sensual anticipation. She moaned and curled into her pillow, hoping for sleep, except she had a man's elbow up her nose and an insistent pounding at the door.

The elbow shifted and a strong arm drew her closer. Fiona savored the exotic male smell, then wiggled her hips against temptation. She moaned again, this time in delight, at the discovery he was again ready for a romp.

A firm hand gripped her curls and held her back as she tried to kiss him. Sleepily opening one eyelid, Fiona peered at her husband. His Grace looked the part of rogue or worse with his jaw bristled with stubble and his thick hair tumbled in all directions—until he smiled. Smiled. The mighty Duke of Anglesey actually smiled, and in the morning too.

Fiona offered, a slow, almost timid grin in return. He was, after all, a man of far greater experience than she, and he'd generously offered to teach her more.

"I don't suppose the door is locked," he asked as the pounding at the door was replaced with a maid's voice calling for "Fiona," followed by a hastily corrected, "Your Grace."

Momentarily startled at the title applied to herself, Fiona sought the rebellion that should erupt at the appellation, but Neville's gaze dropped to her breasts, and any thought at all evaporated.

"There's not much point," Fiona croaked as she realized she was shamelessly uncovered. Striving for insouciance, she continued, "Few of the rooms have keys and Michael's made copies of them all. He's trying to find some way of cutting them so they fit the locks missing their keys."

"I could lock it against the maid," he suggested, raising a leering eyebrow.

Remembering the destruction they'd wreaked last night, she propped up on one elbow and peered over his shoulder. "The tapestries will hold the maids out a while longer."

"It's time and past to be up, your holy worships," Michael called from the far side of the door. "The looms and orphans cannot wait. You can honeymoon later."

"But they will not stop the bloody earl. Couldn't you throw another temper tantrum and tell him to go away?" Fiona inquired hopefully.

"You liked that, did you, brat?" Neville shifted to nuzzle his bristly jaw along her ear. "But you're the one who wishes to spend her dowry on

McGonigle and the orphans, remember?"

Fiona pressed her fist against his muscled chest and tried to wriggle from his grip. "And Michael holds the purse strings, as usual," she said dryly, squealing only a little when he nipped at her nape.

"He owns us," Neville agreed. "Or rather, Blanche does. She just lets Michael have his way—unless I raise serious objection, of course."

"The unholy triumvirate," Fiona muttered.

"We've got McGonigle and his Whiteboys agreeing to leave Aberdare alone and to turn their energies to helping with the looms. I apologize if I did not have time to dance with you," he said, holding her close to nibble her neck.

"If you're not out of there within the half hour, I'll tell Cook to put breakfast away and you can go without until dinner," the earl shouted through the panel.

Neville grimaced, turned over, and flung his pillow at the door. Apparently satisfied with his response, the intruders departed.

"Apology accepted," she agreed, knowing Aberdare was more important than a dance. Although she admired the view of her husband's smooth, broad back, Fiona sighed and pulled the sheet up to her neck. "I'm starving."

"Why can't someone bring breakfast on a tray?" Neville grumbled as he turned back to find her covered.

"No one is trained for the job." Fiona shrugged. "Besides, then we wouldn't get up, so Michael wouldn't let them." She noted the gleam of lust in his eye and warned, "I don't know about you, but I scarcely had a bite of our wedding breakfast, and if you will remember, we had no dinner at all."

Neville swallowed that reminder with obvious regret. "If we were at Anglesey, we could have trays delivered to our door and not leave bed for a week."

Fiona grinned at his frustration. "Not if Michael wanted you in London. He would blow open the door or come through the window and hold us at gunpoint or some such. I'm sorry, but you've married into the wrong family, if it's rationality you want."

Neville frowned, appearing to contemplate that problem for a minute. Before Fiona could strike him for his insulting thoughts, he straddled her and buried his bristly lips against her throat. She squealed and shoved at his wide chest.

"Cry 'enough,' my shrew," he murmured, running kisses up and down her easily-bruised skin.

"Never!"

And rather than obediently climb from the bed, they tumbled out in an avalanche of sheets and blankets.

*January, 1823*

"I cannot believe Michael's done this to me," Fiona muttered as the wind whipped the sails and the yacht set sail from Dublin some weeks after it first arrived. "Whatever did I do to deserve the witch?"

Watching to be certain no one overheard, Neville leaned back against the rail and pulled his sulking wife into his arms. "Michael only wanted you to have someone from home with you. He means well. I couldn't tell him I prefer your curls all tumbled about your face rather than pinned and proper. The widow was trained as a lady's maid, and she was the only one willing to make the journey."

"But she'll fuss and mother me and write everyone back home of everything we do." Fiona snuggled against his chest, though her temper was still evident.

"Another reason Michael chose her," Neville replied dryly. "Should I neglect you in any way, our black widow will notify him immediately, and probably with great satisfaction."

"What if she's the murderer?" His coat muffled her words.

Neville wrapped her in the lengths of his greatcoat and steered her toward their berth. "If she had the money, she would have run far away by now."

"And Colin? What is his excuse for sending Colin to train your yearlings?" Fiona popped her head from the folds of his coat to glare at him.

"To keep you from doing it?" he suggested wryly. "Because, if he were the murderer, he would be on his way to America now?"

"Not Colin," Fiona scoffed, throwing off the protection of both his coat and his embrace as they reached the companionway. "He could have paid his gambling debts or gambled and drunk it away before he ever bought passage. And surely Michael would not have left the orphans to McGonigle if he thought him the murderer."

Anticipating the night ahead with his wife and the yacht rocking on the waves, Neville didn't ponder the mystery. "McGonigle appeared just a little overwhelmed this morn, didn't he? It gave me great pleasure to see him with a toddler dangling from each arm. I think we have the wrong suspects, Fiona, my own. Now let us seek more pleasant subjects."

Restlessly, Fiona paced the elegant Anglesey drawing room, not seeing the beautifully carved blue and gold rug beneath her feet or admiring the gold brocade of the sofa, scarcely even noting the floor-to-ceiling windows undraped against the gloom of a January day. A fire burned in the grate, but she didn't linger beside it, even when her fingers turned blue with cold.

While they'd been in Ireland, Parliament had set aside the Catholic Emancipation Bill, but Neville and Michael were working on finding enough votes to pass the crime reform bill. Fiona supposed she should be glad that they worked for such a worthy cause, but she was losing her mind for lack of anything to do.

She had chosen Anglesey over London. Neville only had rooms in London, and he'd obviously been relieved that he needn't worry about her climbing the walls while waiting for his return each night. She could have stayed with Blanche and Michael in the townhouse, but she'd wanted a home of her own. She'd wanted to feel needed and useful.

Foolish notion. Anglesey had run smoothly for years like a mechanical toy one wound up and let go. Kept oiled and wound, it needed no further attention.

Unfortunately, she did. She'd had scarcely a month in Neville's bed, yet the physical intimacy had become like a drug in her veins, and she craved it. She'd known she'd played with fire from the moment he'd first kissed her. She just hadn't known she'd crave fire forever after.

The head housekeeper scratched at the open door, then coughed to announce her presence. Grimacing, Fiona swung around to confront the iron-haired matron. "Yes, what is it?"

"Would Your Grace care to go over the menu now?"

The menu. She was the only one besides the servants in the whole blamed house, and they wanted a menu? She could live on tea and muffins for all she cared.

But she had nothing better to do. At least the servants were trained to hide their feelings toward their penniless Catholic mistress. The least she could do was keep them from despising her more.

"All right, Mrs. Hanna. Bring the menu into my writing parlor, and have someone douse the fire in here. There is no real reason to waste fuel heating this great cave just for me."

If the woman looked appalled at dousing even one of the dozen or more fires heating the living quarters of this palace, she had the grace to conceal it as she curtsied. Accustomed to the drafty halls of Aberdare, Fiona didn't think she'd suffer greatly without this one fire. Surely it consumed more fuel than all the others put together.

After sitting in the cozier comfort of her small parlor, studying the elaborate menu in her hand for half an hour, Fiona raised her head and stared out the frost-glazed window.

She thought of the starving orphans surviving on potatoes and rain water. She remembered going days without meat. Sometimes, in winter, she'd lived on half a loaf of bread so she could take her meals to the women and children in the village who needed it more. She hadn't really thought twice about it at the time.

She looked down at the menu in her hand again and shook her head in disbelief. Every dinner had seven courses. She'd look like McGonigle's prize pig if she ate all that. Did the kitchen staff get the leftovers?

She hadn't eaten more than a tray of light supper these past two nights since her arrival. Why in the name of heaven would they think she needed more?

Ringing the bell, Fiona sent for the cook. She might as well begin as she meant to go on. They all despised her anyway. Or her religion. Or her foreignness.

The cook was a tall, gaunt man with a shadow of a beard even this early in the morning. He looked down his long nose at her from a distance of some feet since she sat and he didn't. Fiona had never dealt with a male house servant before. She could talk to the stable lads easily enough, but how did one address a chef? "The menu is quite exceptional," she said.

He nodded regally.

"However, I'm not planning on entertaining until the duke comes home. I eat very little on my own."

The man made no effort to ease her plight.

Irritated, Fiona tried again. "Who eats what is left over?"

The chef stiffened even more if that was possible. "I make only enough for the one."

Fiona raised her eyebrows and glanced down at the menu again. "A brisket of beef? Quail pie? Leg of mutton? You make enough for one what? One army?"

"If Your Grace is displeased..." He leaned over the desk to rip the menu from her hand.

Fiona tugged back. The page tore in two and they both deliberately shredded the halves they held. Fiona thought she detected the man's eyes widening in surprise.

"The menu is excellent if we are entertaining," she informed in her best imperious manner. "However, we are not. I will have a light repast in the evenings, whatever everyone else has. I need only tea and muffins in the morning, or a bit of porridge. And the noon meal is the same—whatever is prepared. I trust the staff isn't starving, so I shan't either."

The chef looked horrified. "But Your Grace, you do not need me if you would eat the same slops as the swine."

Fiona bit back a giggle. Her cook's opinion of the English wasn't much higher than her own. Pigs, the lot of them, especially if they ate this much on any given day. However, she greatly suspected the cook and the upper servants consumed the majority of these delicacies.

"His Grace needs your talents, Mr. Girouard. He would be truly distraught without you." Fiona suspected she lied through her teeth. Neville never noticed what he ate. But he would eventually want to entertain, and she couldn't shame him by driving away his excellent cook. Inspiration struck. "However, I would economize on the household budget while His Grace is away so I might purchase newer kitchen equipment in the future. You certainly deserve one of those new stoves, don't you agree?"

Girouard nodded with eagerness. "I understand completely, Your Grace," he replied. "A new bride cannot ask for a larger budget so soon. His Grace would be most displeased. I will do my very best, Your Grace, and if I might suggest, the carving knives are a disgrace. We have desperately been in want of new ones."

Pleased with herself, Fiona vowed to buy knives with her first savings. It didn't matter that the cook at home used the same knife for everything and probably had for a thousand years. She would reward anyone who helped in her economizing.

Heady with her small triumph, she sent the cook away with a request that he have the steward bring the household books to her.

She spent the remainder of the day studying the vast pages of accounts, frowning and scribbling, scratching out figures and jotting in new ones. Her education might be limited, but her mind was not. The utter extravagance in maintaining the household appalled her. She wished she had Blanche here to question. But even the amounts entered in Blanche's fine script from several years ago were extensive. Surely Anglesey hadn't entertained that much back then.

With renewed purpose, Fiona called in Mrs. Hanna again. Ignoring the housekeeper's haughty glare, she tapped the pages of the account book. "I know for a fact that His Grace has not entertained widely this past year, yet the butcher bills have increased. Why is this?"

"Prices have increased, Your Grace. There is apparently a shortage of good beef and pork."

"Fustian." Fiona slammed the book shut. "Why do we not raise our own animals?"

The housekeeper rolled her eyes heavenward. "Anglesey has very limited pasturage, Your Grace. You would do better to discuss this with His Grace's steward."

She didn't need the steward to explain that most of the land surrounding Anglesey belonged to Blanche, and she rented it to the highest bidder. Fiona had figured that out for herself. She didn't know how much Neville rented, but he would have to earn the highest profit possible from each acre to pay the rent. Raising cattle for use on Anglesey's tables would not have a high profit margin. She doubted if Neville had ever looked at the household accounts to note the false economy of profiting on land and losing on butcher bills.

"Very well. Is there a local butcher instead of this one from the city?"

"Yes, Your Grace, but he seldom carries beef as he cannot sell enough before it goes bad. There is little coin for fresh meat here."

"With our current monthly expenditures for meat, we could buy two cows and two sheep from my Uncle William, have the local butcher process them, feed the entire staff, and still afford to give the remainder to charity, with money left over. These amounts are exorbitant, Mrs. Smith."

The housekeeper appeared puzzled but willing. "Yes, Your Grace. Shall I purchase cattle from your uncle, Your Grace?"

Fiona bit back another grin. With a careless wave of her hand, she dismissed that suggestion. For now. "That's a possibility after I speak with the duke. In the meantime, see if the local butcher cannot purchase livestock at some reasonable price, and we will calculate the costs involved. I've already instructed Mr. Girouard to cut back on the menu, so we'll need less than before. I suppose Lady Blanche kept a list of households needing food baskets?"

"In her head, Your Grace, but I'm certain one can be constructed. Might I make a suggestion, Your Grace?"

"By all means, Mrs. Hanna."

"Many of the staff support families in the village. They haven't received increases in some years. If, instead of charity, you included the excess meat as part of their wages, it would give them greater pride."

Fiona beamed her approval. "Excellent idea. And if we can create a savings at the end of the month, perhaps we could purchase sufficient yardage to begin making up new uniforms and livery."

It was the housekeepers turn to beam. "Might I say it's a pleasure to have a duchess in charge of Anglesey once again, Your Grace?"

"Why, thank you, Mrs. Hanna. It's my pleasure. We'll take a look at the candle inventory next. We don't need beeswax for every day." With that encouragement, Fiona dived back into the books again.

Finally, she'd found a way of making herself useful.

# Twenty-eight

"Your Grace, I know it is most presumptuous of me to take time from your busy schedule, but I really thought I must come to town to inform you. The souls of your tenants are of too much importance to relegate to a letter."

Neville rubbed his head even though it no longer ached. He'd listened to the vicar's angry diatribe for half an hour now. Perhaps he should have followed Michael's advice and pretended he was still dicked in the nob. Then he could just stare blankly at the smarmy little man until he took his ugly little cap and went home. Since when did English vicars begin wearing silly little hats anyway? Perhaps they wore them in the city.

Realizing he was supposed to say something at this point, Neville bounced his pen against his blotter and nodded knowingly. "Of course, Ravensworth, I completely understand. I appreciate your bringing the matter to my attention. I'll look into it immediately." He'd said these phrases so many times before that he could repeat them in his worst nightmares. Unfortunately, this time, they related to the Duchess of Anglesey, his wife, and he was damned tired of making excuses. "The duchess is young and impetuous. I'll see what it's all about, Ravensworth. Don't worry yourself."

"She could be making papists of them all, Your Grace," the vicar warned. "I'd not have that on your soul."

"No, of course not." Neville stood, effectively dismissing the man since he didn't seem to know when to leave on his own.

"And she's buying supplies from that Gypsy, Meiner!" the vicar turned from the door, remembering still another complaint.

"Meiner is a Jew, not a Gypsy," Neville answered wearily. "Thank you for coming, Ravensworth."

Neville watched with relief as the vicar finally bumbled out, only to discover the Marquess of Effingham waiting his turn in the doorway. This was the problem with living in town—too damned many people.

Scowling, the duke dropped back in his chair. "What do *you* want?"

The broody marquess seldom smiled, but cynical humor wrinkled the corners of his eyes now. "The grasshopper visiting plagues upon the fields of heathens?" he inquired, flinging his long frame into the chair the vicar had just vacated.

"Close enough. She had an argument with the vicar about using church funds to aid women with children, even those with no visible husband.

When he refused to aid sinners, she found a clergyman from heaven knows where and installed him in the Anglesey chapel. The village vicar is morally incensed."

The marquess steepled his long fingers together and nodded. "Surely our Fiona had more sense than to hire a Catholic clergyman?"

Neville ran his hands through his hair. "I think the church has to do that. No, I've already heard the tale from the butler. Fiona is much more ecumenical than you give her credit for. When she discovered most of the staff has Methodist leanings, she hired a Methodist."

The marquess choked on what sounded suspiciously like a laugh. Rubbing his hand across his mouth to hide any smile, he sat back in his chair. "Definitely a breath of fresh air. Have you reserved your room in Bedlam yet? You'll never survive."

Neville fought an unusual urge to chuckle. "Bedlam won't take me after Fiona's done. She's quit dealing with the mercantile Anglesey has used for generations in favor of dealing with an itinerant Jew. She has the estate gardeners learning to thatch roofs, and she's asked my steward if she might have one of the fields for garden plots for the tenants in exchange for them making their own repairs on the cottages. The reports come in regularly from all sources."

This time, the marquess did laugh out loud.

Neville restlessly rearranged his inkpots and pens. "I'm glad you find it so damned humorous. I'll probably be stoned next time I set foot upon my own land."

Shaking his head, Effingham controlled his laughter. "I'm totally delighted you're the one who ended up responsible for her. After spending one summer chasing her through the slums of London when she wasn't teaching the children how to play 'banshees,' I figured Michael would have to export her to Australia. I didn't think even the Americans could handle her." He shrugged. "And your tenants and staff won't stone you. They'll adore you. It's your aristocratic neighbors who will want your hide nailed to the wall."

Neville muttered a pithy curse describing what the neighbors could do with themselves. "It will get worse if Townsend has his way. He already has half of Parliament demanding an investigation into Fiona's 'traitorous' activities. If the other half gets wind of her reformist notions, they'll start screaming bloody murder too. She's my *wife*, dammit. What the devil do they think she can do? Tear down the Tower with her bare hands?"

The marquess's expression sobered. "That's why I'm here. Townsend is determined to have that cabinet vacancy, and he'll accomplish it at any cost. You're his only obvious competition. If he can bring you down, he'll not only have the position, but he'll destroy any chance we might have of eventually passing the emancipation and crime reform bills. We can't allow that, Neville. Michael and I can stomp out the rumor mill, but you have to keep Fiona in line. As an American born and raised, I truly despise saying this, but she'll antagonize the entire Lords if she continues heedlessly thumbing her nose at time-hallowed tradition."

"I'll talk with her," he agreed with a sigh. "I'll clear my schedule for the next few days and ride out to Anglesey. Fiona can be made to see reason. I'm just not entirely certain that I can. If she wants to hire Jews and Methodists, that's her concern. She's the one living out there."

Effingham stood up. "Were it any other woman, I'd say bring her to London and let her fritter her time shopping. I'd bite off my tongue before suggesting that of Fiona. Are you sure your brain wasn't cracked when you agreed to this marriage?"

Neville stood up and pointed at the door. "Friendship goes only so far, Gavin. Out."

Bowing acknowledgment to that observation, the lanky marquess strolled from the room and down the corridor.

With a groan of despair, Neville sank into his chair again. He didn't need this distraction. They were only a few votes short of passing the reform bill. He'd worked too hard to push the damned thing through to drop his campaign now. He loved London. He loved what he did.

But the whole time his mind protested, the rest of him sang songs of deliverance at the thought of going home—to Fiona.


Wanting to make a speedy journey, Neville rode instead of taking a carriage to Anglesey.

If Townsend truly wanted him dead before the next session started, he'd have to come looking for him. Neville had told no one of his plans to leave the city.

The fall session of parliament had ended while he'd been in Ireland. They'd stayed at Aberdare through Christmas, arranging more beds for McGonigle and the orphans, ordering the looms, and setting up the manufacturing operation in the castle's great hall.

It was February now, and the House wasn't yet in session, but he had a million things to accomplish before everyone arrived. He simply didn't have time for Anglesey. Never had.

But Fiona preferred the country, and if the truth was told, he preferred thinking of Fiona in the country. He liked the image of his fairy sprite in forest green dashing across the countryside on her spirited horse. He'd made certain she had the best mount he could afford. He didn't like the idea of his Irish bride displaying herself in all her glory to the jaded gazes of London society. He wanted to keep her to himself.

He didn't know if that was selfish or not. He'd ask Fiona about it when he saw her. She might frustrate him beyond the borders of reason, but he could always talk to her. He missed talking to her.

That revelation jerked him down to earth. Staring at the magnificent sprawl of Anglesey across the horizon, Neville played with this new idea of missing Fiona for more reason than the physical. Was he that devoid of intelligent friends that he needed a rebellious female to converse with?

It didn't matter. He was almost there. Someone had seen his approach and his flag was rising on the flagpole as he watched. That kind of loyalty and pride almost made him homesick.

Leaves hadn't been raked from the fence rows, he noted as he rode up the drive. The gravel drive hadn't been raked either. Even though he operated on next to nothing, Anglesey had always been well tended, thanks to his cousin Blanche's generosity. Surely she hadn't cut back her funding of the servants. They were family retainers. Blanche would never do that.

Remembering the letter from his steward about Fiona's unusual use for the gardeners, Neville turned from the main road into the lane leading toward a row of tenant cottages.

The cold February wind threatened to blow his hat away, and Neville instantly regretted his decision. He'd much rather be sitting in front of a roaring fire, sipping mulled cider, and pulling his lovely wife into his lap. He must be insane to take this circuitous route for no good reason at all.

But he had to see for himself. His steward had told him there was no money for repairs, that all the harvest proceeds must go into acquiring additional land so the estate could eventually break even. The tenant cottages would have to wait.

Fiona, naturally, had disagreed.

She'd scarcely been here a month, and she'd already turned the entire estate upside-down. Neville didn't want to lose a good steward. But he hadn't liked leaving those cottages in disrepair, either.

As he rounded the bend, he focused on the roof of the first house. She must have started there. New thatch gleamed golden against gray winter clouds. It looked sound. Could Fiona really turn his gardeners into thatchers?

Riding closer, he studied more of the cottages. Several sported new roofs. A crowd in the lane ahead indicated the current project. Instead of the leisurely process he remembered of one man tying up bundles of straw, dragging it up a ladder, and laboriously tying it to the other bundles already fastened there, the scene in progress resembled a manufactory.

Several groups busily tied straw into thick, tight bundles. Others carried the completed bundles up several ladders to the roof, where a team of laborers skillfully lashed them into place. Roofs formed before his eyes. And one small figure kept the process running smoothly, pointing out where a bundle was needed, scrabbling up a ladder to hand up new rope — *Fiona*.

His wife, the Duchess of Anglesey, potential mother of his heir — scrabbling up ladders and thatching roofs!

He wouldn't have believed it if he hadn't seen it with his own eyes. Or maybe he would have.

Neville dismounted and stalked through the crowd. His tenants fell silent after the first greeting failed to bring a smile or nod of recognition. He'd never ignored or condescended to his tenants. Right now, though, he had other things on his mind.

"Your Grace!" Neville shouted loudly from the bottom of the ladder he'd last seen her ascend.

Startled, Fiona teetered backward. His heart caught in his throat as he watched her regain her balance. "Fey-onah Perceval," he shouted, his anger escalating, "get yourself down here this second!"

Green eyes brimming with curiosity peered over the roofs edge. "Neville? What the divil are ye doin' here, then?"

Uh oh. The Irish brogue didn't bode well. But the sight of her leaning precariously over a roof a good ten feet above his head gave him heart palpitations. "I'm ordering you down here where you belong, you idiot! Or must I go up after you?"

The loud bellow of his command descended into astonished silence. Caught off guard by the sound of his own voice, he glanced around. Even the children stared. *At him*. Realization dawned slowly.

He was shouting. In front of his tenants. He was standing here in all his dirt, squalling like a hog farmer at his wayward livestock. *Him*. The Duke of Anglesey, who never raised his voice or presented himself in less than impeccable attire. He must be mad. He truly had dicked his noggin.

To his immense relief, Fiona scrambled down of her own accord. Instead of flinging herself into his arms in welcome — a welcome he'd had some foolish hope his homecoming might inspire — she propped her hands on her hips and glared at him.

"Are you after bein' the death of me then, scaring me like that that?" she demanded.

"No wonder nobody understands the Irish. They don't speak the same damned language!" Uncomfortably aware that they created a scene the entire countryside would talk about for weeks, Neville still couldn't control his fury. Or his terror. Mental images of her tumbling off that roof on her curly head paralyzed his mind.

Without giving a second thought to what he did, Neville scooped up his obstreperous wife before she could unleash another diatribe, and flung her into his saddle. He was up beside her before she could climb back down.

"What the divil do ye think ye're doin'?"

"Taking my wife home where she belongs," he said calmly, although he felt far from calm. Terror gave way to scents of lilac, the brush of soft curves, and the teasing of a headful of auburn curls against his chin. Behind him, he heard a male cheer of approval as he kicked his horse into motion. He'd never sought the approval of his tenants before, but triumph surged now.

"You're behavin' like a blitherin' idiot, your worship! Put me down. I've left my horse back there."

Neville adjusted her more comfortably against his thighs, glad that Anglesey wasn't far. A nice wide bed would be more suitable than a saddle.

"I'll send someone to fetch the horse. If I'd known how you'd abuse your freedom, I'd never have given you a horse."

"Abuse! And how am I after abusing anything by seeing your people with decent roofs over their heads, I ask you? I've done naught more than any decent-minded landlord would do. Put me down at once, Neville! I'll not be hauled around like a bit of baggage."

Neville reined his horse to a halt at the bottom of the graceful stone staircase to Anglesey's main entrance. Throwing the reins to a groom, he dismounted and hauled Fiona down before she could do it herself. Giving orders for the retrieval of her horse, he carried his wife, protesting every step of the way, up the stairs. The door opened silently without need of his knock, he noted with relief.

His relief only lasted long enough for him to discover no fire warmed his bedchamber. "It's freezing in here!" he shouted, irate at the shattering of still another homecoming illusion. "What happened to the damned fires?"

Almost humbly, Fiona pointed to the connecting chamber. "There's usually a small one in there. If you'd warned me you were coming, the others would have been lit also. I've just been saving on fuel."

Neville gave her woebegone expression a look of disbelief and proceeded into the next room, still refusing to put her down until he achieved his objective.

Someone had apparently hurried in here and stirred the grate. Flames danced merrily, releasing a cozy warmth.

Fine then, her room it would be. Neville abruptly dropped Fiona in the center of her bed. Before she could dash off the other side, he fell on top of her, neatly trapping her beneath him.

"What...what are you doing?" Wide-eyed, Fiona stared up at him as if he'd well and truly gone mad.

Maybe he had. But he'd never felt so completely in charge of his life as he did now, with his wife firmly caught under him and the sturdy walls of Anglesey shutting out all else.

"I'm working on our herd of heirs, my dear," he informed her, before pinning her shoulders to the bed and drowning her protests in his kiss.

# Twenty-nine

Happiness and fear warred within Fiona's breast as Neville crushed her into the bed and covered her mouth with his.

She'd missed his kisses, missed finding his arms around her in the middle of the night, even missed the challenge of arguing with him every waking minute. She'd simply been filling up the days, waiting for his return. Silly, foolish thing to do, thinking like an abandoned wife.

Remembering their wedding night, she relaxed and enjoyed the confrontation. Neville had a temper as strong as her own. He'd just learned to curb it better. Apparently, he didn't see the need to curb it with her. She thought that might be a good thing. Indifference from Neville would be truly terrifying.

His hands no longer pinned her shoulders but tore at her bodice. Near breathless from his kisses, Fiona struggled to return the favor, ripping at his waistcoat and cravat. But he was faster and she had fewer fastenings. She gasped as his cold fingers warmed around her bare breast.

"This is where I want you," he murmured, nuzzling at her lips and the line of her jaw as his fingers wreaked havoc with sensitive nipples.

He drove her insane. She wanted him inside her, wanted to tear him apart as he did her, wanted a thousand things all at once. She didn't want to be told her only place was in the bed, however.

"I'll not be your whore!" Fiona protested before Neville shut her up with the clever play of his tongue. The practiced skill of his palms as they slid over her breasts drove her into a frenzy. She tore at his clothing, wanting him to know it was her and not just any female.

"My wife," he asserted firmly, neatly avoiding her hands by bending to suckle at her breasts.

It had been too long since she'd felt his mouth there, and Fiona cried out with the joy of that welcome touch. To hell with this senseless argument. In this, they wanted the same thing.

She helped him pull the gown and chemise over her head. He shucked his coat and waistcoat with ease, but lost patience as she tackled the knotted ties of his shirt. He pressed her breasts together so he could pleasure himself there. Then he cupped her buttocks so he could lift her for more intimate kisses. He'd taught her these things once, but she'd forgotten the lesson. His touch between her legs rendered her mindless.

He used his tongue to drive her almost to the pinnacle and drew back, teasing her. He didn't move fast enough. Brashly, Fiona attacked the buttons of his trousers and triumph surged at his shout of freedom.

Swiftly, he rolled over and pulled her on top of him. Startled, Fiona gazed down into silvered eyes, heavy-lidded with desire. Golden brown hair fell over Neville's noble brow and the bristles of his beard shadowed his jaw. He still wore his lace-edged shirt, although it lay half open, revealing the brown hairs curling against his muscled chest. Desire heated her blood, but the look in his eyes shot straight to her heart. "Love me," he commanded.

Foolish man, to think he could command such a thing as love. But she wasn't at all certain that he knew what he was saying. Perhaps this was what he thought love was—a passionate tumble between the covers. If so, she would provide it for him. Fiona realized she needed his happiness to complete her own.

"Show me," she whispered.

He obliged, lifting her to accommodate him. He still wore his muddy boots and trousers. She was as naked as the day she was born. Wild abandon swept her as she thrilled to the power of her new position. Joy bubbled out as laughter as he surged upward and into her.

She couldn't thrust fast enough for him. He rolled her onto her back and took charge again, plunging deeper and more powerfully with each stroke until Fiona lost all consciousness of everything but the deep driving need for completion.

It erupted in a burst of wildfire and molten lava, consuming them so swiftly, Fiona could scarcely catch her breath. They quaked together, perspiration oiling their flesh in all the places where they rubbed. The musk of their mating perfumed the air around them.

And Fiona realized how much this had become a part of her life. She didn't want him to leave again.

That thought scared her even more than Neville's temper. As their over-heated bodies cooled, he pulled the covers around her, and sat up to remove his boots. As they did so often, they said nothing, although the air between them thickened with unspoken words. Somehow, they must learn to speak of these things, Fiona thought as Neville lay down beside her, bootless, and pulled her into his arms. Terrified that this might be all they had between them, she couldn't bear to disturb the beauty of it with words.

So she snuggled against his shoulder and slept, leaving all the words for another day.

~

"I'm sorry, Neville, but the man is a stiff-rumped snob of the worst degree, and I'll not have him dictate to me or mine. I swear, I shall sell your family jewels and fund a cathedral before I'll set foot in that man's church again. For all I know, I've given up my eternal soul for you, but I'll be damned if I suffer the torments of hell before I must."

Neville tried to keep his lips from twitching at the fiery tirade as his petite wife paced up and down the carpet of his study for all the world as if she were as large and strong as Effingham. He could span her waist with his hands, throw her over his shoulder with no more effort than a sack of grain, but her attitude was twice as large as her puny size. Or her current size, anyway. He grinned inwardly at that amendment.

"The jewels are entailed. We can't sell them," he informed her, knowing perfectly well that his composure only drove Fiona to greater heights of fury. He sat back and sipped his brandy in the firelight and watched her go up in flames.

"Then I'll bloody well pawn them!" she shouted, flinging her hands in the air, and dislodging her auburn curls until several tumbled over her shoulders. "I'll not set foot in that hypocrite's church, Neville. I won't!" She stamped her foot for emphasis.

"All right, don't." He kept as straight a face as he could muster beneath her disbelieving stare. "His living comes from Anglesey, though. Would you deprive the entire village of his services?"

"I would," she grumbled mutinously, crossing her arms over her chest. "I'd not put a farthing in that pinch-penny's cup. The village can attend chapel here, with us. If I can endure that Methodist sermonizing, so can they."

Neville sincerely hoped the new Methodist preacher had sense enough to avoid topics that raised his duchess wife's ire, but knowing the breed, he expected further rebellion in the ranks. Perhaps it was time to teach Fiona the responsibilities of so much power. She had certainly grasped its uses quickly enough.

"Ravensworth has a family, a poor brow-beaten wife who has favored him with five lovely daughters. They're all well-behaved, unspoiled chits who go behind his back to help those in need. Would you put them out of the only home they know just because you disagree with their father's stiff-necked prejudices?"

Fiona's mouth opened, but nothing emerged. With some practice, Neville thought he might become good at this. He did have a few more years of experience than she.

Before she could find an adequate reply, Neville continued without a trace of admonishment. "I think we can adequately fund your Methodist as well as the vicarage, since the chapel is already here and needs regular maintenance whether used or not. But you must realize that once this new man comes to rely on Anglesey income, he'll start planning a life of his own—a wife, children, a house of some sort. Should you decide you dislike his teachings, you will face the same difficulty dislodging him as we face with the vicar now. The power we wield over peoples' lives is a dangerous thing, Fiona."

She stared at him, wide-eyed, as she absorbed this lesson. Neville had no doubt she would have learned it sooner or later on her own. He gave her credit for an intelligence equal to his. He just didn't want her learning the hard way.

"I've been playing duchess, haven't I?" she asked, huddling within herself as she stood in front of the fire.

Satisfied he'd made his point, Neville set his glass down and crossed the room to stand before her. "No, you are playing the part of Fiona, savior of the world, as always. You were born to be a duchess. I could not have chosen better had I searched the heavens."

A tear winked briefly in her eye as she turned toward him. "I'm not born to the silver, your honor. You've seen that for yourself. I can't not help with the thatching, or interfering with the vicar or the steward or any of those other things I've done. It's not in me to be idle."

"You will learn soon enough that the more power you assume, the more work you must do. At some point, you'll have to delegate some of your authority to others and hope for the best."

He cupped her face in his palm. He was so full of joy at this minute, he thought he might burst. Joy, and pride, he admitted, without conceit. He'd had so little of those things in his life, he savored them now. Had he a choice, he would shut out London and Parliament and all his worldly duties, and remain here, basking in the contentment of home and family. He hadn't thought such emotion possible, not for him. Fiona had taught him otherwise.

He kissed her, and her response told him the time was ripe. He wanted to share this new found joy. Gently, he stroked her sides, cupping the fullness of her breasts, spanning her waist with his hands. Was it his imagination, or was there a gap between his fingers that hadn't been there before?

Smiling at the thought, Neville lifted his head and watched the shadows flit across Fiona's lovely face. "Your list of responsibilities already grows greater, does it not? In a few months time, you will be supervising a nursery. I understand that is a considerable task."

Fiona's breath caught in her throat as she stared into Neville's sparkling eyes. She had never seen such pure joy there, not even when they made love. She could scarcely conceal the leap of hope in her heart. "How did you know?" she asked, searching his face for clues. "I'd thought I'd wait until I was further along to tell you, so you needn't worry more than you must."

She thought his smile the most beautiful she'd ever seen. She loved the way Neville's upper lip curved, and the way his lower lip beckoned to be kissed. Daringly, she rested her palms against his waistcoat and admired this awesome duke, her husband.

"Did you think I did not memorize every inch of your lovely body, my Fiona? How your breast weighs just so in my hand?" He cupped her through the wool of her gown. "How your waist fits the span of my hands?" He measured her there again, as he had before. "Did you think I'd not notice my thumbs no longer meet and that your breast weighs heavier?"

His expressive eyebrows raised, revealing the glint of humor in his eyes. She loved his dry humor. She ought to smack him for hinting she had grown fat. But she was proud of that extra inch of waistline.

"What will you do when I grow so big and round your arms cannot encompass me?"

"I'll hug you from behind," he whispered in her ear as he showed her how well she still fit within his embrace.

"What if it's a girl I carry and not your precious heir?" she asked defiantly, biting her lip to hide her fear.

"I will be overjoyed that we must take another wedding journey and try again." He chuckled when she pinched him through his waistcoat. He captured her hands, pulling them behind her. "Let us not get out of practice while we wait to see what it will be. You will not deny me now that you've done your duty?"

As if she could, Fiona thought wildly as Neville's mouth descended on hers. That was the last coherent thought she had before the very proper, very staid Duke of Anglesey laid her on the carpet before the fire and had his way with her.

~

"Durham, you're a sapskull! You've accomplished absolutely nothing except cementing the relationship between that unholy triumvirate more thoroughly than ever. Effingham is laughing in our faces and Aberdare threatens to cut off the ears of the next person who defames his cousin. The duke doesn't need to say a word," Townsend shouted at the man standing in front of his desk.

Slump-shouldered, Durham brushed at his receding black hair and toyed with his threatened ears. "I had Aberdare's people up in arms and ready to burn the castle, but the earl interfered with his lies. Then McGonigle reneged on his promises, all because of the duke and that damned female. Who would have thought the duke would fall for that pestilent chit? I never gave her a thought."

"You were supposed to keep Aberdare and the duke in *Ireland* and out of London entirely. Instead, you got some poor peasant robbed and killed and set all Effingham's spies after us. It's time you started earning your way around here."

Durham tugged nervously at his ear. "Burke's death was an accident. I keep telling you, nobody was supposed to get hurt."

"Right. You loose a band of ruffians to burn a castle and think no one will get hurt? Don't be a lobcock, Durham. People get hurt all the time. Power goes to the strongest, and the weak get hurt. That's how the world operates. I swear, if you weren't my son-in- law, I'd..."

Durham straightened his shoulders and tugged at his tweed coat. "I can do it, sir. I can have all three of them out of London before the bill comes to a vote. You just need to raise the majority, and the cabinet post is yours, sir."

The older man behind the desk looked vaguely placated. "See that you do, Durham. I'm not rich as Croesus and my daughter's portion dwindles with every minute we waste here."

Holding his shoulders rigid and his paunchy stomach in, Durham nodded briskly. "Right you are, sir. I'll take care of the matter."

He marched out, not seeing the balding, bespectacled clerk holding the door for him.

The clerk's worried frown would have given him away had anyone looked, but men of wealth and power never noticed ten-shilling-a-year clerks.

# Thirty

"Must you go so soon?" Fiona asked as Neville shrugged into his caped greatcoat.

Surely a warm fire would be much more pleasant than a ride to London in the wintry gloom. Shouldn't dukes have the right to do as they pleased? She didn't ask the question aloud. She already knew her noble husband's response.

"I've already lost all my work on the Emancipation Bill while I dallied with you in Ireland, Fiona. I cannot afford to let the crime reform bill die, too." With his usual gruff impatience, Neville fastened his coat and jerked on his gloves. "The lives of too many people are at stake."

"I cannot believe a wee bit of paper will save them," Fiona replied bitterly. "The bloody English never let bits of paper stop them before. They'll just find new and more infernal ways of disposing of those who annoy them."

Neville brushed a kiss across her forehead. "I've already explained the importance of this bill and I'll not argue, my love. There's no time. Write me a nasty flaming letter excoriating the entire government if you will, but if I'm to reach London by dark, I must set off now."

"You're taking riders with you this time?" she demanded.

"I can't afford to waste coins on nannies to watch over me. This isn't Ireland. The roads are well-traveled. I blend in with the crowd. Now, will you promise me you'll try to behave while I'm gone?"

"I'm not a child, Neville," she replied peevishly. "I'll not execute any vicars or import the Pope, if that's what you mean."

"Well, the Pope's blessing might help, but his presence definitely would not. Take care of yourself. No more roof thatching."

With that last admonition, he swept out the side entrance to the horse waiting under the portico. Fiona watched him go with a wretchedness she could not endure. She had tried pretending that he was the irritating arrogant duke she once thought him, but she knew better. He'd ignored her barbs, calmly brushed aside her arguments, and though he spoke as if annoyed by their dallying in Ireland, he kissed her as if she were the trusted and beloved wife she wanted to be. She knew she wasn't any such timid creature, and he'd discover it soon enough.

Through the rain splattered windows, she watched Neville's proud, upright form ride past the gate. The emptiness in her heart echoed as loud as the mansion's cavernous banquet room. It was a terrible, dismaying feeling, knowing that Neville took a part of her soul with him when he left.

Perhaps it was the child, Fiona thought as she turned away from the window. She wasn't particularly frightened of the natural occurrences of pregnancy and childbirth. But perhaps that state required the extra reassurance of a husband's presence. If so, how had poor Aileen endured it?

If that poor woman could manage seven pregnancies without a husband in sight, then surely a duchess could manage while surrounded with wealth and comfort. Cursing herself for her weakness, Fiona sought refuge in the study with the estate books. If she couldn't thatch roofs, what could she do to occupy the empty hours?

She stared at pounds and shilling columns and doodled on a scrap of paper, but she couldn't concentrate. Her mind drifted to Neville's look of joy when he'd declared her pregnant. *He'd* announced it, the arrogant monster, but she couldn't resent it for a minute. She'd never seen him so happy. It kind of ached inside her knowing she could produce that response. Usually, she provoked the opposite of happiness. She'd certainly been shouted at and cursed enough to know people's opinions of her.

But Neville hadn't yelled—once he recovered from the scare of seeing her on the roof. He'd not even complained of the changes she'd made. In fact, once he'd come down off his high horse, he had actually approved the improvements.

Fiona smiled at the memory of Neville's terror when he'd seen her on the roof. Maybe he did care for her, just a little. He hadn't known of the baby then. It was *her* well being that had concerned him. Or maybe he'd thought it beneath his dignity to lose a wife to roof thatching.

Grimacing, Fiona chewed her quill and contemplated her neat rows of numbers again. She hadn't had enough time to make a difference. Surely she could find more ways to check the extravagance of...

A knock at the door distracted her. Heaven only knew, she was ready for any distraction. Calling, "Come in," she crumpled her scrap of paper and looked up expectantly.

Both the Widow Blackthorn and Colin stood in the doorway. The widow had made a surprisingly good ladies' maid these last weeks. Fiona had come to rely on her good sense and Irish brogue to ease her homesickness. She had seen little enough of Colin, but he'd mentioned bringing his wife and new babe to stay now that he had a house. She'd thought maybe he'd matured somewhat these last months. Michael was a good judge of character.

Their worried expressions roiled her stomach. The babe had never caused a minute's unease, so she couldn't blame her sudden nausea on anything but fear.

"What is it?" she demanded. When they did not enter, Fiona scowled. "Come in. Close the door. Sit. Must I order everyone these days?"

"You've done a fine enough job of that all these years," Colin remarked with a hint of sarcasm as he partially obeyed her commands. He didn't sit but closed the door as they entered. "Why stop now?"

"Cut the blarney, Colin. The two of you haven't come here together to announce you're running away to the Americas and getting out of my hair. So what is it?"

The widow squeezed Colin's arm to restrain him. "She's upset because the duke's gone and left her behind again. Mind your manners. We've more important things to do than quarrel."

Colin rubbed his handsome head of curls and visibly struggled with his temper. "Your pardon, Your Grace," he responded bitterly. "It's a little difficult seeing the babe you grew up with wielding her wealth and power like a princess, but it's what Fiona has always done, I suppose, just with less of the ready."

Fiona grimaced. "Go away with ye and your flattery, Colin." Pointedly, she turned her attention to Mrs. Blackthorn. "What is it, Mrs. B.? Is there some news I should hear?" She couldn't adopt the arrogance of calling her maid by her given name as a duchess would. The widow deserved the same respect she'd received before Fiona had come into her title.

"There is, child," the widow replied sadly, "though we're neither of us sure it's our place to tell ye. But the news came after His Grace had left, and we thought someone needed to hear it. I don't know that there's aught to be done now, though."

Fiona pressed her fingernails into her palms and tried to restrain her impatience. "What news? Spit it out quickly."

"McGonigle sent one of his men," Colin interrupted. "He says he's not to blame, it's some other faction. They've destroyed the looms, lass. Not only that, the army came in and arrested everyone in sight. They took the boy, Fiona. They've locked him away in Dublin gaol, accused of theft. McGonigle swears Sean didn't do it, but it's his word against an officer in the damned army. He'll hang, Fiona. That's what the damned redcoats do to thieves, regardless of age."

Fiona blanched. Not Sean. Aileen's orphan was as honest and hard-working as any man she knew. And with McGonigle to provide, he'd no need of stealing. And the looms! They'd cost a bloody fortune. Neville had used her dowry and bought the best he could afford. There hadn't been time to earn even the smallest profit to replace them. Who would do such a thing?

She was on her feet and aiming for the door before she gave it any thought. "Have the carriage readied. Send a rider ahead to prepare the yacht. Pack us some warm clothes, Mrs. B. You'd best go with me. Colin, will you ride with the driver?"

"What about the duke, Fiona? Should you not notify him first?" Colin asked anxiously, following in her wake.

She hesitated, considering the idea. "He needs to know where I'm going, but he's terribly busy. Let's not drag him away unless we cannot do this ourselves."

"You *cannot* do this yourself!" Colin argued. "We need your husband and the earl!"

"A body would think you're with the Tories who want the duke drawn from the crime bill." She cut off his argument with disdain. "Should I think this all a sham to draw the duke away from London—again—when he's most needed? I can handle it." Arrogantly, she swept up the stairs, head high, though her heart pounded with terror. Neville would kill her for this, of a certainty. Yet he should have known what kind of woman he married. Parliament was his burden to bear. The tenants were hers.

It was far more important that Neville pass the bill that would save boys like Sean from being hung than to argue with a band of drunken louts. She'd send him a note so he knew she had not run away. Once she assessed the situation, she could let him know if they needed to bribe some official to free Sean.

There was naught either of them could do about the looms.

Her growing sense of unease did not fade as the carriage rolled down the drive with the Widow Blackthorn and Colin as her servants.

The Prime Minister pushed back the winged chair in front of Neville's desk and scrubbed his hand over the gray pallor of his face. "I don't like it, Neville. You know demmed well I don't. But if this is what the country wants, I'll have to accept it. I'll admit, transporting the beggars has a certain appeal, but how long can we afford that?"

"The times are changing, sir," Neville said, tapping his finger on the documents he'd presented. "Someone must face the facts, and you're the man to do it. I don't know how you'll convince His Majesty. He's as set in his ways as his father ever was. But we're not a nation of rural villages anymore. We must look to the future."

The PM glared at him. "It's not done yet, you young pup. I can't believe you and your radical friends can sway all those old squires to anything. I'm just saying, *if* you do, I'll consider your case." His expression grew thoughtful. "We need strong leaders, Your Grace. Much as I hate admitting it, we've buried our heads too long, pretending nothing will change. But you have to win first, my boy. Otherwise, I'll never have the support to give you the position."

As Liverpool departed, Neville consulted his pocket watch and breathed a sigh of relief. He had a few minutes before the session began. Fiona had never sent him a letter before, and he'd saved the note until he'd had time to savor it. He wondered if it would contain flames and vitriol.

It amazed him that he could actually look forward to opening a letter full of Fiona's angry diatribes. That blow to his head had definitely addled his brains. But Fiona's temper usually dissipated as quickly as it appeared, leaving ephemerally lovely joy in its wake. He couldn't describe the feeling any better than that. He just knew he felt it when he woke in the morning to find her tousled curls on his shoulder, her sleeping features peaceful as a child's. Or when she came into his arms all hot kisses and explosive passion.

Neville pried off the wax and unfolded the note. He'd seen Fiona's heavy, slanting scrawls in the estate books and recognized it now. Her penmanship reflected her personality: strong, blunt, and slightly quirky. He grinned at the thought. He stopped grinning as he read her words.

Ireland!

He slammed his fist against the desk, flung the paper down, and stalked to the filthy window of his office. *Ireland.* She'd said nothing of being homesick when he'd left. She'd talked only of the improvements she'd wished to make at Anglesey. He'd thought she'd safely transferred her loyalty from Michael's estate to his, as a loyal wife should do.

She could have come to London if she was lonely. He would welcome the distraction of her presence right now. The pressure of passing this bill and what it would mean should he succeed weighed heavy on his shoulders. He needed her sensible outlook.

He didn't need to know she was taking a reckless journey to Ireland in uncertain winter weather. Anything could happen. Who had she taken with her? Anyone?

He grabbed up the letter again and re-read it. She didn't say, damn her.

"My cousin, the grasshopper, has struck again, has she?" a voice asked lazily from the doorway.

Neville glared at the intruder. "Does she never stay in one place?"

Aberdare strolled in rolling several wooden balls between his fingers. "Not within my memory. She didn't happen to say she was returning to Ireland, did she?"

The earl tossed the balls between his hands as if he hadn't a care in the world, but Neville knew him better. Fear shivered down his spine as he laid the letter down and examined his friend's bland expression. "What is happening at Aberdare?"

For a moment, Neville thought the earl wouldn't tell him. He contemplated various tortures designed to drag the truth from him before Michael reluctantly responded.

"Eamon reports someone has destroyed the looms. The army came in without invitation and left the usual destruction in its wake." He hesitated a moment longer. "And they arrested the boy, Fiona's protégé, the one McGonigle adopted."

"Sean." Neville sank to his seat in disbelief. "They had no right arresting that boy. He wouldn't harm a fly. We'll have to look into the matter." As the knowledge seeped in, he shook his head. "Fiona will have all their heads. She'll go after them with swords and set the whole countryside on fire. We need to go after her."

Michael dropped the balls into the capacious pocket of his outmoded coat and leaned over the desk. "Which is why she didn't tell us. She knows we can't leave now. We have to pass the reform bill. Your position in the cabinet is riding on it. If we lose, Townsend will have that position. Fiona is accustomed to taking on problems without help."

Neville clenched and unclenched his fists. "I know. But I can't let Fiona go out there alone. I can't." He tightened his jaw and glared at his cousin-in-law. "She's carrying my child."

With a nod of approval, Michael stepped back. "I'd hoped you were man enough to say that. I'll find Gavin. We'll monitor our resources and see what's to be done."

Neville watched Michael walk away. He had a sinking feeling that he was becoming as arbitrary and whimsical as the notorious earl. And he didn't care.

For the first time in his life, he had someone to worry about besides the invisible masses who had held his attention all these long, lonely years.

What he intended to do was not morally correct. The country was more important than one impetuous female. But he couldn't help himself.

Even though—or perhaps because—one small unpredictable female thought to save him this moral dilemma, she had become more important to him than all his high-minded ideals.

# Thirty-one

She had gone off half-cocked again.

As the Anglesey carriage raced through mud puddles, splashing its shiny paint so badly the crest couldn't be seen, Fiona stared miserably out the splattered windows and wished she hadn't been quite so impetuous.

She desperately needed Neville's confidence right now, if only his approval of what she was doing.

That's what bothered her most. She should have told him everything, and together, they should have decided on a course of action. She'd been acting as her former self and not the wife with responsibilities that she was now. There was time to fix that.

As the carriage pulled into an inn yard for fresh horses, she comforted herself with knowing that after she explained everything, Neville would admit that she could do this one small thing without his aid. Perhaps she needn't travel at all. She simply needed his advice on what a duchess could do.

No one opened the carriage door after it stopped, but Colin wasn't a trained footman and he'd substituted McGonigle's messenger for the regular driver. She'd lay wager the substitute knew nothing of the niceties either. Fiona gazed down at the ocean of mud in dismay. Ugh.

She glanced around for help. Colin and the driver conversed with the stable groom as they unharnessed the horses. She could yell like a fishwife or wade through the muck. If she'd been wearing her rags, she'd have simply waded. But now she was a duchess wearing skirts and petticoats. So as a duchess, she could damned well do whatever she wanted. She yelled.

Colin's head jerked up, and she could see his frown through the sleeting rain. He shook his head and returned to what he was doing.

From behind her, Mrs. Blackthorn shifted nervously in the seat. "What is it, Your Grace? Is there trouble?"

Fiona flopped back on the seat and glared at the rain. "I need to send Neville another note and wait for his reply."

"If you let him know that you're in good hands and he's not to trouble himself, isn't that enough?"

That sounded eminently sensible on the face of it—had Neville been the stolid, care-for nothing type who would nod and yawn and go back to his port. Fiona had tried to paint him into that corner once, but she knew better now.

"That's not enough." With determination, Fiona kicked open the outside latch. Lifting her heavy traveling skirt and petticoat, she lowered her booted foot into the muck of the yard.

Colin looked up with alarm as she approached. "What the divil are ye doin' out of the carriage, lass? You'll catch your death out here."

The rain was turning to an icy sleet that bounced off her cloak and froze to her gloves. They'd be fortunate to reach the coast by nightfall. Instinct was right. There had to be a better way. "I want to turn around."

Colin frowned but nodded. "If ye're sure, lass. This is bloody awful weather, I'll agree. But we'll not make another start if you change your mind again. It's like to turn to snow before long."

Fiona hesitated. They could be snowed in and never reach Sean. But maybe Michael and Neville could send someone by ship from the Thames. That would probably be much faster and safer.

"I'm certain. Harness the horses and let's go home."

They were already backing fresh animals into the traces. Fiona looked them over with approval, cursed her mud-coated boots, and climbed back into the carriage. Slamming the door against the blowing sheets of ice and water, she almost felt warm again.

Mrs. Blackthorn watched her anxiously. "Will they turn about then?"

"We'll never make it in this weather anyway. Neville and the earl can send someone from London. I'll have to learn that money paves an easier road, I suppose."

Mrs. B. relaxed against the squabs. "We've not any of us had much experience with the power of dukes. You'll learn. That husband of yours means well."

Fiona nodded in silent agreement. The carriage rolled away from the inn yard a few minutes later. It was strange having someone she could rely on after all these years of doing everything herself. She still wanted to leap in and fix it, but she'd learn better ways.

It took a few minutes before she realized their direction did not seem to be what it ought. She hadn't paid attention when they pulled out of the yard, but she distinctly remembered a charming old church set back from the road as they'd entered the village. Mrs. B. had pointed it out to her since it had been on the widow's side then. It should be on Fiona's side now. Only open countryside sprawled across the view from her window. Had she missed it?

Frowning, she concentrated on orienting herself. She had quite a good sense of direction, fortunately for some of her childish escapades.

The sun, or what there was of it, would be directly overhead at this time of day, so it wasn't of any use even if she could see it through the clouds. The view from the window looked unfamiliar.

"Change seats with me," she ordered.

Mrs. Blackthorn looked surprised but obligingly shifted to the forward seat while Fiona slid across the squabs. The view still looked unfamiliar. Not bothering to puzzle over it longer, she knocked on the trap door behind the driver's seat.

No one responded.

Remaining where she was, Mrs. B. looked worried. "What is it, Your Grace?"

"Nothing, probably. I just wish to speak with Colin, but he's ignoring me." Leaning over her maid, she unfastened the latch of the door and looked out. She could see only McGonigle's man whipping the horses faster. Where was Colin?

"Driver!" she shouted against the bitter wind rushing through the door. He didn't answer.

Damn the contrary, disobedient Irish. Why in the name of all that was holy had she allowed one of McGonigle's rebels to accompany them? They should have left the spalpeen to find his own way home.

Finding the umbrella Mrs. B. had insisted she carry, Fiona poked it through the trap door at the driver's back. "Halt the damned carriage!" she shouted in her most authoritative voice. She'd drive the thing herself if necessary. She still wasn't certain of their direction, and the idea of Neville out in this weather scouring the countryside for her did not sit well on her conscience.

Someone leaned over, grabbed the umbrella, and flung it into the road.

Damn, but she was in trouble now.


"The bill will come to a vote at the first of next week," Effingham reminded them, pacing the narrow confines of Neville's office. "We cannot all chase after your errant wife, Your Grace." He used the title with sarcasm.

"I'll go after her," Neville said. "Your job is to get the bill passed without my vote."

"If you're not here to lead the opposition, you'll lose that position in the cabinet," Effingham warned. "There's no guarantee Townsend will get it, but you're risking a great deal."

"I risk even more if I don't follow Fiona," Neville answered, staring out the rain-streaked windows but seeing nothing. "I realize she's capable of taking care of herself, but the roads aren't safe, and she has a tendency to look after others before herself."

"We'll take care of things here," Michael assured him.

Neville couldn't see what bit of nonsense the earl juggled now, and he really didn't care. He simply knew if he had the earl's word that he'd take care of business, he could count on it. "Then I'd best be off. She's been out on the road since morning and has a twelve hour lead over me. If I ride all night, I might find her by tomorrow. We may be worrying for naught."

"Umm, gentlemen?" All three of them swung at the feminine voice interruption from the doorway.

Neville swore beneath his breath as he recognized Lady Gwyneth. Today, she wore a dowdy brown gown that draped her statuesque figure like a toga. He'd once considered marriage to this woman, but he thought it more likely he considered marriage to her wealth and golden hair. It paled in comparison to Fiona's fiery tresses and nature, however. Fiona was flame compared to Gwyneth's cold gold.

"My lady, may we help you?" he asked as gently as he could under the circumstances. Despite her size, Gwyneth always gave the impression that she would flit from sight like a butterfly if accosted too abruptly.

"I think there's something you should know." She glanced nervously over her shoulder at the corridor.

Perceiving her anxiety, Neville crossed the room, urged her inside, and checked the hallway. Gwyneth's abigail glanced at him from a safe distance near a corner intersection of the corridors, but there was no other to see her entering these all male chambers.

He closed the door and urged her into a chair. "Something quite extraordinary must have brought you here, my lady. You've met Effingham and Aberdare?"

She nodded without looking at either of the two gentlemen. "It's about Her Grace. And you. And the crime bill," she said hurriedly, as if trying to speak all the words before they froze inside her.

"All right. Take it slowly and tell us what you know." Despite an instinctive shiver of fear, Neville rested against the edge of his desk, trying not to look threatening.

"It's Townsend," she whispered, "and Durham. They're conspiring against you."

Effingham snorted rudely. "Tell us something we don't know."

She darted him a sharp look. "Durham is responsible for the near riot in Aberdare and is apparently in some way responsible for the murder of a man named Burke."

That brought both Effingham and Aberdare to their feet, Neville noted. He'd known Gwyneth had intelligence. He just hadn't realized what sort of intelligence. "Durham. That's Townsend's son-in-law. He's an incompetent idiot. How could he accomplish anything?"

Gwyneth returned to staring at the floor. "I don't know, precisely. He owns an estate in Ireland, though. And he's been assigned the task of keeping the three of you out of London until the reform bill dies."

The earl relaxed against the wall again. "And how are you aware of this, my lady?" he asked in the quiet voice he often used to reassure young children.

"I have..." She hesitated, glancing at Neville, then back to the floor again. "I would not confess all, gentlemen. Just let me say that my plans have not fully coincided with yours in the past, but in this case, I can see you may be right, and I could possibly be wrong. If the reform bill can be passed by normal means, then I would see it done so. But I fear Townsend will win unless I tell you all I know."

Effingham took the chair behind Neville's desk and began scribbling across a sheet of parchment. "Our Lady Gwyneth entertains radicals under cover of her afternoon gatherings. I thought to amuse you some day with that knowledge, Neville, but you made the tidbit moot when you married Fiona. Go on, Lady Gwyneth. My spy network seems to have failed me where yours has succeeded. How does Townsend mean to get us out of town, as if we haven't already guessed?"

Neville watched surprise raise the lady's eyebrows. *Radicals.* The shy, unforthcoming Lady Gwyneth entertained a nest of radicals. He would have thought it of Fiona before Gwyneth. Gad, he was an idiot.

"Your word goes no farther than this room, my lady," Neville reassured her. "We've already heard there's been an uprising at Aberdare. My wife is on her way there now. Anything you can add would be of great service to me and to the country."

Gwyneth's eyes widened with alarm. "You must keep Fiona out of this! Townsend and Durham are capable of anything, including murder and kidnapping. They've done so before. They were responsible for your beating, Your Grace. I do not know who they hired to murder the poor man in Ireland, but they are quite without conscience in their belief that they act in the good of the country," she said bitterly. "Men rationalize so very well."

"And you do not when you follow your radical inclinations?" Michael asked without accusation. "That people should die for the greater good has been the cause of more grief than actual good throughout history."

Gwyneth darted him a troubled look but did not respond directly. "People die every day, but poor people die faster and in greater quantities." She glanced back to Neville. "I do not know what Durham has planned for you. I suspect he has caused unrest in Aberdare to draw you out. If Fiona has gone to Aberdare, I should think kidnapping would be the most obvious step to bring all three of you running. If a highwayman cracks your heads on the journey, none would be the wiser."

Effingham threw down his pen, sprinkled powder over his hastily scrawled note, and folded it. "Excellent, my lady. You have given us fair warning. I'm sending a note to my wife to take the children to the earl's townhouse and bar the doors. That should eliminate any other easy target. I should think it wise if you would sequester yourself somewhere safe for the nonce in case Townsend's people noted your presence here today. I'll have a footman accompany you home."

Surprised, she actually looked at the scarred marquess. "You believe me then? You do not think me an hysterical woman?"

Effingham stood up impatiently. "Of course we believe you. We all have wives who would knock us senseless if we did not."

Neville's lips quirked at the dry humor behind Effingham's reply. The marquess's diminutive wife would have to take a brickbat to reach his rock-hard head. But he spoke naught less than the truth, Neville realized with a modicum of pride. Fiona stood as brave and strong as either of the courageous wives his friends had taken. She was just a bit younger and more impetuous. A lot more impetuous.

And in a great deal of danger. He tried to hide his panic behind his usual stoic demeanor.

"What about Fiona?" Gwyneth demanded. "She is out there all alone."

"She is no doubt out there with her usual scoundrels and scalawags," Michael corrected. "I'll send word to my men to keep an eye out for her."

Gwyneth looked distinctly reluctant to leave but when silence followed Michael's commands, she rose. "Thank you for hearing me out and not reprimanding me too harshly. If there is anything I can do..."

"Keep yourself safe," Neville ordered curtly. "We have more than enough on our hands for now."

He clutched his hair in despair as the door closed behind her. "Now what do we do?"

"*You* don't do anything," his companions replied in tandem.

"Your leaving is exactly what Townsend wants," the marquess explained.

"Like bloody hell will I stay here." Neville stalked out, leaving the two damned conspirators to do their conspiring without him. He preferred a direct approach, like wringing Townsend's scrawny neck and asking questions later.

# Thirty-two

Fiona considered her problem as the carriage raced toward the coast. Sleet skittered across the muddy window pane as the overcast day descended into early evening gloom. She would prefer escaping while some daylight remained. The thought of walking these roads at night, in the freezing cold, caused grave trepidation. She had the child to think of as well as herself.

The longer she wavered in indecision, the further from the safety of Anglesey they traveled. She didn't hesitate when the first opportunity of escaping arrived.

A cow wandered into the lane from a village green. A dray stopped to let it pass, blocking the road to all other vehicles. Fiona heard her driver cursing the dray, the cow, and anything else within earshot. Inattentiveness was one result of fury, she mused as she quietly opened the door latch she'd already broken. With an audience to watch, what could he do to stop her?

She turned and glanced at the Widow Blackthorn. "Will you come with me?" Not trusting anyone, Fiona didn't care how her maid replied.

The woman looked anxious, but nodded. Taking a deep breath for courage, Fiona leapt from the high carriage step into the rutted, freezing mud of the lane.

The driver continued his cursing. Fiona didn't look back to see if the curses were meant for her or the cow. A lighted inn beckoned ahead. In the evening gloom, she stuck to the hedge shadows, scurrying past dray and cow and toward safety.

She glanced over her shoulder to see if Mrs. Blackthorn followed. The dray had moved on, and the carriage abruptly jerked into motion. The door she'd left open slammed closed from the force of its own weight, suggesting that the driver had indeed been shouting at the cow and hadn't seen her escape. In the twilight, Fiona could see nothing of her maid either. As the carriage rolled past, she realized she was alone.

She'd walked many a street alone in her life. She just rejoiced that she'd escaped that madman of a driver. She would worry over Colin and Mrs. Blackthorn once she was warm and had arranged transportation.

The farmer tugging his cow back to pasture gave her a look of curiosity as she stalked past, dragging her expensive traveling cloak through the mud, but curious stares had no effect on her either. The temper that had simmered quietly while she explored her plight now held full rein.

*Someone had tried to abduct her!* She would have them swung by the neck except she was too cold and too worried to figure out the details of catching them.

The inn she approached was obviously not a coaching inn. A neat picket fence closed off what would certainly be a garden of flowers in warmer months. The dead branches of Michaelmas daisies leaned over the green new growth of jonquils as she opened the gate and hurried down the cobbled path toward the front door. She scraped mud off her boots on the stone, and her cold toes sang hallelujahs.

A burst of warm air and light hit her as she entered, and she halted just inside, blinking as if she'd encountered sunshine. With the door closed against the cold and her enemies, Fiona rubbed her hands for warmth and wondered if she shouldn't wait there while she sent word to Neville.

A tall, large-boned woman hurried toward her, drying her palms on her crisp white apron. "It's a terrible day, isn't it?" she sang out agreeably, as if continuing a conversation with an old friend. "Would you be taking a room for the night?" She glanced eagerly over Fiona's shoulder, apparently looking for a companion.

Fiona hesitated. Once her kidnappers discovered her absence, they would return, if kidnappers they truly were. And if Mrs. Blackthorn were one of them, she could tell them precisely where Fiona had left the carriage. But the idea of traveling farther did not smack of safety either. She gazed uncertainly at her hostess.

"I don't suppose there is a carriage for hire, is there?" she inquired.

"A carriage?" In surprise, the woman dropped her apron and stared. "On a night like this? I should think not. No man in his senses would strike out now. It's almost dark."

Fiona bit her bottom lip. The inn tempted her with its warmth and coziness, but she could not think it safe. Still, she must trust in someone. "If I might have a private parlor and a bite of something hot to warm myself, I'll travel on then. But you must not tell anyone of my presence."

With obvious shock, the woman studied Fiona. Apparently reaching some conclusion, she nodded, almost dislodging her mobcap. "This way then, my lady. I'll stir the fire for you and bring hot cider directly."

She led Fiona to a small parlor, lit a lamp, and threw coal on the embers in the fireplace. With the door closed against the public hall outside, the landlady spoke more freely as she worked. "I do not inquire into the business of my patrons, my lady, but I cannot think it a good night to be about, and you a lady all alone."

Fiona sighed and sank into the chair near the fire, propping her boots on the andirons to toast her toes. "I cannot think it is either, but it seems safer than the alternative. There was a town not too far back, I believe. I could inquire about transportation there."

The innkeeper shot her a sharp look. "We have an excellent mutton pie this evening, my lady. Shall I fetch you some?"

Fiona nodded wearily. "Yes, please. Is it still sleeting?"

"That it is, and by way of being a blizzard, if you don't mind my saying so. No living creature will survive the night out there."

With resignation, Fiona realized she didn't have Neville's strength, and she had a child to protect. Swords and guns were not her weapons of choice. She must use her wits.

"May I trust you, Mrs...." her voice trailed off questioningly.

The woman nodded. "I'm Doreen White, not missus anything. My da owned this place until he died. I keep it now. I'll be happy to be of help, but I cannot recommend a body being out in this weather. The wind blows fair cold off those moors."

Fiona shivered at the thought. "I don't think I have much choice, Miss White. I have reason to believe I have just escaped an abduction, and the man responsible will return here once he learns of my escape. For all I know, he could be out there waiting for me now. I must reach my husband as soon as possible. It is extremely important."

She didn't mention her title or name. She didn't like throwing about her position as if it mattered whether she were queen or pawn. And she thought it might not be safe for this outspoken woman either.

Miss White drew a sharp breath and glanced at the shuttered windows as if thieves already stole their way through them. "The times are terrible indeed when a lady is not safe in her own home. I'll call for the boys, then, and we'll see what we can do."

Before Fiona could protest that "boys" were scarce sufficient against determined kidnappers, the woman hurried from the parlor with an admonishment for Fiona to lock the door behind her.

In no hurry to brave the icy wind, Fiona did as told for a change. Perhaps "the boys" would know of a carriage she could borrow to at least take her to the next town. What if her kidnappers had used her as a means of drawing Neville from the safety of London?

The thought gnawed at her as the minutes passed. They had nearly killed him once. She hadn't seen him after that episode, but she remembered how he'd looked stretched so pale and helpless after Sean's blow. What if he were lying in the fields beside the road now, knocked senseless once again by the blows of murderers?

She lost her taste for the pie that Miss White brought. Standing, she paced the room, rubbing her hands for warmth and to keep them occupied. She couldn't just sit there, warming her toes. She must leave. She must reach Neville. Urgency overwhelmed caution.

A sharp rap on the door jerked her back to the present. Her hostess's voice reassured her from behind the panels. "It's me, my lady. I've brought the boys."

Fiona unlocked the door and allowed her would-be protectors to enter. She couldn't send children out in this weather. Perhaps she could purchase some extra wraps for warmth. Perhaps a lantern would provide sufficient flame to warm her fingers occasionally. She would ask...

Fiona looked up at the newcomers. And looked up some more.

Two towering giants filled the space in front of her. Shoulders broad as oxen blocked out sight of the entire wall. She blinked and looked again. They did not diminish in size upon second look.

"Young John says as he'll get word to your husband, my lady, if that's all right with you."

Fiona searched between the two behemoths for some view of her landlady. Miss White stood directly behind them, but Fiona could only catch a glimpse of a white apron and mobcap as the two young men nodded earnestly.

"My horse isn't so fast as some," one of the pair explained, belatedly pulling off his cap. "But he's sound and sturdy and will carry me far."

"And I'm at your disposal, my lady," the other giant assured her. "I'll guard your door and see naught disturbs you."

The idea of this young giant waiting outside her door all night gave Fiona heart palpitations. Breathless, she tried to think quickly. Thinking did not come easily under the circumstances. She backed away and slipped into the chair near the fire.

"And your names are?" she inquired, postponing any immediate decision.

"Our manners are lacking, my lady. Please forgive us." Miss White hurried forward. "This here's my nephew, John, and the other is his brother, Luke. They're my sister's boys. They help their da on the farm, but in this weather, there's naught to do, so they help me around the place a bit. You can trust them, my lady."

Fiona looked up into two eager young faces, extended her trust, and prayed. "I'm the Duchess of Anglesey, and I must return to my husband at once."

She didn't acknowledge how good the last part of that sentence sounded. She'd never had anyone to turn to in times of trouble before, but she had a trustworthy hero on her side now.

The object of Fiona's thoughts wasn't in a state conducive to rationality. Having arrived at Anglesey in a raging blizzard to learn Fiona had taken only her Irish miscreants with her, Neville nearly had an apoplexy. His grooms, never having seen His Grace in a roaring temper, cowered in a stable corner, hoping the violent storm would pass without causing too much damage.

"She's my wife, you blockheads!" he roared. "She carries the heir to Anglesey and you let her out in weather like this with naught but fools for escort? Have you lost your bloody minds?"

"Beggin' your pardon, Your Grace," one of the older grooms replied hesitantly, "but Her Grace didn't say as to where she was goin'. She didn't pack no boxes. Ladies don't travel far without boxes," he added in a tone intended to soothe.

Neville clenched his fingers in his hair, remembering the single satchel Fiona had brought with her from Ireland. Other ladies might not travel without "boxes," but Fiona did. Blanche had provided her with a dowry of gowns suitable for a duchess. He would be fortunate to discover she wore even one of them and not her usual traveling clothes of boys' attire. Fiona could travel the earth with a single satchel.

"All right, then. Check the village, if you will, and saddle a fresh mount. I think I know her direction." Exhausted by his frantic journey from London, Neville didn't consider resting. By morning, the snow could cover the roads. He'd be as far on his way as possible.

"Willie and I will go with you then, Your Grace," the outspoken groom announced. "It's no night for you to be about either, sir."

At another time, Neville might have rejected the insult to his ability to take care of himself, but not tonight. If Townsend had arranged this misadventure, he might need the aid of his men to rescue Fiona. He prayed it wouldn't come to that.

The sleet had changed to a sloppy snow by the time the horses were saddled and the men provided with lanterns to canvas the village. Neville had little hope of their finding any trace of Fiona. He hoped the exercise would have his men thinking twice before allowing the brat out in a carriage without appropriate escort next time.

Wrapped in his greatcoat and his heaviest cloak and muffler, Neville wheeled his best stallion down the drive. The horse breathed plumes of steam into the freezing night air and champed at the bit, not the least intimidated by the weather. In a fit of desperation, Neville gave the animal its head. He needed the gallop as much as the horse did.

Away from the familiar environs of Anglesey, he slowed his mount to a canter. His grooms followed in the distance, and Neville checked his pocket for the pistol he carried there. He didn't expect thieves on a night like this, but he took no chances.

All his life, he'd watched the irrational passions of others with cynical amusement. Never, not in his wildest moments, had he ever considered falling victim to such emotional desperation that he rode his stallion through a raging snowstorm in pursuit of a hoyden with more courage than brains. Had he any sense at all, he'd sit in front of his fire and send messengers to his yacht rather than be out on a night like this, as any proper thinking gentleman would do. As he would have done, had Fiona been anyone but Fiona.

He refused to lose his wife. It was a matter of pride and possession. Or so he told himself as his horse slogged through the increasingly deeper drifts. The fury driving him now had more to do with Townsend and his tricks than with the fear and panic rising like bile in his throat.

The sight of two towering shadows on plow horses appearing through the blizzard of wet snow ahead startled Neville from his grim thoughts.

He reined in, blocking the road and waiting for his grooms to catch up. It was a sign of his growing insanity that he imagined Fiona behind the unexpected appearance of the twin giants. In any case, he couldn't miss the opportunity of questioning anyone arriving from the direction of the coast.

Through the sleeting snow, Neville discerned a smaller pony trailing in the wake of the giants, its small rider blocked from the wind by their greater forms. His heart lurched and his mouth grew dry as the trio proceeded cautiously, eyeing him warily as they did so.

A feminine cry of recognition and joy cut through the bitter cold air, and Neville closed his eyes in silent prayer. He opened them again with a roar of fury and kicked his stallion into a gallop as the pony broke free of its guardians and aimed toward him.

"I swear, I'll chain you to the walls and lock you in the tower if you ever pull this again, Fey-onah MacDermot Perceval!" he shouted into the wind as he caught her by the waist and hauled her up in front of him, where he could feel her safe and warm in his arms again.

Fortunately, his grooms rode up in time to prevent her stalwart bodyguards from attacking him with the stout cudgels they carried. With a shout for all the riders to desist, Neville wrapped his wife's slender form inside his cloak and held her as tightly against him as their clothes would allow.

The way she wrapped her arms around his waist and buried her face against his coat decimated all remaining anger. She'd run to him instead of the other way around. That knowledge warmed his veins all the way home.

# Thirty-three

"He's scarcely speaking to me," Fiona murmured as Blanche arranged a small white orchid in Fiona's hair.

Fiona fretted about Sean, she fretted about the looms and the village, but Neville's tight-lipped fury threatened her entire existence. She hated that. She needed his reassurance right now, while she played in cozy comfort and her friends suffered. And Neville plotted who knew what dangerous deed.

"You terrified him out of his wits," Blanche replied, admiring the result in the mirror. "He had the flowers sent out for you, didn't he? He never does that."

Fiona's reflection revealed dark circles of worry around muddy green eyes.

When she didn't acknowledge the explanation, Blanche smiled and patted her shoulder. "Neville isn't accustomed to being terrified. He prefers a well-ordered, uneventful existence. He's never known anything else. Has he told you anything of his family?"

Fiona shook her head, not seeing the flattering cut of her pale green gown in the mirror, recognizing only the anxiety gnawing at her.

"Neville's father was the youngest of my grandfather's three sons. He never had any hope of acquiring the title. From what little I can tell, his father was a narrow-minded, despicable little man whose one goal in life was to live like the duke he'd never be. Neville is an only child, and his father's nasty temper prevented his ever having much to do with the rest of us his family."

Fiona didn't meet Blanche's eyes in the mirror as she touched a drop of lilac water to her wrist. She didn't like invading Neville's privacy like this, but she didn't want to live in an armed camp either. She had seen his joy once. She would have it again if she could.

"Anyway, Neville's father taught him his parsimonious ways. They lived in a fashionable part of town because his father bought up the deed from a man who gambled and needed cash. They furnished it with trappings bought at bankruptcy auctions. Neville was taught from the day he was born that he must earn his own way in the world, that his wealthy grandfather would never provide for him. I suppose his mother must have shown him some affection when he was young, but she died of a stomach ailment while he was still in school. I doubt that he ever knew anything but his studies and his father's instructions after that."

Blanche glanced reflectively at the door leading to the glittering ballroom below. "I suppose his father was right. Our grandfather left all the wealth to me and a penniless entailment to Neville. He's never known a moment of childhood or pleasure, really. He inherited Anglesey while he was still at Oxford and has carried the burden well. I've seldom heard him complain. I've done what I could, but his pride won't allow more."

Fiona's heart ached at the tale. She'd known poverty, but she'd never suffered from a lack of joy or love or any of the other human passions. She'd never known a hunger of the soul.

She didn't know how to deal with Neville's detachment now. She had wanted to go directly to Ireland and save Sean and the village. Neville had insisted they stay in London until his legislation passed. She thought she might explode with impatience. And Neville's aloofness wasn't helping matters any.

"He needs you," Blanche murmured as Fiona rose from the chair and fidgeted with the spray of tiny orchids pinned to her sash.

Feeling naked in the fashionable gown with the minuscule sleeves and narrow bodice, Fiona clutched her arms at her waist and tried to comprehend what Blanche was telling her.

There had been times before the abduction that Neville had held her as if she mattered, laughed with her and at her. And even when she'd been foolish, he'd rode frantically in pursuit of her. Those weren't the actions of an uncaring man. Neville cared. He simply didn't *like* caring. Fiona smiled at that realization.

She annoyed the devil out of the mighty Duke of Anglesey, and she would continue to do so for a lifetime.

"Let's go down then, shall we?" she suggested, taking Blanche's arm. "If I'm to be a prisoner in me own home, then 'tis a gay prisoner I'll be."

"You're not a prisoner," Blanche scolded as they strolled out the door. "Our husbands are just excessively nervous. You must admit, they have some right to be."

Fiona shrugged. "I do not see it, myself. I escaped, did I not? The bill comes to a vote tomorrow. What can anyone do at this late date? Either they have the votes or they don't. I just can't imagine any of those pompous old goats caring enough to stir themselves. No, 'twas McGonigle's men behind it all, I'd wager."

"Those 'pompous old goats' steer the country, Fiona. I'm not fond of them, either, but this bill is important to our husbands. Reform must come someday, and if they can carry this off, then it will be easier for them next time. Neville stands to take a position in the cabinet if this is successful."

The cabinet. Fiona shuddered. He would need a wife who could stand by him and shake hands, smile dutifully and speak intelligently. He must have been out of his mind to marry her.

Pasting a smile across her face, she entered the foyer under the scrutiny of three pairs of male eyes. Only the one pair mattered.

Desire heated Neville's blood as Fiona drifted into the room on a cloud of soft green lace resembling the new spring leaves on the branches outside. She'd tucked the tiny white orchids he'd sent her here and there about her person, enhancing the impression of a goddess of springtime. The fiery mound of her curls above a porcelain cream complexion warmed the heart as well as the eyes. He wanted nothing more than to carry her up to the bed they hadn't shared in days. Instead, he remained where he was, hands frozen behind his back as Aberdare and Effingham exclaimed over the women.

Effingham's wife had taken on the task of overseeing the party. Blanche and Fiona had no business here at all, given their delicate conditions. Neville didn't know how he'd been persuaded to agree to this public charade. They should have locked all three women in the rooms above and posted bodyguards around them night and day.

Steadying his shaking nerves, Neville offered his arm. Fiona took it with fingers that lacked the strength to so much as tweak his nose. He couldn't protect *himself* from Townsend's thugs. How in the world could he protect a delicate creature like this, one with the additional impediment of the child she carried?

"I shall persuade your guests that the reform bill will set terrible criminals free in our midst and create chaos in our streets if you do not speak to me, your worship," Fiona said dryly.

So much for the illusion of fragility. Neville glared down at her. "I'll nail your tongue to the roof of your mouth if you try."

Her smile nearly blinded him. "Perhaps I should cling to your arm and insult you before all your friends, then," she continued. "Or command the musicians to play a jig and dance for them."

She didn't need strength in her fingers to tweak his nose. She had it in her cursed tongue. Neville almost smiled at the idea. Almost. "I can still chain you to the tower walls."

Fiona shrugged. "And drop your heir on its head when its time comes?

I think not."

Aberdare interceded before Neville could voice his outrage. Catching Fiona's arm, the earl pulled his cousin from Neville's protective grasp. "Our son escaped his nanny the first day he learned to crawl," he told Neville. "You might consider bouncing your firstborn on his head as a precaution against the MacDermot wandering ways. Come along, cuz. I'll try to keep you out of trouble for the evening."

Neville fought the overwhelming urge to commit violence on both the MacDermot cousins as they disappeared into the ballroom. Beside him, Blanche watched with amusement.

"It's not easy, I know," the countess agreed without his saying a word.

Neville glared at her. "It's all your fault, you realize. You should never have encouraged the bastard."

Her trill of laughter didn't ease his confusion in the least. Irritated and not knowing why, he dragged Blanche in the wake of their unconventional spouses. He still didn't know how he'd got himself into this predicament. Obviously, brains went begging when lust came into play.

As was expected of him, Neville led Fiona into the opening quadrille, but she thought he'd rather be almost anywhere else. Aside from cavorting in the bedchamber on their wedding night, she'd never danced with him.

She studied his grim demeanor as they executed the steps of the dance. Her husband honestly didn't understand that this was supposed to be fun, that they could dance and flirt and laugh and tease with these light steps. She fluttered her eyelashes and focused a blinding smile on him until he blinked in surprise.

Blanche's revelations had her heart aching for the lonely boy he'd been. That wouldn't prevent her from tweaking him a time or two, or even exploding with fury if he pushed too far. But right now, right this minute, she wanted to make him happy.

"Smile," she whispered as the pattern of the dance brought them together. He looked startled and didn't comply as he moved on to his next partner. "I shall flirt with Townsend if you don't smile," Fiona warned when next they came together.

"What the devil do I have to smile about?" he asked warily.

"Oh, that did it your royal majesty," she warned, pinching his fingers where he held her too tight. "If achieving your goals makes you happier than dancing with your new wife, then I shall assure that you are very,

very happy."

"Fiona, I have too damned many..." The dance carried him away before he could finish.

She knew what he would say anyway. She should be hurt by his actions, but she'd never known rejection and wouldn't accept it now. She would force him to admit some feeling for her.

For the remainder of the dance, she threw her smile at every man who looked in her direction and reserved her frown for her husband. He was a hard man to teach, was her duke, but he would learn. After all, she'd been assured he wasn't stupid. Just single-minded.

At the end of the dance, he led her toward Blanche, who sat sedately with the other matrons in a corner of the room. "You'll be safe here," he informed her. "I've several people I must talk to before the vote tomorrow. I'll try to return for the supper dance."

"Oh, don't worry your pretty head about me," Fiona said with a dismissive wave. "I'm quite capable of entertaining myself. You just go ahead and twist a few arms."

Some emotion battled for expression on Neville's implacable features, but his stubbornness won out. Nodding curtly, he delivered her to Blanche and stalked off.

He looked every inch the arrogant aristocrat in his finely tailored black trousers and frock coat, Fiona thought as she watched him walk away. Her noble duke was light-boned and of average height, but she knew all too well the coiled strength disguised beneath his formal evening clothes.

"You might tell your noble cousin sometime," Fiona suggested as she took the seat beside Blanche, "that if the only way I can get his attention is by running away, he'll not find me on his doorstep very often."

Blanche didn't look particularly perturbed. "One of Neville's most interesting qualities is his ability to focus his mind completely on one task at a time. The task tonight is passing the reform bill. Tomorrow night, after the vote, it will be an entirely different story."

Fiona smiled. "I know. And I have decided I shall help him accomplish that so we'll both be very, very happy tomorrow night."

Before Blanche could question or protest, Fiona caught the attention of one of her former suitors and without a word of farewell, departed the staid matron's corner of the room for the frivolous swirl of the dancers.

# Thirty-four

"How festive you look, my lady." Viscount Bennet bent his balding head over Fiona's hand before escorting her into the dance. "I'm pleased to see the duke has finally allowed you to visit London."

"Allowed me?" Fiona laughed, fluttering her fan and her lashes at her former suitor. "You make it sound as if I'm a prisoner in my own home. I'm a country girl at heart, sir. I've merely come to town to celebrate my husband's triumph when he wins his legislation on the morrow."

The viscount clucked his tongue in smiling disapproval. "Now, now, dear, there is no certainty of any such thing, and it's scarcely a topic for young ladies."

Fiona would gleefully have pulled out the remainder of the viscount's graying hair, but a proper duchess had other methods of whipping her teams into line. Her smile never faltered. "Nonsense, sir, celebrating is always a topic for ladies. I wish to have an exclusive soiree and invite all my husband's friends after his bill passes. I do hope we can count you among our friends. I have in mind the most perfect young lady I would like you to meet. She's so charming, I know you'll love her." She lowered her voice conspiratorially. "And her father is a nabob."

The viscount practically blushed pink in eagerness.

She had few female friends in London, so the promise of wealthy daughters would not work for everyone. She suspected a party would not lure the type of men who preferred hiding in their clubs, but behind every successful man lurked a nagging woman. She could be quite as single-minded as Neville when she chose. For her next victim, she picked Neville's old friend, Morton.

She located him as the dance ended, and with a welcoming smile, she had him bowing over her hand before Bennet could return her to Blanche.

"Mr. Morton! I'm delighted to see you again. I have something I want to tell you." Making her farewells to the viscount, she latched on to Morton's arm and steered him in the direction of the refreshment table where the men not playing cards congregated. "I crave a sip of lemonade, if you do not mind."

"I'm honored to be of service, Your Grace. I suppose that ramshackle husband of yours has deserted you for some smoke-filled chamber where he's jawing about politics?"

"Of course, and he's very good at it, too. I wouldn't dream of interfering." She halted beside a lady she recognized as the wife of one of

Townsend's cronies, near the lords at the table, but not among them. "I will wait here, if you do not mind, Mr. Morton. I would not intrude upon the gentlemen's discussions."

"I'm sure they would be delighted to have their dull talk interrupted by a lovely lady such as yourself." Morton said politely, concealing his relief that she did not expect to be introduced to arguing politicians.

Fiona bestowed a smile on the dour-faced woman beside her as Morton strode off. "It is so very warm in here tonight, is it not? The gentlemen really should not monopolize the refreshment table."

The woman creaked a slight curtsey in Fiona's direction as her escort returned carrying the requisite cup of punch. "As you say, Your Grace."

Fiona loved it. Hot coals wouldn't have persuaded those words out of the woman's mouth had Fiona been a plain Miss MacDermot, nobody cousin of an Irish earl. But as a duchess of Anglesey...

This could be fun. "I believe we met last fall, Lady Whitton. How is your husband faring these days? I believe he was a trifle under the weather the last I heard."

Morton frowned at Fiona's conversing with the enemy, but etiquette required he acknowledge the lady. Fiona flashed him another smile as she accepted her cup. Power definitely could be a heady elixir.

"I was just telling Lady Whitton I missed seeing her husband here tonight. The duke would so like to talk with him about a few matters he's been considering. But it's a pity to spoil a party by talking politics." She turned her head flirtatiously toward Mrs. Whitton's anonymous partner, another crony of Townsend's, she suspected.

"And you, sir, how is your health? So many of our older, wiser heads have retired or are considering retiring from the public arena, it seems. It's a pity that my husband and his friends carry more and more of the burden these days. I'd much rather keep him at home. But duty calls and the good of the country is more important, I suppose. I do hope he finds more men like you to help him."

The lady's escort frowned. "As you say, Your Grace, but I cannot recollect anyone retiring lately."

Fiona gave a trill of embarrassed laughter. "Have you not? Oh, I am so very sorry. I must be speaking out of turn. That's the reason Neville never brings me to these things, you know. I'm such a prattlebox. I'm supposed to hear everything and say nothing, but I vow it's a hard lesson to learn."

One of the gentleman standing close by intruded. "Someone in the cabinet is retiring, you say? Can't think who. Liverpool won't let 'em."

Fiona covered her smile with her fan. "Oh, and I'm sure I have it all turned about. I remember Neville mentioning several people who will be offering their resignations when the reform bill passes. He said something about it was time they retired, and I took it to mean..." She trailed the sentence off uncertainly.

Another gentleman took up the lapse. "Nonsense. The reform bill hasn't the votes to pass. Liverpool's cabinet will stand solidly behind us on that."

Fiona fluttered her lashes above the fan. "Oh, I'm certain I know nothing of cabinets and such, but my husband is quite positive about the bill. He's promised me, you see, and he told me just last night he had the votes. That's when the topic of retirements came up, but I most likely misunderstood that part. But I did understand when he said I could give a select dinner for his friends to celebrate his success. I do so hope you all will be able to come," she said with a trace of wistfulness. "Neville has this terrible habit of dismissing anyone who disagrees with him." She brightened again. "It's a good thing Effingham and my cousin agree with him then, is it not? I shall always be able to count on their presence."

Closing her fan and smiling fatuously, she took Morton's arm, bade her farewells, and practically steered him into the ballroom.

"Since I know demmed good and well Neville didn't marry an idiot, could you please explain that performance?" Morton demanded as they walked the perimeter of the ballroom, out of the way of the dancers.

"Don't be such a slow-top," Fiona scoffed, scanning the room for her next victim. "I told them the bill will pass, Neville is almost guaranteed a cabinet position, and that he'll demand the resignations of all those who don't support him. And then I promised them they'd be rewarded with invitations to the first entertainment Anglesey has ever given if they step in line."

"My word," Morton exclaimed, tallying the number of lords she'd just bribed. "You've a devilish mind beneath all that hair. Does Neville know?"

Fiona shrugged. "He knows. He just doesn't understand it yet."

"I say, Your Grace, your wife has a flare for words, don't she? I hadn't thought of your reform bill in quite those terms before."

Neville turned with a forbidding frown and examined the intruder with his quizzing glass. Turner, son-in-law of Lord Whitton, Townsend's party, he deduced warily. He would have dismissed the man summarily had his words not caught his interest.

"In quite what terms?" he asked coldly.

"H-hungry children," Turner stammered. Gathering his courage, he straightened his shoulders and continued. "It costs more to transport or hang a child caught stealing bread than to feed one. We're wasting money on trying petty thieves for capital crimes when we could send them to the mills and put them to work instead."

Send them to the mills? Neville almost repeated the preposterous suggestion aloud, but he bit his tongue. He heard Fiona's Irish tale-telling behind this, and he really didn't want to hear the whole of it. He had difficulty enough keeping a straight face as it was.

"We'll need someone to look into all the ramifications, of course," Neville said, maintaining as solemn a tone as he could muster.

"I'd be delighted to help in any way I can," Turner responded eagerly, just as Neville had known he would. "My wife would kill me should I let this opportunity pass. She has three unmarried sisters, you know. You can count on my support tomorrow."

Three unmarried sisters? Neville tried to assemble that irrelevant information as Turner walked away, then scowled at the appearance of a laughing Aberdare.

"If I forget to vote tomorrow, will you ban me from the Event of the Season, your honor?"

"Event of the season?" A tingling at the base of his spine warned Neville that this would all make sense shortly, but he wouldn't necessarily like it. One of Michael's favorite hobbies was laughing at Neville's discomfiture.

"Aye, and our Fiona is personally organizing the guest list as we speak. She's rearranging the cabinet too, but Liverpool hasn't seen fit to show his face so she hasn't informed him yet."

"The cabinet?" The tingling transformed into a decided sinking sensation. "I don't suppose you tried to stop her?" he inquired with resignation.

"Stop her?" Michael asked incredulously. "Would you stop a frigate in full sail? Heaven forbid. I'll salute her as she passes and stay out of her way."

That's what Neville had thought. That's what everyone had done all of Fiona's life. The woman didn't know the meaning of boundaries. Neville wondered if he really wanted to be the one to teach her.

But he'd lived his life by caution, and he couldn't help thinking caution a necessity now. Someone had already attempted to abduct her once. If she was personally choreographing the passage of the reform bill, they might not stop at abduction next time. Remembering the gang of thugs and the blow to his head, Neville rubbed his skull.

Leaving Aberdare to his own devices, Neville stalked toward the ballroom and his interfering wife.

"My dance, I believe?"

Fiona looked up, startled, at her husband's voice. She hadn't heard him approach. She read nothing in Neville's expression, but she sensed his tension. She really ought to refuse his offer, but aside from the suspicion that he wouldn't accept her refusal, she wanted to dance with him.

She took his offered arm and nodded to her audience as regally as any duchess. Leaving them open-mouthed, she followed Neville onto the dance floor. The orchestra struck up a waltz, the brutes.

"That was abominably rude, your highness," she taunted as her husband wrapped his arm around her waist. The full force of Neville's hot gaze threatened to ignite a raging inferno as he swung her into the dance.

"I'm a duke. They'll excuse my rudeness," he replied arrogantly. "You'll learn that soon, if you haven't already. You've certainly learned the role of duchess quickly enough."

"You would prefer I remain barefoot and ignorant?" Fiona asked with what she hoped was an arrogance akin to his.

"I would prefer you remain just plain bare and in my bed," he replied in a gruff tone and with a look that quaked Fiona to her toes, "but I can see my preferences have little enough to do with anything."

Caught on the broadsword of his gaze, Fiona didn't answer. The heat of Neville's palm burned through the frail silk of her gown. He held her closer than the dance required, and his thighs brushed hers as he spun her around the floor. His expressive eyebrows had pulled together in a frown, but she didn't think it was an entirely disapproving frown so much as one of indecision. Her heart pounded while his powerful mind worked through all the alternatives. She knew the moment he gave up the task and surrendered to the flames already eating her alive.

"I think it's time we bade our farewells," she suggested.

He didn't do any such thing. As the music swelled to its end, Neville spun her off the dance floor, caught her waist, and half carried her past the crowd to the ballroom entrance. Fiona had a glimpse of Lady Effingham's startled gaze as they swept by, but one look at Neville's face apparently convinced her not to intrude.

Since the men had decided it would be simpler to guard their wives if they were all in one establishment, Fiona and Neville had rooms upstairs in Effingham's town house. Neville steered her up those stairs now.

"Neville, this is abominably rude," Fiona whispered as she realized where they were going. "Blanche will worry — "

"No, she won't. She has better things to do. If she worried about you at all, she would have halted your performance." Neville threw open their bedchamber door and pushed her through.

Fiona resisted, but not hard enough. He slammed the door behind them and turned the key in the lock.

Hands on hips, she whirled to face him. "If you brought me here only to scold, you've wasted your time."

"Scolding is the very last thing on my mind." Without warning, Neville dragged her fully against him and captured her mouth with his, preventing any further argument.

Hot coals and summer breezes whirled inside her. Fiona hated how easily he turned her into quivering blanc mange. She tried fighting it by pushing at Neville's chest, but her fingers curled in his shirt instead. Closing her mouth against his kiss never occurred to her. Her mind defiantly resisted as he cupped her hips in both hands and pulled her toward him, but the rest of her didn't cooperate. She pressed against him and desire spiraled through her at the evidence of his arousal.

He pushed her against the wall until their hips ground together and their clothing was all that prevented their melding there and then. Fiona moaned as Neville thrust his tongue deeper, claiming her in this way instead. She had no idea when he'd unfastened her gown, but it fell off her shoulders under his marauding hands. They could fight some other time. She needed him now. It had been too damned long.

She tore at his waistcoat and cravat to get at his shirt fastenings. She needed to feel his flesh. He wouldn't release her long enough to succeed. He had her half undressed and she couldn't touch him.

Furious with frustration, Fiona caught his hands where they plundered her breasts and shoved him away. Startled, Neville stepped back a fraction, and Fiona grabbed the opportunity to wriggle out of her gown. His eyes lit with the heat of admiration as she stripped naked, but still he didn't understand. Fiona tugged on his cravat until he nearly choked. He pulled it off then.

He pulled off his coat and waistcoat too, his gaze never once straying from hers. She shivered at the determination she read there, but she wanted to be the focus of his attention for a change. It was her turn. She had earned this.

She slid her hand over his muscled torso as he jerked his shirt over his head. Heat scorched her palms. His bare arms pulled her against him, until flesh met flesh, and heat wrapped around them. Tilting her head, she accepted his kiss again, and gave herself up to the explorations of his tongue and hands. They might never agree on anything else, but they would always be together in this.

Fiona didn't waste time wondering if lovemaking was enough. She'd chosen her path, made her bed, and now she would make the best of it. She reached for the fastenings of Neville's trousers.

They never quite reached the bed.

# Thirty-five

As the first rays of dawn lightened the draperies, Neville bent over his beautiful, sleeping wife and pressed a kiss against her forehead. Deeply shaken by the prior night, he needed time to think. Quietly, he slipped from the bed.

He held his breath as Fiona stirred at his departure. She needed her sleep. He had kept her awake far longer than was good for either of them, but worse for her. Circles shadowed her brilliant eyes, even in sleep. Shards of pain rendered his insides. No matter how much courage Fiona possessed, no matter how strong she pretended to be, she couldn't do everything.

He wanted to take care of her and keep her safe forever.

Slipping into his clothes, hardening his heart against the need to crawl back in that bed and love her once again, Neville gathered up the things he needed, unlocked the door from the inside, stepped out, and with determination, locked the door again from the outside.

"She's gone!" Dillian, Lady Effingham, exclaimed, running up as her husband and his brother entered the townhouse later that afternoon, still celebrating their triumph.

"Who's gone?" Effingham asked with a frown as he dropped his gloves on the table and looked around for their usually hovering butler. "And are our bags packed and ready?"

"We sent your bags to the yacht, as you requested. And who do you *think* has gone?" Blanche asked sarcastically. She glared at her insouciant husband who twirled his hat on the tip of his finger and leaned against the wall without bothering to remove his outer garments. "Locking Fiona in her room is not the best way to acknowledge how she helped you win that bill."

Finally noticing the Irish earl's suspicious behavior, Dillian also focused her glare on him. "Why isn't Neville with you?"

Michael shrugged, popped his tall hat back on his head, and pushed away from the wall. "Don't know. I'll find out, shall I?"

"Where's that damned butler?" Effingham grumbled, reaching for his hat again.

"Out looking for you. We heard the bill passed hours ago and you didn't come home! We fretted all afternoon." Dillian glared at her husband. "Fiona refused to wait any longer. You have to find her."

Wearily, the marquess glanced at his adopted brother. "The docks?" he inquired.

Michael shrugged. "Where else?"

Without further explanation to their worried wives, they retraced their path out the door.

"I take it since you're here, that you didn't go directly to Fiona after the vote," Michael said idly, tucking his hat under his arm, out of the river breeze. He scanned the yacht's deck almost with disinterest.

Neville ran his hand through his hair, shoving loose strands out of his eyes as he glared at his cousin-in-law. "We couldn't have won today if Fiona hadn't twisted arms last night. She only did it so we can hurry back to Aberdare. I had to make certain the yacht was stocked for our journey before I fetched her. Fiona isn't exactly a seafaring man."

"No?" Michael's gaze caught on the figure of a cabin boy scurrying up a rope ladder to the top mast. "Tell that to Fiona, then. She's not in her room, you realize."

Neville felt himself pale. "What do you mean, she's not in her room? I locked her in there myself. Don't say things like that. I'm a wreck enough as it is."

Michael grinned into the fading sun. "I see that. She's got you bound and gagged, hasn't she? I wish you well of her." He headed toward the companionway.

Neville grabbed the earl's coat collar and hauled him back. "Where is she?" he shouted against the brisk wind.

Michael turned him a shrewd look. "Where do you think she would go?"

"Nowhere! She wouldn't leave without me. She knows I'm only protecting her."

Having satisfied himself that sufficient stores were aboard, Effingham returned to the deck, took instant stock of the situation, and removed Neville's grip from Michael's collar. "You should never have locked Fiona in. You may as well have dared her to escape."

"We can't leave until we find her!" Neville turned to signal the captain.

Michael caught his arm. "The tide's turning. It's time we're off. I have a village under siege, your bloody worship. We've fulfilled our part of the bargain, now it's time you fulfill yours. The damned ship leaves as scheduled. Fiona can take care of herself."

Driving his free arm sharply backward, Neville aimed for Michael's ribs.

Aberdare dodged the blow but released Neville as the sails unfurled. Neville swore under his breath. He raised his hand to signal the captain to halt, but ran afoul of Gavin's powerful grasp.

"We're sailing now and not twelve hours from now. You won't find Fiona unless she wants to be found. You're wasting time," the marquess admonished.

"You know where she's going, your noble worship," Michael added wryly. "You may as well arrive ahead of her."

They spoke sense, Neville knew, but terror still reigned. He could jump. The Thames was so thick with foulness at this point, he could likely walk across.

But Michael's words gradually took root in his fear-addled brain. Fiona would head straight for home. He couldn't find her in London, but he could find her in Ireland. Surely, now that the reform bill was law, Townsend would have no further use for her. It was just the normal dangers of travel she faced. She would seek a ship...

*A ship.* Slowly, Neville swung his gaze to observe his immediate surroundings. She would seek a ship. At the docks.

No wonder the damned earl was so casual about leaving his female cousin loose in London. Neville swore a litany of curses and began a systematic search of his own damned ship.

He started with the traditional hiding places for stowaways. Torn equally between fear and fury, he rampaged from hold to cabins to galley, sending grown men fleeing from his wrath. He'd known an occasional brief anger, but nothing to the extent of this. He thought he might strangle Michael in Fiona's place if he did not find her.

Neville burst up the companionway onto the deck. They were reaching the mouth of the Thames already, and the captain had ordered full sail. With the tide and the wind in their favor, the yacht skimmed over the water, aborting any hope of returning to London. Despair washed over him as land dwindled from view.

He had meant to take Fiona with him. He just wanted her safe while he was otherwise occupied. He'd hoped she would sleep until he returned. He'd kept her awake most of the night. Surely she understood what he hadn't said.

Stupid. Women needed *words*. Pinching the bridge of his nose, Neville fought the unfamiliar burning behind his eyes and tried not to worry.

But the whitecaps on the water reminded him of the orchids Fiona had worn in her hair last night. The tiny flowers weren't half so delicate as his wife, nor nearly as beautiful. The sun lowering in the western sky couldn't compare with Fiona's magnificent hair, the hair he'd buried his hands in last night as he'd kissed her senseless. And she'd kissed him back, with passion and desire and all the things he'd craved in a wife.

He would do well to practice indifference with Fiona if she insisted on behaving like a common hoyden. Let her come and go as she pleased. What difference could it make to him?

But it did. He'd hoped that she would be pleased if he expressed his gratitude for her aid by setting sail immediately for her home. He'd thought of making love to her in the gently rocking berth below. He'd planned on marching into Aberdare like a knight with sword drawn, freeing the village from the dragon in exchange for her love and laughter. He was a damned arrogant fool.

He didn't have to do it all himself. Fiona wanted to march with him.

His gaze drifted upward to the ghostly sails billowing against the evening sky. The yacht was built for pleasure and the platform on the mainmast was mostly decorative, with a polished brass rail. It had no purpose. But he could see a dark figure sitting there cross-legged, leaning against the timber. None of the men had any reason to be up there. Perhaps Michael...

That wasn't Michael. With a sinking feeling in the pit of his stomach, Neville willed that stubborn figure to look at him. Surely even Fiona would have sense enough not to risk their child like that. Terror for her safety warred with elation at finding her. He would wring her neck.

As if his thoughts had truly winged upward, the slight figure rested, elbows on knees, and leaned forward.

Even through the dusk, Neville could see Fiona's laughing eyes. His spirits soared to insane heights at the realization that she was safe and here with him, even as his temper turned murderous. He would kill her as soon as he got his hands on her.

Wrapping his hands around the prickly hemp of the rigging, Neville hauled himself upward, occasionally glancing ahead for the reward of Fiona's laughing gaze turning to one of alarm.

"I surrender! I'll come down. Just get off that rope, Neville, please!" she cried.

"I think I'll cut the rigging and keep you up there," he snarled in return.

"You'll kill yourself! I'm coming down. Watch. I promise." Fiona firmly secured the rope as she anxiously watched him.

Good. Let her suffer some portion of the torments he'd suffered these last hours. Unrepentant, Neville continued climbing. "Don't you dare climb down," he yelled at her.

Ignoring his warning as usual, she threw her breeches-clad leg over the railing, caught her foot in the knot, and began her descent.

Heart slamming against his chest in fear as he watched her scurry down , Neville cursed and slid down his rope as fast as he could go. The burning pain in his hands couldn't compare with the terror in his heart as her rope swung wildly in the evening breeze.

"Fey-onah MacDevil Perceval, I'll kill you for this!" he shouted against the rising wind, just before his feet hit the deck and his legs almost buckled under him.

"Aye, and I'll be murtherin' you in your sleep should you lock me behind closed doors again!" she screamed back.

Before Neville could reach for her, Fiona darted across the deck and down the hatch, out of sight.

Without caring about his abused dignity, Neville raced across the deck after her.

Behind him, the crew snickered.

# Thirty-six

Neville found Fiona without much trouble. Hiding places were few and far between on a yacht, and she hadn't bothered looking for one. She sat cross-legged on the berth he'd hoped to use for much more pleasurable purposes than a confrontation. Her defiant posture with arms crossed and chin tilted warned him this would definitely be a confrontation.

"Don't you ever dare lock me in again," she growled the moment he entered.

Neville slammed the door behind him and leaned against it, crossing his arms as he did so. "I can throw commands around too," he said calmly. "Don't you ever run away from me again."

Her eyes lit like emerald fires. "I did not run away from you. I ran to you, your noble worship. You're just not after havin' the sense to see it."

Neville sighed at this roundaboutation. They would never see eye to eye because they were never on the same level of the whirlwind she spun around him. Maybe if he stayed fixed in one spot, she might eventually bounce to his level once in a while. He fought the urge to smile at the image. She'd damned well terrified him. She would pay for that.

"You endangered our child as well as yourself while running around the streets of London alone, then climbing into the tops. Will you ever grow up?"

Wounded, she flinched as if he'd struck her. But her tongue wouldn't surrender. Straightening, she glared. "No, I think I won't. It's exceedingly boring having two stuffed shirts in the house. Our child must know there is some fun in this life, that it's not all duty and responsibility and propriety."

Neville slammed his head backward against the door and stared at the bulkhead, wishing he could knock himself silly without need of finding someone to cudgel his brains out. "Fine then, we shall raise a herd of heirs to believe it's all right to dangle from the chimneys and slide down the roofs instead of paying attention to their studies and learning how to run the estate. I'll be the dull bore who does that."

"The ones who would dangle from chimneys will dangle regardless of your opinions," she informed him. "And the ones who would study will do so despite whatever influence I might have. And you may as well prepare yourself. The one who dangles from chimneys could be your heir and the one who studies could be your daughter. Do you think you can personally rearrange your children to your liking?"

His entire world had descended into chaos from the moment Fiona stepped into it. He might as well acknowledge that he would never achieve any level of order ever again. At that acceptance, the tight, terrified knot inside him sprang free.

Neville returned his gaze to his willful wife. If he was perfectly honest, he would admit Fiona wasn't truly beautiful. Her features were much too strong and sharp, her eyes far too knowing, her magnificent mane of hair much too unruly. But it was just that combination of imperfections that made his blood race.

His gaze drifted lower to the bosom straining against her boy's shirt. For the first time in his life, he undressed a woman with his mind, and from that point on, his mind had little to do with anything.

"Well then, our studious heiress may run the estate for our feckless heir," he proposed, advancing toward the berth.

She dropped her arms and eased backward. "You'll not settle our argument like that again, your noble worship. I'm not your fine mistress to run into your bed whenever you dislike losing."

"I haven't lost this argument. I'll hire a gaggle of governesses and a throng of tutors to keep the herd of heirs off the roof. You, I'll manage myself, in bed with any luck, on the floor, if necessary, or anywhere else we deem appropriate." He caught her as she tried to dodge him. Gently, Neville pushed her back against the mattress.

"Don't you dare," she warned, falling back against the pillow beneath his greater weight.

"Don't I dare what?" he asked mildly. Without waiting for an answer, he leaned over and applied his mouth to hers.

Maybe they should never talk, he thought as Fiona's lips responded heatedly beneath his pressure. They communicated much better this way, while prone and inside one another's clothes. His palm slid beneath her coarse shirt and he groaned at the glorious feel of silken flesh.

She didn't bother fighting him. Her fingernails dug into his arms through his coat and practically shredded the material as his tongue marauded the interior of her mouth. Within minutes, her hips rose in search of his.

With no compunction whatsoever, Neville reached down, ripped her breeches buttons loose, jerked the fabric out of his way, then leaned over and kissed her there, where he'd imagined her bare just moments before.

Fiona screamed like a wildcat, dug her fingers into his hair, then shuddered and thrust upward so he could take her more thoroughly.

He'd never done this to a woman before, had never really imagined it until Fiona came along. One did not normally do such things to a wife. But this wife...

Excitement exploded in Neville's veins as she thrust and twisted and begged for more of what only he could provide. Perhaps there were advantages to having a woman who climbed up masts.

Releasing his sex from the tight restraints of his trousers, he took what she offered so boldly. Beneath him, Fiona cried out with her own release. He knew, without an ounce of conceit that she would cry out again before he was done with her. She gave him something he'd never known he'd possessed, and the power of it freed them both.

Watching the misty green rising on the horizon, Fiona shivered and wrapped her cloak tighter. "What will you do when we arrive?" she asked in what, for her, was a subdued tone. Neville had turned her brain to mush again, and she hadn't quite shaken off the effect.

"The army is camped at Aberdare. They're too late to save the looms, but they're protecting it against further attack. We need to catch the men who destroyed them and give them something better to do than burn the means others have of making a living."

Neville stood beside her, not touching but keeping a distance while in the public eye. They both knew what happened when they touched.

"You'll not do it with an English army," she answered wearily, expecting her protest would go unremarked.

"You have a better suggestion?" The tone of his voice implied she would not.

She'd given it a great deal of thought these last days. The people she knew in the village had wanted the looms. They would not have burned their own livelihood. Even McGonigle on his worst day would not have destroyed the means for his own mother to make a living, even to make one of his damned rebellious points. The people of Aberdare were bitter, not stupid.

So it struck her that the army punished the innocent by posting its minions in Aberdare. They should be searching farther afield, to those jealous of what Aberdare had accomplished. Or worse, to those who did the devil's work for another purpose entirely.

Fiona sent her stern husband a thoughtful look. What happened in Aberdare was none of his concern. He could have left Michael to deal with it himself, but instead lent his power and authority for the sake of friendship as well as kinship.

"What if all this has nothing to do with secret societies and rebels?" she asked, waiting until he looked at her before continuing. She would give Neville credit for at least listening. Satisfied she had his full attention, she formed her words carefully. "Durham has an Irish estate." At his nod, she continued more confidently. "If Durham was behind the earlier attack on you, he might also have been behind the troubles at Aberdare. He may have hoped Effingham would run to help Michael, thus drawing him out of England also. Durham's a rather inept sort, I believe. It sounds like the kind of thing a man like that would do to draw away his opponents."

Neville returned his gaze to the land rising from the horizon. "We've considered that possibility, but we have no proof. And I don't see how any of this is involved in Burke's murder."

"Durham wouldn't dirty his hands doing anything himself. He would hire someone. That someone may have been told to steal the money to stop the looms. But if Burke intervened in the theft, the thief may have carried his orders a little farther. When one encourages anarchy, one cannot expect control."

Neville nodded thoughtfully.

Encouraged, Fiona continued. "I think we must be even more devious than he. I think, if we're to end these insurrections, we should set a trap."

Neville cast her a startled glance. "A trap? What kind of trap?"

The cobwebs fled from her brain beneath the full impact of his attention. "You aren't going to like this."

Neville scowled. "If it involves you, you're damned right I won't like it."

"Oh, no, your noble lordship. It involves you."


"You've got maggots for brains, little cousin," Michael stated firmly as they observed the progress of the cart down the rutted road toward Aberdare.

"And your head is stuffed with more cotton batting than Neville's if you're after believing that, your worthy lordship," Fiona replied without rancor, her gaze fixed anxiously on the cart.

Behind them, Effingham rolled his eyes heavenward. "That's enough, children. Let us proceed with the next step of this farce. At least I needn't pay for my entertainment while in your company."

Both red-headed cousins turned green-eyed glares on him. It was like watching twin fireworks, Effingham observed. Infinitely entertaining. He nodded toward the waiting horses. "Shall we let the games begin?"

As they watched the two-wheeled cart filled with straw wobble down the road carrying the precious contents of the mighty Duke of Anglesey, Effingham shook his head in appreciation of the irony. The impeccably tailored duke with his damned arrogant expression and annoying quizzing glass now lay ensconced in straw, garbed in tattered rags, reeking of cheap whiskey, with a shabby eye-patch concealing at least one of his recognizably bushy eyebrows. Remembering the night he'd watch the duke lift an eyebrow and rap a walking stick to dismiss the powerful Lord Townsend, Effingham almost smiled. This was a battle worth watching.

His gaze drifted to the duke's capricious wife. With Anglesey jewels glittering at her ears and throat, wrapped warmly in a fur-lined cloak, she stood as regally as any princess, watching her husband disappear into the distance. Only the furrow between her eyes gave away her concern. Considering husband and wife had argued and spat during the entire journey, Effingham thought her apprehension enormously amusing. The termagant had definitely met her match. He just would never have expected it to be in the form of the studious, unruffled duke.

"You look like some pagan princess sending her consort off for execution," Michael grumbled as he helped Fiona into a well-sprung traveling coach.

"It was your idea to dress me up like an Egyptian queen," Fiona complained as the men climbed in after her. "I feel ridiculous."

"Good. Maybe if you're weighed down with a fortune in jewels you'll think twice about picking up your skirts and running off to join Neville," Michael replied smugly.

Fiona shot him a nasty glare, opened her mouth to speak, and apparently deciding it wasn't worth the effort, snapped it closed again. She settled more comfortably into her seat.

"Brava," Effingham called. "You've just learned the first lesson in dealing with annoying gnats like Michael. Freeze them out."

Behind the hood of her cloak, Fiona smiled and turned her attention to the carriage window.

"That's like telling a fire to become frost," Michael complained from the seat opposite hers. "She'll burst a gasket trying."

"Silence, Michael," Effingham said serenely.

The carriage rolled down the road a safe distance behind the humble country cart.

All thoughts rested on the dangers awaiting them should their plan fail. It couldn't fail. Too many lives and the fate of countries depended on it.

# Thirty-seven

"I don't like this. We're mad to try it," Fiona muttered, wringing her hands and watching the farm cart roll away in a different direction. "It will never work."

"If it doesn't work, then we've risked nothing," Michael replied. "As you pointed out, Durham's a bumbling incompetent, not a murderer. I wouldn't wager my savings on Townsend, but he's not here."

"Townsend is an unscrupulous mercenary, but I can't say even he would stoop so low as murder. He might hope someone else will carry the matter too far, but I doubt he could carry it out on his own." Effingham lifted the carriage curtain with his walking stick and peered out as they approached their destination.

Fiona wrinkled her nose at Durham's deteriorating mansion in the distance. The carriage jolted to and fro in the pockmarked lane, and her stomach protested the jostling. She had to do something to keep her mind off the days ahead, so she studied her surroundings. It wasn't much of an estate, she concluded.

The tenant cottages were in total disrepair, fit only for pigs, but she could see faded splotches of laundry draped over rocks and bushes between the houses. Smoke rose in wisps from holes in roofs that might once have contained chimneys. It was a wonder they didn't burn the places to the ground.

Even as she thought it, she saw the charred remains of a cottage between two other teetering dwellings. She hoped the occupants had survived, though she didn't like to think what kind of life they might have if they did. These hovels could scarcely hold one family, and certainly not two.

Her gaze drifted back to the sprawling edifice ahead. Vines covered brick walls, concealing any defects, but Fiona was familiar enough with the area to know what vines could hide. They crept in through loose window sashes and ate through mortar, letting in damp and drafts and rot. She'd seen vines curl around interior windows and push through warped floors if left unchecked. Few landlords actually lived in Ireland. They drained the country of its resources and spent their wealth in the comfort of their London town houses. Durham would be such a one.

Her observations didn't settle her protesting stomach. For the first time in her pregnancy, nausea swelled in her throat. Choking it back, she rejected the role of helpless female, even as her nerves tightened. Maybe

Durham wasn't there.

That hope died once the carriage halted in front of the house. Their driver applied the knocker to the front door, and a footman opened the warped oak. The marquess clambered from the carriage, lowering the steps so Fiona could climb down. As she did, a stiffly erect rider approached on horseback. Nerves shot, Fiona clutched Effingham's hand. She knew Durham by sight, and that wasn't him.

It was Townsend.

Unreasoning terror gripped her. Effingham's hand squeezed hers as she gagged and tried to hold down the bile.

"Well, well, my friends, I didn't expect you to make this so easy for me." Townsend halted his horse a safe distance from the carriage. "To what do we owe the honor of this visit?"

"The duchess is ill. We didn't dare ask her to travel farther today. We stopped to ask for your hospitality."

Fiona heard the barely disguised sarcasm in Effingham's voice.

Townsend smiled in evident enjoyment of their plight. "By all means, invite the duchess in. As a matter of fact, I insist." He glanced over their heads. "Durham, have your soldiers arrest these traitors."

Fiona swung toward their only means of transportation. Before she could take a step, a dozen men wearing ragged uniforms and carrying muskets surrounded them.

So much for the protection of the English army.

Without warning, Fiona gagged, bent double, and spewed the remainder of her breakfast on the marquess's muddy boots.

Behind her, Michael murmured wryly. "Well, that visibly confirms our story."

She wanted to smack him, but she couldn't. The whole world spun around, and she could see three Townsends climbing from three horses, just before the world went black and she fell face forward toward the trampled grass.

Neville fared little better. The straw itched, unknown creatures bit and scratched, and the cart hit every rut and hole with a force nearly propelling him from his bed. He cursed Fiona, he cursed Michael, and he cursed the marquess. Most of all, he cursed himself for falling in with Fiona's insane plan. True, they had no other means of identifying the source of the violence. That didn't mean he had to play the part of village idiot until they did.

He could be in London now, in front of a roaring fire, drawing up plans to resubmit the Catholic Emancipation bill. That seemed much more likely of success than drawing out kidnappers and murderers while wearing a feeble disguise.

Yet he couldn't sit in the safety of his study while the men who had attempted to abduct Fiona were on the loose. It had been a hare-brained attempt at best, but that didn't alleviate the terror they had caused. Fiona could have lost the child attempting to escape. She could have been so terrified that she might have done something dangerous to herself. No, the kidnappers must be found, and the sooner, the better.

So he scratched the flea bites, dug his feet into the straw, and endured the stench of whatever the cart had hauled last. No one would think to find the Duke of Anglesey traveling like this, and that's the way he wanted it. He didn't want anyone knowing of his presence in Ireland.

He just wished his wife and her wretched cousin had dreamed up a more elegant disguise.

Exhausting all other alternatives, Neville closed his eyes and slept part of the way into the sleepy little village of Aberdare.

The driver's cries of alarm as the cart lurched to a halt woke him just before they traversed the last section of road into town.

Neville opened his eyes and gazed into the cold barrel of a musket.

"On the ground!" the soldier with the weapon shouted, while another—not waiting for the command to be carried out—shoved his bayonet into the straw behind Neville's head.

"What the devil!" Startled, Neville sat up, opened his mouth to give the commanding officer a royal set down, and got shoved from the cart with a gun butt for his efforts.

Cursing, he landed on his feet and glared at the rag-tag bunch of soldiers surrounding him. They didn't look like any army he knew, but then, he had never inspected the mercenary armies the government had installed in Ireland to keep peace and order. Neville grabbed the musket barrel at his back, jerked, and swinging, slammed it against its owner's shoulder.

"Now keep your bloody hands off me!" he shouted. "And show me to your commanding officer."

Within seconds, the motley soldiers turned their attention from tearing apart the cart to slamming Neville to the ground and beating him with any weapon at hand.

Outraged, furious beyond all measure, Neville swung his purloined musket, smacking it against kneecaps. He tumbled away from the worst blows while jabbing the bayonet at boot-clad ankles. The howls of pain from his victims couldn't hide the fact that he was outnumbered. A crack against his head sprawled him backward into the mud and someone grabbed his weapon before he could tighten his grip.

Neville doubled up with agony as a booted foot kicked him in the ribs. These were soldiers, damn it! They were supposed to uphold the law, not twist it to their own devices.

The memory of Fiona's hatred for the British rose foggily in his mind. This, then, was what inspired her loathing. He had only to show himself as a British lord and not the vagabond he appeared, and they would run like hell. But even if he could prove who he was, he didn't dare for fear of endangering Fiona and the others. Their plan rested on the hope that Durham would believe him safely in London.

The driver he had hired cried out in pain and once more, Neville swung his aching body into action. He couldn't let the man suffer on his account. Uncurling, he hooked his hand around another musket butt, swung to one side, and hauled the weapon with him, catching its owner off balance. The man screamed and stumbled, and Neville leapt to his feet, musket in hand.

To his astonishment, the soldiers suddenly lost interest in his activities. Glancing up, Neville stared in mixed relief and fear as a pitchfork-waving mob of villagers poured over the hillock and through the field in the direction of Neville and the soldiers.

They would get themselves killed. The soldiers were armed, even if they didn't have much training with their weapons. They could shoot the villagers from a distance, take to their horses, and run them down before the local people could do any damage whatsoever.

The realization that they came to rescue him galvanized him into action. Neville grabbed the reins of the nearest horse from its astonished owner, leapt on, and fighting the animal's rearing protest, aimed for the one man he could distinguish as an officer.

The mounted captain raised his weapon too late as Neville bore down on him. Using his musket, he struck the officer's bayonet, spinning the gun into the mud.

"Order your men to lower their weapons or I'll dismount you with the point of this damned knife," Neville commanded.

"I'll be damned—" The officer clamped his mouth shut as Neville aimed the bayonet at him. He bowed to the authority he recognized in his captor's speech. Raising his hand, he signaled his men to hold fire.

The villagers were on them in minutes, pouring in and around the soldiers, grabbing reins, keeping the horses from trampling all and sundry. Neville sought his driver, discovered the old man being helped to his feet by a recognizable figure, and sighed. *McGonigle.* He supposed, if he looked close enough, he'd see half the orphans amidst the rabble, outfitted on his own money. Or Michael's, if he wanted to look at it that way. That made him feel slightly better.

Keeping the officer at knife point, Neville shouted to the rebel leader. "What the devil do we do with them now?"

At the sound of the duke's voice, McGonigle almost broke his neck looking up. His jaw gaped open as he recognized the ragged beggar on horseback. Glancing around, he signaled another of his cohorts to take the officer's reins, then gestured for Neville to follow him to the side of the road.

"Y-your Grace," he stuttered, obviously fighting the urge to tug at his forelock in full view of interested observers. "W-we didn't know.

"You weren't supposed to know," Neville replied curtly, climbing down so he could meet the man face to face. "What the devil is the meaning of all this?"

McGonigle stiffened and replied in his more usual tones. "They've kept us blockaded for a week. We can't go in or out. I can't even see Sean. The poor lad must be past terrified by now. I've tried sending word to the earl, but I've no means of knowing if the messenger got through. I just know he hasn't come back."

"He got through," Neville replied grimly, keeping an eye on the villagers as they disarmed the soldiers. "The earl's here. We're trying to get to the bottom of this nonsense, but I've reason to hide my identity for now. What are you planning on doing with this scurrilous lot?" He nodded in the direction of the incompetent band of soldiers.

McGonigle shrugged. "Disarm them, take their horses, and send them back to Durham. He's the one behind this, he is."

"We need proof. What does he hope to gain by inciting insurrection?" Before he received a reply, Neville watched another familiar figure lope over the hillside in their direction. For Fiona's sake, he'd even put up with the likes of Eamon O'Connor.

The lanky Eamon caught up with them in a few long strides. His grin at the sight of the rag-bedecked duke tightened into a grim expression. "I was about to curse your soul to hell, your bloody honor," he growled.

Rubbing his aching side, Neville held his temper. For whatever reason, O'Connor was a friend of Michael's and Fiona's. In a hostile environment, he'd do well to cultivate all the friends he could. "I'm certain that was done a long time ago, so you may as well save your breath, O'Connor. What's the trouble this time?"

"Fiona," Eamon replied curtly. "She's ill and at Durham's place."

Neville breathed a little easier despite his aching rib. "She's not really ill. She's with Michael and Effingham. They're searching for evidence against Durham, and Fiona's playing the part of invalid to keep him unaware."

Eamon scowled. "That's not what that devil's spawn, Colin Moriarity, said. He said one of Durham's men posed as a messenger from McGonigle, abducted Fiona, and threw him off the coach for dead. Colin tracked him all the way here from England, and saw Fiona for himself, but he couldn't talk with her. So he bribed one of the maids who said she's taken to her bed."

Neville shook his head, hoping to knock all the pieces of this puzzle back in place, but nothing in this bloody country made sense. He clung to what he knew for certain. "Fiona escaped the kidnappers. If Colin truly tracked them, he tracked empty-handed villains. We've not heard word of the Widow Blackthorn. Maybe she posed as Fiona. I just know I saw my wife this morning and she was in the company of her cousin and Effingham. They were on their way to Durham's."

Eamon's grim expression did not ease. "Then Durham has an earl and a marquess as well as a duchess to use as pawns. Townsend's with them, and word is, he's told the PM the country is threatening insurrection and Aberdare is the leader. He's having them all beheaded."

The whole country was Bedlam run by Irish fairies. The straightest distance between two points was by way of the moon. Glaring at McGonigle and Eamon, Neville couldn't even discern the heroes from the villains. He wished he'd never heard of Ireland.

But then he would never have known Fiona.

The Irishman's challenging glare burned through Neville's immediate denial. Fiona was ill and in Townsend's hands.

Neville's hands shook as he lowered the gun and blindly watched the activity around him. Surely not. Surely she was safe and in Effingham and Aberdare's care...

Panic seeped into his blood as he watched the villagers binding wounds and the soldiers hurriedly retreating. The panic multiplied and raced faster.

He had to find Fiona and see for himself that she was safe. To hell with all her damned plans and schemes. The whole country could incinerate as far as he was concerned. He just wanted Fiona safe and back in his arms. He'd never let her go.

The thought of never seeing Fiona's laughing, taunting eyes again threw fuel on the inferno, only this time, his fury didn't erupt in rage. Every thought coalesced into the cold, calculating determination to find Fiona and take her home, where she belonged.

Neville glanced around at the ragged villagers hauling off their booty of guns and horses. Several of the men stood guard between the soldiers and the women and children, holding the soldiers' own guns against them. Thieves, the lot, but they were Fiona's thieves. They'd saved his life, unwittingly or not.

Neville took a deep breath to force back the panic. "All right, I'll need pen and paper," he ordered. "Water and rub down those horses. We'll need them later. Is the castle safe? I need somewhere to work." As he rapped out his commands, he strode briskly in the direction of the village.

Without even realizing it, he usurped the leadership of the rebel band. The two Irish miscreants, McGonigle and O'Connor, fell into step behind him.

# Thirty-eight

Neville gasped as a small elbow jabbed his bruised rib. Adjusting the youngster on his lap, he bent over the drawing his informants had compiled over the last few hours. He knew precisely in which room each of the hostages was kept, but his finger lingered over the one where Fiona was held. Pain nagged at him, not from his injuries, but from guilt. He should never have agreed to this. Never. No matter how many cousins or earls or marquess's agreed to protect her. No matter how incompetent the enemy.

His wife had the courage of a pride of lions. She would defy her captors. She would spit in their faces.

She would be terrified and recklessly endanger her life.

Clenching his teeth, Neville forced his thoughts back to a military standpoint. If he allowed his emotions free rein, he'd be on a horse, tearing across the countryside, prepared to rip Townsend and Durham into bloody little pieces. He couldn't risk it. Too much was at stake, and not just Fiona's life and that of his unborn heir. The whole countryside was a powder keg with a lit fuse. Townsend hadn't completely lied to the authorities. Insurrection was imminent if someone didn't douse the flame.

McGonigle gently lowered a sleeping infant into a makeshift cradle while his wife set cups of steaming rich tea on the table. Neville gulped half the cup without flinching. He hadn't eaten anything the better part of the day. Tea alone fueled his blood.

He surrendered the toddler in his lap to his hostess. He no longer thought of his unborn child as a symbol of his title and ancestry, as another duty he had undertaken. That child was a living, breathing bundle of arms and legs as much as the orphans crammed into McGonigle's drafty cottage. The future duke would yawn and cry and suck his fist like any other infant. And Neville longed to hold him as much as he longed to hold Fiona again.

With white knuckles, Neville clutched his pen and scribbled out still another letter. He had messengers scouring the countryside, sailing the sea, riding hell-bent for Dublin and parts unknown. The signet of the Duke of Anglesey sealed the wax on each letter that went out. At times of war, dukes could command armies. Neville was positioning himself to command his.

In a rising breeze portending a storm, the cottage door blew open, sweeping in Eamon. "The horses are saddled."

Neville stamped his ring into the hot wax he'd dripped onto this last letter. This one would go directly to the king himself. His Majesty wasn't a particular friend of his. George IV had grown narrow-minded and bigoted since his regency. But even the corpulent king wouldn't stand for insurrection. This letter was insurance and would only go out if something happened to Neville or the hostages.

He laid the missive in Mrs. McGonigle's hands. He'd explained its purpose earlier, and she looked grim as she tucked the document into a high drawer of her kitchen cabinet. She said nothing as the men donned their outerwear and prepared to leave.

"It's an hour's ride," McGonigle said as they slipped out of the cottage to the waiting horses. "The men from Roscommon are already there. Soldiers should be there soon. Durham has some militia with him, but most went home in disgust. We have numbers on our side."

"But they have Fiona on theirs," Eamon reminded him, arranging his lanky frame in the saddle.

"Aye," McGonigle said sadly. "It's a stalemate I'm seein'."

Neville grunted in disapproval. "I'll remind you, gentleman, that you're talking about Fiona. Durham will be damned lucky if she doesn't have him trussed and stuffed up a chimney by the time we arrive."

Laughing softly at this image, the other two men rode into the night. Neville double-checked the girth of his mount, then slowly followed in their wake. He wished he could inspire his own confidence so easily. McGonigle and O'Connor didn't know Fiona was with child. Neville was desperately aware of it.

Holding himself stiffly erect, Neville tried concentrating on organizing his troops as they crept out of field and hedge to join him. He had a formidable concentration, he'd been told time and again. He could personally shove a bill through recalcitrant committees, past the old stick-in-the-muds in the Lords, and into the right hands in the Commons. He could conquer continents if he so chose.

Fiona was an unprincipled rebel just like these Irish scoundrels he traveled with, but right now, all he cared about was getting her back. Hell, the way he felt right now, Townsend could bloody well keep Aberdare and Effingham if Neville could just have Fiona. Since Fiona wouldn't appreciate his generosity, he would have to rescue the lot of them.

"We're almost there, Your Grace." McGonigle sidled his horse next to Neville's. "There's a thicket off to the right where ye can wait safely. O'Connor and I will check the positions of our men. I'd not storm the place if I could prevent it. We've kept the tenants quiet, but there's always one in every bunch..."

Neville shook his head. "These are not feudal times. Townsend has no authority here. His wits have gone addled, if I do not miss my guess. Find some pretext to draw him from the house, and I'll deal with him."

Eamon eased his horse close enough to hear and shook his head in disagreement. "These *are* medieval times. This is Ireland. The law belongs to whoever takes it into his hands. You are not in your safe London study, your nobleness. Keep out of sight. If we lose you, we'll lose the war of a certainty."

Neville knew if he could only draw Townsend out, he could end this bloodlessly, but he also knew Eamon had a point. They had very little physical evidence against Townsend. It was the word of a band of Irish rebels against a lord of the realm. Townsend had no idea the Duke of Anglesey was even in the country, or he would have thought twice about this escapade.

As soon as Townsend realized his plan had fallen through, he would become even more of a loose cannon than he already was. Even as Neville argued with himself, the point became moot. A scream from an upper story window shattered the moonless night.

Neville recognized that scream as clearly as he would recognize his own face in the mirror. Without consulting his two sergeants-at-arms, he kicked his horse into a gallop straight toward the house. It had never occurred to him that a poor specimen of manhood like Durham or an old madman like Townsend would actually molest Fiona. He'd feared their physical abuse if she applied her biting tongue. But Fiona wasn't screaming in terror. She was screaming with murderous rage. He would kill them if they'd touched her, if Fiona didn't kill them first.


Fiona smacked Durham so hard his head should have spun off his shoulders. It didn't, but she had a solution for that. Picking up her skirt, she didn't waste time kicking his shins with these ridiculous slippers. Instead, she raced for the door he'd so conveniently left open while he'd offered his insulting proposition. She'd seen swords mounted in the billiard room the last time she'd escaped this room.

Durham roared with anger and raced after her. He had the advantage of breeches instead of her hampering skirts, so it wouldn't take long for him to catch up. She wished she knew where they kept Michael and the marquess. She wished she knew if they were all right. Without any resources but her own, she did what little she could.

She grabbed the arm of a rusted suit of armor adorning the upper corridor. She'd had some hope of knocking it over in Durham's path, but the metal pulled loose in her hands. Giving it a look of disgust, she turned and flung it as hard as she could in Durham's face. *Then* she shoved the armor over.

Durham roared in pain. As the armor clattered and splintered across his path, she picked up her skirt and ran. She'd seen the billiard room when they'd first arrived. It was in the front, where a proper salon should be. Men! They lived like pigs on their own.

A woman screamed below. *Mrs. B.* Fiona scowled but didn't slow her step as she passed the stairs. Her erstwhile lady's maid and Colin had both been on the premises when she'd arrived. Mrs. B. swore they had followed the kidnappers in hopes of capturing them, but Fiona didn't believe anyone right now.

She heard Durham's awkward gait close at hand. She could nearly smell the stench of whiskey on him. Stupid fool. Surely he didn't really think she'd welcome his overtures or believe his lies?

"Damn you, you Irish hussy!" her tormentor called as she slammed the billiard room door in his face. "I'll wager you've spread your legs for half Ireland before this, and I'll have you before this day's done."

There was no fool more stupid than one who thought with that worm between his legs, Fiona thought spitefully as she clambered onto an ancient blackened oak chair. The chair's massive weight held it in place as she stood on the arm and reached for the rapier just above her head. She'd carve the wretch into stew meat.

Durham pulled the chair out from under her just as her fingers gripped the rapier. Fiona grabbed a shelf of filthy tankards, and still clinging to the rapier, leapt from the chair arm, slowing her descent to the floor by hanging onto the shelf. The shelf jerked loose from the crumbling plaster and heavy tankards bounced across the warped wooden floor, but she was on her feet again, rapier pointed directly at Durham's bulging belly.

"Don't be a fool, woman." Durham hiccuped, batting at the thin sword point with his arm. "You'll all hang for treason before the month's out. I can save your pretty head if you'll just give me what I want."

Fiona didn't give this nonsense the courtesy of a reply. With an agile upward twist of her wrist, she split all Durham's buttons. He tottered in a puzzled attempt to catch one. When it came right down to it, she hadn't the courage to split his guts in the same way. Just the idea of blood nauseated her. She backed away while he drunkenly studied their predicament.

Concentrating all her thoughts on the immediate enemy, she didn't hear the first shouts in the yard, but the rising noise through the cracked window panes caught her attention now. Michael! Michael had escaped and roused the household. Fiona didn't know whether to cheer or be afraid.

"That was my last decent waistcoat, you slut!" Durham cursed, looking down at his shredded clothing. "I'll make you and your damnable husband pay for that."

"You want my coin now, or after you're behind bars?" a calm male voice inquired from the doorway.

Neville! Fiona's eyes widened at the sight of her husband still garbed in rags yet striding into the room as if he wore a suit of armor. The blasted man didn't even have a weapon! She would kill him when this was over and done. Did he think himself invulnerable as well as omnipotent? All the same, her heart thrilled at his appearance.

To her surprise, Durham shrank into a whimpering, stoop-shouldered caricature of a man as he backed toward the far wall, out of Neville's reach. "I never hurt her, I swear."

"Watch it! He's after the sword," Fiona cried as she caught the glint of metal in the dim light of the room's one lamp.

"Give me yours," Neville commanded, holding out his hand while keeping his gaze fastened on Durham.

At any other time, with any other man, Fiona would have hesitated at surrendering her hard-won weapon, but not with Neville. She flung the light rapier toward his outstretched hand.

He caught it easily, swinging it in an experienced grip before pointing it at the hapless Durham. "How would you like to do this, Durham?" Neville asked, as if discussing a hand of piquet. "Shall I cut you into tiny ribbons, or will you come peacefully and tell all to the authorities?"

"Don't be ridiculous," Durham sputtered, jerking a broadsword off the wall with some effort. "I've not done anything any other man hasn't tried." He tilted to one side before adjusting to the weight of the sword. "You can't attack a man for no reason in his own home."

"If I did not mistake, I believe you just insulted my wife," Neville continued in a voice of deadly calm. "You'll get down on your knees and beg her forgiveness."

Fiona couldn't believe her ears. They stood in a house occupied by two treasonous Bedlamites, surrounded by who knew how many enemies, and the arrogant duke played gentlemanly games of honor? She'd rip the ears off his head if that tone in his voice hadn't warned her to stay clear.

She'd never heard that tone before. If she didn't know better, she'd believe it nothing short of murderous. Not Neville. Not her stoic duke. Surely he wouldn't...

"I'll not—" Durham began to protest.

The rapier lunged, whirled, and returned, at ease, to Neville's side. Durham's waistcoat and shirt fell in shreds to the floor, and he stared blankly at the X just beginning to leak red across his chest. With a groan of anguished shock, Durham dropped any pretense of holding the heavy sword, slipped to his knees, and stared at his chest.

"I didn't hurt her, I swear," he whispered, vainly stanching the blood with torn pieces of linen and the rough tweed of the coat he still wore.

"Apologize," Neville commanded curtly.

Something about that coat struck Fiona as familiar, but she had no wish to linger and ponder the puzzle. "Neville, let's just get out of here," she urged. "We must find Michael and Effingham."

Her skin tingled in terror as the full impact of Neville's determined stance hit her. Neville meant to kill the man just for insulting her. She could see it in his eyes. Never, in all her life, had she thought her studious duke would resort to such violence, but he was on the edge of berserk. He was doing this for her. The knowledge scattered her thoughts to the winds.

"Effingham won't be going anywhere soon," a new voice intruded.

Before she could so much as squeal, a hard arm caught Fiona's waist, hauled her up against a tall frame, and slammed a hand over her mouth.

Townsend.

# Thirty-nine

Fiona bit at the hand covering her mouth. Townsend smacked her.

Her cheek stung, and she didn't need to look to see how her husband took this new development. Neville's rage swept the room in a force so powerful she thought the storm striking outside had entered through the windows. She slumped forward, dumping all her weight on Townsend's one arm. She damned well wouldn't stand between Neville and this object of his fury.

Townsend staggered at the unexpected drag of her full weight. Neville's rapier whooshed over Fiona's head before she even reached her knees. Fortunately for her, she was well-balanced. Townsend screamed in pain and released her, and she rolled to the floor, before crawling indecorously out of the field of battle.

Safely behind the huge oak chair, she finally dared to observe the situation. Blood dripping from the gash on his cheek, Townsend hauled a battle-ax off the wall and wielded it expertly. A battle-ax against a slender rapier—Neville didn't seem to notice the disparity. Roaring, he slashed at his opponent.

Thunder crashed outside, startling Fiona. In a flash of lightning, she saw Durham lift the broad sword again.

With no more effective weapon at hand, Fiona grabbed a cue stick and lurched to her feet.

"Good show, cuz, but I really don't think he needs your help," Michael drawled from the doorway. "Our illustrious duke appears capable of tearing His Majesty's Navy into tatters right about now."

Breathing a sigh of relief that the earl had escaped, Fiona glanced toward the door where her noble cousin leaned lazily against the frame, arms crossed over his chest. He wasn't looking at her, however. He was glaring at Durham.

The frightened lordling had regained the broadsword and raised it over his head, prepared to strike. Before Durham could act, Neville spun from his first target, sliced his rapier across Durham's bare midsection, and returned to cutting Townsend's weapon arm into neat pieces.

Fascinated, Fiona stared as Townsend cried out in pain, staggered, and dodged the repeated blows, waving his ax with faltering strength, never once coming close to the more nimble duke.

"You're the magician, Michael. Turn him off." Effingham appeared behind the earl, watching the duke's furious attack in almost as much fascination as Fiona.

Michael snickered. "That's Fiona's job. Let her at him."

She shot a glare of fury at both the lackwits. Neville was in the process of single-handedly murdering two men, and the two nobles stood and watched as if it were some entertaining play of Shakespeare's. Men were all mad.

As the next burst of lightning illuminated the grim scene, she located a pewter tankard rolling on the floor. Dodging the melee to grab it, she slammed it over Durham's head before he could lift his sword again. He slumped to the floor and stayed there.

Townsend was still reeling about the room, attempting to reach Neville with his ax. She had no idea exactly of which crimes he was guilty, but his actions proved his murderous intent. She couldn't hope to reach his much taller head with any degree of the strength.

Grabbing her abandoned billiard cue, she slipped into the shadows closest to the battling pair, waited her moment, and jabbed the stick between Townsend's legs. With a howl of dismay, he tripped and pitched forward.

Fiona watched in horror as the tall lord stumbled directly toward Neville's pointed rapier. She hadn't meant to kill the man, but Neville...

She gasped her relief as Neville easily sidestepped, allowing his opponent to crash to the floor. Before Townsend could consider rising again, Neville pointed his rapier at the back of his neck.

"Had I a cudgel, I would give you a taste of how it feels, your bloody lordship," Neville growled.

"There's always one of Fiona's tankards," Michael suggested as he sauntered into the room. "I vote we *each* crown him one before hauling him to the authorities."

"I vote we find out what the devil is going on before beating him senseless." Effingham strolled in behind his adopted brother. Without compunction, he smashed a wooden chair against the hearth and threw the pieces into the dying fire, stirring a small blaze to light and warming the room.

Fiona was beyond hearing them. Heart stilling, she stared at Neville, who stared back at her. He'd lost his ragged cap and his golden hair fell across his brow, framing eyes that commanded orders she was finally ready to accept. Despite the cold and damp of the room, perspiration streaked his filthy face. He looked far from the impeccable duke she'd first known. Yet standing there with his sword pointed at his enemy's neck, he looked more the duke than ever. Her heart pounded as she finally accepted that she'd married a man she could respect, and respect required understanding and recognition of his wishes.

Battening down all her raging emotions, she wordlessly lay down her billiard cue and left the room.

At the sight of Fiona's departure, Michael lifted a questioning gaze to Neville. "Perhaps you should go after her."

Neville shook his head. "No, Fiona's leaving this to us. She's gone to see about the others." Fury still coursed through his blood, but the sight of his brave Fiona obediently leaving the battle scene to him tempered his violence with wonder—and with an odd tranquility, as if something had been settled between them.

"She should be going to her bed and resting," Effingham protested.

Neville smiled. "Would you care to suggest that to her?"

He wouldn't tell them that he ached to rush after her, gather her in his arms, and haul her screaming and protesting straight to the first bed he found. In the moment she'd met his eyes, they'd made promises to each other, or so he hoped. His heart still swelled with all the knowledge that look had imparted. He'd seen her respect, her willingness, and something he prayed he hadn't misinterpreted.

He'd had little enough experience with the softer emotions, but he'd thought he'd seen it in the way her full lips softened, her eyes brightened, and her cheeks blushed. He could do no less than offer her the same respect she gave him. She would do what was best for her and for their child, without his interference.

Neville thrilled with the knowledge that he could do what he must, and Fiona would support him in whatever way he needed. He hadn't married just a wife or a brood mare; he'd married an equal partner.

The idea was such a new one to him that he needed to study it further, work it over in his mind. But for now, he exulted in the freedom his wife offered.

Swinging his attention back to his friends, he threw down his rapier and kicked Townsend in the ribs. "Who murdered Burke?" he demanded.

Gowned in a thick night shift against the damp air of Durham's derelict castle, Fiona leaned against the massive headboard of some long-forgotten Irish chieftain, and sipped her hot chocolate.

"It's that grateful I am that it's all done and said." The Widow

Blackthorn bustled around the room, pressing clothes with her fingers and folding them into neat stacks in Fiona's trunk. "He's a butcher and a knave and no two ways about it."

"Durham?" Fiona asked idly. The last hours had taken a toll on her strength, and she reserved it now for the scene yet to come. She'd spoken with Eamon and McGonigle, but the men in the billiard room had not condescended to explain anything to her as yet.

"Aye, Durham, the wicked, wicked creature, and he with a lily-pure wife who wouldn't so much as let a drop of cream pass her lips."

Mrs. B. had a warped way with words, Fiona mused as she sipped her chocolate. Had she not already pried some of the story from Eamon, she would be at a loss for reply.

"He seems little more than a blithering idiot to me, completely under his father-in- law's thumb."

Mrs. B. snorted. "Did he look a blithering idiot when he came to your room? Oh, don't think I don't know about it," she warned, shaking out Fiona's traveling cloak. "For all your clever ways, I still worried when I saw him drinking as he does when he's into one of his fevers. I worked in this house far too long not to recognize the signs. He's a mean drunk, is what he is. But it's usually the servants he goes after, not the guests. There's not a thing one of us can do. It's a pure blessing the duke brought him down like he has, although what will become of his tenants, I cannot say."

"You could have locked him in his room when he started drinking," Fiona suggested, although her mind already explored the paths opened by her maid's words. She knew about mean drunks. Drunkenness was simply an excuse for carrying out their loutish depredations. She'd not heard of one to abstain to prevent the act from happening again.

"Oh, and it's that simple for the likes of you to say," Mrs. B. said scornfully, with her usual lack of respect. "You'd not be beat to a puddle and turned off the next day. We tried it this night, Colin and I did, when we saw how it was to be. But Townsend caught us at it, he did. Evil man, that. He didn't know us from Adam, thought we were naught but a lot of heathen peasants. We taught him better, we did," she added triumphantly.

Fiona hid a smile behind her cup. Colin and the widow had to be almost as inept at heroics as Durham was at villainy. But they had eventually freed Michael and Effingham from the attics, after Neville's army had already arrived. She'd give them credit for trying. "Aye, and I'm certain it is you saved our necks," she agreed.

"Well, and that's how it should be when we near cost it believing that spalpeen was McGonigle's messenger. It's sorry enough we are for that. And didn't I try and pay for it by staying the way with him so he'd not notice it was an empty carriage he drove?"

The more emotional she became, the more the widow's speech degenerated into the accents of her youth. The lilting phrases eased Fiona's spirits, and the familiar half-truths and self-exculpations soothed her humor. The widow and Colin were equal scoundrels, she'd wager, always looking for the easy path, but they weren't utter blackguards like Durham and Townsend. The two Englishmen had the advantages of a proper upbringing, making their villainy doubly evil.

"Now, if we only knew who murdered poor Burke," Fiona murmured, setting aside her cup and wearily curling against her pillows.

"Aye, and it was Durham, himself," the widow replied smugly. At Fiona's questioning glance, she shrugged. "We've been listening outside the door. He admitted he didn't have the coins for paying a thief, and he thought to use the village's funds for himself since he'd gambled away his allowance. Cursed Townsend for keeping him on short shrift, blamed it all on his miserliness. Terrible, what the young have come to these days."

Oh, Jesus, Mary, and Joseph, poor Burke, murdered by a spendthrift lordling. Remembering the tweed coat now as the one on the intruder they chased through hill and dale, Fiona buried her face in the pillows. It didn't seem quite fair that a murderous drunk could end the life of a decent man. But then, maybe the courts would let Ireland hang the scoundrel. That would be justice indeed.

She closed her eyes and wished Neville would hurry.

Neville scowled as he met Colin propped on a chair outside the room he'd been told Fiona had taken. "What the devil are you doing here?" he demanded.

Colin shrugged and lowered the chair legs to the floor. "Eamon ordered her guarded round the clock. I'm just following orders."

"Oh, and you're very good at that," Neville mocked. "I've found the man Durham sent to abduct Fiona. He said you believed him when he told you that McGonigle wanted her gone without me. Precisely whose employ did you think you were in?"

Standing, Colin crossed his arms defiantly, but there was a trace of sheepishness in his expression. "Fiona's," he admitted. "I tried to get her to send word to you, but she wouldn't. And I wouldn't go against her wishes."

Neville rolled his eyes heavenward. Of course. These people were loyal to Fiona. It didn't matter the color of the coins that paid them. He couldn't fault them for that. But he could fault them for being fools. "Next time, think twice about endangering her like that or I'll have your head on a block. Is that understood?"

Colin understood that "next time." He still had a position. Nodding eagerly, he stepped out of the duke's way. "I'll not let her out of sight without word from you, Your Grace, and I'll tell Mrs. B the same."

That wasn't precisely what he'd meant, but it would suffice until the young moonling was trained. All Neville really wanted was to be in that bed beside Fiona. His other duties could wait. With a nod, he dismissed Colin. "I'll take over guard duty."

He waited until Colin was gone before opening the door. He wanted Fiona completely to himself for a while. He had a lot of things to say, words he should have said long ago, if only he'd had the sense. He prayed she'd welcome them this late. He didn't know what he would do if he discovered she didn't feel the same. It might possibly drive him as mad as poor Townsend.

Cautiously opening the door and examining the darkness beyond, Neville slipped inside. Startled by a movement in a far corner, he reached for the sword he'd kept at hand.

A familiar whisper stopped him.

"It's about time, then, your worship. She's been dead on her feet for hours. The poor lass needs her sleep, she does, but she kept waiting for you."

Mrs. Blackthorn. Damn. A body would think that out here in the midst of rural solitude, one could shake this squadron of servants. Scowling, Neville jerked his head toward the door. "Get out." What little patience he may once have possessed had dissipated entirely.

Mrs. B. huffed. "Well, and if that's the gratitude one can expect, I'll be serving my notice now, Your Grace. I've only the duchess's best interests in mind, I'm sure. She needed someone to talk to, and you weren't here, I'll remind you."

He was never here. He was always somewhere else when it came to Fiona. That would stop soon enough. "Get out, and if you're not with us in the morning, I'll send someone to hunt you down."

Finally taking the hint, the widow hurried out.

Sighing with relief, Neville set his candle down on the table and pulled off his coat and waistcoat. In the lamplight he could see his wife's thick auburn braid against a white gown. She wore a frilly cap over the rest of her curls. Fiona never wore caps.

He supposed she protected herself and the babe from the damp chill of this place. She wasn't entirely irresponsible, was his Fiona. Irrational upon occasion, impulsive mostly, but not irresponsible. Smiling, Neville stripped off the rest of his clothing and slipped between the heavy covers beside her.

"I love you," he whispered in her ear as he slid his arms around her.

She snuggled closer into his warmth without waking.

"I love you madly and I'll go insane if you ever go off on your own again like that." Settling into the feather ticking, Neville tugged her into the angle of his arm and shoulder and played with her breast. "I don't ever intend to leave your side again."

"I heard that," a soft voice whispered. "You mean to drive me mad, do you?"

Neville caught his breath, but a giggle and a small hand stroking his chest reassured him. Sometimes, he wasn't entirely sure when she was jesting. He'd had far too little humor in his life. Through the fabric of her gown, he cupped her breast and played with the aroused crest. "You're already there, my love," he whispered in return. "I mean to drive you back."

She pinched his bare side. Neville yelped, pushed her back against the mattress, and swiftly covered her with his length.

She surrendered to his plundering mouth immediately. And she surrendered a good deal more before the night was done.

It was even odds which one was the captive.

# Forty

"Sean! Sean! He's back!" Screaming children poured into the courtyard of Aberdare Castle.

The crowd swarmed around Neville's horse, surging toward McGonigle who was holding the lad in front of him.

People, young and old, streamed from the castle and the hedgerows and from down the lane until a crowd of laughing, cheering, weeping adults and children packed the muddy yard. Atop his gelding, Neville swept the crowd in search of the one figure he longed to see more than any other. To his disappointment and concern, she was nowhere in sight.

McGonigle lowered the boy into the arms of his wife, who hugged him so hard, Sean could do no less than cling to her neck and bury his head against her pillowy breast and weep.

Neville choked back his weakness at the sight. He was a duke. Dukes didn't need soft shoulders and welcoming arms, even when they'd saved a child from hanging. He'd only done his duty. He didn't need a mob to tell him so. He needed only one slight woman.

He'd left Effingham and Aberdare behind in Dublin to deal with Townsend, Durham, and the law. If the noble pair had any say-so, they wouldn't have opposition from Townsend or anyone in the madman's family for a long time to come. Neville's position in the cabinet would be affirmed. But that didn't matter to him at the moment.

He hadn't wanted to leave Fiona, but they'd needed his authority in Dublin to release Sean, and Fiona had wanted to stay with her people at Aberdare while they patched their lives together again. He'd promised to pay for repairing the looms. Perhaps she was with the men who worked on them.

From the ground, Eamon muttered in disgruntlement. "She's up there, your noble lordship."

Ignoring the man's rudeness, Neville cast a glance upward, where a movement on the castle ramparts caught his eye. The heart he would have sworn he didn't own leapt at the sight of a billowing cloak disappearing through the tower door. *Fiona.* Fiona had been watching from the ramparts for his return.

He hadn't heard her repeat the words he'd whispered to her in her sleep, but then, in all probability, she hadn't heard him say them either. They'd simply made love that night and fallen into exhausted slumber. And in the morning, there had been ten dozen other tasks and people awaiting them. There hadn't been time.

He would have to make time. He wanted her to know what she meant to him, but he didn't know how to go about saying it. As it was, he felt as if he'd slit his chest and exposed his insides for all to see. Even the crowd of excited, congratulatory villagers bustling in the courtyard had sense enough to step out of his way as he dismounted and hurried toward the castle entrance. They knew how he felt. Why couldn't Fiona?

Neville strode briskly into the dim interior. He would inspect the looms in the Great Hall. Fiona would know to find him there.

"Neville! Neville!"

He halted in the gloom of the foyer and glanced up the high stone stairs at the slender figure racing down, cloak billowing behind her. As she hit the first landing, the faint rays of sunlight through the leaded glass windows played red and gold in the auburn of her hair. Did he imagine it, or was that excitement alighting his wife's face as she hurried down, her eyes sparkling and her lovely lips parting with dancing laughter? Was all that light and love for *him*?

Gulping, he glanced over his shoulder, certain Aberdare or some other had entered. But the door was closed and no one else occupied the hall. She had called *his* name.

Blood pounding, Neville took another stride forward. No one had ever greeted him like this. Surely it was just his own desires that read more into her greeting than was there. This was Fiona, the brat who had run from him, taunted him, loved him, and left him. He could never know for certain.

"Neville, you're home!" Without further warning, she flew from the last step and into his arms and smothered his face in kisses.

Had he not needed to protect her from a tumble, he would have fallen backward in surprise. Instead, Neville braced himself, squeezed her waist so hard it should have broken, and swung her in circles of pure delight, his heart near to bursting.

"I love you," he whispered against her wayward hair. "I love you, I love you, I love you."

Her lips descended on his without the least shyness. There was nothing shy about his Fiona, and that knowledge filled his heart to overflowing.

"You are an arrogant, impossible man, my noble duke," she murmured against his mouth, "but I love you into eternity and beyond. Thank you for Sean. Thank you for the looms. Thank you for being arrogant and impossible."

Fiona's laughter warmed Neville more than the sun on the hottest day of June. She was a wicked spoiled woman, but she was *his* wicked spoiled woman. He nibbled at her ear and held her off the floor. "I'll thank you for the nearest bed, my lovely wanton wife. It's been too long already."

Her laughter trilled through the castle air, tinkling even the iron chandeliers. Sweeping her up in his arms, Neville took the stairs two at a time. He didn't think he'd ever known joy before. He knew he'd never known love. He didn't know if the two were related, but he was about to burst from an excess of both. He recognized only one way to release these reckless tides.

From the upper library, a sturdy figure limped out, an ancient leather volume in his hands.

"Fiona, Your Grace!" Fiona's Uncle William waved the book in excitement. "Look at this." Fiona buried her face against Neville's neck and groaned. "Not now, Uncle, please. I'm welcoming Neville home."

Rapt in his own world, William paid no heed as he hurried toward them, still waving the open book. "I've been looking into your father's antecedents, Fiona, just for the fun of it, you understand. I can trace his family back..."

Halting before the young couple, he looked momentarily puzzled at the sight of Fiona in the duke's arms. Finally understanding that perhaps he should hurry his tale, he pointed at the open page. "It says right here, your father's family produces at least one set of twins in every other generation. Your mother didn't have twins, Fiona."

He said this last with such excitement that his audience stared at him with momentary incomprehension.

And then it sank in.

Their eyes met. Neville grinned wickedly as understanding dawned on Fiona's face. "A herd of heirs, my dear," he whispered before she could even open her mouth, "lots and lots of little heirs."

Indignantly, she tossed her head. "And heiresses, I'll remind you. I'm probably carrying two right now, I've grown so fat already."

"Shall I measure how fat you've grown, my lady?" He headed down the hall in the direction of the bedroom he remembered so well.

"Oh, much too fat for what you're thinking," she answered tauntingly.

Behind them, William cried out, still consulting his books, "Your grandfather produced two sets of twins and one set might possibly have been triplets!"

Uproarious laughter greeted that genealogical news report.

Scratching his head, William retired to the library and his books again. The younger generation simply didn't have the proper respect for their ancestry.

# Author Bio

With several million books in print and *New York Times* and *USA Today's* bestseller lists under her belt, former CPA Patricia Rice is one of romance's hottest authors. Her emotionally-charged contemporary and historical romances have won numerous awards, including the *RT Book Reviews* Reviewers Choice and Career Achievement Awards. Her books have been honored as Romance Writers of America RITA® finalists in the historical, regency and contemporary categories.

A firm believer in happily-ever-after, Patricia Rice is married to her high school sweetheart and has two children. A native of Kentucky and New York, a past resident of North Carolina, she currently resides in St. Louis, Missouri, and now does accounting only for herself. She is a member of Romance Writers of America, the Authors Guild, and Novelists, Inc.

For further information, visit Patricia's network:
http://www.patriciarice.com
http://www.facebook.com/OfficialPatriciaRice
https://twitter.com/Patricia_Rice
http://patriciarice.blogspot.com/
http://www.wordwenches.com

Made in the USA
Las Vegas, NV
05 October 2024

96347438R00163